THE
BONE FLOWER
THRONE

BOOK ONE OF THE BONE FLOWER TRILOGY

THE
BONE FLOWER THRONE

BOOK ONE OF THE BONE FLOWER TRILOGY

TL MORGANFIELD

FSB

THE BONE FLOWER THRONE
BOOK ONE OF THE BONE FLOWER TRILOGY

copyright © 2013 by T.L. Morganfield

Interior map, cover art and design by TL Morganfield

Published by Feathered Serpent Books
Thornton, Colorado

Printed in the USA

ISBN 978-0-9909207-0-0

PRINTING HISTORY
Panverse Publishing, LLC edition published October 2013
Feathered Serpent Books edition published November 2014

For Jeff and the kiddos

to the northern desert

Tollan

The Basin of Mexico
10th Century CE

Tultepec

Teotihuacan

Acolman

Lake
Meztliapan

Chapultepec

Culhuacan

Xochimilco

Xico

Chalco

Xochicalco

PART ONE
THE YEAR THIRTEEN RABBIT

CHAPTER ONE

In my sister Cualli's love stories, a woman's wedding day is always the happiest day of her life, but none of them had to marry their cousin when they were only seven. Though things could have been far worse; I might have had to marry one of my older brothers, like Itzcoatl, who thought it was funny to blow his snot at my older sisters. My cousin Black Otter at least was well mannered, and my best friend. But none of my sisters had to marry so young.

"It's because your father needs to secure an heir," Mother told me as she finished primping my feathered wedding dress. The handmaidens had finally cleared out of my nursery, leaving us alone with the murals of snakes, birds, and butterflies.

"But why can't he just name someone his heir?" I asked, kicking at the wicker baby basket that hung from the ceiling by a braided rope. No one but my dolls had slept in it since I'd started sleeping on a regular reed mat.

"As the king's only legitimate child, you carry the burden of succession." Though I read the unspoken part in Mother's frown: she too wished this could wait until I was older, and her mood had been just as cloudy as mine for the last two weeks since she'd first told me the news. She fretted over my long braided hair a moment then sighed. "You look beautiful though."

I didn't mind wearing my everyday dresses, but this one went all the way to my feet, and the skirt was stiff with hundreds of red parrot feathers. The handmaidens had covered my face with the traditional yellow tecozauitl paint, which felt like packed clay, and I wore my mother's heavy gold, turquoise, and quetzal-feather necklace. Hopefully I wouldn't always have to wear such smothering finery from now on. I could hardly climb trees and chase lizards dressed like this.

"How am I supposed to go to the calmecac this year, so I can learn to be a priestess like you were? Priestesses can't be married." I tried out some tears, to see if that would change anything.

Mother smiled though. "They'll still let you in, dear. It's a marriage only in name. For now anyway." Though she seemed to be saying it more for herself than me.

I wasn't going to get out of this wedding nonsense, so I held Mother's hand as we left the nursery for the Great Hall. Still, I pouted the whole way.

"This is a lot for both of us to deal with," Mother said. "The happiest day of my life was the day you were born, and it grieves me to have to give you over to someone else so soon."

I wouldn't have described her as happy on the day I was born. One of my earliest memories: Mother smiling down at me with tears that turned to sobs when a stern, mean woman told her I was the only child she'd ever have. I once told my sister Jade Flower about my memories of that day, but after she told everyone in the play yard about it, and my brothers and sisters spent weeks calling me Princess Lying Butterfly, I decided I should keep those memories to myself.

Nor did I want to remind Mother that her barrenness was why I had to marry Black Otter today. She usually hid her burden well, but the last couple of days I'd often walked into her room late at night to find her still awake and crying. If my marrying Black Otter would help her sleep through the night again, then I could live with it.

My uncle Nochuatl greeted us outside the Great Hall, wearing his best mantle and a headdress of scarlet macaw feathers. He bowed, kissing his fingers before sweeping them across the ground at my sandaled feet. "You look lovely, My Lady. Black Otter is a lucky boy."

I half-hid behind my mother, embarrassed for the delightful attention. I adored Nochuatl; he'd sit me on his shoulders at the festivals, so I could see over my siblings, and he made me necklaces of flowers and bear teeth. If I wasn't marrying Black Otter, Nochuatl would've been my second choice.

"The king awaits you, My Lady." He offered me his arm and we went into the Great Hall, Mother following a few steps behind.

The Great Hall was the largest room in the palace, where my father put on the weekly feasts attended by most of Culhuacan's nobility. Red and blue feathered banners hung from the white plaster walls, adorned with the city's symbol: a hilltop with the crest bent to the left, like an old man hunched over his walking stick. A hearth taller than a grown man was built into the wall at one end of the hall, and my father's reed throne—decorated daily with fresh flowers—stood on an elevated platform at the other end. My mother's smaller reed throne sat next to Father's, with stalks of white bone flowers sticking up along the top of the backrest like lovely, delicate spears. I loved sitting in her throne, surrounded by the sweet, vanilla-like fragrance.

My father stood near the hearth, a crowd of nobles around him, though he stood a good head taller than all of them. He wore a green macaw feather mantle, gold-woven sandals, and a jaguar-skin cape with the head draped over his bulging shoulder. In his crown of long, flowing quetzal feathers, he resembled an emerald sun.

My earliest memory of Father: when the midwife brought me to see him for the first time, he'd refused to hold or even look at me. Only Nochuatl convinced him to. *She's as precious as a butterfly, Mixcoatl.* And when Father had finally looked down at me, the disappointment had slowly melted away and he'd taken me into his strong arms with a distant, dreamy smile. *Yes, my precious little Butterfly,* he'd agreed, and that was how I'd gotten my childhood name.

And for six years I'd enjoyed my father's doting attention, the walks in the garden, the rides in the royal canoe, and even getting to sit on his lap in his throne. He used to tickle my nose with the feathers on the royal headdress and tell me stories about the gods, like how the Feathered Serpent Quetzalcoatl stole the jade bones from Lord Death to make us, or how he lured the love goddess Mayahuel down from heaven, enraging her earth monster grandmother.

But when I turned seven, the gods cursed me with the name I'd wear for the rest of my days, and I was no longer my father's beautiful little Butterfly. Instead I became Quetzalpetlatl, a Feathered Mat, something that everyone slept on and so it wore out quickly. Now the only time I saw him was when he came to my room with lectures about how proper Tolteca women behaved.

Today though, he granted me one of those smiles he used to give me, and my heart swelled. "You're radiant today, Quetzalpetlatl," he said, setting a firm hand on my shoulder. I beamed at him, basking in the warmth of his attention. He directed me to the long reed mat laid out against the north wall. We sat, with me in the middle between him and Mother, "Because today's your special day," he told me.

I was expecting to have fun, with dancers and musicians and maybe some acrobats painted up like the gods to play out stories for me, but instead I spent the next few hours until dark listening to a stream of noblewomen admonishing me to be a good, honest wife. "Keep your loom busy and your husband's house ready for his return, whether he's gone to the temple or off to war." It sounded suspiciously like they were telling me to be my husband's servant—ridiculous since I was a princess, not a commoner working the maize fields from sun-up to sundown. But at least Mother led me through how to reply to all of this the first couple of times.

But by the tenth bored recitation of the same false thanks, one woman snarled at me, "What a spoiled little disgrace to the gods you are! I'd hold you over the chili roaster if you were my daughter!" Her venom scared me, and I clutched at Mother's wrist.

Mother reacted smoothly though, with astonishing poise. "Please forgive Quetzalpetlatl's youthful selfishness, Lady Silver Flower. Rest assured she appreciates your heartfelt words, and she will gift you the first blanket she completes on her own." The old woman nodded curtly then moved off. Mother then whispered to me, "I know it's a long process, but try to keep your spirits up."

Finally the last noblewoman bestowed her "wisdom" upon me, then Father set me onto a litter attended by four serving girls. The young women hefted me up on their shoulders while a fifth girl sounded a pink conch shell, then they carried me out onto the patio. We passed through the garden and up the stairs to the portico where the commoners went to petition the king. The crowd of noblewomen followed as we set out into the torch-lit city.

The only time I ever left the palace was to accompany Mother to the temple, so this was my first time seeing Culhuacan's other quarters. I'd been most looking forward to this part of the wedding ceremony, and as soon as we passed out of the palace gates, I completely forgot the boredom of the Great Hall.

Paintings of the gods decorated the whitewashed courtyard walls of the houses in the noble quarters while the fragrance of fried corn and spicy meat clung to the air in the merchant quarters. Whereas the houses in the upper class sections of the city were made of stone and stucco, out in the peasant quarters the houses were drab mud huts no bigger than my nursery, topped with thatch roofs, and grubby, naked babies playing in the dirt outside them. The people were cheerful though, many handing small bundles of flowers to my serving girls as we passed. Girls my own age watched with rapt interest, and a few waved to me before their mothers scolded them. I smiled and waved back at them, to tell them I didn't mind their admiration.

Statues of the Feathered Serpent god Quetzalcoatl stood at every intersection, all with garlands of flowers draped in their open mouths, and his temple in the sacred precinct had large, open-mouthed serpents built into the sides of its grand staircase as well. In Culhuacan, Quetzalcoatl held the highest throne.

Eventually the procession wound its way back to the palace and to the Great Hall. My cousin Black Otter now stood in front of the giant hearth, wearing a red and blue patterned cloak and matching loincloth. His parents stood with him—my mother's sister Eloxochitl, and my father's eldest brother Ihuitimal.

Eloxochitl helped me down from the litter and complimented my dress. "It's missing something, though." She tied a large white Magnolia flower to my wrist with a bit of twine. I whispered a shy thank you before shifting my gaze over to my uncle.

Ihuitimal thankfully never paid me any mind. He wore a perpetual scowl, and his suspicious eyes looked too large for his skull. He'd even filed his teeth to sharp points, "To look ferocious in battle," Nochuatl once told me. On the rare occasion he did smile, the nasty scar on his left cheek—that went from his mouth to his ear—turned him into a grinning caiman and made my insides curl up. Father had scolded me more than once for not showing him proper respect. "War scarred him, and he deserves your attention every time he enters the room." Though why did Father care, since Ihuitimal snapped at him like a hungry dog all the time?

Luckily, Black Otter shared nothing of his father's face, or personality;

in fact, he looked just like Nochuatl; hence my affection. He gave me a secretive smile as we knelt together on the reed mat, but when I giggled, Ihuitimal told us to be quiet.

"Let us begin with gifts!" my father announced. Mother set a feathered mantle and loincloth—both big enough to fit my father—in front of Black Otter, while Eloxochitl set a woman's dress in front of me. I'd seen them working on these in the Women's Hall several months earlier and I'd thought they were for the children of one of my father's allies. *So silly, giving me a dress I can't wear for many years,* I mused.

Father then took the corner of my wedding dress and tied it into a knot with the corner of Black Otter's cape. "From this day forward, the two of you are bound in marriage. Bring forth the wedding cakes!" Father called, the crowd cheering.

A servant brought tamale maize cakes on a gilded plate, and Father set it between Black Otter and I. "Eat your first meal together as husband and wife, and may you enjoy many more in the years to come!"

Black Otter made to eat his, but I elbowed him. "We have to feed them to each other," I whispered.

Black Otter held his out to me, grimacing. "Don't slobber on me."

Grinning, I mashed mine into his chin. He did the same to me until we were both laughing, but we also earned a stern reprimand from Father. "Respect the solemnity of the day," he scolded. Whatever that meant.

The servants soon brought in clay plates, bowls of food, and jugs of drink, filling the Great Hall with so many exotic aromas I couldn't begin to describe them all. Musicians played flutes, drums, and rattles while young girls danced, and everyone was laughing and talking. Children were rarely allowed at the royal feasts—though Black Otter and I had been caught more than once spying on them from the doorway—so I watched everything with enthusiasm and a giddy feeling that I'd magically become a grown-up by marrying Black Otter.

But just as the celebration was starting to heat up, Mother told us, "Time to go pray." I knew it was too good to be true. I looked back regretfully as she led me out of the hall by the hand.

Black Otter and I followed our mothers down the hall, leaving the laughing and singing behind. "But it's our wedding, so why don't we get to stay to enjoy it?" Black Otter complained as we passed through a curtain decorated with the city's royal crest. Several hallways branched off from there, but we followed the blue-and-red painted one to the royal family quarters. Guards bowed to Mother as we passed between them.

"The wedding couple prays for four days," Eloxochitl told Black Otter.

"Four days! Ayya!"

"Really?" I asked Mother, hoping it was an exaggeration.

Mother nodded. "And on the fourth evening, both of you will lay quetzal feathers and jade stones on your marriage bed, to bring you good luck in having children."

"Is that why you keep those stones and old feathers on your bed?"

She nodded again. "I re-lay them every day."

"But they weren't very lucky for you."

Eloxochitl shot me a startled glance, but Mother said, "They brought me you, and that's enough for me."

I smiled, tickled by her kindness.

Mother took us to a room a few doors away from her own; it used to belong to my grandmother before the Black Dog came for her last year. The hearth's orange glow lit half the room while moonlight from the open door curtain at the back lit the rest. Wooden folding screens stood in the corner, and two prayer mats lay on the floor in front of the fire.

"Now offer prayers to the gods, so they'll bless you both with a long, happy marriage," Eloxochitl told us.

Kneeling on my mat, I shut my eyes and cleared my mind, as Mother had taught me. I then quoted the prayers she said before bed every night:

"I honor you, Xilonen,
For the maize that fills our bellies.
I honor you, Tlaloc,
For the rain that makes the maize strong.
I honor you, Xipe Totec,
For the fertile land that nurtures the seeds of life.
I honor you, Nanahuatzin,
For lighting the days.
I honor you, Metzli,
For bringing light to the darkness."

And, like her, I saved the most important prayers for last. Quetzalcoatl had given us the sacred calendar for counting the days, and writing to record the deeds of our kings; but most important, he'd given us life by bleeding his tepolli—his manhood—upon Cihuacoatl's metlatl grinding stone. "No god deserves our prayers and sacrifices more," Mother always said. She'd been a priestess of Quetzalcoatl long ago, and I often overheard her praying to him for one last child so she could give Father an heir. I'd taken to backing up her request with prayers of my own:

"Oh Great Feathered Serpent,
Watch over Mother and Father,
Over Black Otter,
Over Nochuatl,
And my aunt Eloxochitl,
And my uncle Ihuitimal.
Hear Mother's prayers,
And grant me a brother.
I promise to be a very good sister to him.
I honor you, oh Merciful Quetzalcoatl,
For my family,
For my friends,
For my life."

I looked up when Black Otter tossed some pebbles into the hearth. "This is boring," he moaned. "What do they expect us to do in here? One need only pray so much."

I laughed. One could never pray enough.

"I'm hungry," he added.

My stomach rumbled again. "Me too."

At the door, Black Otter called to a passing servant. "My wife and I need dinner."

"The wedding couple must fast the first night, My Lord," the servant replied.

Black Otter glared at him. "The Princess is famished, practically falling over dead of hunger, and you dare argue with me?"

The servant startled at his tone and glanced past the curtain at me, but he backed away when Black Otter pulled out an obsidian dagger.

"I should cut your head off this very moment, you disobedient wretch!" Black Otter growled.

I gasped, appalled. Boys had to be tough, especially when the other boys teased them about their best friend being a girl, but I'd never heard Black Otter speak so nastily to anyone. It wasn't often I saw his father in him.

The servant promised to bring us food, then hurried away.

When Black Otter grinned at me like a pleased ocelot, I demanded, "How could you say that?"

He rolled his eyes. "Father says it all the time when the servants argue with him."

"My father never threatens the servants."

He laughed. "They wouldn't dare argue with the king."

I turned away, arms folded.

He knelt in front of me, giving me pup eyes. "I'm sorry, Papalotl. I'll apologize when he comes back, so please don't be mad at me."

And since he kept his word and muttered an apology to the servant when he came back, I had to forgive him. I liked him more when he acted like Nochuatl rather than Ihuitimal.

After devouring the roast duck stew and the maize-bread tlaxcallis we ate with every meal, we discussed trying to sneak back to the Great Hall. I pointed out that with the guards standing watch at the head of the hall, we were unlikely to make it far.

"Then let's see what's out there," Black Otter said, pointing to the curtain at the back of the room. I followed, but gave him a shove when he failed to hold the curtain open for me.

We stepped out onto a flagstone patio with a small private bath house off to the side, complete with bathing pit and steam bath, but what lay beyond it was far more interesting. Vine-covered stone walls enclosed a yard twice the size of the room, and a large copal tree stood sentry at the center, its branches spread across the yard. Flowers of every color choked the beds, many of them still droning with bees even at this late hour. "This must be my garden," I whispered.

"Yours? Maybe it's mine. My father has one just like this off his room."

"Father always visits Mother, so this has to be my room, because you're visiting me." I'd never been to Father's room either, so I wondered what he kept in there that he didn't want us women to see.

"My father never invites Mother to his room either," said Black Otter. We wandered the yard for a moment, but when I found a pond at the back, I called him over and we lay on our bellies, watching the tiny fish and frogs swim in the moonlit pool.

"Maybe this can be our garden, to share," I suggested.

Black Otter knocked his shoulder against mine in silent agreement. I splashed him with a fistful of water, which he returned with equal abandon. We wrestled around in the dirt a moment, laughing and cursing before he pinned my arms behind me and I called him the winner. He always won, but someday I'd get the better of him.

A glint in the water caught my eye, so I reached in to find a warm stone among the reeds. I rinsed the silt off as I brought it out.

"What's that?" Black Otter asked.

"A piece of jade." It resembled the stones Mother kept on her bed with the quetzal feathers, except it grew hotter as I held it. How did one of my mother's precious jade stones get out in the pond?

But then suddenly, something bit my wrist.

I squealed and swung my arm around, tossing something long and hissing across the yard. It landed on the flagstone behind Black Otter. "A snake!" I shrieked, clutching my wrist. "It bit me! It bit me!"

Black Otter pushed a rock onto the snake, pinning it down, then cut off its head.

"Get over here!" I held my throbbing hand out, the pain surging up my arm. "You need to suck the poison out for me!"

"I'm not sucking anything out of you," he said, sticking his tongue out.

"At least look at it," I insisted.

He pulled my wounded wrist close to his face and squinted. He glared at me. "You said it bit you."

"It did!"

"No it didn't."

I looked at my wrist, expecting gaping puncture wounds, but instead my sandy-brown skin remained unblemished, not even a scratch. The throbbing continued though.

Black Otter returned his knife to its sheath with an indignant huff. "That wasn't funny."

"It did—I felt it!" I stared at my wrist, flustered. Had the snake merely brushed against me and I'd overreacted? Embarrassment burning my cheeks, I muttered, "I'm sorry. I really thought it did."

Black Otter patted my shoulder. "At least it wasn't poisonous."

My stomach sank when I looked at the snake again. "You shouldn't have killed it. Snakes are sacred to Quetzalcoatl, and now he might curse our marriage."

Black Otter laughed.

"It's not funny! We must make a sacrifice to make amends for this affront." Mother would've scolded me for saying such a thing, for Quetzalcoatl was good-natured and merciful, unlike most of the gods, but she'd also taught me that one should always try to correct one's mistakes.

Black Otter hesitated then said, "My father won't like this." When I asked why, he shook his head. "Never mind. Let's just do this."

We knelt over the snake. Its white body shimmered in Metzli's pale light, but when I touched the scales, they were feathers. *Like Quetzalcoatl,* I thought. I tried to push that silly notion aside, but with my entire arm throbbing, my worry built all over again.

Black Otter scooped up the head. "What do we do with it?"

"We have to burn it..." I poked the body once more, my trepidation growing. "Doesn't it look kind of...strange?"

"It's just a black and white snake."

I laughed. "Did you actually look at it?"

Black Otter looked again. "So?"

"It has feathers."

"No it doesn't."

"It does too, like Quetzalcoatl."

Black Otter blinked. "You think it's Quetzalcoatl?"

My cheeks blazed. "I didn't say that."

"You think it's the Feathered Serpent!" he cackled. Propping the head between his fingers, he moved the lower jaw and spoke in a comically booming voice, "You killed me, Papalotl, and now I will smite you!"

I almost gave him a shove, but then I saw the long emerald feathers drooping like wilted flowers from the snake's severed neck—feathers like those on the statues of Quetzalcoatl around the city. *Oh my gods! It is Quetzalcoatl! Black Otter killed my beloved god!*

I ran screaming back into the palace and down the hallway. I tried to cut between the guards at the curtain, but they grabbed me. "Nantli!" I shouted through hot tears, still yanking to get away. "Nantli! Help! Nantli!"

Both Mother and Father burst from the Great Hall. Eloxochitl followed, but Ihuitimal remained at the doorway, glaring at me. "What happened?" Mother demanded, scooping me into her arms. "Are you hurt?"

"He killed him, Nantli!" I sobbed.

"Killed who?" Father demanded, fear straining his voice.

"Black Otter killed Quetzalcoatl!"

Ihuitimal finally joined us. "The child's obviously dreaming."

"I am not!" I wiggled from Mother's arms and led her by the hand down the hallway, back to the room. Up both sides of the hallway, my father's concubines and my siblings peered out from behind their door curtains, many asking what was going on, but Father sent all of them scurrying back inside with a gruff order.

Black Otter was still in the garden, the dead snake at his feet. He cowered as his father approached. "I didn't mean to scare her—"

Ihuitimal slapped him aside and looked down at the headless serpent. He narrowed his eyes then snarled at me, "This is your precious Quetzalcoatl?"

The serpent was only a small black and white banded snake.

I would have flung myself at Black Otter with fists flying if my mother didn't have hold of me. "What did you do with it?" I shouted.

"I did nothing with it," Black Otter retorted, tears spilling down his cheeks. "You're the one who thought it wasn't a regular snake."

"You two are supposed to be praying, not playing in the garden," my father rumbled. "And just look at your dress, Quetzalpetlatl! It's covered in dirt and you've crushed all the feathers!"

I cowered behind Mother.

"I'll go and assure everyone that all's fine," Ihuitimal said.

Father turned to me, his expression fierce. "Such behavior is unbecoming of Culhuacan's future queen. You're nearly eight now!"

"Mixcoatl—" Mother started.

But he cut her off. "You coddle her too much, Chimalma. This kind of hysteria could cost people their lives."

"She's a child, not a warrior!" Mother snapped, startling me. I'd never heard her talk back to my father.

"Then it's a good thing you never bore me a son, if that's how you would've raised him too," he replied, then stalked from the garden.

Mother stood red-faced, clenching her fist before hard-fought tears snaked down her cheeks. When Eloxochitl put an arm around her shoulder, she broke into hiccupping sobs. "He didn't mean it, Chimalma. He's just scared," Eloxochitl assured her.

Seeing Mother cry quickly made me do the same. "I'm sorry I got you in trouble, Nantli," I wailed, clutching her dress.

Mother smiled through her tears. "You have nothing to be sorry about, dear. Think about it no more."

The servants laid out bed rolls on opposite sides of the room and set up the wooden screens around them. Once in my nightdress, I watched the servants gather up the remains of the snake. "I thought it bit me, so Black Otter killed it," I told Mother with more tears. "Will Quetzalcoatl curse us?"

"Quetzalcoatl will forgive, so don't worry," Mother assured me.

"Can we take the snake to the temple in the morning and make an offering of it to him, just to be sure?"

"Offerings are always a good idea." She kissed my forehead. Mother always knew how to make me feel better.

As I turned to my bed, I saw the jade stone sitting inside the back doorway, glimmering in the moonlight. It must have landed there when I threw the snake. I picked it up and held it out to Mother. "I'm sorry I made Father mad at you."

"It's all right." She turned the stone over in her hand. "Where did you get this?"

"I found it in the pond."

She frowned. "Are you sure you didn't take it from my room?"

"I'd never take your stones. I know how much you love them."

"Maybe it's Eloxochitl's, though I think she keeps hers in her wedding basket. Maybe Black Otter took it."

"If it's not hers, I want you to have it," I said. "Maybe it'll bring you good luck, and Father won't be mad at you anymore."

She hugged me. "Forget what your father said. He didn't mean any of it."

I couldn't forget, though. I lay in bed, my chest aching with anger and guilt.

"Papalotl?" Black Otter peered at me from the edge of my screen.

"Go away." I pulled the blanket over my head.

But he tugged it down. "I'm sorry."

"I said go away!"

He cringed as my voice carried. "I mean it, I'm sorry. I shouldn't have made fun of you about the snake."

I sat up against the wall, my knees pulled to my chest. "I don't know why I thought all that. I'm sorry I scared you too."

He sat next to me. "We're still friends?"

"Of course. But you must come to the temple with us tomorrow, to make the offering to Quetzalcoatl."

"I doubt my father will let me."

"Why not?"

He hesitated then whispered, "You must promise never to tell anyone."

"I won't."

"No, you have to swear on something important...swear on Quetzalcoatl that you'll never tell anyone."

"I swear on the Feathered Serpent," I said, intrigued.

He checked the hallway then came back.

"What are you doing?" I asked.

"Making sure no one's spying on us."

Sometimes Black Otter was truly silly. "Are you going to tell me or not?"

He took a deep breath, then whispered, "My father hates Quetzalcoatl."

I laughed. "It's impossible to despise the Feathered Serpent—"

"But he does. My father is the high priest of the dark sorcerer god Smoking Mirror, the Feathered Serpent's mortal enemy. Father tells me the god sent him here to spread his worship among the Tolteca."

"I've never heard of any Smoking Mirror."

"My father learned about him when he lived in the northern desert, with the Chichimecs."

I frowned. Everyone said Chichimecs ate their own children, so what must their god be like? "What does he do?"

"Father says I'm too young to know the god's secrets yet. I only know that he makes warriors fierce and fearless, and he feeds on their hearts. Father says the Smoking Mirror will think me weak if I make offerings to Quetzalcoatl, and he even said he'd sacrifice me if he ever caught me worshiping the Feathered Serpent."

"Being a sacrifice is an honor, not a punishment." Or so Mother had told me.

"I don't want to die," Black Otter said. "My father will flog me if he

24

finds out I told you any of this."

My wrist throbbed again and I rubbed it, worried. "You won't make me stop worshiping Quetzalcoatl, now that we're married?"

He smiled and slipped his arm over my shoulder. "Never! We're friends."

We talked of other things, but the worry remained at the back of my mind. *You should tell Mother about this,* I thought, but I'd given my word.

Eventually I leaned against Black Otter's shoulder and drifted off to sleep, dreaming that when he laid me down, he kissed me on the cheek. But he'd never do something so disgusting.

Later, the dream shifted, to laughter out in the garden, and when I went to investigate, I found a boy hunched next to the pond. I liked him immediately; he had my mother's kind eyes. "Will you play boats with me?" he asked, so we sat next to the pond, blowing autumn leaves across the surface, watching them float like canoes on Lake Meztliapan. Whenever I met his gaze, a pleasant heat filled my body, strange as an out-of-reach memory. His smile made my heart soar like a hawk.

When the wind picked up, I looked up to see storm clouds gathering in the north. Thunder rumbled, growling like a jaguar stalking prey in the forest, waiting for the right moment to spring.

CHAPTER TWO

Mother returned in the morning in high spirits. "Did you and Father make up?" I asked as she braided my hair. Black Otter sat sulking against the wall, stewing after his father told him he needn't tag along after us "women folk".

"We made amends." Mother took my hand and I waved goodbye to Black Otter as we left the palace, a few servants following behind.

"I didn't want to say anything in front of Black Otter, but I have exciting news," Mother said once we reached the market, surrounded by shouting merchants and crowds of nobles and peasants shopping at the blankets laid out in lines. The guards kept close ranks around us as we pressed through towards the gates of the sacred precinct.

"What is it?" I asked.

"The Feathered Serpent came to me in a dream last night."

"He did?" I gaped, awestruck. "What did he say?"

"That I'll have a son soon, an heir for your father."

"I'll have a brother—a real blood-brother?"

Mother took the jade stone from her dress pocket. "Remember this, from last night? Quetzalcoatl told me to swallow it, and it'll grow into a baby inside me."

I stared at her, baffled. "In your stomach?"

She laughed. "Well, not in my stomach, but in my abdomen."

"How odd! Black Otter says that the goddess Cihuacoatl leaves newborns in the kitchen pot and that the mothers' bellies swell with milk."

Mother laughed louder. "That's not exactly how things happen."

"You're going to swallow it, aren't you?"

"Of course. I wanted to make offerings first."

"Is Father excited?"

"I haven't told him yet. I don't want to get his hopes up, in case it was just a dream."

Quetzalcoatl's temple sat atop the biggest pyramid in the sacred precinct, and the soothing smell of copalli incense greeted me at the door, covering the pungent smell of decay. I found the latter oddly alluring. Mother claimed it took years to get used to the temple's smell, so surely the fact that it didn't bother me meant I was destined to be a priestess too.

We knelt on the reed prayer mat before the gilded serpent idol and sang a hymn, honoring Quetzalcoatl for everything he gave us. Mother pulled a long gray snake from one of our baskets and slit its throat with her knife. The blade fascinated me, with its stag horn handle carved in the likeness of Quetzalcoatl, and how the blood pooled in its open mouth. She bled the snake over two grass balls in a clay bowl then repeated the process with five more.

When she finished, I held my hand out and she pricked my middle finger with a maguey thorn tied to a rope of more thorns she kept in her pocket. I winced as she squeezed my finger over the grass balls until a single drop fell. I used to dread that part most, but I was tougher now, and it was nothing like what she did to herself.

While I watched, Mother closed her eyes, meditating. She then opened her mouth and stuck the first thorn through her tongue, slowly dragging the string of thorns through, coating the rough maguey fiber with her blood. She never flinched—oh, her tenacity!—and when she finished, she set the rope in the bowl and held it up.

"Oh Great Quetzalcoatl,
I honor you for blessing my family,
For filling me with life once more,
For giving Mixcoatl an heir,
For giving Quetzalpetlatl a blood-brother,
And for giving Culhuacan her future.
Fill my son's head with wisdom,
So he grows to be a great and respected king.
Fill his heart with love,
So he honors you and his family always.
And fill his stomach with courage,
So he will be a great but just warrior."

When she handed me the bowl, I cleared my throat then said:

"Oh Merciful Quetzalcoatl,
Please pardon Black Otter's mistake.
The fault is mine,
I honor you and ask you spare our marriage from disaster,
Accept this blood to undo my dishonor,
Oh Great Feathered Serpent."

I dumped the bloody grass balls into the idol's gaping mouth.

"The high priest will burn the snake's body with the nightly sacrifice and all will be right again," Mother assured me.

But I was eager for more important things. "Now will you swallow the stone?"

"Bring me some water."

I hurried to the jar by the door and returned with a bowl of water. I watched anxiously as she murmured another prayer then put the jade stone on her tongue. Once she drank down the water, she looked woozy. "Do you need more?"

27

"It was just difficult to swallow." She touched her belly. "I feel like Lord Sun Himself just lit up inside me."

"Does it hurt?"

"It tickles, like magic swelling." She smiled. "He's growing already."

I bounced, too excited to stay still. "Can I carry him home?"

She laughed. "He'll be in there a while yet, Papalotl, thank the gods."

"But how long?"

"At least until winter."

"But that's so long!"

"Nine months isn't all that long, and once he gets here, you'll wish it was still just you."

"I won't." I'd prayed for someone to share the lonely nights in the nursery with for far too long. "Can I tell Father about the baby?"

"You should leave the good news to me," Mother suggested.

¤

But when I saw Father in the portico out front of the palace with Nochuatl and Ihuitimal, I couldn't help myself. "Father! Father! I'm going to be a sister!" I shouted as I ran up the stone steps to him.

"Then you've heard about Lady Tlallixochitl?" Nochuatl asked me with a crooked smile. "I've never seen you so excited about such things."

"No, Mother's going to have a baby!"

Ihuitimal laughed like a coyote. "Your mother's incapable of bearing children anymore, Quetalpetlatl."

Mother put a hand on my shoulder, but I couldn't stop the excited words pouring out of my mouth. "I found a stone in the garden last night and Quetzalcoatl told Mother to swallow it so it could grow into a baby boy, for Father, so he'll have an heir!"

"He already has an heir," Ihuitimal shot back.

When Father turned to Mother, confused, she sighed. "I really wanted to discuss this with your father in private, Papalotl."

"Then she speaks the truth?" Father asked.

She cast a wary gaze at Ihuitimal, but said, "The Feathered Serpent visited me in a dream last night."

Roaring joyously, Father wrapped his arms around her. I tried to stifle giggles as he kissed her passionately in plain view of everyone at the city registrar's office! Father never showed her such affection in public—Mother said they had to be careful to prevent jealousy among Father's other women. Mother's face flushed once Father released her.

"You actually believe this nonsense, Mixcoatl?" Ihuitimal snapped.

"How can't I? I trust Chimalma to know a real vision from the god when she has one." He set a friendly hand on Ihuitimal's shoulder. "Don't worry about Black Otter's position. He's married to my daughter and is still the heir until my own son is old enough, and even then he won't be forgotten. He'll have very high rank in the war council, and I shall still call him my son. In fact, Nochuatl and I will start taking him with us on our weekly hunts, so he can learn to bear a spear. A man must know how to handle men's weapons."

The veins on Ihuitimal's neck stood out. "You think I haven't taught my boy to be a man?"

"Not at all. You're just very busy, and any potential heir should begin his weapons training early. My own boys started sleeping with play swords in their baby baskets."

Ihuitimal still glared at Father. "I assure you that Black Otter won't disappoint you."

"Of course not. He's his father's son," Father said, smiling, but Ihuitimal strode away down the hall. Mother watched him go, a worried expression on her face.

"Why's he so angry?" I asked.

"Don't worry about him," Father said. "Your uncle's just a grouchy old bear."

Hopefully Black Otter took my good news better than his father did.

¤

"You made the prayers for me? Quetzalcoatl isn't going to curse me for the snake?" Black Otter asked, anxious.

"Everything will be fine," I said. "But never mind that. I have fantastic news! I'm going to be a sister!"

Black Otter scowled. "That's not so special. You have more brothers and sisters than anyone I know."

"All by Father's concubines, you tamale-head. My mother is having a baby!"

"But she can't have any more. That's why Father said we had to marry."

"The Feathered Serpent blessed her. Remember that piece of jade I found last night? She swallowed it, and Quetzalcoatl put a baby in her stomach."

"In her stomach?" He looked incredulous. "But won't he drown?"

"Mother said it's not like that."

"Lord Green Water lied to me!"

I nodded. "I bet babies come from their mothers swallowing the jade stones and feathers they get during the marriage ceremony."

"I'm going to ask my mother to swallow one of her jade stones," Black Otter said. "I want a brother too."

Once the servants delivered our early afternoon atole, we drank the bowls under the copal tree, filling our bellies with watery cornmeal mash to settle us until the evening meal. Black Otter then scaled the tree and beckoned me to follow. "You have to see something."

I hiked my skirt up past my knees and followed him up. We sat on one of the branches above the wall, and I could see all the way to the lake. Many walled gardens lay beyond our own, each paired with a room and backing up to a secret passageway watched by guards. I noticed that the vines hid an archway in our outer wall.

"It goes all the way from the lake to the main gardens," Black Otter said.

When I looked down the line of gardens, I spotted Mother and Father in one, holding hands and smiling. "I've never seen my father so happy," I said with a pleased sigh.

"My father's never happy, and he never holds Mother's hand like that." After a pause, Black Otter said, "I don't think they like each other. He never does anything nice for her, and she's always sad." He pursed his lips, looking as if he'd never considered any of this before. "That won't be us, though. We're going to be happy, like your parents."

I'd always pictured Mother and Father being happy together, but after the outburst in the garden last night....

But we didn't have to be like that either. "You promise?" I asked.

"I promise." He then leaned in and kissed me.

It wasn't like the kiss Father gave Mother earlier, but I almost fell backwards out of the tree in surprise. Black Otter pulled me back though, leaving me feeling hot and dizzy and bewildered. "What was that for?" I demanded.

He laughed, his cheeks red. "It's all right. We're married."

Though my parents were busy gazing at each other, I knew that if my father had seen us, we both would have gotten held over the chili roasters in the kitchen. He'd only done that once, when I'd stolen a doll from one of my sisters, and sometimes even now, when I passed by the kitchens, the smell of the roasting chilis brought burning tears to my eyes. "Don't ever do that again!" I punched Black Otter in the shoulder and climbed back down the tree.

Black Otter joined me on the ground again, avoiding my gaze. "Let's just pretend it never happened." I agreed, and we returned to our room where he tossed pebbles while I tried to focus on my silent prayers.

But my mind kept wandering back to the softness of his lips, the warmth of his breath. The memory renewed the strange, hot feeling inside and I couldn't help giggling like a crazy old woman.

Eventually we returned to the garden and watched the minnows swim in the pond. By evening it was as if the kiss had never happened. And I felt sad about it.

¤

On the fourth evening, servants brought in a stack of large reed mats and several armfuls of bear and wolf skins. They laid everything out under my father's watchful gaze, covering the mats with the skins, and the skins with colorful cotton blankets. Then Mother handed me four jade stones, and Eloxochitl gave Black Otter some quetzal feathers. "Having completed your prayers to the gods, we've now laid the marriage bed for you, my son, my daughter," Father said. "Lay upon it the rich plumes and precious stones it will bring you."

Black Otter laid the emerald feathers on the blankets. "These are the daughters you will give to Quetzalpetlatl, so she'll have women-kin to keep her happy when you're away at war," Father said. I then set the jade stones atop the feathers. "These are the sons you will give Black Otter, so his memory and influence don't die with him," he said.

Mother washed the yellow paint from my face and put me in a new dress with red, green, blue, and yellow feathers. "Now you get to celebrate," she said with a smile.

31

Cheers greeted us in the Great Hall, and for the rest of the night the nobles gave us so many gifts: jewelry, clothing, blankets, tapestries, statues, and beautiful birds. The high priest of Quetzalcoatl sprinkled us with water and octli, and then we feasted. I sat with Black Otter for a while but climbed in my mother's lap after the meal and fell asleep. I missed her soft skin and the smell of her bone flower perfume.

Eventually Father carried me to bed. He smelled sweet with tobacco—a scent I'd missed much longer than my mother's. I latched my arms around his neck and snuggled against him.

"I wish her to sleep with me tonight," Mother said when we reached her doorway.

"But I was planning to stay with you tonight," Father said.

"I miss my daughter and want her close tonight."

Father sighed, then handed me over to her. "Tomorrow night she goes back to the nursery. She's too old to share her mother's bed."

"But you won't stay with us?"

"I must stay with one of the others."

"Of course," Mother said with a sigh. She wished him good night, and I puzzled over Father's regretful look as the handmaiden closed the door curtain on him.

Someday that will be Black Otter waiting outside your door, I realized, struck with a strange sense of clarity. *And that's supposed to be happiness?*

CHAPTER THREE

When Mother and I came to the Women's Hall in the morning, Father's concubines were chattering in a flurry of heated, indignant discussion which fell silent as we walked through the doorway. They watched us as we wound through the many looms spread about the stone floor to our mats on the open patio overlooking the royal gardens, but Mother held her head high in spite of them. Many of my sisters watched us too, though mostly they wore expressions of curiosity.

"She finally deems us worthy of taking breakfast with again," someone whispered.

I looked around—no one spoke nastily about my mother—but Mother pulled me along. Finally we sat next to my sister Jade Flower and her mother Zeltzin in the sunlight stretching under the stone eaves, and a servant brought us bowls of honeyed atole.

When the conversation settled, Zeltzin leaned closer and whispered, "Is it true, Chimalma? Did the gods grant you another child?"

"A son," my mother confirmed.

Zeltzin smiled. "I'm glad we made that trip to Xochicalco last spring to make offerings to Quetzalcoatl." She cast her gaze around, and some of the other women stiffened and turned away. "Not everyone's pleased though."

"There's no pleasing some of them," Mother answered.

"Why not?" I asked. When I looked to one of my older sisters nearby, the girl sneered at me, so I stuck my tongue out at her.

"Mind your manners," Mother reminded me, but smiled.

Once I finished my atole, I started my daily work. Mother taught me weaving, and the fine art of being a good wife, and I rather liked the first but found the rules of the second annoying. Girls were expected to be proficient at weaving by age seven, but thanks to Mother's teaching, my own skills excelled. We made intricately-patterned rugs and blankets as gifts for Father's allies, though the tapestry of fish and snakes we were working on now would hang in the meditation room of the high priest of the rain god Tlaloc.

Jade Flower's mother was already unraveling most of the work her daughter had done the day before. Shameful, considering Jade Flower was almost two years past her Naming Day, but she didn't seem to care. She preferred gossip to weaving lessons. "What's it like being married?" she whispered, so our mothers wouldn't overhear.

"All right, I guess." Nothing had really changed.

She gave a dreamy sigh. "You're so lucky, Quetzalpetlatl. Black Otter is so handsome."

I snickered. Black Otter *was* handsome, but nothing short of black magic would make me admit so to her. She might be my sister and a friend, but she couldn't keep secrets.

"Does he kiss you?" she asked, breathless. Heat traveled up my face as some my older sisters turned to listen as well.

"Of course we don't!"

They giggled behind their hands and Mother looked up from her weaving, questions in her gaze. "We don't do such foul things," I spouted.

Jade Flower laughed, but her mother said, "Such talk is uncalled for, and inappropriate. I won't have anyone saying I'm raising you to be anything but a proper king's daughter."

"Yes, Mother." Jade Flower grinned at me.

But when Jade Flower and I left the Women's Hall to join the rest of our siblings for afternoon play in the yard, the other girls followed us, crowding around and tossing out questions: "Does Black Otter come to your room in the middle of the night, like Father comes to my mother's room?" or "Did he give you that flower in your hair?" or, from one of my oldest sisters, "Has he gotten you with child yet?" My face burned so hot I felt dizzy. They all cackled.

I shoved the oldest in the chest, making the others gasp. She gave me a "how dare you!" look, so I put up my fists, just like Black Otter had shown me. I didn't have to take such nonsense.

"What's going on here?" Nochuatl suddenly asked behind me, and the girls scattered.

"They were making fun of Quetzalpetlatl," Jade Flower said, and I broke down into sobs.

He gathered me into his arms and stroked my hair. "They don't mean real harm."

"I hate every one of them!" I sputtered.

"They're just curious."

"And jealous," Jade Flower added.

Nochuatl laughed. "And that. Don't worry about them. They'll tire of it, and everything will get back to normal. You'll see."

The royal play yard was next to the kitchens, so Jade Flower and I picked up a couple of tlaxcallis to eat before going outside. Most of the yard was covered in plastered flagstone so the boys could practice the sacred ball game with their rubber balls while the girls watched and made fun of their mistakes from the shade of the trees at the edge of the patio.

But today, no one was playing Tlachtli; instead everyone was gathered in a chanting mob around two boys beating each other up.

I searched for Black Otter—we never missed a fight—but I couldn't find him. The old matrons who usually made sure we behaved were gone, probably finding someone to break up the fight. I squeezed through the crowd, headed for the front. Jade Flower held my dress to keep up.

My oldest brothers crowded the front line, and they elbowed me back when I started worming past them. I prodded a few into looking down at me and they grudgingly stepped aside. Being the Princess of Culhuacan had its advantages.

Jade Flower gasped and pointed. Black Otter was in the center of the crowd, red-faced and swinging fists at my much larger brother, Itzcoatl, who held him back by a fistful of his hair, laughing and taunting. "Your arms are too short, Lake Monster!" Itzcoatl crowed, then rammed his knee into Black Otter's stomach. Black Otter keeled over, heaving, and Itzcoatl leaned over him, laughing. "Next time get into a fight with a girl, so you don't get the piss beaten out of you."

"Princess Black Otter!" my brothers sang.

Incensed, I shoved the nearest one, sending him stumbling from the circle and slamming into Itzcoatl, knocking them both over. Itzcoatl glared until he saw me; then he laughed. "Now your wife must fight your battles for you? Pathetic!"

Black Otter glared at me, filling me with shame, but then he lunged at Itzcoatl, taking the larger boy by surprise. They swung fists and cursed, rolling around on the hard ground, but soon Itzcoatl started howling and kicking. "Get him off me! Get him off me!" he screamed, as he struggled to his feet. Black Otter had got his hands up under his mantle and dangled like a large rock tied between his legs, but when he twisted, Itzcoatl's knees buckled and he collapsed, his high-pitched wail raising the hairs on my neck.

The oldest boys descended on Black Otter, kicking and punching.

Ihuitimal shoved me aside as he broke through the crowd and tossed the boys aside. Black Otter only let go once his father cuffed him on the cheek. Itzcoatl lay in a heap, sobbing. An old woman knelt beside him, stroking his sweaty hair. "You should have broken this up immediately, My Lord. The king will be very angry."

"He should think twice before picking on someone smaller than him," Ihuitimal replied. Black Otter wiped his bloody nose as Ihuitimal pulled him over to one of the doorways.

"Oh, he's so brave!" Jade flower crooned.

I glared at her, then followed them over to the doorway, keeping at a distance as Ihuitimal squatted to talk to Black Otter.

"Always remember there's no such thing as dirty tactics," Ihuitimal said. "The teachers at the House of Warriors will try to fill your head with nonsense about honor and fair fighting, but in the real world—in real battle when the enemy will drag you off to the sacrifice—if you must cut the stones off your enemy to get away, you do it. You're Culhuacan's heir, and that takes precedence over everything else. Understand?"

"Yes, Father," Black Otter said.

"But men also don't accept help from any woman. Quetzalpetlatl's duty is to be silent and follow your orders, and if she fails, deal with her swiftly, just as you would any soldier in your army."

Black Otter flicked his gaze over at me before slowly nodding.

I felt struck through with an arrow. *How could you agree, Black Otter?* I thought, tears threatening. *You promised we'd be nothing like your parents.* The phantom pain in my wrist—where I'd thought the snake had bitten me days ago—returned. When Mother and my aunt came out of the kitchens, I ran and clutched Mother's dress, my insides boiling.

Eloxochitl gasped. "What happened?" she demanded, as she knelt and dabbed at Black Otter's wounds with the hem of her dress.

Ihuitimal swatted her away. "Leave the boy alone. A bloody nose now and then won't hurt him."

Seeing the old matron helping Itzcoatl limp inside, Mother asked, "What happened?"

"Lessons in battle tactics and underestimating your enemy," Ihuitimal said with a creepy smile.

"The play yard isn't the place for teaching battle tactics."

"You have no sons, so I wouldn't expect you to understand."

Mother's face flushed, and I wanted her to say something nasty back, but she held her tongue, like a good Tolteca woman was expected to.

Father and Nochuatl stepped out of the doorway, and Mother bowed in greeting. "What's the matter?" Father asked. "You look upset."

"I'm fine," she murmured.

"I heard there was a brawl but I trust you took care of it, Brother?" When Ihuitimal nodded, Father bent to scrutinize Black Otter's face. "None the worse, I hope?"

"I'm fine, your Majesty," Black Otter replied.

"Good. Today you'll join me and Nochuatl on a hunt."

Black Otter smiled wide.

To me, Father added, "And you'll spend the afternoon with Ihuitimal."

My stomach dropped. An entire afternoon with Ihuitimal? After what he said to Black Otter?

Ihuitimal was as unenthused as me. "Whatever for?"

"You must oversee her spiritual transition into your son's household, to show her what's expected of her as Black Otter's wife," Father replied.

Dear gods! He's going to make me worship that evil Smoking Mirror!

Mother cast a sharp stare at Father.

To my relief, Eloxochitl stepped up. "My husband is very busy, your Excellency, but I'd be honored to tutor Quetzalpetlatl for the afternoon." I wanted to hug her.

Father considered for a moment, and Mother said it was an excellent idea, but after some hesitation, Ihuitimal said, "No, she'll come with me. I won't shun my duty." He cast a spear-like gaze down at me. "I was on my way to the menagerie to feed some of the animals."

That didn't sound so bad. I liked watching the servants feed the tapirs and otters.

"Excellent." To me, Father said, "Be respectful and well-mannered, Quetzalpetlatl."

"Of course, Father." Why did he think he always had to remind me?

Mother lingered a moment after the others left, still worried, but then finally disappeared into the darkened entryway.

Ihuitimal gave me a skeptical frown. "Come." He then strode through the entryway too. I ran to keep up with him. He took a basket from a servant standing in the hallway and shoved it into my hands. "You will carry this." Its weight surprised me, as did the jostling as something inside tried to nudge the lid open. Ropes kept it secure, though. "Now hurry. I'm late."

We cut through the kitchens to the back hallway leading to the portico. Ihuitimal snapped for me to keep up as we descended the stone stairs and headed towards the archway marking the entrance to the royal menagerie. I sweated under the heavy load, trying not to kick the basket. My arms felt like melting wax.

We passed the tapirs and monkeys, and I noticed no servants out feeding the animals. *That's because they feed them in the morning*, I remembered. I followed Ihuitimal past the mangrove trees to where the pumas, jaguars, and ocelots lived. He waited for me at a stone bench next to one of the jaguar pens.

Father had three black and yellow jaguars, but this one was an unusually large, solid black one I hadn't seen before. I eyed it as I set the heavy basket on the stone bench. It stared back, ears twitching and nostrils flaring as it rested on a log in its cage.

"Proper women don't keep their men waiting," Ihuitimal scolded. I almost said I could have kept up better if he'd carried the basket, but that would just get me into trouble. "You have much to learn about being a proper wife, but you're still young and easily molded."

I bowed, hiding my scowl. "Of course, Uncle."

"You will address me as 'My Lord'. I've earned that right."

"Of course, My Lord."

"First, always remember that your husband doesn't need your opinion or actions when it comes to dealing with other men. Like today when you shoved that other boy."

"But he called Black Otter names!"

"That's his dishonor to deal with. You only worsened his humiliation."

"He would've come to my defense." Anger slithered into my voice.

"Because you're a woman...or rather, will be, someday."

"But we're friends...and friends defend each other."

"He's your husband," Ihuitimal corrected me. "The days of you two carrying on any other way are over. Your place is at the loom, not climbing trees and killing snakes."

My wrist started itching and I scratched it behind my back. "Yes, Uncle—I mean, My Lord."

"A proper woman also formally addresses her husband at all times, just as you would address me. Nor will he address you by that childish name you had as a baby."

I felt as if he'd slapped me. With all these stupid rules, I didn't want to be married to Black Otter anymore.

"This is much to take in, but you'll grow used to it," Ihuitimal said. "Embrace your proper role, and all will be fine."

This word "proper" seemed no better than a wooden slave collar. I despised the very sound of it.

"You'll best serve Black Otter when he's king by keeping the perfect image of the supporting wife. It's why correcting your bad habits now is important," Ihuitimal went on.

"But what if Black Otter doesn't become king?" I asked.

Ihuitimal raised an eyebrow. "Why wouldn't he?"

"Quetzalcoatl gave Mother a son." How annoying that I had to state the obvious.

He flashed me a ghastly smile. "It still remains to be seen whether there's truly a son or not."

He still didn't believe? "Quetzalcoatl is a great and powerful god, Uncle—I mean, My Lord—and he promised Mother a son, so he will give her one."

"Maybe, but the boy must then survive childbirth, no small feat considering that your mother lost many children in the womb even before she had you. Bearing a child is dangerous enough without involving the gods. She should cast it away or she'll never see her own grandchildren."

I frowned, confused. "What do you mean?"

"Your mother nearly died giving birth to you, and having another child will kill her, and the baby. She's foolish to even consider carrying this child."

My heart flopped like a dying fish in my chest. Surely mother didn't wish to die. "But then why is Mother so happy?" I asked, sure he wasn't telling me everything.

"Blind faith can be very dangerous, Quetzalpetlatl. What do mortals truly know about the intentions of the gods?" He removed the lid from the basket and pulled a rabbit out by its ears. When it squealed, he cradled its bottom with his other hand.

The jaguar perked up its ears and twitched its nose, suddenly interested. As Ihuitimal approached the cage, it jumped from its perch, tail swishing. "In my experience, the gods are like jaguars," Ihuitimal said. "They care not whether they kill their keepers; they just want their due." He held the rabbit out through the bars of the cage.

He's crazy! I wanted to look away, just knowing the cat would tear his arm off, but a strange excitement kept me watching.

The jaguar hissed and backed away, but then snatched the rabbit from Ihuitimal's hands. The rabbit's scream jolted me, and I started inexplicably sweating, my heart thudding painfully in my chest. The jaguar quickly silenced the rabbit, but that did little to lessen the alarming distress coursing through me. It was like watching a brother or sister die, rather than an animal. I had to look away.

"Don't ever turn away from the sacrifice, or someday you'll find yourself the one on the sacrificial stone," Ihuitimal warned. "Everyone must eat, even the gods. Your mother's taught you admirable devotion to the Feathered Serpent, but never forget that Quetzalcoatl doesn't rule the heavens alone. Every god must be given due, and I'll properly educate you so you're prepared to serve your husband's chosen god."

But I don't want to worship your Smoking Mirror, I almost said, but bit back the words. *You promised—swore on Quetzalcoatl—and you can't break that.*

"That's all for today." Ihuitimal turned his back on me.

That's when I saw the glimmer of emerald and white from the corner of my eye. I looked towards the bench where I thought it was, but saw nothing. My wrist started throbbing though, and dizziness swept in and words filled my head like a song desperate to burst forth. So I obeyed. "The Feathered Serpent is merciful, but he is also fierce, so beware your meddling lest he crush you in his divine coils." Once the last word left my lips, the dizziness lifted, leaving me feeling very happy.

Ihuitimal stared at me, incredulous for a moment, but then he narrowed his eyes. "What did you say?"

That look killed my peace. "I bade you farewell, My Lord, and thanked you for your wisdom." I swallowed hard.

"Did you?" He sneered. "Beware the words your mother puts in your mouth, little one. You're just like her, and see what befell her? Left barren and telling her only daughter to trust in dreams from the gods." His words rekindled my anger, but before I could snap off at him—and likely get a lashing—he added, "Run along and play. The days will only get shorter now." He didn't turn from me as I walked away this time.

CHAPTER FOUR

I'd hoped life would go back to normal after the wedding, but soon I wished I'd never married Black Otter. I quickly tired of the adults nagging me, particularly the old matrons who now kept an even closer watch on me in the yard so Black Otter and I could no longer sneak away to the aviary or spy on the servants tending the gardens.

Though with the other boys increasing their torments of him, Black Otter had little time to sneak away anyway. Packs of my brothers tailed him everywhere, goading him into fights he usually lost. Soon he didn't want to talk to me anymore and ran when he saw me. Everything I'd feared came true.

"I wish I was married to Black Otter," Jade Flower often told me. "It's so romantic, like a love story. Do you think he'll have concubines, like Father does? Oh I hope I'm one of them!"

I wanted to punch her, but Mother had told me that jealousy was an ugly beast undeserving of a princess's company. "If marriage was a love story, Black Otter wouldn't hate me now," I told her instead.

But I had my own reasons to hate him too. I could tolerate his ignoring me, but I couldn't stand him moving in on my father's affections. He sat at Father's side in court, listening to the peasants fight over land boundaries and turkeys, and they spent every afternoon in the men's private yard, practicing with swords and spears. He even hunted deer with Father and Nochuatl once a week. Whereas my heart had missed Father before, now it burned with resentment.

"I wish I was a boy," I told Mother as we walked through the market on our way to the Temple of Quetzalcoatl, to make offerings to honor his miracle. I hadn't wanted to come along—already I hated my unborn brother, for he too would enjoy my father's company—but it was better than being spied on by old women. "It's not fair! Why wasn't I born a boy, Mother?"

"Because the gods wished you to be a girl," she said. "Being a woman is difficult, but men go off to war, many to die and never see their loved ones again. Everyone makes sacrifices."

"It's still not fair," I huffed. "Everybody hates me; the old women, Ihuitimal, Black Otter, even Father."

"Your father doesn't hate you."

"If I was a boy, he would love me."

"That's enough, Quetzalpetlatl." Mother only used my proper name when I was in trouble. "Maybe your father's right. I don't wish to send you away to calmecac already, but perhaps you need the school's strict rules to remind you of your place."

I hung my head, seething inside. *Father has turned Mother against me too.*

Mother knelt before me. "I understand how you feel, Papalotl. I didn't understand why my own father distanced himself from me—"

"What did we do wrong?" I cried.

"Nothing. The world has an order: men and women cross paths for certain reasons, but other than that, we all live our own lives."

"I don't want to live apart from Father, or Black Otter, or Uncle Nochuatl. I'm happy when they're around."

"They make me happy, too." Mother smoothed my hair and sighed. "I'm sorry the world is not fairer. The gods know I don't want you to be miserable, and you deserve better than this life your father thinks is best for you." She thought a moment, then smiled and said, "When we finish at the temple, we'll go down to the lake and see if your father will let us watch him and Black Otter spearing ducks."

I smiled and nodded eagerly.

¤

We followed the path behind the temple down to the lakeshore. Fishing boats dotted the lake, the afternoon sun shining brightly off the cerulean water and making me squint. Seeing the boats reminded me of the trips Father and I used to make in the royal canoe, and how I loved to stare at his wavering reflection in the surface off the side.

The memory brought a smile to my face, especially when I saw him sitting on a log a little further down the beach. His guards waved us by when we neared them. My happiness melted away, though, when I saw Black Otter sitting next to my father, listening intently as he showed him how to grip an atl-atl stick.

Seeing us approach, Father rose to greet us. "Is something the matter?"

"We're finished making offerings, and Quetzalpetlatl wished to come see you and Black Otter," Mother answered.

Father frowned. "A woman's place isn't out hunting with her husband—"

"She just wants to watch."

"Surely she has weaving that needs doing—"

"I finished my weaving for the day," I said, giving Father a bow.

Father scrunched his brows, but Mother took his hand and led him away a few steps. "Please, let her have this one little favor. She misses you so much."

"It's not appropriate."

"She's not your best friend's wife. She thinks she did something wrong and you're punishing her."

"I am not!"

"Then give her a little of your time."

Father pulled Mother further away so I couldn't hear them anymore, so I turned to Black Otter. He ignored me as he loaded an arrow into a notch at the end of a wooden baton. "What's that?" He said nothing, so I pushed on. "Can I see it?"

He gave me a scathing look before going back to work. I watched, numb with anger. We'd been friends a very long time—for five of my seven years—and for him to so suddenly turn on me stung as if I'd inhaled chili powder. "Why do you hate me so?" My choked voice spoiled my anger.

He turned still further away. "I don't hate you."

"Why don't you talk to me anymore then?"

"You wouldn't understand."

"Yes I would!"

"No, you wouldn't. You don't know anything about being a man—"

"And neither do you."

He turned on me, furious. "You're just a little girl, so shut up."

I had to tolerate such nastiness for my uncle, but I wouldn't abide it from my best friend. Embracing the rage rising inside me, I lunged, knocking him into the wet sand, pummeling him with my fists. I said nothing, just gritted my teeth and bloodied his nose and cut his lip, and I would've bashed both his eyes in if Father hadn't yanked me back.

"Great Feathered Serpent! What are you doing?" Father pinned my arms to my sides. "What demon has possessed you?"

"Who's just a little girl now?" I screamed. Black Otter stared at me, wide-eyed with fright.

My father squeezed, cutting off my breath until I stopped flailing, then he set me down. "What's gotten into you?"

"I hate you!" I shouted over my shoulder at Black Otter.

But then Father smacked me; just a small strike across the face to draw my attention, but hard enough to leave my cheek numb and my heart thrumming like a hummingbird's wings. Concern rather than anger filled my father's eyes; an expression shared by my mother a few steps behind him. "You will go back to the palace and sit in the nursery," Father said, his voice trembling. "In the morning, your mother will take you to the calmecac and the priestesses will teach you to have respect for your parents and your husband." He pushed me away.

Mother reached for my hand, but I wrapped my arms around Father's leg, trying to keep him from leaving. "I'm sorry, Father," I sobbed. "I didn't mean any of it!"

"Remove yourself from my sight or the guard will do it for you," he snarled. "You've dishonored me. Now I must explain to my brother why I bring his son back abused and bloodied at the hands of a girl. Maybe I should give you over to Ihuitimal for punishment."

The thought sent spikes of terror through me. I'd never envied Black Otter for his father; Ihuitimal punished Black Otter harshly for the slightest infraction, so I didn't dare think of what he'd do to me. "Please no, Father! Hold me over the chili roaster or make me help in the kitchen every day for the next year, but please don't hand me over to my uncle! He's the high priest of a demon god who hates Quetzalcoatl and he threatened to kill Black Otter if he worshiped the Feathered Serpent! He will surely feed my heart to his awful Smoking Mirror!"

Father stared me agape but then turned to Black Otter. Black Otter stared back at us, fear and betrayal painted on his face. My stomach dropped. I'd broken my oath on Quetzalcoatl's good name.

"This is true?" Father boomed. When Black Otter didn't answer, Father sprang upon him like a puma, yanking him to his feet by his hair. "Has your father brought that abomination into my city? Does he worship him in my palace?"

"Yes, Your Highness!" Black Otter shouted, tears streaming down his face.

"And what about you?"

"I worship as my father tells me to!"

Father twisted Black Otter's hair. "Then I wedded my favorite daughter to some spineless demon worshiper?" I imagined him gutting my best friend right there next to the lake.

But I wouldn't let him. *Bite his leg, then Black Otter can break free and swim across the lake. You'll get a lashing for sure, but it'll be worth it. This is your fault.*

I made to rush at Father, but Mother grabbed me, clutching me with both arms. I struggled, but her strength held, leaving me only one option. "Please don't hurt him, Father! I'm sorry, Black Otter! I didn't mean to tell, I swear!" With all my fight drained, I wept against Mother's arms while she whispered that everything would be all right.

Father regained his composure, perhaps moved by my sobs. "We're going back to the palace." He shoved Black Otter over to one of his guards, then started up the hill.

¤

The argument raging down the hall was so loud that Father and Ihuitimal might as well have been right outside my nursery's door curtain.

"I warned you not to bring that deceitful Chichimec god into Culhuacan, but you dare flaunt your treachery by setting up an altar to him in my own palace?" Father roared.

"I dare?" Ihuitimal shouted back. "You talk endlessly about your merciful Feathered Serpent, but where was he when I was being tortured by the Chichimecs? Where were *you,* Brother?"

"We're not discussing that now—"

"It's never a discussion for you, because you're afraid of the truth. You owe me, Mixcoatl, for everything you took from me—"

"And I repay that debt now by not executing you and your son for treason. Leave my palace and never darken my lands with your shadow again!"

Everything fell silent. I pulled aside my door curtain, but the guard pushed me back in. "Don't come out again," he warned, so I peered out the crack between the wall and curtain.

Ihuitimal passed by, surrounded by guards. I couldn't see Black Otter, but I heard him pleading, "I'm sorry, Father. Please forgive me!" Ihuitimal said nothing, his face livid. I sank into the corner and wept.

Mother finally came for me and took my hand. "Your father wishes to speak with you."

But I didn't want to go and made the guard carry me down the hall to Father's room.

Nochuatl looked up at me with a sad smile, but my father paced, fists clenched. The walls' murals of bloody battles made me more anxious, especially when Father stalked towards me. Only Mother's supportive hand on my shoulder kept me from bolting. Father said, "What did that traitor's son tell you, about his father and this Smoking Mirror?" I only blinked, startled, so he shook me. "Tell me, Quetzalpetlatl!"

"She's just a child, Mixcoatl," Mother scolded him. "She doesn't know what you're asking for." She knelt and wiped my tears away. "Can you tell me when you first learned of Smoking Mirror?"

"On my wedding night. Black Otter said his father wouldn't let him come to the temple with us because his god was Quetzalcoatl's enemy, and that worshiping the Feathered Serpent made him weak."

"What else?"

"He said Uncle Ihuitimal would bring Smoking Mirror's worship to the Tolteca—"

"I knew it!" Father barked. "How dare he lie through his sharpened teeth?"

"Is there anything else your uncle might have said that upset you?" Mother pressed.

I nodded, eager to tattle on my wicked uncle. "That day, in the menagerie, he blasphemed against Quetzalcoatl and said Black Otter was going to be king after Father, and that keeping the baby was going to kill you. But he just wanted to scare me, didn't he?"

Mother looked ready to say something, but Father interrupted her. "Of course he lies. That's all he knows how to do." To Nochuatl, he added, "You were right, Brother. If I'd died before Black Otter came of age, Ihuitimal would've taken the throne himself, and no doubt killed my son, to ensure Black Otter's claim." He punched the wall, breaking off the plaster, then he turned on me, his eyes dark and accusing. "And you! Why didn't you immediately tell someone about this?"

"Black Otter made me swear on Quetzalcoatl's good name," I sobbed. "He said his father would flog him like a criminal if I told anyone."

"The boy's lucky *I* didn't beat him for keeping such a secret," Father snapped.

"You're being unfair, tossing him to the coyotes like this," Nochuatl said. "If Father had told you to keep a secret, would you have questioned it?"

"Our Father never would've made us privy to dangerous secrets, for our own good. If the boy had come to me, I would've protected him. But he didn't. My brother can do with him as he wishes."

Nochuatl gave him a sharp stare.

"But we're married, Father, so Black Otter is as good as your son, right?" I asked, hopeful.

Father shook his head. "I've dissolved that union and sent his family into exile in the north."

Black Otter was going to live with the barbarian Chichimecs? I trembled, guilt stabbing my heart.

"You should execute Ihuitimal rather than exiling him, Brother," Nochuatl said. "Eloxochitl and Black Otter are innocent in all this—"

"They both knew, so they aren't innocent," Father snapped. "As for Ihuitimal, I owed him a debt and now I've repaid it. I won't discuss it anymore." He scowled when he saw me crying. "Why are you carrying on again?"

"Will I ever get to see Black Otter again? I didn't even get to say goodbye." Or to tell him how sorry I was for betraying his trust.

"Stop being emotional over a demon-worshiper. It's time to send you off to calmecac, so you can learn to control yourself, like a proper woman."

"Brother, have mercy on her," Nochuatl said. "You can't expect her to snuff her feelings out for her best friend like you would blow out a lamp."

"When you've finally let go of the past and taken a wife and sired a few more children, then you may lecture me on how to raise my daughter. Now out, everyone. I need peace after all this nonsense."

Mother and I followed Nochuatl, but he vanished into his room, a wake of anger behind him.

¤

I shared Mother's bed that night so I wouldn't have to be alone, but even her soothing humming couldn't bring me sleep. I pressed my cheek against her belly, staring at the painting of the Feathered Serpent that covered the wall next to her bed and feeling I might never move again. "Close your eyes and try to sleep. We have to get up early to go to the temple," she said.

"Then you're taking me to the calmecac tomorrow?" I choked.

"I think it best you stay here with your sisters a while longer, so I'll speak with your father in the morning, when he's in a more reasonable mood."

That loosened some of the painful knots in my chest. "I'm sorry I disappointed you, Mother. And Father too."

"I'm not disappointed. Your father just forgets what it's like to not live life fearing that people are trying to harm you."

"But why would anyone want to hurt him?"

"It's one of the perils of being king." She kissed my head. "Now try to sleep."

But instead my bitter words to Black Otter repeated over and over in my head. I'd never get to chase him through the gardens again, nor get to tell him that I really hadn't minded the kiss that much. *I wish that statue were really Quetzalcoatl, so he could crush me in his coils,* I thought as I stared at the small stone idol next to the bed. Mother prayed in front of it every night. *It's what I deserve, for breaking a promise I made on his good name.*

I startled when something pushed against my back. I turned, but Mother was asleep. I poked at her dress, wondering if a mouse had crawled up into it, but I felt only her slightly-swollen belly. *You're so tired you're imagining things.*

But then I felt it again, this time where my hand rested against Mother's stomach. "Great Feathered Serpent!" I gasped as a bulge slid under my hand. "What is that?"

"Your brother," Mother whispered.

"Truly?"

She nodded. "He's moving already."

"Is he supposed to?"

"You did the same, just not so soon."

I followed the moving bulge with my hand for a moment then asked, "Did you swallow a piece of jade to put me in your belly, or was it a feather?"

Mother laughed. "How you came to be in there is a discussion for when you're older."

I set my cheek against her stomach, amazed at my brother's movements. It was like seeing a distant light when I'd been sure I'd have to spend the night out in the cold rain. The pain of Black Otter's leaving lessened a bit.

"I'll be your friend, Brother, if you'll be mine," I whispered to him. I smiled as he pressed against my cheek as if in answer. "I think he said yes!"

She smiled. "I hope the two of you grow up to be the best of friends."

CHAPTER FIVE

Father said to forget about Black Otter, but I couldn't. Where was he, and had his father made good on his threats? Hopefully they were exaggerations, like the way my brothers always said they wanted to kill each other but never did. The adults whispered about Ihuitimal's departure while my brothers and sisters made up stories as to why. Even those who'd bullied Black Otter showed surprising concern for his absence.

Jade Flower took a different tack. She refused to talk to me, so I spent my afternoons with my mother in the Women's Hall, working on my weaving. I passed a few months working on a blanket for my unborn brother, but I tore out more work than I finished as I made mistakes over and over again. Mother offered me advice, but she mostly left me to my work.

But when the weather turned cold and damp with the first signs of fall, Mother came to me with bad news. "You're starting calmecac next week," she said as she tucked me into bed. When I started crying, she said, "I was your age when I started calmecac, and I was very afraid too. This is when we'd planned to send you even before all this mess with your uncle, so we're not punishing you. It's just your time. And you won't live in the dormitories until the beginning of the year. Everything will be fine; you'll make new friends, learn to read and write and keep the calendar, and you'll have a few years as a priestess before your father calls you back to do your duty to the family. Just as I did." Her voice faded with a hint of regret.

"Did you like being a priestess?" I asked.

"I loved being a priestess."

"Do you wish you were still one?"

She sighed. "What I truly wanted was that I could've married Mixcoatl, but also remained a priestess. Unfortunately, I had no choice either way; as my father's eldest daughter, I had duties that superseded anything else." She hugged and held me for a moment. "If the gods would grant me one wish, it would be that life treat you better than it has me."

I thought of Mother's words often over the next three weeks as I spent my days at the Temple of Quetzalcoatl. The priestesses were strict; failing to sweep behind the gold Feathered Serpent idol got me a switch across my palms; if I spoke out of turn, they held me over the chili roasters in the school kitchen; and if I was late for my day's duty, they kept me well after dark with extra chores. I missed the afternoons with Mother in the Women's Hall, particularly now that she'd opened up a hidden door into her life and showed me what was inside. I wanted to know so much more about her.

I stayed home during the last week of the year, for tradition said no one should work during these dangerous Leftover Days, which were unaccounted for on either our harvest or festival calendars. The Tolteca didn't even wage war on those days, for it might anger the gods. Everyone kept their heads covered so the gods couldn't see them, and they spoke in whispers. Most people remained in their rooms, to be safe.

A few days before the beginning of the new year, Mother came to the Women's Hall where I was working on the blanket in front of the hearth and told me Father wanted see me in his quarters. Remembering how he'd acted the last time I was there, it struck me through with fear when Mother said she wasn't coming with me. "He wants to speak with you alone," she said. I felt I was walking to my doom as I left the Women's Hall.

Luckily I met Nochuatl in the hallway, and his cheerful greeting eased my nerves. "Are you enjoying calmecac so far?" he asked, as we walked together.

"Not really."

He laughed. "It's a big change," he admitted.

"I don't like change."

"We've had more than our share of it," he said. "While we must move on, we don't have to forget. I miss Black Otter too."

I swallowed back a spike of anguish. "Do you think he's all right?"

Nochuatl didn't answer right away. "I hope so."

"Do you think we'll get to see him again?"

"I don't know. The bitterness runs deep between Ihuitimal and the king."

"Why?"

"It goes a long way back, before your father became king. Ihuitimal has a right to be angry, but we have to let go of the past, before it completely destroys us."

"Is that why Father told you all that stuff about getting married?" I asked. But seeing the stricken look on Nochuatl's face, I regretted saying anything.

When we arrived at Father's doorway, Nochuatl smiled at me. "Yes, that's why your father told me to move on."

"I'm sorry I upset you, Uncle."

He hugged me. "You haven't anything to be sorry about," he said, then left me to face Father alone. I rang the copper bells on the hem of the door curtain.

Father called me inside. He sat on the floor in front of the hearth, burning copalli incense and wearing a cloak that didn't cover his head. He smiled the way he had on my wedding day, easing my mind a little. "Come sit with me, Quetzalpetlatl."

I sat near the unlit hearth with him; no one lit the house fires during the Leftover Days. He didn't say anything for a moment, but then asked, "So the big day approaches? Finally moving into the dormitories at the calmecac? I was very frightened my first night in the House of Warriors, but just knowing Ihuitimal was a few beds away made it better. He'd been there two years already, learning the art of war, and he would've rather have shaved his head than have me dogging after him, but still, he was a comfort to have around." The way he spoke about Ihuitimal seemed nostalgic and kind. I found it puzzling. "Remember that you have older sisters at the calmecac, and they'll help you if you need it. You'll do well though. Your faith in Quetzalcoatl is your strength. Your mother did an excellent job of raising you to respect the gods and she's very proud of you. So am I."

I smiled shyly, unused to him praising me anymore.

He paused, taking a deep breath, then said, "I know I've been very hard on you, and that I wasn't any source of comfort or trust for you when Black Otter left, and I'm very sorry for that. I hope you can find the strength to forgive me my faults."

Father's admission shocked me; and though I also knew it took him a great deal to admit this, at first I didn't entirely trust it. I'd spent so long trying to be what he wanted me to be that this sudden change baffled me.

He took my hand in his. "I don't want you thinking I put you in calmecac to get you out from under my feet. Your mother was right. I always showed you more favor than any of my other daughters, so it shouldn't have surprised me that pushing you away hurt you so. But I want to repair the damage I did. I'll visit you twice a week and I'll take you to the market or out in the royal canoe, or we'll just walk the gardens and you can tell me everything you're learning."

"Truly?" I asked, daring to raise my hopes.

He nodded. "And if you haven't anything planned for the rest of this afternoon, you can stay here and I'll teach you to play patolli."

That startled me even more. "But patolli is a man's game."

He leaned forward and whispered, "Just don't tell your mother. She would kill me for teaching you to gamble."

Not caring about decorum or rules, I flung my arms around his neck like a baby monkey and hugged him tight. When he hugged me back instead of pushing me away, I let slip a few tears. I'd finally gotten my Tatli back. "I love you," I whispered.

"And I will always love you, my little Butterfly, no matter what."

¤

"How much longer?" I asked Mother when I touched her belly, checking if my brother was moving. He usually touched my hand while I sang him a song, but tonight he sat very still. Mother had grown very round in the few months since I'd first felt him moving around.

"A while still," Mother said, pulling my blanket up to my chin. "He'll come no sooner than his time."

"You'll tell me when he's born, and bring him to see me?"

"I'll summon you when it's time." She smoothed my hair and smiled. "Did you and your father have a nice talk this afternoon? I haven't seen you so happy in months."

"He promised to come and see me at school twice a week. Will you come too?"

"Of course. But now to sleep with you. It wouldn't do for the gods to see us up late whispering during the Leftover Days." And she blew out the flames on the nursery's lamps.

¤

I awoke when my itching wrist flared up again for the first time in months. I tried not to scratch but couldn't help myself. *Maybe washing it will help,* I thought. I pulled a cloak over my shoulders against the evening chill then padded down the hall to the side corridor that led out to the bathhouse.

A small torch burned over the large water jar near the doorway, giving me enough light to examine my wrist. Four ugly red bumps stood out, two on top and two on the bottom, like a snakebite. I poured cold water over them but it did nothing, making my stomach knot. *Wake Mother and have her look at it,* I decided, so I dried my hands then turned to the hallway.

A coughing sound—like the call of the jaguar—echoed from the main corridor, and a shadow moved in the darkness. When yellow eyes flashed at me, my heart jumped into my throat and I stumbled backwards, knocking over the water jar. There was a jaguar in the palace!

But when I looked again, I saw nothing. The sweet smell of tobacco smoke wafted out of the doorway. *It's probably just a guard,* I told myself, but fear held me captive. If it was a jaguar, it had me trapped.

Hot pine pitch dripped off the torch onto my shoulder, scalding my skin. I scratched it off quickly and glared at the torch as I moved away, but then remembered having seen the servants use one to force Father's jaguars into cages so they could clean the pens. Maybe I could use the torch to get past this jaguar. *Better than waiting to get eaten.*

I'd hoped holding the torch would strengthen my confidence, but I shivered like a cold dog as I approached the main hallway. I stuck the torch around the corner but the hall was empty in both directions, not even any guards. Father's doorway stood open, moonlight creeping through; he never kept his curtain open.

I crept to Mother's room, next door to Father's. Her curtain was closed but her bed was empty. I checked her private bathhouse, but she wasn't there either. "Nantli?" I whispered, wandering around the small garden, looking for her. My panic intensified. She was always in her room in the middle of the night, to give me comfort when I woke up from a nightmare.

Wake Father. I'd surely get scolded for it, but what else could I do? I ran into Father's room, praying he'd understand.

But I slid to a stop and gasped when I saw the black-robed monster hunched over Father's bed mat. Its long, matted hair glistened in the moonlight, and it sang in a harsh voice that sounded like bones snapping. I screamed, my heart thudding as if trying to break out of my chest.

The creature whirled on me, so I swung the torch, shouting, "Get back! Stay away!"

"Quetzalpetlatl! Put that down before you hurt someone!" It wasn't a demon's voice, but rather my uncle Ihuitimal's. A painted gold stripe split his face but I recognized his hideous scowl.

I dropped the torch and ran to him, wrapping my arms around him, relieved. "Thank Omeyocan you're here, Uncle!"

He pushed me away and straightened his robe as if I'd mussed it up. I opened my mouth to ask him why he was dressed like a priest of the Sun, but he said, "I said I would come back."

"Is Black Otter back too?"

"Your husband is here," Ihuitimal replied, his voice chilly. "And wiser now."

I didn't like how he said that. "Is he all right?"

"He's fine."

"Can I see him?"

"In time."

Remembering what had driven me to my father's room in the first place, I said, "There's a jaguar loose in the palace, Uncle! I saw it in the hall by the bathhouse." My wrist itched worse than ever, so I rubbed it against my side.

"I didn't see anything," Ihuitimal said. "You were just having a nightmare, child."

"I was not!" I snapped. Why did he always think I was dreaming or imagining things? And why did my wrist constantly itch around him? *You should have known better than to think he'd changed at all,* I thought, so I tried to step around him. Father at least would listen.

But when Ihuitimal blocked me, I blinked up at him, startled. "I must speak with Father."

"He can't talk right now." But then Ihuitimal seemed to reconsider. "Forgive me, fool that I sometimes am, but I forgot he'd asked me to give you a gift."

"A gift?" I asked, excited.

"To let you know how much he loves you. You must close your eyes and hold out your hands, for it's a surprise."

I did as he asked, eager. *I hope it's a necklace he made for me, so I can wear it every day and remember him while I'm away at school.*

But Ihuitimal put something heavy and wet into my hands. *Like a little dog with its skin pulled off,* I thought, then shuddered. *Don't be stupid. Father would never give you something so disgusting.*

"You may look now," Ihuitimal said, amused.

I stared down at my hands with shocked confusion for a moment before realizing what I held: a heart, warm and covered in blood. But why would he give me...?

But even before I looked up to see that Ihuitimal had stepped away from the bed, the truth struck me like a poison arrow: this was my father's heart.

Father lay on his bed, his throat cut so deeply he looked as though he had a second, gaping mouth that drooled blood. His chest was open too, his ribs snapped aside like a butchered animal. I stared, reeling, intense heat filling me. *It has to be a dream. Great Feathered Serpent, don't let this be real, this can't be real this can't be this can't be!*

But my father's sticky heart oozed in my hands. I felt as if someone were squeezing my stomach. I had to get out of there.

Dropping the heart, I turned to flee, but Ihuitimal grabbed me like an eagle seizing a rabbit. I tried to scream, but instead my stomach tossed my dinner all over the front of his robe. He roared, disgusted. My second attempt came out loud as thunder. Ihuitimal tried to clamp his hand over my mouth, but I snapped at him like a crazed dog, screaming and yelling, "Murderer!"

He threw me down on my father's dead body and struck me so hard my jaw popped and tiny stars invaded the corners of my vision. "Be quiet!" he hissed. I would have defied him, but I suddenly faded away into darkness.

But I soon awoke again, my body sluggish, and my nightdress warmly wet and clinging to my legs. Ihuitimal shook me and said something I couldn't hear at first, but like water escaping a broken dam, the sound suddenly rushed back, loud and painful. "Where is she, Quetzalpetlatl? Tell me and I'll spare you further harm," he whispered.

"What?" I muttered, confused.

"Tell me where your mother is and I'll take you to see Black Otter. You want to see him again, don't you?"

I looked over at my father again, surprised to see him; I'd forgotten he was there, what Ihuitimal had done to him, but not anymore. Even if I knew where Mother was, I wouldn't tell him. He'd kill her too.

"Unhand her, Brother, or I'll relieve you of your head," Nochuatl shouted from the doorway, sword drawn.

Ihuitimal yanked me around, twisting my arm behind my back until it threatened to pop loose of my shoulder. I wailed. "Come get me, Brother, or is your heart too soft to kill the girl to get to me?" He put an obsidian blade to my throat. I couldn't breathe.

Nochuatl backed down and my heart failed me. "Please don't leave me, Uncle," I sputtered, my tears spilling fast. "Please!"

"I won't leave you. I promise," Nochuatl said.

"Always so loyal, even in death," Ihuitimal sneered. "But then what choice did you have when Mixcoatl could turn your secrets against you at a moment's notice? Mixcoatl had no honor when it came to women, but did you really think you were clever enough not to get caught? How could I not have noticed your face when I looked at Black Otter?"

"Leave the boy out of this," Nochuatl said, taking a step forward.

"You think I'd harm him, after all the time I've invested in raising him to be *my son*?" Ihuitimal asked, mock hurt in his voice. "Maybe you had something to do with him coming into this world, but I'm the one he calls Father, I'm the one he looks to to learn about being an honorable man, a concept neither you nor Mixcoatl know anything about."

"Using a child as a shield against your enemies isn't honorable," Nochuatl snarled, but he still didn't move. Why all this talk of nonsensical things instead of rescuing me?

"I'm taking back what Mixcoatl stole from me. Step aside and she won't get hurt; fetch me Chimalma and I'll forgive your betrayal and let you live. Accept me as the rightful king of Culhuacan and you can have Eloxochitl," Ihuitimal said.

"I will never kneel before you as the king," Nochuatl said.

Guards burst into Father's room and my heart leapt, until they turned their spears on Nochuatl. They disarmed him and held his hands behind his back.

"I tried dealing fairly with you, Nochuatl, but now you leave me little choice." Ihuitimal shoved my arm up higher, making me squeal and kick. "You will bring Chimalma to me or I'll pull the wings off her precious little Butterfly. Have you ever seen a butterfly with all her wings plucked off, Brother?"

"I'll kill you if you harm her, Ihuitimal!" Nochuatl shouted.

"Then bring me her mother and our deal can still stand."

I squeezed my eyes shut against my stinging tears, but when I opened them again, I saw a flash of emerald and white, this time slithering under the logs in the hearth. My wrist flared hot and suddenly fire erupted in the hearth.

The guards jostled away, startled. Even Ihuitimal stepped back, dragging me with him.

But the flames extinguished as if doused by water and smoke billowed out, forming a giant snake. The guards fled, screaming as it rushed them. The smoke engulfed Nochuatl and his one remaining guard, reducing both men to coughs and gags, then it rushed at me and Ihuitimal, hissing.

Ihuitimal shoved me and I shrieked, but I fell through the smoke. I looked up to see a smaller smoke serpent split off from the larger mass. It swam down to me, its eyes burning orange like hot coals.

Follow me, and it moved towards the garden doorway. Smoke filled the room and I heard scuffles and cries in the dark, so I hurried after it, holding my breath against the pungent cloud around me but not daring to close my eyes even as they burned and watered.

Out in Father's garden, the smoke-serpent disappeared among the vines hanging over the back wall. I pulled aside the thick mat to find an opening into the secret pathway. I looked over my shoulder, hoping to see Nochuatl coming out of Father's room along with the billowing smoke.

Hurry! the nahual whispered beyond the vines, so I swallowed hard and pushed my way through.

The passageway was empty and the smoke-dragon flew to the right. I followed, my wrist itching less the further away we went. "When you bit me...you gave me something that would warn me...you knew my uncle was a bad man, didn't you?" I panted as I jogged after the nahual.

It is one of several gifts the god has given you, it replied. *It will help keep you and those you love safe.*

We ascended a steep set of stairs and I had to stop to catch my breath. We hadn't passed any doorways in the wall for a long time now and by the time we reached the top I had no idea where we were, but ahead the path bent to the left. Hopefully that meant we'd reached the main garden.

You must hurry, the nahual said as it swam over my head. *Your mother is waiting for you.*

"But what about Nochuatl? We can't leave him behind."

Suddenly two guards charged around the corner, their thick bodies scattering the nahual's smoke. "Come along, Princess," one of them said, while the other man grabbed my hand. His touch shot hot pain up my arm from my wrist. I tore free but he grabbed me from behind. "Calm down. We're taking you to your mother," he said.

"Liar!" I wiggled down to my armpits, but he tightened his grip, so I bit his arm.

He bellowed, letting me go, but the other man wrestled me to the ground. "Bloodsucking brat! I should give her a good thrashing for this. That's going to leave a scar."

The other man laughed. "Can't you even handle a child, Calli?"

Suddenly Nochuatl was there. He grabbed the first man from behind and threw him down the stairs, taking his sword in the process. The guard holding me down went to his knees to reach for his sword, but Nochuatl kneed him in the mouth. I huddled on the ground while the men fought, peeking up when I heard one of them gagging. Nochuatl had the guard pinned with his knee across his throat, his sword raised. "Turn away, Papalotl," my uncle warned. I hid my face again and covered my ears until Nochuatl scooped me into his arms. "Keep your eyes closed, lest you see something no child should see," he whispered, so I buried my face in his chest as he ran. Behind my eyelids though, I still saw my father's dead body as if the image was burned into them.

"You can look now," Nochuatl finally said, his breath labored. I opened my eyes to see a dark stain on the side of his mantle.

"You're injured?" I gasped.

He winced with each step but said, "It's nothing. Ihuitimal stuck me with his knife, but don't worry. It's not deep."

I didn't believe him.

We descended another stair to the mouth of a cave. Nochuatl lit a torch in the pine pitch burning in a clay kettle brazier in the alcove. "Where are we?" I asked, gazing uneasily into the darkness ahead.

"These caves run under the city and let out under Quetzalcoatl's temple, but also along the lake shore, under the shadow of the temple."

I held onto him a little tighter as we went inside.

The deeper in we went, the more I was glad Mother had never taken me to the temple this way. Dripping water echoed in the dark, and fang-like rocks on both the ceiling and the floor made it look as if we were moving through a monster's ugly mouth. I shivered, reminded of those nightmares I sometimes had in which I walked down to Mictlan to face judgment before Lord Death. The trail twisted, climbed, and fell, and once Nochuatl had to backtrack when we came to a dead-end.

"Now we're on the right path," he murmured when we came to a pool of water. He put me on his shoulders and I bent low to avoid hitting my head on the teeth sticking out of the low ceiling. Our progress slowed when the water reached Nochuatl's chest, but ahead I saw the gray glow of the cave exit.

Before we reached it, we came to the bow of a canoe. Mother sat inside, looking sick with worry, but her tear-stained face lit up when she saw me. "Oh my dearest Butterfly," she murmured into my hair when Nochuatl put me into her arms. I clutched her, overwhelmed to be holding her again. "I feared he took you from me forever." One of my mother's handmaidens sat with her, shivering while two guards in thick cotton armor stood ready with poles in hand. "Thank you so much for bringing her to me, Nochuatl."

"I wouldn't let you leave without her, but now you must go. The royal litter awaits you on the opposite shore, manned by my closest comrades, and my most trusted friend Lord Blood Wolf leads them. He'll see you safely to Xochicalco. I've already sent word to Cuitlapanton, and he'll take you and the children in without hesitation. May the Feathered Serpent bless your journey, My Lady." He stepped away from the boat.

"You're not coming with us, Uncle?" I cried. "But you must! It's not safe here...and you're hurt—Mother, Ihuitimal stabbed him! We must take care of him. Make him come with us."

He kissed my forehead. "Someone must stay and stand against Ihuitimal."

"But that should be someone who's not injured." I gave him a fierce hug and wiped my tears against his neck. "Please don't stay. I couldn't stand it if Ihuitimal killed you too, Uncle."

"Don't worry about me. You must watch after your mother, and when all's well again, I'll bring you both home—and your brother, if it takes that long."

"You promise?"

"I promise." He gently pried my arms off his neck then set me back in Mother's lap. "But until then, pray to the Feathered Serpent for my health."

"We will, every day," I assured him.

Nochuatl stepped away again and motioned the soldiers to shove off. "I love you, Uncle!" I called back as we approached the cave's open mouth.

He waved back. "I love you too, little Butterfly."

My heart grew anguished as Nochuatl faded from view, as if the shadows of Mictlan itself had swallowed him up.

CHAPTER SIX

While the soldiers pushed us across the dark lake, Mother and I murmured prayers, asking Quetzalcoatl to watch over Nochuatl and our beloved city. My uncle had once told me that invaders usually burned the temple and the palace, but Culhuacan glowed pale, none the wiser that she was without a king, and that her queen now fled to escape death. How had Ihuitimal gotten back into Culhuacan and past my father's guards? Maybe he used the same passageway Nochuatl and I had used to escape? I'd hoped prayers would calm the sick feeling in my stomach, but now I could do nothing but shiver.

"Your dress is wet." Mother touched my stomach with panicked fingers. "You're not hurt, are you?"

My cheeks flared with heat. "When Ihuitimal grabbed me...he scared me so much I...." An embarrassed sob escaped my throat, preventing me from going on.

Mother understood though. "It's all right," she assured me with a tender hug. She stripped my dress off me and cleaned it in the lake water over the side of the boat. I wrapped my naked body in my cloak to keep warm. "We'll say no more about it," she said as she wrung the water out as best she could.

As we neared shore, one soldier mimicked an owl call and someone soon answered with an identical hoot in the distance. When we reached the bank, soldiers hurried to help Mother and me from the boat. "Your litter awaits, My Lady," one of the soldiers—Lord Blood Wolf—told Mother as he helped her up the grassy bank. She held her large belly and winced, looking tired. He hurried us into the canopied litter, and before we'd settled in among the blankets, the soldiers—three to a side—lifted the litter and headed off into the forest.

I sat at the curtains peering out, but the dark left little to see. The forest was alive with shrieking monkeys and chirping insects, but when I heard the coughing growl of a jaguar, I shrank back to Mother's side and snuggled up close to her. The sound of her steady, soothing heartbeat blocked out all the scary sounds outside until I finally fell into welcoming sleep.

But nightmares of Father woke me at dawn. Mother whispered comforting words and slipped my still-damp dress back on me, but when she gasped in pain, I forgot my own woes. "Are you all right?" Noticing how she held her belly, I asked, "Is my brother punching you?"

She smiled. "It's little wonder your brother wishes to make an attempt to come forth now, but he'll calm down. The Leftover Days are a bad time for a baby to be born, so he'll wait until they're over." The worry lines on her face kept my stomach twisted with trepidation, though.

We huddled together all day, stepping outside only to relieve ourselves. Mother mostly slept, waking whenever more pain gripped her.

"How much longer until we're there?" I asked one of the soldiers when we stopped to eat cold, dry tlaxcallis and rest along the side of the dark dirt road. We had no fire, just the moon, which made it feel all the colder. A dampness that smelled of rain hung in the air.

He ignored me though, instead watching Mother's handmaiden speak with Lord Blood Wolf. She twisted her hands together and glanced back at the litter where Mother rested. "Can the men go on through the night?"

"Does the queen's condition demand it?" Lord Blood Wolf asked.

"Her labor has slowed, but she won't make it past morning. If we delay...do any of the men have medical training?"

"Nothing beyond dressing wounds and mixing tonics." He looked past her at the litter too. "Can't you deliver the baby?"

"The queen knows more about delivering children than I do, but when the time comes, she won't be able to direct me." When Mother started moaning again, the handmaiden said, "Please don't leave the life of the king's son in my incapable hands."

She made it all sounds so serious, reminding me of what Ihuitimal had told me that day in the menagerie. *He can't possibly be right,* I thought. *He'd wanted to scare me. Mother's going to be fine.*

Before Lord Blood Wolf could answer, several soldiers called out an alert and everyone came to their feet, weapons ready. A few closed in around me just as a pack of new soldiers jogged around the bend in the road ahead, carrying yellow and white banners. Everyone relaxed but I crawled back to the litter, not trusting these new strangers. I climbed inside and peered cautiously past the curtain as a tall man dressed like a bird stepped up to Lord Blood Wolf and gave a bow.

"I am Lord Spear Fish, war chief to King Cuitlapanton of Xochicalco," the man announced. "We come on behalf of His Highness, to expedite the queen's arrival."

"And none too soon," Lord Blood Wolf said. "She must get to the city as soon as possible, but my men are almost spent."

"And My Lady will give birth before sunrise," the handmaiden added.

"We'll set off immediately." Lord Spear Fish pointed his men towards the litter.

They tossed all but two blankets out of the litter and I rode on one soldier's shoulders from there on. Light rain fell as we set off into the night.

It soon gave way to a downpour. Lord Blood Wolf trotted with us, insisting he must keep his promise to ensure our safe arrival in Xochicalco. His loyalty to Nochuatl warmed me in the cold rain.

Mother's moans soon became cries, and those intensified into screams and sobbing. Unable to see well now that clouds blocked the moon, I imagined monsters ripping her apart, but everyone continued on as if it were completely normal. I tried jumping from my soldier's shoulders to help her myself, but he held me by the ankles. "Calm yourself, child," he rumbled. "We can't afford to slow down."

"But my mother needs me. *Mother!*"

"Be strong, Papalotl," Mother called back. "Trust in Quetzalcoatl; say prayers for me, to take your mind off what you hear."

So I closed my eyes and whispered under my shaking breath:

"Oh Great Feathered Serpent,
Watch over Mother,
Over Black Otter,
Over Nochuatl,
Over Eloxochitl.
Watch over me and give me strength."

We finally tromped out of the woods, and through the haze I saw dim lights in the distance. "Are we there?" I asked, and my soldier nodded. Soon tall white walls coalesced out of the darkness, reaching into the heavens as if dropped there by Lord Sun himself. The soldiers manning the great gates held torches to help us find our way in the darkness of the Leftover Days.

On the last day of the year, people stayed in their houses until the king relit the city's fires, signaling all was well, but my mother's screams brought more than a few people to their doorways. Seeing a few of the women whispering anxiously together, my own fear for Mother came roaring back.

When we reached the large, empty main plaza, the soldiers turned towards a tall, sprawling building surrounded by stone walls.

"Not the palace!" the handmaid shouted. "My lady wishes to go to the Temple of Quetzalcoatl."

"The palace is closer," Blood Wolf said.

"Stop the litter!" Mother called, and the soldiers slowed to a stop. "He must be born in the temple," she panted from the curtain. When Blood Wolf shook his head, she screamed, "Take me to the temple, *now!*" She let out another keening cry that raised the hairs on my neck.

Blood Wolf helped Mother out of the litter, then he and another soldier carried her up a broad stone staircase leading up the darkened hillside off the square.

By the time we reached the top, the clouds had cleared, letting the moon spill light on Xochicalco's sacred precinct. The flat hilltop hosted several stepped pyramids and a long, rectangular building with a stone-ringed cistern out front. Mother's cries brought out still more people, but those at the tallest temple ran down to meet us. Two priestesses in white cotton robes took Mother and carried her up the stairs into the temple. I followed as soon as my soldier let me down.

Priestesses scrambled about inside the temple, preparing a bed of reed prayer mats on the blue stone altar in the middle of the room, in front of the gold Feathered Serpent idol. Still more hurried to light the large clay kettle braziers. "Fetch Nimilitzli," one of the older priestesses ordered as she laid numerous obsidian knives at the foot of the altar.

What in Mictlan are those for? I clutched the handmaiden's dress as she stood next to me, looking around just as bewildered as I felt.

"I'm already here," a new voice spoke from the doorway. "I heard her in the plaza and came from the king as quick as I could." A tall, imposing woman wearing white robes embroidered with two gold feathered serpents on the front strode down the three steps into the temple. She tossed aside her waist-length black braid when she stopped at the foot of the altar.

She's the one I saw the day I was born, I realized. *The nasty woman who made Mother cry by telling her she'd never have another child.* Noticing me, she asked Mother, "Do you wish the child be here, Chimalma?" Who was this haughty woman who thought she could send me away when Mother most needed me?

As the priestesses helped her onto the altar, Mother panted, "She *must* be here when he's born." She broke out into another agonized cry.

I ran to her side, gripping her hand. "I'm here for you, Mother." I tried to keep my voice strong.

Nimilitzli knelt at the foot of the altar and told the handmaiden, "Keep me supplied with clean cloth as needed."

The handmaiden paled but nodded.

One of the priestesses set a blanket over Mother's lap while Nimilitzli pushed her knees up. "The head's crowned, Chimalma," Nimilitzli said. "I need to cut you, so when you feel the need to push, resist it."

Mother nodded but I didn't share her strange calm. "Cut you, Mother? But why?"

In answer, Mother rose into another scream, crushing my hand in hers. I added my cry to the din ringing off the plaster walls. What was happening? "Mother! Mother!" I sobbed, wanting to crawl into her arms so she could hold and comfort me.

"Push!" Nimilitzli shouted. Mother's face reddened, tendons standing out on her neck. I shut my eyes to block out the terrifying vision, trying to remember her beautiful, carefree smile. Only when she fell silent did I dare open my eyes again. She breathed fast, but blissful relaxation painted her face. I let out a gasp of relief. Finally it was over.

"Cloth," Nimilitzli told the handmaiden, and the sickly-looking girl obeyed.

Mother stroked my hair. "I'm so sorry your father's not here for you, Papalotl," she murmured. "He wanted to make up for past wrongs, but Ihuitimal has no honor. What kind of madman attacks and kills his own brother during the Leftover Days? May the gods curse his reign to be short, if it all—"

She suddenly tried to pull her hand away from me, but I held it tighter, refusing to let her go. But her grip turned bone-breaking, renewing my panic and fear. I screamed with her, the pain shooting up my arm, but I didn't try to break free. I'd hold onto her even if Lord Death himself came walking through the doorway.

When a liquid squalling filled the temple, I looked up to see one of the priestesses holding a wiggling infant in a blanket. Mother's handmaiden stared over Nimilitzli's shoulder, wide-eyed. "Is she supposed to bleed that much?"

"Hold your tongue," Nimilitzli scolded her, then glanced up at me. She whispered to another priestess who then hurried out into the night.

The priestess sat my brother in my arms, and he immediately fell silent. "You have the special touch," she said with a smile. My sore hand hurt under the weight of his head, but I forgot all about it when I looked down at him for the first time.

I'd seen many of my younger brothers and sisters when they were only a few hours old, all tiny with wrinkled skin and sleepy eyes. By contrast, my brother was smooth-skinned and plump as a baby that had been nursing a few months already. He gazed up at me with large, alert eyes, and his grip on my fingers was strong, but not as strong as it was on my heart. Would Nimilitzli call his strange appearance a bad omen and try to leave him to die in the woods? *I won't let her, Brother, I promise.*

When I held him out to Mother, she shook her head. "I'm too weak to hold him." She stared at him a moment before her face twisted with sadness. "He's so beautiful," she whispered. Taking my hand in hers, she added, "Take good care of him. He's special, and someday he'll reclaim what your uncle stole, from both of you. But until then, he'll look to you for his strength." She then looked to Nimilitzli. "What day is it?"

"One Reed, My Lady," the girl in the doorway answered. "I saw the king light the fire just as the boy was born."

"Bless you, oh Merciful Feathered Serpent," Mother murmured. She turned to my brother and after a moment's thought, she said, "My Xocoyacatl."

"Are we going to call him Little Reed, Mother?" I asked.

She nodded, her eyes brimming with tears.

Hearing footsteps at the doorway, I looked up to see the young priestess had come back with a priest. His matted hair hung in clumps around his face, his lower jaw painted black.

I'd seen one like him a few days before my grandmother died last year. Mother had called him Tlazotlteotl, the Eater of Filth, who came to listen to the confessions of the dying, so they could journey into Mictlan without the burden of their bad deeds. Sickening heat spread over me. *No! Not Mother too!*

When the priestess took Little Reed back, he burst out crying again. A second priestess took my arm. "Let me go! I'm not leaving! *Mother!*" I screamed, reaching out to her.

"She has only a short time left, child," the priestess said, dragging me away. "She must prepare herself for the journey to paradise in Teteocan. She's earned that right sacrificing herself in the childbed, so be happy for her."

Once we reached the door, I saw Nimilitzli knelt in a pool of blood, the tails of her white robes stained crimson. "No!" I fought loose and ran back to Mother, falling into a sobbing heap at her side. "Please don't leave me too! I need you!"

Mother wept into my hair then held my face in her hands. "You're strong, Papalotl, and you'll take excellent care of your brother for me. The Feathered Serpent trusts you, so trust yourself and all will be fine. I love you so much." She kissed my wet cheeks. "Now go, and don't dwell on what happened here today. And remember that I'll always be here if you need me." She set her hand over my heart.

"Please, Mother, no!" I whimpered. What would I do without her?

Who would take care of me and Little Reed? Who would protect us from Ihuitimal if he came after us? How could she leave me when I needed her most?

The priestess gathered me into her arms but I didn't fight her this time. I might as well have been dying too. I stared back with stinging, watery eyes as Mother's pale, ghostly figure remained behind, Tlazotlteotl kneeling next to her.

The next time I saw her would be only in my memories.

¤

The priestesses took us to a line of small houses behind the temple and they ducked through the curtained doorway of the one at the end, leaving the copper bells tinkling. My priestess laid me on a bed mat then went about stoking the fire while the other paced the floor, trying to quiet Little Reed with sweet words. But he wailed relentlessly.

Once the fire glowed in the hearth, the room came into focus: a loom stood near the rear window, and jars and baskets lined the shelves above the hearth. A metlatl maize grinding stone sat near the door, next to a basket of shucked maize. Unlike the walls of my father's palace, these were simple, unpainted plaster. If not for the sturdy stone construction, I would've thought it was a peasant's house.

Nimilitzli came in, now wearing a clean robe. "Inform the king of what's happened, and tell him I'll bring the children to the palace at daybreak," she said, taking Little Reed from the priestess. Once the others left, she sat on the mat next to me. "Do you wish to hold your brother again?"

I said nothing, just lay staring at the fire, wishing Lord Death had taken me as well. Nimilitzli tried to stroke my hair but I flinched away and tucked my head under my arms. From this woman who let Mother die, any touch was vile and unwelcome.

"You think you can't feel anything but pain ever again, but that too will pass, little one," she said with a maddeningly understanding voice. "Have faith in the Feathered Serpent to heal your heart's wounds. Your brother needs you."

"I don't want him," I muttered. "This is his fault."

"He's hardly had enough time to have done such evil."

"He killed Mother." I squeezed my eyes shut against the suffocating pain in my chest.

"Don't blame him for another's fate. Many mothers give their lives capturing a baby from the gods. It's an unparalleled honor to die trying, especially for your mother; she sacrificed herself bringing forth the son of the god. I assure you she bore no regret for having answered Quetzalcoatl's call."

I gave her an indignant snort. Who was this woman who presumed to know Mother at all?

"I don't suppose your mother ever spoke about me," Nimilitzli went on. "We were good friends when we were younger; we served together in the priesthood, before she married. She sent me a letter not long ago telling me Quetzalcoatl gave her a great task, and that when you were old enough, she wished me to teach you in the calmecac. Both of your parents have friends in Xochicalco; your father and the king served together in the campaigns against the Chichimecs, and he was a nobleman of Xochicalco before he became king of Culhuacan."

Now that I gave her my full attention, I noticed she was older than I'd first thought; but her posture was relaxed and her demeanor soft. Strands of gray hid in the contours of her long black hair and the wrinkles at her eyes lent her the air of a wise woman. *Mother trusted her as a friend*, I thought, so it felt wrong to continue hating her.

"What's to become of me and Little Reed?"

"The king will place you in the care of one of his women." Nimilitzli looked down at Little Reed again as he continued crying in her arms. "You're sure you don't want to hold him?" She held him out again.

He fell quiet again as soon as I took him to my lap, and just looking down at him, the joy he brought me burned away the terrible grief in my heart. "I'm sorry, Little Reed. I didn't mean what I said about you," I whispered through tears, resting my head against his.

"Of course you didn't," Nimilitzli said. I didn't shrug her off when she hugged me this time, instead leaning against her side for comfort. We sat that way until sunrise.

Chapter Seven

King Cuitlapanton leaned forward on his war staff and smiled as he presented me with a bundle of flowers when I greeted him on the steps of the palace. He would've been very tall if not for the hump on his back. I found it odd that his parents had allowed him to have such an unfortunate name as "Hunched Shoulder," for we Tolteca were very superstitious when it came to names. I remembered Cuitlapanton from my wedding; he'd sat with Father at the feast, the two of them laughing like old friends.

Like back home, the halls were painted according to the city's colors—yellow and white here in Xochicalco—but everything else seemed so different. There were so many hallways going off in so many different directions, and every door curtain was a different color, with a different symbol woven into the fabric in the middle, and every room we visited was decorated with flowers, both real and painted. Cuitlapanton showed me the Women's Hall, filled with countless women and girls; he had at least twice the number of concubines my father had had.

The boys were in the huge stone-paved yard, practicing swordplay under the watchful gaze of warriors who corrected their grips and techniques with gruff words and the occasional flick of a switch across the backside. One boy my age stopped to look at me, following me with a piercing stare until his sparring partner whacked him in the shoulder with a feather-covered wooden macuahuitl sword. "Oh! Sorry, Brother!" the other boy squeaked, lowering his practice sword. The first boy responded by shoving him over. "You've got rocks for brains, Mazatzin," he hissed. I scrambled after Cuitlapanton, hoping to be gone before the boy could look back at me again.

Once we'd finished touring the palace, Cuitlapanton led us to the living quarters and introduced me to his queen, his sister Lady Emerald. She was tending to their newest child, an infant girl named Rain Bird, and by the look of her round belly, she had another baby on the way. Lady Emerald was very tall—taller than her hunched husband—and looked like a lake reed with a bulge. She also exuded coldness the same way my mother had once given off warmth and kindness, and my stomach twisted when Cuitlapanton informed me that Lady Emerald would care for me and

Little Reed for now on. "The children of my best friend shall be raised side by side with my own first heir," he said with a proud smile.

It turned out that this first heir, Prince Red Flint, was the boy who had stared at me in the yard, and I soon found out he was mean as the scorpion he put under my blanket in the nursery that first night. He spent the second night spitting wads of cornmeal that he'd hid in his arrow pouch at me. I missed my old nursery with its paintings of butterflies and bees, and when I awoke crying from a nightmare, Red Flint yelled at me, "Stop your bawling or I'll put you in the baskets with the other two criers." I prayed nightly to Quetzalcoatl, begging to go home again.

I feared Nimilitzli had forgotten about me, but a week into my exile, she visited the palace to check on me. She accompanied me up onto the city's west wall; usually one of the servants took me up there so I could watch the road in hopes that Nochuatl would soon rescue me from Red Flint's nastiness. The climb up the long stone stairway was good for letting me stamp out my anger with whatever new awful thing he'd said or done to me.

"You seem unhappy," Nimilitzli said, once we reached the top and I'd leaned against the wall in a huff, dangling my arms over the edge.

"Red Flint is a mangy dog," I said. "One wouldn't know he's a prince, as nasty as he is. But at least I won't have to put up with him much longer, because my uncle Nochuatl will come for me and Little Reed, and I'll never have to see Red Flint ever again." I blew out an exasperated breath. "I'd have rather stayed with you."

"You belong with other children, not with a childless priestess. You'll go into the calmecac soon enough, and then we'll see each other more than you'd care to." She gave me a knowing smile.

In the fields below us, the farmers tended the maize, beans and squash. The sun's rays hadn't yet turned the white walls into cooking stones, and the cool breeze felt like a good omen. I knew today would be important. We passed the time guessing which cities' merchant caravans were coming into the gates below.

"Xochicalco is the trade hub of the whole central valley," Nimilitzli told me. "Goods come in from the south and we sell them to the local trade caravans, and the taxes pay for Xochicalco's many splendid temples and buildings." She pointed to the hilltop behind us.

I only watched the road when I came up here, so I'd taken little notice of just how beautiful Xochicalco was. At twice the size of Culhuacan, it sported three times as many temples, all of them tall and white, like the walls. And flowers grew everywhere, on rooftops and in the many public gardens; they even grew in clay boxes up here on the walls, and their potent fragrance hung in the air like perfume. As its name claimed, Xochicalco was indeed a house of flowers.

"When I return to Culhuacan, I'll plant a huge bed of bone flowers in my mother's honor. She loved them so." I sniffed my wrist, to see if I could still smell the cream she'd let me use the night before we left; but like her, it too was gone.

I glanced back down at the road to see a column of soldiers headed for the city, the front ones holding feathered banners. "Oh! Who's that?"

Nimilitzli shielded her eyes. "They're wearing red and blue—"

"My father's colors! Oh, I knew Nochuatl would come back for me! I must change my dress and fix my hair. Come and help me." I grabbed Nimilitzli's hand and pulled her back down the stairs.

"Don't get ahead of yourself, Quetzalpetlatl," Nimilitzli warned. "You don't know if it's him."

"Of course it's him! He promised."

□

While Nimilitzli went to speak with Cuitlapanton, I hurried into a blue and white dress Lady Emerald had given me and begged one of the servant girls to braid vines of flowers into my hair. When Red Flint came to fetch his practice sling, he grimaced at me. "Just when I thought you couldn't get any uglier." He laughed, but I tripped him when he started to leave, making the servants gasp as he called me a stupid bitch then ran out, shouting for his mother like a baby.

Yes, all the omens pointed to this turning into a very good day indeed.

Nimilitzli stood outside the Great Hall with the king and a priest who said, "What's the child doing here?" when I came up next to her.

Nimilitzli glared at him but then told me, "I think you should wait in the nursery, Quetzalpetlatl."

"But I want to see my uncle," I said.

She pursed her lips a moment. "It isn't who you thought it was."

I didn't believe her, until I noticed that my wrist itched. To my shame,

I'd ignored it in all the excitement. It seemed I hadn't paid attention to the right omens. I swallowed back tears. "It's not?"

Nimilitzli shook her head. Cuitlapanton and the priest turned to leave us, but I screwed up my resolve and declared, "As the Princess of Culhuacan, and the king's eldest heir, I will sit in court for my brother, just as my mother would have for my father if he couldn't go himself."

Cuitlapanton looked thoughtful.

"Surely you're not giving this ridiculous request consideration?" the priest said.

"What does it matter to you if she attends, Ahexotl?" Nimilitzli asked.

"I'm thinking of the child's well-being. Hasn't she been traumatized enough already?"

I stood straighter. "You needn't worry about me, Lord Ahexotl. I hold my mother's strength in my heart."

"That's *high priest* Ahexotl." He glared at me. "Show respect to Quetzalcoatl's high priest."

Something about the way Ahexotl carried himself bothered me, but the god had chosen him so I bowed and kissed the earth at his feet and begged his pardon. Still grumpy, he followed Cuitlapanton into the Great Hall.

"You're sure you want to do this?" Nimilitzli asked.

The thought of seeing Ihuitimal again carved a pit in my stomach, but I couldn't afford to be a fearful child anymore. I had to be strong for Little Reed, and for myself. "Someday Little Reed will want to know what was said here today."

¤

Cuitlapanton's Great Hall was twice as big as my father's but decorated similarly, with large feather-banners depicting the city's sigil—a house with a bundle of three-petal flowers inside the doorway—in the city's colors. The entire left side of the hall opened onto a limestone patio with stone columns holding up the eaves, so there was a clear view into the splendor of the royal gardens. Captive parrots squawked from their tethers in the trees.

I sat next to Nimilitzli on feathered mats while Cuitlapanton took to his reed-woven throne upon a raised platform. He muttered to Ahexotl as servants fitted him with a large quetzal-feathered headdress and adjusted his mantle of yellow and white parrot feathers. The heavy gold jewelry around his neck made him stoop a little, concealing his hump to all but the closest scrutiny; that he wasn't bent double was testament to both his strength and pride. Eventually he told his guards to bring in his visitors.

The guards brought in a group of ten men, led by a tall, fur-clad warrior with black and blue tattoos on his bare chest. He held a head by its hair in his hand, and he tossed it at Cuitlapanton's feet. The whole group bent to their knees, though the man in the middle stood again while the others remained kneeling.

Ihuitimal looked the part of warrior-king, his mantle covering his cotton armor and a headdress of black turkey feathers on his head. In one fist he gripped a spear with a small obsidian mirror tied to it. A shard of jade hung by a string of gold from his nose. "Most Honorable Lord Cuitlapanton, in accordance with our traditions, I've laid the head of the traitor Nochuatl before you as proof that I alone stand as guardian of the city of Culhuacan."

I leaned forward to see if it was truly Nochuatl's head, but Nimilitzli held me back. Ihuitimal gave me a sweet, deceitful smile, and even bowed his head.

Cuitlapanton dropped a cloth over the head and said, his voice cold and formal, "Why do you seek my counsel, Lord Ihuitimal?"

"Now that peace has been restored, I request the return of the queen and my niece."

"Lady Chimalma has left this world."

Ihuitimal frowned. "And what of the child she carried?"

Cuitlapanton hardened his expression. "Mixcoatl's son survived."

"Then I welcome him with open arms. As the children's only living relative, it's my duty to see the boy is raised to manhood and takes his rightful throne."

I'd spent the last week wishing I'd never walked into my father's room that night, but had I not, Ihuitimal's concern for me and Little Reed now would've fooled me. My wrist burned and itched badly, but rather than feeding my fear, it stoked my anger.

"I don't wish to keep kin apart," Cuitlapanton answered, "however, if you think I don't know what transpired in Culhuacan, you must think my hump is filled with stupidity, Lord Ihuitimal. I'd gladly avenge my old friend's murder if not for him now having a son who's claimed that right

73

as his to exercise once he reaches manhood."

Ihuitimal's mask of kindness slipped. "With all due respect, Culhuacan's internal conflicts aren't yours to judge. You never meddled in my brother's affairs and I ask you grant me the same respect. I settled a matter of personal honor with Mixcoatl—and with Nochuatl—and that concerns no one but me."

"I respect that, but Mixcoatl's children aren't prizes of that outcome. I'm not ignorant of the nature of your quarrel with Mixcoatl, and if I gave them to you, you would scatter the boy's brains on my beautiful white walls as you left. There's only one man I'd relinquish them to, and unfortunately his head rests at my feet." Cuitlapanton motioned the servants to take it away.

Ihuitimal's frown deepened. "I understand your reasoning, your Majesty, but surely you see I hold no ill-intent against the girl. She's my son's wife—"

"Black Otter and I aren't married anymore," I said, no longer able to keep quiet. "Father undid it when he sent you away."

"Your father isn't the law in Culhuacan anymore," Ihuitimal snapped. "You're still Black Otter's wife." He softened his sneer then asked, "Wouldn't you like to see your friend again? He's very eager to be reunited with you."

I missed Black Otter, but not enough to trust Ihuitimal. "You put my father's heart in my hands, and you're the high priest of an evil god who hates my beloved Quetzalcoatl. Never again shall I call you my uncle."

Nimilitzli squeezed my hand and Cuitlapanton smiled at me.

Ihuitimal stepped forward, his neck tendons standing out. "You will come home to your husband, girl."

Fear tickled my stomach, but I had to be strong. "No."

"Then I'll drag you by your ear!"

When Cuitlapanton lifted his chin, the guards descended around me. "The Princess stays here with her brother. When the boy comes of age, he'll settle grievances with you personally."

Ihuitimal summoned his own soldiers. "You will turn them over to me or—"

"You'll do what?" Cuitlapanton roared, coming to his feet too. "You dare threaten me in my own court as if I were no better than a Chichimec dog? I'd take your head from your neck this very moment and toss your carcass from the wall if I hadn't sworn that pleasure to Mixcoatl's son, so get out! And if even so much as a merchant bearing Culhuacan's colors darkens the dirt of my land, I'll declare war on you. Bring your pathetic Chichimec army to my gates, for the Feathered Serpent knows no honorable Tolteca would fight in your ranks."

Ihuitimal's soldiers readied their spears, but when more guards rushed forward, Ihuitimal told his soldiers to stand down. "You've made your position clear, and I don't intend to start an incident a mere week into my reign. My men and I will leave peacefully." He cast me a scathing glare before leading his men out, flanked by Cuitlapanton's guards.

"He knows not whom he trifles with," Cuitlapanton growled. To me, he said, "You were very brave, Princess. Your mother would be proud."

The comment left me sad though, and my heart ached for her.

¤

Back in the nursery, I rocked Little Reed after he'd nursed. "I'm sorry, but we have to stay here longer," I told him, my voice breaking. "Our uncle Nochuatl didn't come back for us after all." Saying it aloud brought forth the scorchingly painful memory of that man holding his head in his hand. *He promised me—promised!—but Ihuitimal made him break that,* I thought, the tears wending down my face.

Little Reed stretched his hands to touch my wet cheeks. *Why do you cry, little Butterfly?* his bright eyes seemed to be asking me.

I laughed. "You're lucky you don't know what's going on. I liked it much better when I didn't either." He gave me a laughing smile and I wiped my tears, my heart melting in strange new ways. Had I even known happiness before he was born?

CHAPTER EIGHT

Life in the palace might have been nice if not for Red Flint and his friends following me around, chanting, "Weeping Woman!" anytime they saw me. Cuitlapanton said Red Flint liked me, but that made no sense; Black Otter had never teased me like this.

Red Flint also took to calling me "the freak baby's sister." Within the first few weeks Little Reed doubled in weight and the wet-nurse couldn't keep up with the demands of both him and Princess Rain Bird, so Cuitlapanton brought in a second woman to feed him.

But Little Reed refused her. When she took Rain Bird to her breast, by the end of the day, the little girl lay dying in her basket.

"Poison," Nimilitzli said when she came to examine the baby. "I can smell it on her breath." Rain Bird passed out of the world by morning, leaving Lady Emerald wailing and Cuitlapanton cursing my uncle.

"This is Ihuitimal's doing," he spat, while he paced in the Great Hall. I sat in the corner, listening, for Nimilitzli said one should know what their enemy is capable of.

"The girl rubbed the poison on her breast, intending to feed Mixcoatl's son," Nimilitzli said. "She tried to refuse to nurse Rain Bird, but the queen threatened her."

"I want her driven through with arrows then beheaded! Oh, my poor little girl! If that dog wants war, I'll give it to him!"

Lady Emerald wanted both Little Reed and I out of the palace, fearing she'd lose her son next, but Cuitlapanton refused to renege on his promise. Instead he put us into the care of one of his concubines, Lady Necuazcatl.

Her only son Mazatzin was just a month younger than Red Flint, but unlike his brother he was kind and serious. I liked him right away. Nimilitzli said he'd someday make a very good priest; he'd believed my story about the jade stone and Little Reed being the god's son with little question, whereas Red Flint had laughed and said I had mud in my head. Like Mother, Mazatzin looked at Little Reed but wouldn't touch him, as if my brother was too awe-inspiring for mortal hands.

After we'd prayed over Little Reed, like we did every night before bed, I lay awake, sleep eluding me. The toy snake on gold wheels sitting near the hearth held me transfixed, and when the green quetzal feathers unfolded from behind its head, I thought I'd fallen asleep and was dreaming. They flowed in the draft coming off the fire. It turned its head, showing me glowing orange eyes. My heart played a drunken beat as the snake slid off the wheels and slithered over to me. It stared back at me a moment before I found the courage to speak. "Are you a nahual?" I whispered.

It flicked its leather tongue at me then spoke in that familiar ethereal voice. *I am the Feathered Serpent's tonal companion,* it confirmed.

I sat up and immediately bowed. "My Lord." Last time we'd spoken I hadn't had time for bows, but I would do it right this time.

I am but a humble servant. It is you I have come to honor.

"Me?"

The nahual bowed, dragging its neck feathers on the stone floor. *The Morning Star has risen, and through my fangs he anoints you guardian of his only son, the future Emperor of the Tolteca, and he gives you the power of his counsel when your need is most urgent.*

I touched my wrist. "You mean—"

You may call upon the Great Feathered Serpent in body and spirit and he will come to aid you, the nahual answered.

My mouth dropped open. "You mean I can summon the god anytime I want?"

Use the gift wisely, the nahual warned. *The sacrifice only becomes greater the more you use it. The gift is meant to protect his son and yourself from those who would harm you.*

My mood darkened. "You mean like Ihuitimal. He sent someone to poison Little Reed."

And this very night, another assassin walks the palace halls.

I pulled Little Reed's basket to my side. He slept soundly. "What should I do?"

There is no safe haven for the god's blood in this palace, so take Lord Topiltzin to the temple, where his father's powers are strongest.

"Lord Topiltzin?" I asked, confused.

That is the name the god himself has given his son.

Our Prince. Fitting, I supposed, but I liked Little Reed better.

My time here is limited, the nahual said. *I spent too much magic and will soon fade away, but I can provide cover for your escape. You will have to find a way to the temple on your own.*

"But I don't know how to get out of the palace without being seen."

"I know a way," Mazatzin whispered, and I yelped in surprise. He crawled over, keeping his distance from the nahual as he spoke to it. "I'll see that she and the god's son make it to the temple."

The nahual whipped its head around, flicking its tongue. *He comes.*

Mazatzin grabbed a toy sword and peeked around the edge of the curtain while I gathered Little Reed into my arms. "Someone's coming up the hall."

I'll use what magic I have left to confuse him, but then you must run, the nahual said.

"Put your brother in this," Mazatzin suggested, taking a bag from the wicker chest near the door. "My mother used to carry my baby brother in this before Xolotl came for him." I slipped Little Reed inside and Mazatzin helped me put it across my shoulder. "He's not too heavy, is he?" He looked as if he didn't relish the idea but would carry Little Reed for me if necessary.

But I was Little Reed's guardian so it was only right I should carry him. "I'll be fine."

The nahual slipped soundlessly under the door curtain, but we made the copper bells clatter like obsidian spearheads spilled on the stone floor when we stepped out. My breath quickened as my wrist started itching.

A servant came up the hall, carrying a water jar on his shoulder. "What are you two doing out of bed? Don't you know the bloodthirsty civatateos prowl the streets after dark, hunting children out of their beds?"

"I'm taking my sister to the bathhouse," Mazatzin said, taking my hand. He was sweaty and shaking.

The servant smiled. If not for my itching wrist warning me, I would never have suspected this kindly-looking man of evil. "And that requires your sword, young Lord Deer?"

"In case I meet a civatateo," Mazatzin replied.

I didn't like how close the servant was to us. "I must go," I insisted, fidgeting.

The man laughed. "Hurry along, before she bursts her dam and I have to clean it up." Noticing the bag on my shoulder, he asked, "What's in there?"

"My brother's soiled clothes." I prayed Little Reed didn't choose that moment to start fussing about his cramped quarters. "I'm taking them to the laundry basket."

"Now?"

"I didn't take them earlier, so now the nursery stinks."

"The servants can do that."

"I don't mind it." When he looked inside the nursery at Little Reed's basket, revulsion rose inside me. "I'll do anything for my brother, no matter how petty the task."

"Then he's lucky to have a loving sister like you," the servant said. "Along with you already." He stepped into the room and closed the curtain behind him.

Mazatzin ran, dragging me after him. But after only ten steps, the curtain jangled and the servant came charging after us.

He overtook us a few steps away from the bathhouse, yanking me backwards by the bag's strap, whipping me away from Mazatzin. I kicked at him with my bare feet but he pulled harder, tossing me off my feet into the wall with a thud that brought the painted plaster off in chunks. I tasted blood on my tongue.

Suddenly the air turned thick as sap, and over my shoulder a blue, spectral feathered serpent rose from Little Reed's bag. The man backed away, shocked, but when the ghostly snake leaped at him, he shrieked and fell over backwards, swinging a flint knife at it.

Mazatzin grabbed my hand and pulled me into the bathhouse. "Follow me." He climbed atop the adobe-brick steam bath at the back and in three moves reached the top of the courtyard wall, but I struggled to find handholds on the rounded bathhouse roof.

Just as I clambered up, the servant burst out of the hallway and snagged my ankle. I rolled over and kicked him in the face, breaking his nose in a gush of blood. He cursed but still held on, bringing his knife around to slice my leg.

Mazatzin smacked his wrist with the edge of his wooden sword, knocking the blade out of his hand. He chopped at the man's other arm, laying open a deep gash. The servant finally let me go and both Mazatzin and I scrambled up onto the wall.

"Keep hold of my hand," Mazatzin said as we shuffled along the wall past the private gardens. Reaching the end, we jumped onto the kitchen roof and ran across to the tall oak tree overhanging the main garden entrance. We climbed down, then, after checking the path, we hurried into the unlit area of the gardens. We crawled behind some bushes and through a crack in the stone wall, though I had to put Little Reed through first to fit.

"Your brother's a sound sleeper," Mazatzin noted as he helped me re-shoulder the bag. "I can't believe he never woke up in any of that."

I checked on Little Reed but he still slept, bubbles on his smiling lips as he made "ah, ah" sounds. "Maybe the nahual put a sleeping spell on him, to keep him from crying." I stroked his hair then covered him again. "Where are we?"

"The royal ball court," Mazatzin said, leading the way. "Red Flint and I sneak out here all the time. I don't think the guards know there's a hole in the wall back there."

We scampered through some winding corridors decorated with reliefs of ritual ball players locked in battle with the sacred rubber ball—and of some being beheaded for losing the game—then came out onto the sandy court. The sloping side walls stood tall as temples around us, and I caught a glimpse of the outline of a stone ring near the top on one side. I'd never been to the ball court in Culhuacan—Mother had called it a man's sport, bloody and full of gambling, and so we never attended any matches, though all my brothers were always playing it in the yard.

When we reached the main entrance, we crouched in the shadows. Seeing no guards, Mazatzin hurried us across the empty main square and up the stairs to the sacred precinct. I had little breath left once we reached the top.

The precinct was empty but kettle braziers at the doors of the calmecac and temples gave off a warm glow. I breathed a sigh of relief on seeing Quetzalcoatl's temple just a jog away.

"What should we say when we get there?" Mazatzin asked, as we walked towards the temple.

"We'll get someone to wake Nimilitzli and I'll tell her about the nahual, and what it said."

"You think she'll believe you?"

"Of course! She's the god's high priestess, so she'll know all about this kind of thing."

I hadn't been back to the temple since the night Mother died, and now the beauty of the stone carvings along its base stole my breath: noblemen counting the days on calendar carvings, and giant, slithering Feathered Serpents painted white, green, red, and blue. If anywhere was heavy with Quetzalcoatl's protective influence, this was it.

Mazatzin suddenly gagged, and I turned to see the treacherous servant had stuck a knife through his shoulder from behind. When the man pulled it out, Mazatzin fell to his knees, clutching his chest.

I screamed but the air sounded thick in my ears, as if I were swimming in honey. I put my hands up as the servant rushed me, swinging his blade. He sliced my palm in a jagged rip and I almost ran backwards into the wall. But I spun around in time to avoid crushing Little Reed, instead hitting the wall with my wounded hand and splattering blood across Quetzalcoatl's stone face. The assassin swung his knife again but shattered the blade against the stone wall.

"Please save us from this evil, My Lord!" I stumbled backwards and fell hard, gritting my teeth. I clutched Little Reed's sling as the killer advanced, a victorious smile on his face. Behind him, a black jaguar stood in the shadow at the temple's corner, staring back at me with burning yellow eyes. Was it the same one I'd seen in the hallway the night my father was murdered? "I promise to hold no god above you, oh Merciful Quetzalcoatl! Please help us!" I cried.

The wall above me exploded in a shower of gravel and stone. I rolled over to cover Little Reed, and when I looked up, the giant stone serpent peeled off the temple wall. The man screamed and tried to run, but the serpent opened its stone jaws, letting out a burst of wind that took him off his feet and up into the air. The wind howled louder than I'd ever heard it before and I hunched over Little Reed to keep the dirt out of his bag, my hair lashing around in the wind.

It died down just as quickly as it came, and in the time it took me to blink away my astonishment, the stone serpent vanished and the temple wall was back to the way it had been before all this. When I looked at the back of the temple, the jaguar was gone too. Mazatzin looked around, bewildered.

Little Reed suddenly burst into hiccupping cries, and though he was unharmed inside the bag, he was red-faced and angry.

"By the Great Feathered Serpent, what are you doing out here, Quetzalpetlatl?" Nimilitzli stood at the edge of the pyramid. But then she gasped and rushed down the stairs, kneeling next to Mazatzin and putting the tail of her robe over his wound. "What happened? Who did this?"

"One of the palace servants." I crawled to Mazatzin too. "He came after Little Reed and...and...oh, please don't let Mazatzin die, My Lord!"

"Calm yourself. You're all safe."

I nodded, wracked with tears.

"Whatever possessed you to leave the palace in the middle of the night?" Nimilitzli demanded. She turned to Ahexotl, who'd come from the calmecac where many people were standing outside, looking into the sky. "Rouse the king and let him know his son's been injured." The high priest glared at me before heading for the stairs at a jog. Nimilitzli gave me a similar stare. "The darkened world isn't safe for children, and you dare bring your brother out into it? How did you three get out of the palace without being seen?"

"There's a crack in the garden wall, behind the ball court," Mazatzin replied, wincing.

"Lay still." She then asked me again, "What are you doing here?"

Her anger scared me, so I stuttered for a moment, trying to find my words. *She's the god's high priestess, so she'll understand,* I reminded myself. "The nahual told us Little Reed would be safest here because the god's power is greatest near his temple."

Nimilitzli furrowed her eyebrows. "Nahual?"

"Quetzalcoatl's. On my wedding day, when I found Little Reed's jade stone, the nahual bit me, and now my wrist itches whenever my uncle or one of his men is close." I showed her my wrist, but the bumps were gone now. I pressed on anyway. "The nahual helped me escape Father's room that terrible night by making smoke flood the room, then it led me out into the secret corridor. Tonight it came back and told me to bring Little Reed here, to escape the assassin."

"Then Quetzalpetlatl called on the god and he came and swept the servant away in a great wind!" Mazatzin said, excitedly pointing towards the forest in the distance behind the calmecac. "The wind blew him so far I couldn't even see him anymore. It was incredible!"

"I told you to stay still," Nimilitzli reprimanded him. She looked at me again, the doubt plain in her eyes.

How could she not believe me? Surely such things were ordinary in a life of a priestess. *Aren't they?*

The king arrived with a physician and guards. "Where's my son?" he called as he ran to us. While the physician stitched up Mazatzin's shoulder, Nimilitzli took Cuitlapanton aside, speaking in a hushed voice. Their gestures soon became a heated discussion and I turned away, uncomfortable that I'd caused all this trouble.

"You were so very brave Mazatzin," I said, once the physician finished sewing up my hand and had muttered a prayer to Quetzalcoatl over it, to ensure its proper healing. "I'm sorry you got hurt."

"It's a small price to pay to serve the Feathered Serpent," Mazatzin replied. "And you were incredible! With a gift like that, surely you're destined to be someone great—maybe even the god's high priestess."

I liked the idea of someday being a priestess. Mother would have been proud if I were. "I just wish Nimilitzli would believe me about the nahual."

"I think she was just scared about hearing that the god had something to do with it." Mazatzin sat up and looked over at his father and Nimilitzli. "So what if the adults don't believe us? I know what I saw, and I shall never forget it."

¤

Nimilitzli and Cuitlapanton argued until dawn's first bloody streaks peeked over the mountains, then the king pulled Mazatzin along with him back to the stairs, leaving me and Little Reed behind with Nimilitzli. "Come, you look tired," she said, cradling Little Reed in her arms as he slept. I glanced back at Mazatzin once more before he disappeared down the stairs with his father, then I moped after Nimilitzli to her house.

She gave me and Little Reed her bed mat, but instead of sleeping I watched her stare into the fire, her face a mask of concentration. "What did the king say?"

She looked startled but didn't chastise me. "All you need to know is that he fears for his own children if he keeps you and your brother in the palace anymore. And after tonight, I can't blame him." She shook her head.

"You think I'm lying about the nahual," I concluded, holding back angry tears.

"I've been a priestess a long time, and I've never heard of the god coming to his followers like that."

That puzzled me. "You've never spoken with the god, or his nahual?"

"The god speaks to us, not the other way around. And I've always had to use special mushrooms or the sacred octli liquor to accomplish that little bit. His intent can sometimes be read in the patterns of nature, though. Were you feeling sick tonight?"

"I feel fine."

Nimilitzli sat in silence a moment. "What did you talk about with this nahual?"

"It told me Quetzalcoatl had chosen me to be Little Reed's guardian, and that he'd given me the gift to call on him, in body and spirit, and I did! Quetzalcoatl came just as he promised—as the serpent on the side of the temple—and he killed the assassin." Seeing the skepticism again, I glared back at her. "It really did happen."

She held her hands up. "I'm just trying to understand what took place. It's obvious you've had visions of the god, and I'd encourage you to keep an open mind about these experiences. With some study of the priestly arts, I'm sure you can come to understand what it all means."

Not exactly the enthusiastic acceptance I'd hoped for, but least she wasn't calling me a liar.

"Perhaps this is all for the best, for both of you. I believe Little Reed is the god's son; your mother carried him only three months and he was almost too large to be birthed. And he grows so fast.... He'd have been tormented and ostracized by Cuitlapanton's sons for being different, so he'll be better off among priests, who will treat him like the gift he is. And you'll be starting calmecac soon anyway."

"Then we're to live with you?" I squeaked with excitement. Finally I'd be rid of Red Flint.

"As your mother's friend and confidant, it's my duty to see her children brought to adulthood with respect for Quetzalcoatl in their hearts. And I'll need your help with your brother, having never had any children of my own. But we can discuss that later, after you've finally slept. Now to bed with you."

I snuggled around Little Reed, smiling. I hadn't felt this good since that night I first felt him moving in my mother's belly: proof of Quetzalcoatl's greatness. *And I'll keep my promise to love and protect Little Reed always, My Lord,* I prayed, and for the first time since coming to Xochicalco, I fell into deep, dreamless sleep, feeling that finally everything was as it should be.

PART TWO
THE YEAR ELEVEN HOUSE

CHAPTER NINE

"You think you're ready for war, but battle is never what little boys think it is," Nimilitzli snapped at Little Reed as we sat on reed mats on the floor of her house eating the beans and tlaxcallis I'd prepared for the three of us. The last ten years had left her with streaky, graying hair, knobby knuckles and thinner skin, but her temperament remained fierce as ever. She was a marvel to watch when pitted against Little Reed.

Little Reed laughed heartily. "I'm hardly a 'little boy' anymore, Mother." Indeed, the accelerated growth he'd experienced early in life hadn't let up, and by the time he'd visited the soothsayer to learn his true name at age seven, he and I had looked the same age. Now age ten, he stood a full head taller than me, and looked a bittersweet mix of my mother and father. I hoped he wouldn't grow too much more or he'd end up a giant. He suffered enough ridicule from Red Flint as it was.

Nimilitzli held up a hand when I motioned with the pot of beans. "You don't look like one anymore, but you also don't even have a young man's life experience yet."

"I have more than you think." Little Reed held out his tlaxcalli flatbread for me to fill with stewed beans.

"Your arrogance is speaking again."

"It's not arrogance to state a fact."

"It's arrogance to assume it's a fact."

Little Reed laughed. "I'll miss these discussions, Mother, but we both know that the longer Ihuitimal holds Culhuacan's throne, the harder it'll be to depose him. He's already building alliances against me. And not only did he not give Mixcoatl a proper burial, he's also outlawed Quetzalcoatl's worship. I can't wait around another ten years for everyone else to think I'm ready to do something about it. By then it could be too late."

Meals at Nimilitzli's house were usually quiet, solemn affairs, but ever since two weeks ago when Little Reed had sprung the shocking news on us that he was leaving for the army, they had argued daily about it. I didn't want him to go, but just the thought of talking about it turned my throat to cotton and my chest into a painful, vibrating drum. I couldn't believe he was leaving me behind so soon.

Nimilitzli showed no hesitation about taking him to task about it, though. "Your uncle is disgraceful, but he's trying to bait you into acting before you're ready. Stay here a few more years. You're ready to take the trials to become a full priest, and you need to build grace with Quetzalcoatl before invoking his name in battle—"

"Using the god's name won't get me anything. The army is full of soldiers who'll demand I earn their respect with my actions, not by the name of my father. You see how Red Flint and his lot treat me—"

"You can't judge others by what Red Flint thinks, Brother," I said. "Mazatzin has always shown you the greatest respect."

"But Mazatzin is a priest, or will be soon, although you're right about Red Flint," Little Reed conceded. "He's just a spoiled royal brat. But I have no reputation among the commoners, and no honorable man will follow me in re-conquering Culhuacan until I prove myself in battle. What's the use in being named 'Our Prince' if I'm only ever a priest and not a king?"

"You will be a king when the time is right," Nimilitzli insisted. "Until then, serve the god."

"The best way I can serve the god is on the battlefield."

"And how do you know that?"

Little Reed sighed. "We all knew this day would come, Mother."

"But after only ten years?" I asked, trying hard not to choke into a sob.

"Who knows if I even have another ten years left to me?"

"Don't talk like that." I had to look away so he wouldn't see the wetness gathering at my eyes.

He set his hand on mine. "I can't ignore that I age faster than everyone else. I'd like to stay, but it'll take me years to amass the troops necessary to retake Culhuacan. I want to have time to rule and produce an heir before this rapid aging escorts me to the road to Mictlan."

All the more reason why you should stay here with me, I thought. By the time Little Reed was two, I'd realized that he was the little boy I'd seen in my dream on my wedding night, but it wasn't until I was older that I understood what that strange fluttering he'd made me feel that night meant. Over the last couple of years, that feeling that used to come only when I remembered the dream started happening whenever he spoke to me, or when he held my hand; and by now it had intensified into sweaty palms, and dreams that I'd blush to describe aloud.

I'd hoped Cuitlapanton would marry us, as Father would have if he were still alive—to ensure the royal bloodline—but to my disappointment, nobody said anything about it. I didn't dare bring it up to anyone; Nimilitzli was so proud that I was taking the trials to become a priestess this summer, and as for telling Little Reed.... Many of the girls at calmecac fluttered their eyelashes at him and giggled behind their hands, and a couple had tried to talk me into delivering notes to him. And though he always seemed to ignore them in favor of focusing squarely on his studies, I couldn't help but wonder: was he merely keeping his interest in someone secret from me, as I kept my interest in him secret? Or maybe he had no interest in such things. He was the son of a god after all, and so perhaps found it easy to ignore such human weaknesses.

Not all of us could be so lucky.

"War is nothing like those battle drills you went through last summer at the House of Warriors, Topiltzin," Nimilitzli continued. "Men lose limbs or become crippled, or worse yet they're dragged off to die in honor of foreign gods. You look like a man to everyone, but you're not mentally prepared for that kind of life. Boys your age are busy catching lizards and learning how to use a bow and arrow—"

"I'm not like other boys. The god didn't put me here to sit back and be afraid of being a man."

I couldn't listen anymore. When Little Reed made up his mind, he never gave other options a backward glance. "I wish to go and pray before my temple duties," I muttered, and left the house.

I wished I could be indifferent to everyone else, like Little Reed, so I too could go on with life without feeling terrible pain for losing someone so dear to my heart.

◻

Across from the temple, Mazatzin stood with Red Flint by the cistern outside the calmecac. Seeing them next to each other, one would hardly believe they were brothers; Mazatzin's broad shoulders and face made him look strikingly like Cuitlapanton, while Red Flint had inherited his mother's lithe build and fine features. Red Flint's smile was his own, though; predatory, like a coyote. His gaze wandered over me as I approached, making my face redden with resentment. I hated it when people stared at me, which seemed to be happening with increasing frequency since I'd attained puberty.

From Little Reed, I wouldn't mind it, but I especially didn't want it from Red Flint. He'd finally outgrown the childish taunts against me; but for the last few years, he'd refocused his attention on Little Reed, especially once Little Reed started catching up to him both physically and mentally. For a while it was just verbal sparring, with Little Reed often getting the better of him, but once Little Reed surpassed him in height, it turned violent.

One afternoon, Red Flint and his friends lured Little Reed to the west ball court and pummeled him with hard rubber balls, breaking his nose and knocking him unconscious. I tried summoning the god but ended up with a bloody palm and no Quetzalcoatl. Only a couple of men arriving to practice early stopped the assault. Red Flint did a year of service to the temple for his actions, but I kept close watch over him from then on.

"You're upset," Mazatzin noted when I reached them.

"I'm fine. Nimilitzli and Topiltzin are arguing again. That's all they've done for the last two weeks."

"So he's still leaving with the army?"

When I nodded, Red Flint snorted. "He made the decision so suddenly, I must question his motives."

"You always do, Brother," Mazatzin said.

I too wondered how much Red Flint's impending army service had played into Little Reed's decision. He couldn't resist any opportunity to show up his boyhood nemesis.

"But I thought he was going to be a priest," Red Flint pressed.

"He'll be one," I said. "He's just chosen to be a warrior first."

Red Flint laughed. "He's no different than any of these other weak little calmecac worms; he'll do his minimum service and call himself a warrior."

"There's nothing dishonorable in doing only the required military service, Brother," Mazatzin said. "Priestly duty is just as important as marching about swinging a sword."

"Kings don't do the minimum."

"Why do you care whether or not Topiltzin becomes a warrior? Are you worried he'll out-sparkle you?"

Red Flint glared at him. "Forgive my being concerned about what his untimely death would do to his family. Particularly to Quetzalpetlatl."

"What's that supposed to mean?" I snapped, my cheeks flushing. I thought I was pretty good about hiding my attraction for Little Reed, but was I instead very transparent?

"Let's be honest, Quetzalpetlatl: you've cared for that whelp since the day he came into this world, but he doesn't care at all that he's hurting you."

I hated the idea of Red Flint being right about anything, but it dug a deep wound in my heart to realize that he was more aware of my pain than my own brother. Just more evidence that I was alone in my foolish infatuation.

"If he cared, he wouldn't rush off bent on impressing strangers while his faithful sister worries about whether he's dead or alive," Red Flint insisted.

"Don't say such things." I tried holding back the tears but failed. Soon Red Flint would break out chanting "Weeping Woman!" at me again, and I wasn't sure I could handle that right now.

But to my surprise, he slid a friendly hand over my shoulder. "I'll watch over Topiltzin while we're gone."

"That's my job," I snapped.

"Topiltzin is a man now," Mazatzin spoke up. "And all men must eventually leave their mothers. Someday he'll come back and become a priest, trust in that. Besides, you have your own future to think about, with the trials coming up in a few weeks."

"He's as callous as Topiltzin," Red Flint said. "Telling you what to think and feel, as if you're not entitled to any of your own. Has Topiltzin even asked you whether you really want to be a priestess?"

Little Reed had never asked me one way or the other, though I'd always thought I wanted to follow my mother's path into the priesthood. But I'd been surprised by just how difficult it was. The lessons were easy, but the calmecac's strict rules punished the slightest transgression, and the fire priestess Mothotli had taken a particular dislike to me, perhaps suspecting I might receive special treatment for being the high priestess's charge. I'd grown weary of the constant sweeping, the raps on the knuckles for not paying attention in boring classes, or Mothotli's constantly probing gazes. Sometimes I doubted I was meant for a priestly life—especially when Mothotli knocked me out of my daydreams about Little Reed with a strike of her switch. But if I didn't want to be a priestess, would Little Reed accept that?

"If Topiltzin is old enough to do what he wants, so are you." Red Flint looked past me with a smug smile. "Speaking of the boar...."

Little Reed came to us, his posture reminiscent of an aggressive turkey. He made a perfunctory bow to Red Flint then said to me, "I thought you were going to the temple to pray."

"Perhaps she prefers actual two-way conversation over the endless mumblings to a god who never answers, Crotch Bleeder," Red Flint said with a sneer.

"He wasn't asking you anything," I snarled. I was used to his offensive pet names for my brother, but I wasn't in the mood for it today.

Little Reed merely smiled back at him and said, "She'll find a more sympathetic ear with the god than with you, Impotent Lizard."

Red Flint moved to draw his dagger, but Mazatzin grabbed his arm. He glared at his brother a moment then told Little Reed, "We'd hoped you'd join us on the pilgrimage this year. There'll be war next year."

"Someday I'm going to make that a false statement," Little Reed replied.

Red Flint scoffed, but Mazatzin said, "I'd hoped to have the great honor of becoming a priest at the same time as you, then we'd march together for our first battle next year."

Little Reed clapped his shoulder. "Then I hope to see you in my ranks next year."

"He'll be in *my* ranks," Red Flint retorted.

"I'll go where the god points," Mazatzin stated. "Now we really must go, Brother, before father skins us for being late."

Red Flint gave Little Reed a glare, but slipped on a smile for me. "Your company is always a pleasure, My Lady." He kissed his fingers and swept them across the ground at my feet with a fluid motion that left me inexplicably breathless. *As nasty as he can be, he's still delicious to watch*, I thought, and nearly gasped aloud. Where in Mictlan did *that* come from?

Once Red Flint and Mazatzin were out of earshot, Little Reed growled, "Stupid dog. How dare he speak so disrespectfully to me?"

I glared at him. "It's not as if you've done anything to earn his respect." I tried not to care about the hurt frown on his face, but I hated seeing him upset. "I'm sorry, but I just don't understand why you two have to act like wolves guarding a kill whenever the other comes around. I can't expect better of him, but I do expect better of you."

Little Reed bowed his head. "You're right, Papalotl. A prince should always have respect for others, especially for his enemy. I'll walk with you to the temple."

I'd never told Little Reed about my childhood name, and as far as I knew no one in Xochicalco knew of it either. But when Little Reed wasn't quite six months old he'd sat next to me one day playing with string while I wove and suddenly blurted out his first coherent word: "Papalotl!" I'd looked around for signs of his butterfly outside the window, but he was staring up at me, eyes bright and laughing. "Papalotl!" he shouted with glee, and he'd called me that ever since.

And truthfully I preferred it, just as he liked me to call him Little Reed. Nimilitzli disapproved of us using our child-names, so we only did so in private.

We knelt side by side on the reed prayer mats in front of Quetzalcoatl's idol. The smell of blood and decay oozing out of the idol's open mouth gave my stomach a funny little jerk and gurgle, so I focused my attention on the baskets of grass balls and obsidian blades next to the gilded statue. That was another thing I never told anyone: the smell of sacrifices made me inexplicably hungry, even after I'd eaten a big meal. It seemed a little too bizarre to risk talking about. I closed my eyes and held my breath against the smell, finding my focus for the prayer.

"You're angry with me, about more than just Red Flint," Little Reed said after we'd finished our silent prayers.

His words dredged up bitterness I'd been glad to be free of while praying. I pulled the wooden blood-bowl to my knees so I didn't have to look at him. "I don't want you to go, I don't like you arguing with Nimilitzli, and I don't like you rushing to keep up with Red Flint—"

"My decision has nothing to do with Red Flint."

"We've been lucky the last ten years, Little Reed. Ihuitimal has made no more attempts on your life, but if you go away...." Mazatzin's words came back to me. But what was so wrong with wanting to protect him? Quetzalcoatl appointed me his guardian, after all. But if Little Reed could fend for himself now, didn't that render me completely useless?

"I understand your concern," Little Reed said. "I'd be a fool if I wasn't afraid. But a man doesn't earn his reputation in safety. I can't stay locked up behind these walls forever."

So why must I? But I couldn't say it. Mother said a woman's lot wasn't fair, and Mothotli's stinging switch taught me it was easier to stay silent about this injustice, but I'd never changed my mind about it; I just simmered with anger.

Little Reed took my hand in his, making my heart skip. "I promise to be very careful out there, Papalotl. I'll make you proud, and with the Feathered Serpent's grace, we'll return to Culhuacan with our uncle vanquished and our fathers avenged. We will be where we belong again."

The thrill coursing through me made all the bitterness vanish again, almost bringing me to tears. "I'll pray for it, Little Reed."

"Will you pray for me too?"

"Every day." It was the only protection I could give him anymore.

◻

Mothotli came at midnight, to make sure I wasn't taking any shortcuts with my duties. Her name—"Chipmunk"—was apt: she had beady eyes and puffy cheeks where she stored her mean words, and when upset she'd shriek like a rodent being savaged by a dog. As fire priestess, she was second to Nimilitzli in power, though someday she'd be the high priestess. I dreaded what life under her rule would be like.

"You've already swept there three times, girl," she snapped. "The rest of the room could use your attention too."

I hadn't realized I'd gone back to the altar again until now. I always swept there first, to get it done quickly before memories of Mother resurfaced. Years ago just being in the temple set off panic, but with time I came to fear Mothotli's switch more than the memories.

Nimilitzli understood though, and had taken me on as an apprentice midwife when I was twelve so I could see that things didn't always go wrong in the childbed. Many of the priestesses were also midwives for the noble class, though as high priestess Nimilitzli cared for Lady Emerald and Cuitlapanton's concubines; she'd delivered every child in the palace. The rational detachment necessary for delivering babies helped me focus my fears into one little area of the temple that I could sweep quickly then move on from.

So why am I lingering so long here tonight? I wondered, as I went to sweep behind the gilded Feathered Serpent idol.

Mothotli checked all the corners of the room with her stern, suspicious stare. "I hear Topiltzin isn't taking the trials this year."

"He's joining the army," I said.

Mothotli shook her head. "That boy's not nearly as brilliant as he thinks. Nimilitzli would do well to put him under the lash more often, teach him humility."

Little Reed could use a dousing in the cistern, but I'd never say so to her. Nimilitzli was strict but never cruel, so I respected her far more.

"He's wasting all the training we gave him. Son of the god, indeed! One wouldn't think a god's seed would produce someone so irresponsible."

I almost said something she'd give me the switch for, but Ahexotl came into the temple and reprimanded her. "Don't disparage Topiltzin to her. She has plenty to worry about as it is." He inspected the braziers and tossed more copal wood into the north one, then told me, "Excellent work as always, Quetzalpetlatl. Have a good night."

I bowed and thanked him for his kind words. As I headed up the steps, he added, "I have to fetch something from my meditation room, so I'll walk with you." He took my broom for me, and as we headed out I caught Mothotli glaring at us, the disdain more vehement than usual.

"Pay Mothotli no mind," Ahexotl told me as we crossed the precinct to the calmecac. "I'd hoped Topiltzin would take his vows before embarking on a military career, but I respect his desire to choose his own path."

I nodded halfheartedly.

"I can't imagine this is easy for you; I know the two of you are close. I'm sure he'll think fondly of you while he's gone. Love of family and faith in the god will see him through the difficult times."

I hadn't expected to like Ahexotl after that first meeting ten years ago, when he'd looked at me as if I was a grub feasting on his tomato plants. For the first couple of years he remained distant and cold towards me, but once I took on priestly duties he took more interest in my progress and encouraged me. He even became something of a father figure to me.

"Are you ready for the pilgrimage next month?"

I nodded. "I'm apprehensive about leaving the city for the first time, though."

"The king will provide us with adequate guards. Xochicalco's soldiers are the best in the land."

We crossed the school's courtyard garden and went into the row of storerooms across from the girls' dormitories. Its four rooms each held different materials: laundry, pottery and baskets, brooms and gardening tools, and an entire room full of copal wood for the temple's braziers. I returned the broom to its hook in the tool room and thanked Ahexotl for walking with me.

"I know these are difficult times for you, Quetzalpetlatl. If you need anyone to talk to, I'm at your disposal," he said with a warm smile. "You'll be one of my priestesses soon and you can come to me with your troubles. You're joining a much larger family, and we're here to support you."

The pain and depression that had built slowly over the last two weeks suddenly welled up inside me; I tried to swallow it but couldn't help frowning.

Ahexotl raised an eyebrow. "Do you need to talk now?"

I almost said "yes," but instead the exhaustion hit hard. "I appreciate the kindness, My Lord, but it's late, and I'm very tired."

"Some other time then. You know where to find me." He then departed, leaving me wondering if I should have taken up his offer. *It might make you feel better,* I thought. But I didn't like the idea of possibly breaking down and revealing my feelings for Little Reed to him.

Only the pine-resin torch at the doorway to the dormitory gave light to lead me across the garden, so when the bushes next to the storerooms began rustling, I stopped like a startled deer.

"Quetzalpetlatl!"

"Red Flint?" I gasped when he grabbed my wrist and dragged me into the bushes. "What in Mictlan are you—?"

"I have to talk to you."

If I was caught in the bushes with a boy…I didn't want to think about the flogging I'd get. And if I must be caught with someone, the last person I wanted anyone thinking I'd been doing anything with was a cur like Red Flint. "It's after midnight and I'm headed to bed."

"I have to tell you something," he insisted, not letting go of my arm when I tried to get up.

"Tell me what?" I snapped, trying to tug my arm free. He finally let me go, so I decided to let him say his piece before leaving.

He pushed branches aside to look into the courtyard, then turned to me again. "I'm not good with words, so hopefully my actions can speak for me," he said, and kissed me hard on the lips, pushing me against the storeroom wall.

My first impulse was to shove him off, maybe even punch him, but a strange haze settled over me and I found myself kissing him back, all concerns about being caught mysteriously gone. When we finally separated I was intensely dizzy, and my skin tingled as if lightning had struck nearby. "What was that for?" I panted.

"I can't go off to war without telling you how I feel about you," he said. When I blinked at him, confused, he continued, "I know I was a scoundrel before, calling you ugly and putting poisonous animals under your blankets, but I was a foolish child who knew no other way to express himself. But I'm a man now, and I know better. I love you, Quetzalpetlatl."

I shook my head, wishing the haziness would go away so I could think straight. What was wrong with me?

"Yes I do," he insisted, then kissed me again.

I should have pushed him away, but again my head swam, and it felt so right to pull him closer instead. In my mind, he was Little Reed, moving his hands all over me, seeking out those areas I scarcely dared touch even while bathing.

Voices in the courtyard finally broke through my stupidity. *You're a breath away from being taken before the entire school and flogged for indecency, Quetzalpetlatl.* I pushed Red Flint away and looked out through the bushes in time to see a couple of priestesses disappear into the calmecac. I closed my eyes and took a deep breath before saying, "The door monitor is expecting me, and if I don't show up on time, she'll report me."

Red Flint sighed but stole one more kiss before I slapped him away. "I must see you again, soon. I march for the army camp in a week, and who knows how long it'll be before I return and can ask you to be my wife."

Oh, Little Reed would hate that! I thought with a disturbing spike of pleasure. I immediately felt bad for wanting to hurt him so.

"When can I see you again?" Red Flint asked.

Befuddled, I muttered, "I...I don't know. I have evening temple duty again in six days—"

"That's perfect. I'll meet you back here again." Red Flint glided gentle fingers over my chin, sending intoxicating chills through me. He then pulled aside the branches. "The courtyard's clear now."

I hurried to the dormitory doorway, sparing a glance back in his direction before going in, but I couldn't see him in the dark. As I walked down the hall towards the girls' dormitory and my head cleared, I started to wonder if I'd just imagined it all. Surely Red Flint had no interest in me, and I certainly had none for him.

Or so I tried to convince myself when my heart raced at the thought of his kiss.

CHAPTER TEN

Nimilitzli and Little Reed were already deep in debate when I arrived at her house in the morning, though they must have been at it for a while. Before I even sat down with my atole, Nimilitzli shook her head and declared, "Well, the king calls you a man now, and men will do as they wish. May the Feathered Serpent watch over you out there."

Little Reed frowned. "I'd prefer you understood my decision rather than just accepting it."

"I do understand, Topiltzin, and I trust I raised you to be cleverer than most noblemen, and that that will see you through it."

"You raised me very well, Mother, and I promise to make you proud." He hugged her but she shooed him away, still frowning. I'd never seen her so disconcerted.

Once he finished his breakfast, he left to go hunting with Mazatzin. "I'll bring you a nice fat deer to see you through the summer," he told us on his way out.

"And so he gets his way," I muttered once we were alone.

Nimilitzli sighed. "Have you ever known him not to?"

"Only with Red Flint."

"When the dislike runs that deep, it's little surprise."

A guilty flush heated my cheeks. It was such a betrayal to set up a clandestine meeting with Little Reed's nemesis. *Why do you worry about what he thinks? He doesn't care what you think about him leaving. He's made his choice, so you should make your own too.*

But if life had taught me anything, it was that women didn't get their own choices. Mother married because her father insisted she did, and she had to give me over to Black Otter at Father's behest. And now Little Reed was handing me over to the priesthood so they could protect my virtue until he had political use for me. As a child I'd thought the priesthood was about serving the god, but it turned out to be mostly an outpost for noblewomen waiting for their fathers or brothers to tell them whom to marry.

Nimilitzli gathered up the dishes. "Perhaps it's for the best. He might be the god's son, but he's flesh and blood like the rest of us, and young men are notorious for their susceptibility to temptation. Best he soothe those desires before devoting himself to the celibate life of the priest."

"How can you speak such things about him?" I asked, my cheeks burning. Her words brought images of him "soothing those desires" with me on the altar in Quetzalcoatl's temple.

"You can't lock him away in your head as a perpetual child, Quetzalpetlatl. Sex isn't a dirty act never to be performed. It serves a very sacred, important purpose."

"Then why must priests and priestesses abstain?" *And why can Little Reed go off to satiate his lusts in the army while I must prove my virginity to be a priestess?*

Nimilitzli gave me a curious look. "Because it's a sacrifice to give that up, and it's our sacrifices that make us worthy of serving the god."

"It hardly seems a sacrifice."

Nimilitzli laughed. "It's a bigger one than you know."

I rolled my eyes. She'd been a chaste priestess all her life, so what would she know about it?

"One should be sure they want to make that sacrifice before committing to the priesthood, so I can't blame your brother for hesitating," she said. "Better he not take the vows than break them. But I'll give him a good whipping if he comes back from war with a week's worth of children and angry fathers demanding he do right by their daughters."

¤

I contemplated that conversation all day long. It distracted me so much that Mothotli shrieked at me during calendar studies and sentenced me to kitchen duty. While scrubbing out the clay pots, my mind went back to that meeting with Red Flint later in the week, and from there the scheming began.

If I'm not an unbroken maiden they won't let me into the order, and Little Reed can't do anything about it, I thought. I loved Quetzalcoatl, but was that enough to endure half a lifetime under Mothotli's switch?

It wouldn't be difficult to coax Red Flint into aiding me to my freedom; as Nimilitzli said, young men were prone to temptation. But would I really make a whore of myself to avoid taking priestly vows?

It wouldn't be harlotry. Red Flint's already mentioned marriage, and if he got you with child, he'd have to make good on that promise early. And what more could Little Reed want for you than to be married to Xochicalco's future king? It's not as if he wants you for himself. Though that left me feeling sad. *No matter what he thinks of Red Flint personally, from a purely practical standpoint it's a good match and would ensure a future alliance between Culhuacan and Xochicalco.*

But was I ready to be a mother? I was of marrying age; many noblewomen married at fourteen and bore their first child within a year. Being already seventeen, if I waited too much longer, I'd squander away my best childbearing years, as well as my marriage prospects.

By sundown, my musings turned to planning. When I took a laundry bag to the storeroom, I stood looking around, thinking, *I could bring Red Flint in here.* Laundry day wasn't until the end of the week, so there would be a large pile of robes and blankets I could build up for privacy. Secrecy was of utmost importance: the penalty for being caught in unchaste activities at calmecac was the direst there was, next to committing blasphemy.

But a woman wasn't guaranteed to become with child with just one attempt, and since I would only get one chance, I needed to improve my chances. There was the chipahuacxihuitl root, usually used to keep a woman from begetting, but Nimilitzli had told me that if it was used at the beginning of one's cycle then discontinued for the remainder of the month, then it actually increased one's chances of conceiving. When I checked her wicker midwife basket, I found some, but I hesitated. She kept track of her medicines meticulously—not because she mistrusted me, but because she hated running out of something unexpectedly. If I took this, I'd be breaking her trust....

I'll tell her one of her patients asked for it. I still cringed with guilt as I brewed the chipahuacxihuitl into a strong tea. But I was choosing my own future, and it would be worth it in the end.

¤

A nervous sickness followed me for the next six days, even up to the evening I had temple duty. I'd thought maybe it was a side effect of drinking the chipahuacxihuitl tea each night, but I'd stopped the day before and still my stomach felt like a simmering pot of hot orange chilis.

Little Reed had kept his promise to bring home a deer, but he was invited to the departure feast at the palace and was expected to be there, so Nimilitzli and I prepared beans and venison for ourselves.

"Are you feeling well?" Nimilitzli asked, for I'd hardly eaten any of my meal.

"I'm fine. My afternoon atole just stuck with me longer than I'd expected," I said, avoiding her gaze.

She continued watching me but said nothing, letting me have my peace. Once we finished and I started cleaning out the cooking pot, she told me, "I have to go and check on some of the women at the palace tonight. Do you want to come with me?"

"I have temple duty."

"I forgot. If you'd like one of the other girls to cover it, so you can go to the celebration with your brother, I can arrange that."

My sour gut told me to accept her offer, but this would be my only chance to execute my plan. "It's a men's celebration, and I doubt Topiltzin wants me hovering around him." And I certainly didn't want to see courtesans hanging on him, for there would surely be many at this farewell celebration.

Nimilitzli nodded then went to her wicker midwife basket and dug around inside. My heart stalled as she looked over everything, but eventually she closed the lid. "I'll see you tomorrow morning, then." She gave me a smile before going out through the curtain. I finally breathed again.

I finished scrubbing the cooking pot then went to the bathhouse. I washed in the cold water pit with copalli soap then put on my best dress and slipped my robe over it. I combed my hair and cleaned my teeth with charcoal powder, then chewed some chicle, to catch whatever hadn't rinsed away when I'd swished with water. I finished by rubbing on some bone flower cream Little Reed gave me last year, making me think of him. *If only I were going to meet with him tonight instead of Red Flint!* I pushed aside the spike of guilt and left the bathhouse.

Next I went to the laundry room. I built an alcove out of the towering pile of dirty laundry, stacking the bags to form a sturdy wall tall enough to hide me and Red Flint; Mothotli often patrolled the grounds after midnight, trying to catch girls out of their beds, so we'd have to be especially discreet.

You're really going to do this, I thought as I examined my handiwork. The sickness returned, but I didn't have time to think on it. The sunset bell rang; I was late for my temple duties.

I walked into the temple to find Ahexotl bloodletting. Women bled their tongues, in honor of Cihuacoatl's breath of life, while men bled their tepolli, in honor of the sacrifice Quetzalcoatl made to bring humankind to life. Male and female students learned their rituals separately from each other, but as full priests and priestesses, they performed them together; and though I'd been taught that the ritual was never shameful, seeing Ahexotl's manhood so plainly felt like catching my father naked.

"You're late," he said, not sharing my discomfort. "I'd hoped you might do a sacrifice with me."

The shame struck hard; there was no greater honor than to make a sacrifice with the high priest, and I'd squandered that opportunity preparing for an illicit meeting. "I'm sorry, your grace. I got caught up helping some of the younger girls." Oh how easily the lies flew from my tongue now!

"Next time, then. Will you say the prayer for me?"

I did so, then poured the blood-wetted grass balls into the idol's fanged mouth. When I turned back, Ahexotl had his hand down his loincloth, and for a moment I thought he was rubbing himself—but that was ridiculous. *He's just adjusting. The high priest of Quetzalcoatl doesn't commit lewd acts, especially in the god's holy temple.* He dropped his robe back down around his knees and smiled at me. "Thank you."

"Of course, your grace." But the uneasiness lingered as I watched him leave.

◻

Mothotli did a thorough inspection, making me sweep a third time behind the idol and refill all the copal wood burners, so I didn't leave the temple until well after the midnight bell. I hurried into the storerooms to put away my broom then went out the other side, to the bushes, my stomach knotting up tighter with every breath. *Maybe he won't show up and you won't have to do this.* I pulled aside the branches on the bushes and whispered, "Red Flint!" But still no sign of him.

Suddenly someone grabbed me from behind, clasping a hand over my mouth. My heart took off at a run, but then Red Flint whispered in my ear, "Why would such a lovely maiden be lurking in the shadows after midnight?"

I elbowed him in the gut and he let me go. "That's not funny!" I tried to hold back the tears but failed.

He gave me a stupid grin as he gripped his stomach where I'd hit him. "Are you really crying?" He wiped my tears away with his thumbs. "I'm sorry."

Hearing voices further down the garden path, I grabbed his hand and dragged him up the stairs, ducking into the laundry room. I listened at the curtain for a moment before finally breathing again.

"I'm really sorry," Red Flint said. "I didn't know I'd scare you so much."

"Of course not, because women just love being grabbed from behind as if you were an attacking Chichimec," I snapped.

"I said I was sorry," he growled. He soon calmed though and pulled me to him. "I promise I'll never do it again." He kissed me, pressing me

103

against a tall shelf stacked with clean robes. With him so close in the darkness I couldn't see anything, but he smelled of tobacco and tasted of greasy, spiced meat.

Like before, the pleasant haze settled over me, but this time I pressed back against him, especially when he started moving his hands over the contours of my robe. He kissed me harder, his pressing body starting to crush me. "I want to touch you," he whispered, voice eager. "Can I touch you?"

"Of course," I said, inexplicably impatient. "That *is* why we came here tonight, after all." This bold, demanding voice coming from my own mouth sounded alien to me.

He worked his hands up under my dress, his fingers and palms hot and sweaty against my skin. He reached for my breasts but my dress shackled his hands just short, so he pulled harder, making it cut into my back. When I shifted it, he clamped onto my breasts like a dog seizing a small animal to shake. I gasped in both pain and pleasure.

"Sorry," he muttered and eased his flexing grip. He thrust his groin against mine, and I closed my eyes, my body inflamed with growing intensity. I could so easily get lost in the sensations, the hungry tingling in my lower abdomen. "A man shouldn't go to battle having never known the pleasure of a woman's love," Red Flint said in a throaty whisper. "I could be carried off by Chichimecs or even die of a festering wound, but all I would think about was how much I wished I'd made love to you, Quetzalpetlatl." He kissed me some more, eager and demanding. "Please let me have you. I want you for my wife; I'll even go to my father in the morning and ask him to marry us before I leave, so you'll be cared for while I'm gone. Just please don't deny me...."

All this talk of marriage inexplicably annoyed me, so to shut him up I grabbed his hand and took him over to the little alcove I'd built.

A lascivious grin crossed his face. "You never cease to surprise me." Abandoning all pretenses of seduction, he removed my undergarment and stripped himself down naked, then he pushed me to the floor and lay atop me.

Nimilitzli had been very forthcoming in educating me about sex, so I knew the basic mechanics for both male and female; and though Red Flint sounded very excited, his tepolli remained disappointingly flaccid, even when I took to stroking it with my hand. A dead snake had more rigidity.

"Squeeze me tighter—oh yes, just like that," he whispered, but that soon turned to frustration. "Not much longer now. I'm almost ready."

I shared his frustration. "My arm's hurting," I said. He mashed himself between my legs, against my delicate tepilli, thrusting and huffing and puffing and grunting. He tried to push himself inside, but what little stiffness he'd managed melted away.

By now I'd tired of the wearying effort. "Is something wrong?" I asked, impatient.

"Nothing's wrong with me!" he snarled. "You're just rushing everything." He pinned me to the floor and kissed me hard. But when he again tried to force his limp tepilli inside me, I dug a knee into his side. He yelped and pulled away. "What did you do that for?" He rubbed his ribs.

"Just go home, Red Flint," I said, sitting up and looking around for my undergarment. The very sight of him filled me with a disturbing, hot loathing.

"I can do this! Just give me the time—"

Of course you can't, the annoyed voice wanted to say, but I held it back this time. "I don't want to anymore." With the lust subsiding, shame now burrowed deep in my stomach. *I never should have come here. Such foolishness!*

"You can't change your mind," Red Flint shot back. "You already said yes, so you can't back out now!"

"I did, and I will," I replied.

He stared at me as if contemplating striking me—and for a moment I thought he would—but then he snatched up his loincloth. "You're a whore."

"And so are you, Impotent Lizard."

Red Flint started shaking. "If you tell Topiltzin—"

"You think I want him to know that I actually let you *touch* me like that?" I said, disgusted, with him, with myself. Why had I ever thought it was a good idea to strap myself to this reprehensible dog? Of all the stupid, childish things I'd done in my life, this was by far the worst.

"You weren't any pleasure to lay with either. That perfume you're wearing made me shrivel up like a dead root."

I was about to fire off a retort, but then I heard voices out in the hallway. I froze.

"And if you think that marriage proposal is still any good, think again," Red Flint said, trying to tie on his loincloth.

I clamped a hand over his mouth. "Shut up! Someone's coming!"

In the silence, I heard Ahexotl's voice clearly. Red Flint peered over the top of the wall, towards the curtained doorway, but when shadows blotted out the light, he ducked back down. "If I get in trouble, you little whore—"

I covered his mouth again and glared at him, not daring to speak. What did he have to worry about? He was under the jurisdiction of the House of Warriors, where the young men took women to bed with them all the time—some would say it was even expected of them. But if Ahexotl caught me with Red Flint.... I hoped he'd have mercy and let me take my own life rather than making a public spectacle of my disgrace and permanently dishonoring both Little Reed and Nimilitzli. I watched over the top of the wall of clothing, praying Ahexotl would move on. *Please make him go away, My Lord, please. If you demand my loyalty to the priesthood, I'll gladly give it. Just please make him go away.*

But Ahexotl threw aside the curtain, letting in a flood of blinding light.

Chapter Eleven

I ducked, feeling faint. *Please don't let him see me!* But since Quetzalcoatl ignored my first prayer, I doubted he would show me mercy now. I closed my eyes, trying to calm myself.

But then I heard a woman's voice: the priestess Xocoyotl. She was a year older than me and usually led the youngest girls in evening prayer and made sure they were on their bed mats at night. I hunkered down as she tossed an armful of dirty robes onto my wall, but when she moved away, I breathed finally. Not daring to peek over the wall again, I opened a hole between the bags with my hand, just big enough to see through.

Ahexotl followed Xocoyotl around the small room, holding a ceramic dish of burning pine resin while she took folded robes off the shelves and talked about one of the girls cutting herself. "Nimilitzli stitched it up and reprimanded her for playing with a sacrificial blade," she finished. "So I think she'll be just fine."

"You do a wonderful job with the girls," he said. "Just today, the god expressed admiration for your dedication during this first year in his service. He's very pleased you're one of his priestesses."

Xocoyotl gasped. "He spoke to you? He really said that?"

I shared her surprise. Nimilitzli said she'd never heard of the god coming to anybody in this way.

"He speaks to me all the time, my dear. The high priest is his earthly vessel, after all, charged with carrying out his desires. He also says you're worthy of being one of his wives, and that's what I came to you about tonight." He put the lamp on the shelf and set his hands on her arms, a proud smile on his face. "The god desires that you consummate your marriage to him."

Xocoyotl took a step backwards. "But Nimilitzli told me the marriage is only spiritual, a devotion to the god's teachings as long as I wear the robes. She said it's nothing like a marriage to a mortal man."

"She must say that, for it's secret priestly knowledge." Ahexotl stepped closer again. "Within the first year, all his priestesses must lie with the god as they would a mortal husband."

Xocoyotl hesitated. "But how?"

I wondered too, and the possibilities terrified me. Would Quetzalcoatl himself manifest, as he did on the sacred precinct that night ten years ago? If he did, he'd surely know Red Flint and I were here. Would he reveal us to Ahexotl? I shuddered, panic blooming.

"As the god's earthly vessel, I perform his will," Ahexotl repeated, then leaned in to kiss her.

I itched as though ants were crawling all over me. I would have preferred a manifested god to the thought of Ahexotl touching me like Red Flint had. How could Nimilitzli lie to me about this? *Except Nimilitzli has never lied to you about anything,* I thought. *Even to spare your feelings. She's embarrassingly honest about many things. Something is very wrong about all this.*

"What's happening?" Red Flint whispered next to me. I clamped my hand over his mouth again but when he stayed silent this time, I let him peer through the hole too.

Xocoyotl tried pushing Ahexotl away, but he pushed her into the wall—exactly where Red Flint and I had stood for our passionate embrace—and pressed his bulk against her, smothering her with a crushing kiss. She squeaked behind his lips and he responded by tearing at her robes as if he was possessed of something terrible and hungry. That couldn't be the god Mother taught me to love, the one who saved me from Ihuitimal.

Ahexotl jammed his hand up under Xocoyotl's robe. She tried to turn away from him, but he followed her mouth, insistent. When he finally stopped kissing her long enough to catch his breath, she cried, "Please stop!" Tears wound down her cheeks and her lips curled into a sob.

"Oh, but you're enjoying it so much, my dear." He smeared his fingers across her cheek, leaving a glistening streak behind. "Why else would you be so wet?"

I had to look away for the hairs rising on my neck.

Xocoyotl cried harder. "Please! I can't do this. I want to go to my bed now."

"You're the god's wife and he demands you submit."

"I'm not ready—"

"If you refuse, I'll have no choice but to take back your robe and denounce you as an unfaithful priestess. There's no room in the priesthood for those who won't obey the god's will."

"Your grace, please—"

"Then you're gone from the temple, and don't come back!" He cast her aside as if she were an animal that bit him. She lay on the ground, weeping. "I had such high hopes for you, but instead you disappoint me. After everything I did for you? I championed your education. I made you worth something. Not all commoners' daughters are so lucky. You would've already been burdened with three children and living in squalor in a shack down in the fields, but I made you into a woman any nobleman would deem worthy of being his wife. And this is the thanks you give me? Disgracing my efforts by refusing to obey the god you took your oath to serve?"

By now, anger had burned away all my discomfort. I wouldn't believe the god was so shallow, so cruel. This was all Ahexotl's disgusting talk. *And to think you actually considered going to him about your problems.*

Xocoyotl sobbed. "I'm sorry, your grace. I've never forgotten your kindness to me."

He knelt beside her and raised her chin. "I don't enjoy this duty, but we all answer to the god. It's not too late; Quetzalcoatl understands you're afraid, but he's not a patient god. Don't throw away all you've worked for. It'll only take a few moments and you'll still be a priestess. You can do this. I have faith in you."

Xocoyotl hesitated but then muttered, "If it's the will of the god...."

I couldn't watch anymore and huddled with my head down and knees to my chest. It was bad enough hearing it all; Xocoyotl's gasp of pain mixed with Ahexotl's boorish grunting. Red Flint continued watching though, a half-smile on his face, as if it amused him. *And someday he's going be king.* I hated him; I hated Ahexotl, and Little Reed too, for setting me up to be violated just like poor Xocoyotl. And there was nothing I could do about any of it.

"Now that wasn't so bad, was it?" Ahexotl sounded winded but pleased with himself. "You did very well. The god's pleased."

"I'm bleeding!" Xocoyotl cried.

"Did no one ever tell you that happens the first time? Don't worry. It won't hurt as much the next time."

"Next time?"

"You're the god's lover now, and I'll call on you to do your duty when he demands it."

"But you said it would only be once—"

"I said nothing of the sort. Keep the god happy, and he'll protect you from the other women. You'd do well to keep this to yourself, lest you become a target of jealousy, particularly from Nimilitzli. The god doesn't call on her to pay wifely tribute anymore, so if she finds out, she'll expel you from the order. But it's far past midnight now, and I have sunrise duties." He departed, leaving the curtain jingling.

Xocoyotl remained behind, still weeping. "What did I do, oh what did I do?" she muttered over and over. Eventually she left, shuffling as she went.

Red Flint poked his head up over the laundry wall. "I was sure we'd get caught."

"We need to leave, right now," I stammered. In the lamplight, I finally found my undergarment and clambered out from behind the laundry, knocking most of it over as I did. When I tried to re-tie my undergarment, I saw I stood over a bloodied robe on the floor and I stepped away, chills scurrying up my back like a hairy spider. "I never should have come here."

Red Flint snorted. "At least I got to see something entertaining, so this night wasn't a complete waste of my time."

I stared at him, incredulous. "The high priest forcing himself on one of his priestesses isn't entertaining."

"She didn't tell him to stop."

"Because he threatened to expel her from the order! You should have done something!"

Red Flint laughed. "Like what?"

"You could have defended her!"

"And interrupt a religious ceremony? Are you crazy?"

"That was nothing but lies, so he could have his way with her."

Red Flint shrugged and started tying on his loincloth.

It was all I could do to not sneer at him. "You're completely unworthy of someday being king. You care about no one but yourself." Though was I any better, hunkered down and thinking only of getting caught while Ahexotl made Xocoyotl submit to his lusts?

"And calling you a whore would be an insult to other whores in my kingdom," he replied with a scathing smile.

I raised my hand to slap him, but a sudden gasp made me freeze mid-motion.

Mothotli stood in the open doorway, staring at us. "What is this?" she demanded, advancing. She gasped again when she saw the bloodstained robe. And with me standing there holding my undergarment and Red Flint still naked, I knew exactly what this looked like.

I didn't expect the switch across the face though. I shied away as she swung at me, so she missed my eye, but she laid open the side of my ear and the corner of my cheek, across the bone. It stung like thousands of wasp bites. I clutched at it, cowering for the next blow, but instead she turned on Red Flint, whipping him across the chest and shoulders, shouting, "You filthy little dog! I'll make sure you can never sit again!"

Red Flint dropped his loincloth as he shielded himself, and fell backwards over the wall of laundry, demolishing the rest of my handiwork. Mothotli clambered after him, screaming and whipping at his naked backside as he turned to right himself. He lumbered to his feet, howling at the switch's bite, and he knocked her over as he pushed past and sprinted for the door.

"Your father will hear about this!" Mothotli yelled as she fought her way out of the ruins of my alcove. I tried to help her up, but she whipped my hands away. "As for you, you little whore," she swore as she struggled to her feet, "your days at this school are over!" She snatched up the bloodstained robe in one hand and wrenched me towards the door with the other.

Her shouting roused the priestess who watched the dormitory door, and by the time we reached the school, we'd attracted curious stares from the windows. Mazatzin, who was returning from the palace, ran to us. "What happened? Is everyone all right?"

"Wake Nimilitzli and tell her to come to the Council Room immediately," Mothotli ordered him. "Tell Ahexotl to come too."

Mazatzin turned his questioning gaze to me, but I couldn't meet it. What must he think of me, standing there with a tear-stained face, messy hair, and carrying my undergarment? He headed for Nimilitzli's house at a jog.

Mothotli dragged me down the hall to the Council Room reserved for meetings between the upper-level priests and priestesses. I'd never been there before, but my stomach fell when I saw the array of weapons on display on the walls: obsidian-studded swords, spears, and atl-atl arrow throwers, like the one my father had been showing Black Otter how to use that fateful day ten years ago. Murals of Quetzalcoatl decorated every wall, and he seemed to glower down at me with dark, vengeful eyes. "Sit down!" Mothotli snapped, pointing at the mats in front of the large hearth.

"Can I please finish dressing myself?" I choked through tears.

"So you can conceal your harlotry?" She snatched the cloth from me. "I said *sit down.*"

I knelt on the hearth stones, tucking my dress over my knees. *This is the spot where I'll die tonight,* I thought, trembling and nauseous. No doubt under the blade of one of the weapons hanging on the wall. Gazing up at the atl-atl again brought on a shameful, hollow sickness. *What would Father have thought of what you've done?*

"What in Mictlan is this all about?" Nimilitzli demanded when she arrived. I turned away when she looked at me.

"I'll explain everything once the high priest arrives," Mothotli said. "Suffice it to say this girl flagrantly violated one of the school's highest rules."

Nimilitzli paled, and this time I couldn't turn away from the fear in her eyes. She came towards me, wringing her hands but not speaking, as if imploring me to defend myself against this accusation. *I'm so sorry, Nimilitzli. I was foolish and desperate, but please—oh Great Feathered Serpent please!—help me now, protect me from my own stupidity!* I wanted to say.

But when Ahexotl shuffled into the room, she shifted her gaze away and the wall went up around her heart. At that moment, I was just another student, to be dealt with accordingly. When it came to priestly matters, Nimilitzli never treated me any differently than any other novice.

I felt betrayed.

"What's this about? I have sunrise duties and I was just about to turn in after a very long night," Ahexotl said.

"I was patrolling the grounds," Mothotli started, "when I came across Quetzalpetlatl in the laundry room, in the company of Prince Red Flint, and he was completely naked, and she was without her undergarment. And I found this on the floor between them." She threw down the bloodied robe.

Nimilitzli turned her stern frown on me, but Ahexotl stared down at the robe, his facial muscles twitching. "In the laundry room, you say?" he asked.

Mothotli nodded, and Ahexotl shot me a hard glare. I shifted my own gaze away, unable to breathe. "She broke the chastity rule. She is not fit to be a priestess!"

"You caught them in the act?" Nimilitzli asked.

"They'd already finished by the time I found them, but the evidence—"

"Is a bloodied robe that could have been soiled by a girl's monthly bleeding?"

Mothotli faltered, then said, "The Prince was naked and she was carrying her undergarment. It's obvious what they were doing."

Nimilitzli turned to me. "What *were* you doing in the laundry room with Red Flint?"

I looked from her to Ahexotl. He glared at me.

"Well?" Nimilitzli pressed, losing patience.

It was useless lying to her, and to try now would only make me look guilty of something I didn't do. I couldn't look at her though. "I met with Red Flint after temple duty and we stole away into the laundry room to...must I really say it?"

"If you think yourself woman enough to do such things, you shouldn't be embarrassed to speak frankly about it," she snapped.

I cringed. "We went there to lie together, as husbands and wives do." I didn't dare look up at her. I didn't want to see the disappointment on her face.

"Then you're responsible for the blood on this robe?" She dangled it in front of me.

"It's not my blood," I said.

"Then whose is it?"

I flicked my gaze over at Ahexotl again, unsure what to say. "Answer her right now," he said, the challenge plain in his eyes.

"I don't know whose it is," I finally said, guilt hitting me like an arrow. I was a coward and ashamed of myself, but fear of Ahexotl kept me from admitting what I'd seen.

"She lies!" Mothotli shouted, the vein on her forehead pulsing like a swollen worm.

Nimilitzli held up a hand. "You've admitted your purpose there, but you say you didn't go through with it?"

"We didn't," I said.

"Why not?"

Because Red Flint's limp snake wasn't up to the task, I almost said, but that would only make me sound unrepentant. "I realized the folly of what I was doing and told him to stop."

"This is ridiculous," Mothotli spouted. "We should make her prove her story by physical examination. That will determine not only if she's broken, but if so, if it just happened tonight."

"I'm not lying!" I cried. "I swear on the Feathered Serpent!" *Why would I have been ready to slap Red Flint if I'd just bedded him, you nasty woman?* I managed to bite my tongue though.

Mothotli glared at me, but Ahexotl said, "Her request isn't unreasonable, Quetzalpetlatl. Given what I've heard here, I believe the examination is in order. There's no sense in continuing your studies if you couldn't pass the physical exam necessary to become a priestess." To Mothotli, he said, "Fetch Ixchell and we'll have it done immediately." He put on a smug smile.

Mictlan be damned, I wasn't about to subject myself to a check of my virginity for the sick amusement of this beastly man. Shaking my head, I shrugged past all of them. Mothotli tried to grab my arm but I ran out of the door. "You can't just walk out. You belong to the Temple—" she shouted after me, but I didn't look back as I ran off down the hall, tears blurring my eyes.

CHAPTER TWELVE

I sat at the top of the stairs descending to the palace square, staring into the darkness and wondering why I'd let all this happen. *What kind of an idiot tries to strap herself to a dog like Red Flint, and all to do what? Defy your brother? Make him jealous when he clearly has no such feelings for you?*

Nimilitzli came up behind me. "She's right, you know. Your mother gave you to the Temple on the day of your birth, and while you're allowed to leave once you've completed your schooling, you can't avoid punishment for what you did as a student."

"So then everyone but me has a say in my future?" I spat.

"If you wanted to marry Lord Red Flint, why didn't you talk to me about it?"

"Red Flint is the last man I'd ever want to marry."

"Then what were you thinking?"

"With Topiltzin leaving...now I'm the child that needs to become a priestess so I'm a desirable commodity for him to trade on in the future."

"He said that to you?" she asked, surprised.

"He doesn't have to. I'm well aware that my worth in this world has nothing to do with what's in my head or my heart."

Nimilitzli sighed. "Our lot is seldom fair, but you assume too much. We both know Topiltzin isn't like other men."

"He's in such a hurry to run off to war and become another empty-headed nobleman," I said.

"You can't run his life for—"

"And he's not going to run mine. I'll determine my own future."

"Even if it means making a whore of yourself?"

She might as well have slapped me. I stood, glaring at her. "My mother never would've called me that."

"Your mother would've been too horrified to say anything at all," Nimilitzli retorted.

"I don't want to talk about this anymore." I pushed past her, tears threatening.

But she followed me. "Your choices don't go away because you don't want to talk about them. You made one, and now you must live with the consequences."

"I didn't give in to him! Why don't you believe me?"

"Then agree to take the test! You only make yourself look guilty by refusing. You made a judgment error, you've admitted as much, but you can still have a future in the priesthood—"

"Just as Topiltzin wants me to."

Nimilitzli sighed, exasperated. "Then what do *you* want?"

We'd reached the temple base, where the Feathered Serpent's relief rested an arm's reach from me. I wiped my tears away then set my hands on the frieze. "I had purpose, given to me by the god himself, but now Topiltzin has taken all that from me."

"You can't build your whole life around someone else, Quetzalpetlatl. People go away; they leave us, whether by choice or not, and then what are we left with? You believed Quetzalcoatl gave you purpose before, so maybe you can find it again, in the priesthood."

Her words made sense, but fear clung to me. "I can't...I can't go through the trials just to throw it all away...to be coerced into breaking my vows to the god."

"Coerce you? Who?" When I didn't answer, she motioned me to follow her to the house. Once she closed the curtain behind us, she said, "Tell me what you saw."

"I can't talk about—"

"It was Ahexotl, wasn't it?"

I stared at her, shocked. She knew?

She went to stoke the dying fire. "I've suspected him of victimizing the young priestesses for some time now but no one's come forward, and not even I would be so foolish as to accuse the second most powerful man in Xochicalco."

"He told her that you would expel her from the order if you knew," I said, relieved to finally be able to speak about it.

"Who?"

I hesitated before telling her; she scowled and tossed wood into the flames. "What else did he say?"

"That Quetzalcoatl demanded she consummate their marriage by lying with him, and that all priestesses had to do it. And when she resisted, he threatened to throw her out of the order. I've never heard such vile blasphemy." I hugged myself. "How could I be such a fool, thinking he cared about me at all?"

"You haven't the benefit of enough years to understand the true shade of his spots," Nimilitzli said. "Even I only had suspicions until tonight."

"But now he knows I saw him," I cried, sitting on one of the reed mats next to the fire.

Nimilitzli sat too. "It's not my intention to tell you how to live your life, Quetzalpetlatl—you're not a little girl, and you should make your own decisions about your life—but you're dismissing what the priesthood can do for you. Your faith and devotion to the god runs deep; deeper than even my own at times, and that's exactly the kind of women we need in the priesthood. We've unfortunately become a place where powerful men send their daughters to make them more appealing as wives, so we need strong women to preserve the little bit of power we still have. Once, long ago, a woman could have been a powerful war-queen…but these days too many men come back from war having adopted the ideals of those they claim to be barbarians. High priestess is the highest position any woman can hold anymore. And why should we relegate all the decisions to men like Ahexotl or Ihuitimal? You're very strong, if you'd just see it, Quetzalpetlatl, and I won't live forever. And though Mothotli is strong, fate has decided that she will never be high priestess. I can't say who will be, but I see great potential in you."

I blinked, surprised. "Me?"

"Your mother had the potential too, but sadly she didn't think she had the choice. *You* have the choice, and I'll beat Topiltzin over the head if he thinks otherwise. I didn't raise him to be wooden-headed."

The notion of someday being high priestess of Quetzalcoatl held surprising appeal, but still.... "What about Ahexotl?"

"You said you wanted to make your own choices, but if even a bit of you wants to be a priestess and you're holding back out of fear, then you're letting him make the decision for you."

She was absolutely right, of course, and I'd be a fool to let Ahexotl make my choices for me. Little Reed at least had my best interests at heart.

"We aren't allowed dreams for long, so don't let him keep you from yours," Nimilitzli said. "You're better equipped to fend him off than the others were; you've seen the true nature of his sweet words. Men like him prey on those they can easily control, but you're not weak. You've seen his tricks, and you can help arm the other girls against him. Together we can keep him from claiming any more victims."

"That would be a worthwhile task," I admitted. "No one should have to suffer like Xocoyotl did."

"And should you find something else that sings to your heart, you can leave the priesthood without fear of angering the god. He will treasure your service as long as you give it." Nimilitzli stood and took a narrow wooden box off one of the shelves above the hearth. "Your mother gave this to me prior to her death. She asked me to give it to you when I thought you were ready. I think now is a good time."

Carved feathered serpents decorated the box's panels, bringing a flash of memory: I'd seen this box sitting at the bottom of my mother's wicker clothing chest and I'd often tried to open it, but the gold latches had been too stiff for my young hands. I'd always wondered what she kept locked in it. My heart drummed as I pulled the delicate gold latches aside and lifted the lid away.

Inside, Mother's sacrificial blade nestled in a bed of graying linen. The carved serpent handle was worn but still beautiful.

"She had only a moment to get away that night in Culhuacan, but she wouldn't leave it behind. It was very important to her that you should have it," Nimilitzli said.

I gripped the handle and ran my fingers over the side of the blade as I sniffed back fresh tears. "Thank you. For this, and for believing me." I hugged her. "I'm sorry for disappointing you."

She hugged me tightly. "I'm not disappointed, Quetzalpetlatl. Even I was young once."

"I suppose I must go submit to that examination."

She nodded. "And again, should you take the trials, but we only grow stronger for facing the consequences of our choices."

¤

The priestess Ixchell—who was also one of Nimilitzli's assistant midwives—performed the examination behind a screen in the Council Room, but as humiliating as it was to have to go through it at all, Ixchell quickly pronounced me unbroken.

"And that settles that," Ahexotl said. "You assumed wrong about her, Mothotli. What have you against her, always accusing her of lying?"

Mothotli scowled at him. "There's still the matter of her conduct. She confessed to engaging in activities unbecoming of a novice, which are grounds for expulsion."

"As foolhardy and disgraceful as her actions were, I don't think expulsion is necessary. She recognized she'd taken a wrong step before taking matters too far, so she's to be commended for that." He turned his steady gaze to Nimilitzli. "What do you think would be a fitting punishment?"

"If she's to stay, a harsh punishment must be rendered. Casual rule-breaking cannot be allowed." Nimilitzli turned to me. "That is, if you still wish to pursue a future in the priesthood."

"I do," I said. "I'll accept whatever punishment you deem appropriate."

Ahexotl nodded. "Ten lashes then, five on each hand. As is customary, the fire priestess will administer them immediately."

That gave me a knot in my throat, but I wouldn't back out just because I was in Mothotli's hands now. *Better than being turned over to Ahexotl.*

Mothotli took my right hand by the fingertips. She struck her switch across the back of it, laying the skin open. I bit my lip to hold back the cries as she hit me over and over, five times on one hand until it was bloody and raw; then she did the same to the other one. "Henceforth look upon your hands and be reminded of how close you came to a far worse fate," she said. I felt faint with pain.

Ahexotl headed for the doorway. "I trust we're done here then? Sunrise is closer than I wish and I've yet to get any sleep."

"I'll be watching you," Mothotli hissed at me, then she raked the curtain aside with a clatter as she followed Ahexotl out.

Back at Nimilitzli's house, I soaked my bloodied hands in the water jar then smeared salve over my wounds. "I don't think I'll ever be able to close my hands again," I said. Just thinking about it made my split skin sting anew.

"You handled it well," Nimilitzli said as she wrapped my hands in linen.

"Stay out of the steam bath for a week while this heals."

"Now I wish Topiltzin had already left, so he wouldn't see what a disgrace I've become. What am I to tell him?"

"The truth is always best. And don't leave out your reason for getting yourself in such trouble." She gave me a pointed look.

Little Reed suddenly tore aside the door curtain and stormed into the house, red-faced and panting. "That wretched, foulmouthed little lake leech!" He stopped short when he saw Nimilitzli wrapping my hands. "What happened, Quetzalpetlatl?"

I struggled a moment before saying, "What are you doing back from the palace already?"

"And what brings you cursing into my house before the Sun has even been born?" Nimilitzli added.

"Red Flint." Little Reed spat his name. "I can't repeat what I heard tonight, and it took all my resolve to not challenge him right then and there, but I fear by morning he'll have crowed his drivel to every nobleman in Xochicalco."

Numbness crept up on me. "What's he saying?"

"I can't say it in front of Mother."

"There's little I haven't heard in my life, Topiltzin," Nimilitzli replied.

Little Reed paced a moment, then blurted out to me, "He's telling everyone that you gave yourself to him like some worthless whore, and that they should all come to you so you can make 'men' out of them!"

I gasped, appalled. "How dare he—"

"And you expected better of him?" Nimilitzli asked, not looking at either of us. I sputtered until the shame took over.

Little Reed stood silent a moment before asking again, "What happened to your hands?"

Nimilitzli stood. "I've already said my piece, so I shall leave you two to talk." She took her cloak off the wall peg. "I need to go and speak with Xocoyotl anyway." She slipped out onto the precinct.

Little Reed took the mat next to me. I turned away, unable to hold his worried gaze. "Please tell me what happened, Papalotl. We have no secrets from each other."

I laughed. "No secrets? What about you not telling us about your plans to leave for the army until two weeks ago?"

"I didn't want to burden you—"

"And I don't want to burden you with my troubles, either." I turned from him.

"I want to be burdened. If I can help you—"

"Don't you mean tell me what to do? To pray to Quetzalcoatl for forgiveness for dishonoring you, and to hang my head like a good little girl? Because it's all about what *you* want and what *you* think is best. You don't care what Nimilitzli and I think, what *we* want, for ourselves or for you. You're a man now and must take your rightful place as our guardian, and make sure we don't do anything to embarrass you."

Stricken, Little Reed asked, "What...where does all this come from, Papalotl? Are you feeling all right?"

"I feel horrible and useless, and abandoned, but you neither notice nor care. You can't wait to run off to prove yourself a man and shove me safely away into the priesthood so my maidenhood will be protected and you can someday make a good marriage of me to someone you desperately need for an alliance."

He gasped, looking as though I'd slapped him. "I don't intend to marry you off to anyone. No one means more to me than you—"

"That will change once you've lived among the soldiers and don't have to answer to Nimilitzli. When you come back, the boy who once listened to me—who used to love me—will be gone."

"I do love you, Papalotl," Little Reed insisted.

"Then you wouldn't have dismissed my concerns and I never would've thought to dishonor myself with Red Flint—"

Little Reed's face reddened. "Then what he said—"

"That I'm a worthless whore?" I snapped.

"Don't call yourself that."

"It doesn't matter what I do, I'll be considered one. I'm cursed if I do and cursed if I don't."

Little Reed rubbed his temples and sighed. "Do you love him?"

"Since when does love matter?"

"It matters to me."

"I'd as soon love a dog."

"Then I don't understand why you did this."

Because I wanted to make you jealous, make you hurt like you're hurting me. But that was such a childish, petty, horrible excuse. "It doesn't matter. I was foolish and I should have just accepted my place and what you required of me."

Flustered, Little Reed shook his head. "I want you to choose your own way, Papalotl, just as I will choose mine. I won't force you to become a priestess; real devotion comes only from a true desire to serve, so if your heart calls you elsewhere, then go there." He went to the doorway then looked back. "I'm sorry I hurt you. That wasn't my intention, and I beg your forgiveness."

"If you must have it," I said, indifferent.

He looked ready to say more, but instead he frowned, bowed his head, and left. I lay on Nimilitzli's bed, exhausted like I hadn't been in years. I stared into the fire, wishing I hadn't let my anger get the last word with Little Reed, and I welcomed restless sleep when it finally whisked me away from my troubles.

¤

When I awoke, an extra bedroll lay in front of the hearth and Nimilitzli was gone, but she'd left me a tlaxcalli in a cloth. I ate it, but when I noticed how little sunlight leaked through the front window, I felt sick. The noontime bell at the calmecac chimed too, confirming my fears: Little Reed had left for the army camp at midmorning and I'd slept through it. *Why didn't Nimilitzli wake me?* I thought, despairing as I pulled my priestly robe on. I never should have let him leave before apologizing for my harsh words.

But when I tossed aside the curtain, Little Reed was coming from the calmecac, dressed in his novice robe. "What are you still doing here?" I asked once he was within earshot. "Hasn't the army contingent left already?"

"I didn't go with them."

I waited until he reached me, then asked, "Why not?" Though I already knew the answer: *He can't trust you to behave yourself. And can you really blame him?*

"Because I stayed up all night thinking about what we talked about, and everything Nimilitzli has been telling me these last two weeks, and you're both right. I'm not ready to go, and perhaps I let Red Flint influence my decision. I should be above such pettiness, and I'll be better off becoming a priest first."

I stared at the ground a moment before saying, "Just because I wanted you to stay doesn't mean you have to."

"I can't go to war worried that you think I don't love you anymore—because I do, and dearly." He drew me into a hug.

I hugged him back fiercely, all my anger and distrust dissolving in a moment of imagining he was expressing that same exhilarating emotion he brought out in me. "I love you too, Little Reed," I whispered, wanting the moment to last forever.

"What's one more year?" he asked once we headed for the temple, still holding hands. "That'll give us both time to settle out our futures."

As we passed the calmecac, I noticed several novice priestesses watching us and whispering. Word of my misdeed had already spread, and no doubt seeing me holding Little Reed's hand wasn't helping the rumors. He looked startled when I tore my hand away from him but said nothing as we continued walking.

When we reached the stairs up to the temple I stopped and asked, "Are you disappointed in me, Little Reed?"

He smiled as he shook his head. "You could never disappoint me, Papalotl. One doesn't learn proper sacrificial technique without once or twice cutting too deep."

CHAPTER THIRTEEN

For the next two weeks, Little Reed and I spent our evenings studying for our upcoming priestly trials and packing for the pilgrimage to Teotihuacan. It would be a long journey, and though we'd have a heavy guard, rumors abounded of Chichimec raiding parties being spotted as far south as Xochimilco just a week before we were to leave.

"Strange that Chichimecs should start pushing into the south end of the valley right when I was about to march with the army," Little Reed noted as we sat in Nimilitzli's house the night before leaving.

Nimilitzli nodded. "Cuitlapanton agreed to increase our escort, but every man should bring a weapon with them. A heavily-armed entourage may discourage any mercenaries we come upon."

Little Reed had also been giving me weapons lessons. "It's nonsense to say women shouldn't handle swords," he told me. "You're no safer from our uncle than I, and I'd rather you put up a defense than be dragged off without a chance." He took me to the exercise field behind the House of Warriors and showed me all the best places to strike an enemy on the fakes made of grass and maguey cloth. Little Reed let me use the sword Cuitlapanton had given him—it had a mahogany core emblazoned with Little Reed's name symbols—and I broke the obsidian blades multiple times missing the target. I fared little better with the spears, atl-atl, or axes. I was best with my mother's sacrificial blade, and took great joy at slashing at the grass man as if he were Ahexotl.

Before sunrise the next day, all the graduating novices gathered in the calmecac's courtyard with packs on. The men came armed. The king allotted us thirty soldiers and four porters, the latter to carry Ahexotl and Nimilitzli's single-seat litters, bringing our full compliment to forty-five.

We departed under predawn's gray light and took the northern road through the fields where the peasants tended the maize, beans and squash. Fires burned bright in the mud houses and farmers stood in their doorways, eating their morning tlaxcallis before heading out to work.

By dawn, we reached the stepped pit where workers quarried limestone for the city's buildings, and we kept to one side as the men lugged the heavy stones to the city. We passed two trade caravans manned with slaves carrying packs of merchandise on their backs, balanced by cotton straps across their foreheads. Our lead soldier spoke to the first caravan's security detail about the road conditions and any encounters with bandits. As we approached the forest, I whispered a prayer to Quetzalcoatl, imploring him to ensure I'd get to see Xochicalco's beautiful white walls again.

Little Reed fell back a few steps to walk with me. "Don't worry, Papalotl. We're unlikely to be set upon while traveling so well armed, and Quetzalcoatl watches over us." But still the forest shade left me cold and uneasy.

Upon reaching the main trade route we turned west, away from the Teotihuacan side of Lake Meztliapan. "We used to take the eastern road and stay overnight in Culhuacan," Nimilitzli told me as I walked next to her litter. "But that was before the war, when the Feathered Serpent's followers were still welcome there. Ihuitimal executes Quetzalcoatl's followers and displays their mutilated remains along the road. So now we take the longer western road. At Tultepec, we'll take boats across the lake."

"When we reclaim the throne, Culhuacan will again be a haven for Quetzalcoatl's followers," Little Reed replied with staunch conviction.

We reached the tip of the lake by nightfall and made camp. With our close proximity to Culhuacan's territory, we hoped to pass the night unnoticed, and so forewent any fires and ate cold tlaxcallis and spoke in whispers. We departed in the dark of early morning but still no one spoke above a whisper until past noon, when the opposite shore was far from sight.

Two nights later, we came upon the military camp on the outskirts of Tultepec, one of our allied cities. Hundreds of tents crowded the open plain, and bonfires left none of it in darkness. Banners hung from tall poles along the road, denoting where each city's army camped: Chapultepec's blue and white, Xochimilco's green and red, and Tultepec's black and white, among others. We made camp at the far north end, behind an empty pole. Was this where Father's troops would camp when Culhuacan was still an ally?

We pitched our deerskin tents around two separate fires, but we all gathered in the women's camp for dinner, singing, and music. We girls practiced our festival dances while Nimilitzli admonished the men about smiling or whispering to each other. Little Reed sat away from the others, watching me with a proud smile he refused to abandon even when Nimilitzli scowled at him. I smiled back clandestinely, imagining it might mean more. Ahexotl closed off the night with a sacrifice of snakes, thanking Quetzalcoatl for helping us arrive there unharmed.

I woke before dawn and went down to the lake's edge to bathe before the ride across the lake. The morning was quiet save for the occasional soft quacking of ducks floating serenely in the distance, the lake surface smooth as an obsidian mirror. The coolness felt wonderful on my aching blisters as I eased my feet into the water. The smell of fried maize cakes mixed with the brackish breeze blowing softly off the lake.

The other girls came down the path a short while later. Two of them—Malinalli and Iczoxochitl—greeted me with smiles, but the third—Princess Turquoise Bells, one of Red Flint's countless sisters—merely whispered to her companions and laughed. Iczoxochitl giggled at the whisper, but Malinalli shot Turquoise Bells an annoyed look. I went about my business while they undressed then waded into the lake.

"I thought Topiltzin was joining the army this year," Turquoise Bells said. The day after my ill-advised meeting with Red Flint, I heard through rumors that she had been betrothed to him since she was five, and so I'd spent the last two weeks making concerted efforts to avoid her, and any confrontations it might bring.

But with the others here, I knew I couldn't ignore her without seeming rude. "He's going to march next year," I said, and avoided her gaze as I washed myself with copalli soap.

"What could have changed his mind, I wonder?"

"It's not our business," Malinalli said. She was a commoner's daughter, gifted with more brains than most noblewomen, and she'd go far in the priesthood. We got on well in our classes but rarely spoke outside calmecac.

Turquoise Bells continued anyway. "I bet it's so he can make sure you don't disgrace yourself again."

"Again?" Iczoxochitl asked.

"Didn't you hear? Mothotli caught her in the laundry room with Red Flint."

Iczoxochitl gasped. "Doing what?"

"Suffice it to say that my brother left with an ocelot's smile on his face."

"Red Flint's a dishonorable liar," I fired back.

"Then tell us what really happened." Turquoise Bells gave me a nasty smile.

I could have told them about Red Flint's problem—the gods knew he deserved such humiliation—but fear glued my tongue to the roof of my mouth. When it came to sex and reputation, I'd seen too many of the young women become like wolves on a kill. Why we should relish beating and maiming each other's feelings, I didn't know, but many wielded it as if it were the only power they had.

All the same, my silence condemned me. "Just as I thought," Turquoise Bells sneered. "You won't tell the truth because it's already there for everyone to see." She grabbed my hands and held my fresh scars up for the others to see. I wrenched them away and hid both hands in the water, my face burning with embarrassment. "You hide your disgrace now, but you were trying to force a marriage to him. But the best you can ever hope for is to be one of his concubines."

Seeing her bristle over someone who couldn't even perform the most rudimentary of reproductive functions brought me an amused smirk.

She poked me in the chest with her finger. "Stay away from him. I may not be the queen yet, but that doesn't mean I can't make your life miserable." She waded back to shore with Iczoxochitl. They dressed, then hurried back to camp.

"Don't listen to her," Malinalli said. "So you made a mistake; who hasn't? Besides, whatever it was, it's between you and your family and the god, and in the end those are the opinions that matter most."

I gave her a strained smile. "Thank you, Malinalli."

"I smell tlaxcallis cooking. Shall we head back to camp?"

"I still need to put balm on my feet, but I'll see you there."

I waited until she was gone before coming ashore and drying off with my linen. As I slipped my dress back on I thought about what she'd said, and something new occurred to me: what if Quetzalcoatl didn't want me for a priestess because of what I'd done? Would he reject me during the vision ceremony where I was supposed to receive his spiritual guidance? Might he even take back the gift he'd given me? I felt as if a lump of cornmeal were stuck in my throat.

"You look troubled," Ahexotl suddenly spoke up. I whirled to find him watching me with a disarming smile on his face. "What's bothering you, dear?"

My flesh crawled at his closeness but fear kept me from springing away. "I'm fine."

"Malinalli's right, you know. The opinions of women like Turquoise Bells account for nothing. She might be queen of Xochicalco someday, but you will be the high priestess of Quetzalcoatl."

Just how long had the evil dog been spying on us? My cheeks burned at the thought he might have seen me undressed.

"The god has made his intentions for you very clear to me long ago," Ahexotl went on. "I made it my top priority to make sure you pursued his wishes, though after that mess with Red Flint, I feared I'd failed. I'm pleased that you were intelligent enough to realize your folly before it was too late."

"I would prefer not to talk about that, Your Grace." I looked past him to the path, wondering if I could get around him.

"I'm glad you saw what you did. The truth can be difficult to accept when one's told lies about her true duties. Obviously Quetzalcoatl wanted you to see the sacred ritual, to keep you from destroying your future."

The creepy smile on his face made the hair on my nape rise. "I should get back to camp."

But when I tried to hurry past him, he grabbed my arm. "It's natural to be afraid. Don't be embarrassed." I tried to yank my arm away, panic setting in, but he held me firm. "Everyone cowers before he who's greater than them, and when the time comes, you will too."

Thankfully the bushes up the hill rattled and Little Reed came down the path, watching where he was stepping. Ahexotl released me before he could see anything though. "It's time to eat, Papalotl. Malinalli told me you were—" He stopped short when he looked up. "Good morning, Your Grace. I didn't know you were down here too."

"I came to wash my feet." Ahexotl slipped off his sandals and sat on a rock at the lake's edge. "You'd better run along, Quetzalpetlatl, before the men eat everything."

I hurried up the hill and once we were away from the clearing, Little Reed asked, "Is everything all right? You're trembling."

Tell him what Ahexotl said, I thought, but what if he said I'd got what I deserved, after what I'd done with Red Flint? "It's nothing I can't handle on my own, Little Reed," I assured him, avoiding his concerned gaze.

"You're sure?"

"It's nothing at all. Now let's hurry. I'm starving." Though as sick as I felt, I doubted I'd be able to eat anything.

¤

We crossed the lake in a small fleet of wooden canoes that dropped us off on the opposite shore, and they'd return for us in seven days. From there, we cut through the woods for several hours. Teotihuacan's giant pyramids became visible once we broke from the forest, standing out against the sky like mountains. We followed a well-worn road running north-south and reached the city limits by noon.

Mostly only the limestone-walled courtyards of the noble quarters remained standing and we women made camp in one off the main road. It was small, forcing us to pitch our tents close together, but flowering trees provided shade against the sun for both us and the plethora of wild flowers and blooming vines. The men pitched camp further down the road from us. Several guards stood watch at our entryway, though any of us could have easily wormed through the hole in the wall behind Turquoise Bells's tent. We spent most of the day setting up camp and preparing the evening meal, and then Nimilitzli sent us to bed early. I fell asleep as soon as I pulled the blanket over my shoulder.

"Time to rise," Nimilitzli called inside my tent after what felt like only a few moments of sleep. "Much to do today."

Not wanting to deal with Turquoise Bells, I waited until the others came back before going to the water yard myself. A large rain jar sat in the back corner, and though the walls of the deep courtyard stood tall, the open doorway had me hurrying to change clothes, wash my feet, and put salve on my blisters before tying my sandals on again.

After bowls of atole and fruit along with the requisite tlaxcallis, we followed Nimilitzli out to a large open precinct bordered by three mountainous pyramids and countless smaller ones. Standing this close to them, it seemed very possible the gods themselves had built them, as the stories said. Teotihuacan was "The Birthplace of the Gods" after all.

"This road we're on now is called 'The Walk of the Dead', for the kings of the past were carried through here on their funeral processions," Nimilitzli told us, her voice small and hollow in the vast openness. She pointed to the largest pyramid ahead of us. "It was on this very spot that the gods gathered to elect the Fifth Sun, where Nanahuatzin threw himself upon the sacred pyre and became Tonantiuh. This is where Quetzalcoatl bled his tepolli on Cihuacoatl's metlatl stone to create the fifth generation of humanity. Back then this was the paradise known as Tamoachan, where Quetzalcoatl and Mayahuel made the Sacred Tree to hide from her grandmother. Later, our ancestors built the city and these magnificent temples."

The pyramid's flat summit had a stone-ringed fire pit in the center. The men were already there, and I joined Little Reed on the southeast side of the pyramid. Lake Meztliapan stretched into the distance, large and greenish-blue in the morning sun.

"Isn't it exciting being here, where the gods themselves were born?" he asked, his face glowing with boyish charm.

"Meditation time, you two," Nimilitzli warned us, so we closed our eyes. I focused on clearing my mind and relaxing my body, though the breeze caressing my skin like a lover's hand made it difficult. I inhaled the fresh scent of flowers and the trees....

Papalotl!

I opened my eyes to find myself in a garden—not any garden I'd ever been in, but still strangely familiar, like a forgotten memory. Little Reed called to me again, but I couldn't see him, so I followed his voice to a tall stone wall covered with ivy. "Little Reed? Where are you?"

You only need to climb the wall to find me, he whispered back. *I'm waiting for you, my love.*

I felt dizzy with joy. "You called me 'my love'," I said, needing to know for sure if it had been a slip of the tongue.

Of course you are my love! But we can only be together once you climb out of your prison.

I tried to climb up the vines, but they snapped under my weight, so I found hand and footholds between the wall's stones and climbed up that way. The wall grew higher the more I climbed, but I knew it was a trick meant to discourage me and so continued on.

My persistence paid off as I clambered up to the top of the wall. But when I looked down, I saw only a jaguar black as smoke but shimmering like obsidian in the sun. It sprang up and grabbed my head in its jaws, pulling me down off the wall.

And now I fell forever, screaming while the jaguar clung to me. *Come meet your destiny, my love,* it laughed in my head. And to my horror, it was still Little Reed's voice....

Feeling a sudden lurch, I snapped my eyes open and looked around, my heart hammering. Little Reed held my arm, but with his laughing voice still fresh in my head, I wanted to tear free. The concern in his eyes brought me back to my senses. "Are you all right?" He held me a moment longer before finally letting go.

Everyone stared at me, their expressions a mixture of curiosity and concern. Nimilitzli came over, frowning. "What's the matter?"

"She almost tipped over the edge," Little Reed said.

I expected a stern reprimand but instead Nimilitzli asked, "Do you need to return to camp and rest some more?"

"No, I'm fine, I was just—"

But when the tall, mangy black dog crested the stairs behind her, I forgot what I was saying. It sniffed the air, fangs bared. "What's that?"

Nimilitzli turned around. "What?"

I pointed at the dog. "That!"

The concern on Nimilitzli's face now changed to annoyance. Turquoise Bells and Iczoxochitl whispered to each other while the men exchanged amused glances. I looked to Mazatzin too, but he gazed back at me, puzzled. *Now everyone thinks me not only a harlot, but a crazy one too.* "Maybe you should go and lie down a while," Nimilitzli suggested.

The dog was now sniffing each person in turn, sometimes lapping its tongue across someone's cheek. So far it was only licking the men, though it sniffed Ahexotl's sandal before moving on around the circle.

"I'll take her, High Priestess." Little Reed pulled me to my feet, but as we descended the stairs, I noticed him watching the dog too.

Once we were out of earshot of the others, I said, "You could see it too?"

"I did."

"What do you think it's doing?"

"You don't recognize it?" When I shook my head, he said, "The Deformed One? The Black Dog?"

"Xolotl?" In our sacred stories, the deformed god Xolotl—so named because of his backwards-pointing feet and hunched back—was Lord Death's servant, the god who led the dead through the nine trials of the underworld, into the land of Mictlan. His nahual was a dog as black as nothingness.

I looked back at the pyramid, stunned. Xolotl's nahual was marking people for death. "But why couldn't anyone else see him?"

"Maybe my being the son of a god gives me special sight, and you've been god-touched."

"But Mazatzin saw Quetzalcoatl's nahual, so why not—" I suddenly gasped. "Did the nahual lick him too?" I started heading back.

"There's nothing you can do for him now," Little Reed said, taking my hand to stop me. "If he's marked for death, then what will happen will happen."

"But we must do something!"

He thought a moment then said, "I doubt Ahexotl would listen to such a warning, but maybe you can convince Nimilitzli."

But given how she hadn't believed me about Quetzalcoatl's nahual or the stone serpent, I doubted she would believe me about this.

◻

I retired to my tent but was too anxious to sleep. I watched the shadows creep along my tent wall, waiting to see Xolotl's nahual coming for me, so when Malinalli came to fetch me, I was even more exhausted. I followed her to the Pyramid of the Feathered Serpent—named for the hundreds of stone feathered serpent heads jutting out of its walls.

"Feeling better now?" Nimilitzli asked as I sat among the others. She already sat behind a small slab of bloodstained basalt stone, a thick, folded codex lying partially open across the ground next to her. Fully expanded, it would've easily stretched from one end of the platform to the other, the pages connected together one after the other with hinges made of animal sinew.

"One of the duties of the priesthood is to divine the future using augury," Nimilitzli began. "We help the king make decisions about war, planting, or alliances. The gods leave clues for us to find in the flight of birds or the patterns of falling stars, or in animal entrails." She pulled a small, hairless dog from the basket behind her, broke its neck, then sliced the belly open and dumped the organs onto the stone slab. "Not everyone is gifted with the Sight, but anyone can learn to recognize omens through study." She motioned Iczoxochitl over. "Examine the entrails and tell me what you see."

Iczoxochitl peered down a moment then said, "I don't know what I'm looking for."

"Then consult the book."

We each took a turn examining the mess on the stone, each person seeing something different. I went last and planned on saying the same thing Malinalli had—a difficult winter ahead—but when I stepped up, the image of the skull was as clear as a real one; not just kidneys laying over the liver in just the right way. A wad of sinew glistened in the sun like a blinking eye. The hairs on my neck stood up.

"You see something?" Nimilitzli asked.

After my strange behavior that morning, who'd believe me divining a death omen? *But Nimilitzli believes in omens, so she needs to see this.* "Would you please look at it for me first? I really don't want to read this wrong."

Nimilitzli stood next to me and looked down at the stone, but showed no sign of recognition. *She doesn't see it,* I thought, crestfallen.

But then her demeanor shifted and she looked back at me, worry painting her face.

"What is it?" Turquoise Bells leaned forward for a second look.

"It's nothing." But Nimilitzli's voice trembled.

Malinalli looked again but this time she narrowed her eyes. "Wait. I think I see...I saw something like that in the book...." She flipped through the still-folded sections of the codex. "Yes, that's it."

When the other two girls crowded around, they gasped. "Who's going to die?"

Nimilitzli shooed them away and folded up the book again. "It's very easy to misread patterns when one's new to the art. Death omens are particularly rare and even then they're often confused with the signs for a harsh winter. Now return to camp and get washed up." She kicked the entrails off the stone, but when they landed in a fan, the omen was still there, even more plain than before. As the rest of us turned to leave, she took to smashing the guts against the stone floor, reducing them to mush.

I remained behind on the stairs while the others left. "Then it's what I thought it was?"

Nimilitzli glanced up and nodded. "You have the Sight, just like your mother. I never had it, and I always envied her abilities, but it's especially strong in you." She slapped her sandals together, knocking the muck off.

"I must tell you something, and I know it'll sound crazy, but...this morning, on the Pyramid of the Sun, I saw another nahual. I know nahuals are supposed to be spiritual rather than physical, but I know what I saw; it was a huge, ugly black dog, and it went around the circle sniffing everyone. It licked the cheeks of some of the men, three that I saw. Paired with this omen...something bad is coming."

Nimilitzli closed her eyes. "Quetzalpetlatl, I could excuse this ten years ago, but you're seventeen now—"

"I didn't imagine it. Topiltzin saw it too." I scowled at her. "Why don't you believe me? You're the high priestess; you're supposed to believe in this kind of thing."

"I saw the omen and I believe it—"

"But you don't believe me." Angry tears wound down my face, and I wanted to say more but it all was spiteful. Instead I ran back to camp and hid in my tent.

But I broke down into hiccupping sobs when I realized that I had no idea whether or not the Black Dog had put his mark on Nimilitzli.

CHAPTER FOURTEEN

For two days I waited for the omen to come true, but instead they passed with nerve-racking quiet. We spent most of our time meditating and practicing rituals, and I saw very little of Little Reed or the other men. Nor did I see any more signs of the Black Dog, or death omens. By our fourth day, I started doubting that I'd seen any of it at all, chalking it up to stress from the pilgrimage and the upcoming trials.

Just before sunset on the fourth day, all the novices gathered atop the Pyramid of the Sun and meditated while Ahexotl and Nimilitzli built a bonfire. Once Lord Sun's last light faded from the horizon, Ahexotl called us into a circle around the fire.

"In a matter of weeks, all of you will be initiated into the order of your choosing; the women will become the wives of their chosen god, or handmaidens to their goddess, while the men will become their god's war companion or their goddess's protector. So long as you wear that robe, you swear to forsake the ways of the mortal world; you'll live a purely spiritual life, devoting day and night to interpreting the will and desires of your god."

I stifled a laugh, hearing Ahexotl, of all people, lecturing us about living a pure spiritual life. Too bad the Black Dog passed him by.

"As part of your trials," Ahexotl continued, "you've come to the very place where the gods first came to earth, so you can meditate on the mysteries of their ways. You've learned their stories, and by now they are as familiar as your own mother's voice; but tonight we tell them again, as the first priests and priestesses told them, under the open skies of the bright heavens, with the elixir of the gods opening your minds and bodies to their divine inspiration."

Nimilitzli filled each of our earthen bowls with octli from the clay jars sitting outside the firelight. "Drink up!" Ahexotl shouted, raising his hands at us. "Imbibe the sacred octli and reach out to the gods!"

I'd never had octli before, for only full priests and priestesses were allowed to partake of it, and it was sinful for young men and women to drink it. The thick, sweet liquor burned my tongue and throat, spreading pleasant heat throughout my body.

Ahexotl threw a fistful of copalli incense into the fire, making it burn orange and smoke white, spreading the spicy aroma. "The world has expired four times now, each to a disaster designated by the name of the Sun that ruled it: the Earth, the Wind, the Fire, and the Water. Each Sun crashed and died beyond the horizon, taking all life with it and leaving the gods to begin anew with their creations.

"And so with the death of the Fourth Sun—consumed in floodwaters that extinguished its light and heat—the gods gathered where they were born and decided that one of them must make a sacrifice and become the new Sun.

"Two gods stepped forward: the handsome but selfish Tecuciztecatl, and the leper Nanahuatzin. To decide who should become the Fifth Sun, the others insisted they each offer four days of penance."

I'd heard this story so many times I could tell it while doing calendar calculations, yet I found myself listening with bated breath, as if I knew not what would happen next. Ahexotl's pacing was like a wave, first up, then down, then sideways, and it all seemed funny yet awe-inspiring all at the same time. My empty stomach gurgled—we'd fasted most of the day—so I filled it with the only thing I had to give it.

"Tecuciztecatl gathered costly tools." Ahexotl grabbed a deerskin bag and emptied it on the ground. He held each item up as he named it. "Quetzal feathers for his fir branches, gold for his grass balls, and slivers of green jade and red coral for his sacrificial thorns. And his incense was the best in the land." He threw another fistful of incense into the fire, turning it red and creating a black smoke that smelled of fragrant hardwoods. "But Nanahuatzin, being only a poor leper, gathered green water rushes, bound in threes for a total of nine bundles. He made his grass balls of dried pine needles, and he cut his spines from the sacred maguey, and painted them with his own blood. And for his incense, he picked off his scabs and burned them." Ahexotl threw more copalli into the flames, overpowering the smell of the other incense. I inhaled deep, enjoying the aroma. I watched Ahexotl run around the bonfire, fascinated, like watching a viper swallow a chipmunk.

"And so the two did their penance and fasted while the others built a great fire—the Teotexcalli. When the two gods finished, the others dressed them for the sacrifice. They gave Tecuciztecatl the finest clothes: a long cotton xicolli shirt and a round, forked heron-feather headdress, and they plugged his earlobes with gold spindles and hung more gold around his neck. Then they dressed Nanahuatzin in paper: a paper breechcloth, a paper stole, and a paper headdress. Then the gods gathered around the fire and implored Tecuciztecatl to cast himself into the flames, to make the sun rise again.

"But when he stepped near the fire, the intense flames jumped so high that he hesitated." Everyone gasped in awe when Ahexotl threw something into the bonfire and the orange flames leaped for the heavens. "He tried again, but again he backed away. Four times he tried to cast himself into the Teotexcalli, but four times his courage failed him.

"So the gods called on Nanahuatzin to make the sun rise, and he flung himself into the fire without hesitation. His body turned to ash and the gods sang his praises and danced in his honor.

"Now to your feet, so we too may dance and sing Lord Sun's praises!" Ahexotl shouted.

We sang and danced around the fire, some of us more clumsily than others. I found a spot next to Little Reed and grabbed his hand, laughing and slurring the lyrics of the sacred hymn to Fiery Lord Sun. The smell of copalli made me feel like I was flying. Ahexotl soon told us to return to the circle, but in a moment of madness, I whipped Little Reed closer and whispered, "I love you." I desperately wanted to kiss him, right in front of everyone, but when Nimilitzli admonished us to get back to our mats, I found the will to let him go. Little Reed stumbled backwards, a half smile on his face as he stared back. He almost stepped over the edge of the pyramid, but Mazatzin caught him and helped him sit down again. Little Reed laughed and clapped him on the back, but he didn't take his eyes off me. I hid my smile by drinking more octli.

"And so Nanahuatzin jumped into the fire and became Lord Fifth Sun," Ahexotl went on. "But Nanahuatzin's courage so shamed Tecuciztecatl that he finally flung himself into the flames as well, and he too burned up. The gods gathered at the four directions, to see where the new Sun would rise, and when he rose in the east, he blinded everyone who dared stare upon his brilliance.

"But another Sun rose as well, and the land scorched and the light blinded. Nothing could live there—"

"And Ehecatl said 'This is no good!'" Little Reed yelled, holding his bowl aloft with a laugh. "'There can't be two Suns!' and he threw a rabbit at Tecuciztecatl and hit him in the face, *smack!* and the cowardly Tecuciztecatl became the Moon." He drained his bowl then asked, "But how could there have been a rabbit there when the Fourth Sun took all life with him?"

I giggled, but Ahexotl gave Little Reed a glare. He might not have liked the interruption, but it was a very good observation.

¤

I don't know how late it was when Ahexotl and Nimilitzli extinguished the bonfire and the soldiers came to escort us back to camp, but Little Reed had passed out before Ahexotl finished his telling of Quetzalcoatl's journey into the underworld to rescue the bones of humanity. I'd given up on the octli shortly after he'd passed out; the whole situation was far less interesting without him smiling and winking at me across the circle.

I felt feverish and so thirsty, and when I tried getting to my feet, the whole world seemed to move under me. Two soldiers had to carry Little Reed down off the pyramid.

Back at camp, Nimilitzli made us drink water and eat some tlaxcallis before letting us go to bed. That quenched my parched throat but the sour ache in my stomach remained; soon I felt I was burning up, and not even taking off my blanket helped. I stripped down to my undergarment, but my tent was like a steam bath and my stomach felt as if someone was squeezing it.

Dear gods, I hope no one saw me leering at Little Reed! I thought, adding to the rebellion in my stomach. I couldn't believe I'd actually confessed my love to him like that. Anyone could have seen and read my lips. *Now everyone will say you've earned the title of whore.* How would I ever face Little Reed in the morning?

I finally listened to my abdominal pains and donned my robe and headed for the water yard, hoping I wouldn't vomit in the courtyard. "You want an escort?" one of the guards asked when I hurried by at a run.

I only shook my head and ran faster.

I made it a few paces inside the yard before vomiting. I fell to my knees, panting and heaving as my stomach convulsed until there was nothing left to expel. I crawled to the water jar and scooped up handfuls of the cool liquid to rinse my mouth out, my nose stinging. I knelt against the water jar, waiting for the overheating to pass and my legs to feel capable of holding me up again.

"Someone should have told you to slow down with the octli," Ahexotl suddenly said behind me.

I spun around, my senses shocked into high alert. My robe caught on the lip of the jar and I almost de-robed myself as I fell over the side of it. When Ahexotl stood there, grinning at my near nakedness, I covered up clumsily. "What are you doing here?"

"I heard someone getting ill, so I came to see if I could help."

"I don't need your help." I staggered to my feet, my head swimming, making my tongue quick to release my rising temper. "I'm just fine. Nimilitzli is waiting for me—"

But he blocked me. "She would've come down here with you if she was really awake." His eyes roved over me as he added, "You owe me a favor and I think I'll collect on that now."

"I owe you nothing. You forget whom you answer to, Ahexotl, and someday that power you dishonor will make you pay."

He grabbed my arms and shoved me back against the water jar, sending a jolt of pain up my spine. "Your righteous indignation makes me hard, my dear. Just remember that it was by my mercy that you're not a prostitute, pleasuring men for whatever they're willing to pay when they come shaking your door bells." He plastered his lips over mine and forced his tongue into my mouth.

I pushed back, but he was too big, and my dagger sheath had slid around to my back. I snaked my hands up under his robe and clawed his bare belly.

He cursed and smacked me, making my ears ring. "If you want it rough, I'll oblige you." He flipped me around, and when I pushed back he held my neck down so my nose touched the water in the jar. "Fight me or make any noise, and I'll hold your head under. Keep your mouth shut and this will be over soon." My silent tears broke loose as he yanked my robe up past my waist. "And don't worry, I'll leave you virginal enough to pass the physical examination, and you can owe me again for that favor."

This can't be happening, dear gods this can't be happening! I fumbled around again for my knife, hoping it was within my reach now. My fingers found the stag horn handle and I snatched the blade out then drove it backwards into Ahexotl's leg, and twisted it.

It didn't go in very deep, but he howled and let me go. I fell over sideways, yanking the knife out as I went down. I slashed at him again, this time slicing through the tendon on his left heel. He tried to jump away, but instead crashed to the ground, gritting his teeth as he clutched his ankle.

I hurried to my feet, and once out of his reach I stood panting and staring down at him, disgust stamping out my fear. "I told you Quetzalcoatl would make you answer for yourself." I spat on him then left, shaking from the pride pumping through my veins. *Now to wake Nimilitzli. He's finally going to have to answer for himself.*

The moon had gone down over the mountains, leaving the passageway in pitch black save for the dim glow from the courtyard doorway still far away. Hearing a patter of feet behind me, I whirled and stared into the darkness, my mother's sacrificial blade still ready in my hand.

Past the water yard, two guards stood sentry in the dim glow from the men's courtyard. *It's probably just an animal,* I decided, continuing on my way. *Or maybe it's Xolotl's nahual again.* I picked up the pace.

The sudden clatter of weapons on stone made me look back again. The guards were gone. I stared, trying to work out where they'd gone, but then realized I was scratching my wrist. It hadn't bothered me in years, but now it itched so fiercely I could claw it raw. I ran for my own camp as fast as I could.

The guards raised their spears and called for me to halt as I emerged from the darkness. One grabbed me by the arm as I tried to run by. Shouts erupted down the passageway from the men's camp and the guard shoved me into the courtyard. "Rouse the others."

I flung the flaps aside on Nimilitzli's tent. "Wake up! There's trouble!"

She blinked at me, disoriented. "What?"

"The omen." I hurried to wake the others.

By the time everyone came hobbling out of their tents, the shouts had turned to screams. "What in the name of the Feathered Serpent is going on?" Nimilitzli demanded at the courtyard entrance.

Another soldier limped out of the darkness. "A Chichimec raiding party has taken the men's camp. We're trying to hold them back at the water yard, but there are at least a hundred of them! If you put the fire out and stay quiet—"

But an arrow pierced his neck and he gagged. Another buried itself in his back and he collapsed through the entryway, falling into Nimilitzli's arms and knocking her to the ground. Turquoise Bells and Iczoxochitl screamed. One guard charged off into the dark, spear ready as he shouted for blood. The remaining guard took an arrow to the head and slid down the wall.

When Malinalli and I pushed the dead man off Nimilitzli, she look dazed and frightened, making me wonder if she'd hit her head. "Everybody out through the hole in the wall behind Turquoise Bells's tent. *Now!*" I shouted. Malinalli and I put Nimilitzli's arms over our shoulders and helped her limp to the back of the courtyard. The hole wasn't big enough for her, so I kicked out some of the crumbling stonework to make way.

Just as Nimilitzli cleared the hole, two raiders crept into the courtyard, one armed with bow and arrows, the other with a flint ax. I ducked down just as an arrow chinked off the stone above my head then I hurried through the hole and crouched beside the others. When one of the men began climbing through, I kicked him in the head, knocking him unconscious.

"Where to now?" Malinalli whispered.

The courtyard we were in now had crumbling walls in the back corner, so I ordered everyone in that direction. "We'll climb over into the passage then go north."

Nimilitzli nodded. "Our best hope is to head for the temples."

While the others crossed over the wall, I helped Nimilitzli climb up, but—to my horror—when she slid over the top, she lost her balance and hit the ground on the other side with a thud and a cry.

"Nimilitzli! What happened? Is she all right?" I moved a few steps down the wall before climbing over myself.

Malinalli and I tried lifting her to her feet again, but she gripped my arm with painful strength. "I think I broke my hip."

"Are you sure?"

She tried to move again but went over immediately.

The distant shouting grew louder again, no doubt responding to my cry.

Nimilitzli grabbed my sleeve. "You need to lead the others to safety, Quetzalpetlatl."

"I'm not going anywhere without you!"

"You must. I'll only slow you down."

I'd already lost one mother, and I'd rather never find eternal rest in Mictlan than leave Nimilitzli to die too. "Malinalli and I will carry you. No one's getting left behind."

Malinalli grabbed Nimilitzli under the arms and I took her legs, and together we hefted her into the air between us. "Fools! Put me down!" Nimilitzli scolded us between gasps of pain as we took off jogging down the passageway, Turquoise Bells and Iczoxochitl leading the way.

We wound through the passages until we came out onto the sacred precinct. The Pyramid of the Moon stood outlined against the starry sky ahead of us. "Go there," I panted. When we reached its base, Turquoise Bells and Iczoxochitl hurried ahead while Malinalli and I struggled under Nimilitzli's weight. By the time we reached the summit, my legs felt afire and I thought my arms might drop out of their sockets.

"They're everywhere!" Iczoxochitl whispered as she crouched at the edge, staring over the city. Moving spots of torchlight spread out in every direction, and the men's camp was ablaze with bonfires. "Do you think they killed all the men?"

"My brother's out there," Turquoise Bells sobbed. "Oh Merciful Quetzalcoatl, please let him be all right!"

I whispered my own prayer for Little Reed. *You must find a way to call Quetzalcoatl,* I thought.

"Oh no, they're coming!" Iczoxochitl backed away from the edge and tripped over the fire ring. Below us, the spots of orange spread out over the precinct, and a few came in our direction. "What should we do?"

Malinalli picked up a stone from the fire ring. "I'm a pretty decent shot with rocks. My brother taught me to hunt monkeys with them." With Iczoxochitl's help, they moved all the rocks to a pile by the stairs and Malinalli started telling her how to throw straight and hard.

I left them to it and returned to Nimilitzli's side, hoping for a little solitude to work out what I needed to do. *Last time you gave blood and promised devotion, but the nahual said each sacrifice demands more. All sacrifices involve blood, so that must be part of it, but what more is required?* I glanced back out over the city again. *Oh, you must hurry! You don't know how long Little Reed has, so focus! What kinds of sacrifices does Quetzalcoatl ask of us? How do we show our devotion to him?*

"What are you doing?" Nimilitzli asked, pain in her eyes.

"Trying to work something out."

"Work out what?"

I hesitated then said, "What sacrifice to make to call on Quetzalcoatl."

"Quetzalpetlatl—"

"I don't have time to argue about this."

"You'd be wiser to focus on getting through the night—"

"I am! Quetzalcoatl gave me something truly powerful to call on when all else fails, and while we argue this, the men are dying. Your hip is broken and we're surrounded by Chichimecs bent on killing all of us. What else can I do?" I loved Nimilitzli, but it angered me that she still didn't believe me.

"I told you to leave me behind so you all could get away."

"And I'm not leaving you behind!" Hot with anger, I went to the back of the summit and sat with my back to her.

Turquoise Bells came over next and I almost snapped that now wasn't the time for her latest jealous outburst about Red Flint. "You're trying to find a way out for us, right?"

"Of course. But I need quiet. It's hard enough concentrating with Chichimecs bearing down on us—"

"I know, and that blasted octli! My head is throbbing. Why do the gods ask us to suffer so much for them?"

I started to ask her to give me some peace, but suddenly there was the answer: *They ask us to suffer for them.* The gods always suffered in one way or another in the stories, like when Quetzalcoatl climbed a mountain of obsidian blades in his bare feet to reach the underworld and rescue the bones of humanity. And he cut his tepolli to give mankind life. For a man there wasn't a more painful place to cut himself.

"Oh no, they're coming!" Iczoxochitl shouted and Malinalli hissed at her to quiet down. I hurried over.

Two animal-skin-clad Chichimecs came up the steps, one carrying a torch but both carrying obsidian-bladed spears bearing red and blue feathers: Culhuacan's colors.

"Aim for the nose," Malinalli said then she threw the first stone. It caught the lead man on the cheek, leaving a nasty red gash and knocking him backwards, but his companion caught him. Iczoxochitl's weak toss landed on the steps well before the men but it bounced and hit the lead raider in the stomach. He charged up the stairs. Malinalli's next shot hit him between the eyes, and this time he rolled down head over feet, almost knocking over the other man.

The commotion caught the attention of others in the precinct and their flaring torches showed them approaching us fast. Soon we'd have more Chichimecs storming the pyramid than we had rocks to throw. I had to do something now.

But what should I give? I looked around. My gaze eventually fell to my hands. *Maybe a finger,* I thought, but my stomach churned. *No, something else, something less—*

Less painful? Just imagine what Quetzalcoatl's feet must have look like after he came down off the mountain of obsidian blades; he cut his most delicate part so mankind might live, and you shrink from losing a finger? Nothing less than two would be a worthy sacrifice.

I knelt next to the stone slab where the altar once stood. "Turquoise Bells, come over here. I need your help."

She knelt next to me.

"Hold my fingers down for me, keeping the first three fingers together, like this, and don't let go. Understood?"

"I think so, but what's this all about?"

I untied my undergarment and set it on the stone too. "When I'm done, if I haven't the mind to do it myself, you need to wrap this around my hand."

"What are you doing?" Nimilitzli asked behind Turquoise Bells, her voice awash with fresh fear.

"I'm making a sacrifice." I drew my blade. The knife felt awkward in my left hand.

"Quetzalpetlatl, this is foolishness—"

"Hold my hand still," I told Turquoise Bells.

"You're going to cut a finger off?" Turquoise Bells demanded. "What craziness is this?"

"Hold my hand."

"Is this some sick penance over Red Flint—?"

"Forget Red Flint! This is about saving our lives, because who knows what demon gods those Chichimecs will sacrifice us to. Now hold my hand down!"

She complied but turned her head and closed her eyes. I took a deep breath and poised the blade over the knuckle of my small finger.

"Don't do this, Quetzalpetlatl!" Nimilitzli tried to crawl to me but fell over in a wail of agony.

"Trust in the god, Nimilitzli." I gritted my teeth and started sawing into my knuckle.

Little Reed had replaced my blade before we left, so it went right through the flesh and sinew, holding up a bit in the knuckle joint. But soon my little finger lay detached on the stone in a pool of blood. And the pain...it burned like a flame, making my hand pulse with agony and throb with heat. I paused to take deep, calming breaths and then I started into the next finger. Sweat slicked my left hand, making me stop halfway through to wipe it dry on my robe. I felt cold and dizzy, and where I could hear my heart pounding in my ears before, now everything fell quiet, as if I were drifting away. I was taking too long and bleeding too much. I needed to finish before I passed out. With two final sawing motions, I cut the finger loose.

Turquoise Bells grabbed my hand and wrapped my undergarment around it as Nimilitzli gave her hurried directions on how to tie it to staunch the bleeding. I watched, marveling at how much blood pooled on the stone. At the back of my mind I wondered if I'd ever be able to grip my knife with my right hand again.

"Isn't this supposed to do something?" Turquoise Bells shouted, looking from me to the stairs. I looked too, feeling as if I was floating. Malinalli threw the last stone and Chichimecs came thundering up the stairs. I was forgetting something....

Nimilitzli pulled my sleeve. "You need to pray to Quetzalcoatl. That's what you told me you did last time, so focus. Remember why you made the sacrifice."

My wits leaped back at me. *For Little Reed, and for you, Nimilitzli.* I set both hands in the blood then raised them to the sky:

"Merciful Quetzalcoatl,
Hear my plea!

Come aid your son,
For he lies in the hands of his mortal enemy,
And those he loves face certain death.
Help me save him, My Lord!
Help me save us all!"

Hot orange flames engulfed the stone in front of me, and I grabbed Nimilitzi's arm and dragged her away as it grew larger. Turquoise Bells fled shrieking. Iczoxochitl and Malinalli looked back at the fire with wide eyes, and the Chichimecs behind them stared too, their mouths hanging open.

The fire formed a towering column that sprouted a serpent head with tentacles of sunlight radiating from its neck. Through the back of its swirling head red spots burned for eyes, and when it opened its flaming mouth, it roared like a devastating wind.

The Chichimecs fled down the stairs, but the fire serpent leaped after them, turning their yells to death screams. I crawled to the edge to watch the flaming serpent race through the precinct, reducing fleeing Chichimecs to cinders. It squeezed down the main walkway, shooting smaller fire snakes into the outlying courtyards and passageways. In the distance a few torch lights fled, but soon the flames were everywhere.

"Great Feathered Serpent!" Nimilitzli breathed.

"How did you do that?" Iczoxochitl panted, staring at me with both awe and fear.

I stared down at the stone. My sacrifice was gone, the fingers reduced to ash and the blood boiled away. *At least Little Reed is safe,* I thought, dizziness seizing me again. Nimilitzli called to me, but the darkness swooped down on me like a cloud of bats, and I vaguely recalled a dull pain on the side of my head as it struck the stones.

CHAPTER FIFTEEN

I awoke to Malinalli tending to me with a cool rag. My hand throbbed and when I lifted it to look at, it was stitched closed where I'd cut off my fingers. "Nimilitzli showed me how to do it," she said. I sat up, my head swimming and my stomach feeling like I hadn't eaten in days. "Take it slowly. I gave you some tochtetepon to keep you asleep while I stitched you up."

I clutched my forehead with my now three-fingered hand. "Where's Nimilitzli?"

"Over there."

Little Reed sat next to Nimilitzli, who lay on a mat in the corner of the courtyard, a half-burned tent giving her cover from the sun. It brought me to tears to see them both alive. "How are the others? How many people did we lose?"

"None of the women, but we lost every soldier and three of the male novices. Only Topiltzin, Mazatzin, and Lord Talking Serpent remain."

"What about Ahexotl?"

"He's alive, but badly burned."

Of all the indignities...if anyone deserved the god's flaming wrath, it was him. "I should go talk to Topiltzin."

Malinalli helped me to my feet. "I'll get you something to eat. That'll help with the dizziness."

While Malinalli went to the cooking fire, I hobbled over to Nimilitzli. Little Reed sprang to his feet and embraced me with crushing strength. "Thank Omeyocan you're all right," he murmured. He took my hand in his and shook his head. "The god really asked that much of you?"

"He wasn't in a talking mood, and I had to make a quick decision." I touched the skin under the stitched gash on his forehead, examining it.

But he pulled away from me, looking uncomfortable. "It's nothing. I don't even remember getting it. I don't remember much of anything about last night. The octli...."

Then he didn't remember my moment of lustful insanity. *It'll spare you the embarrassment of having to explain yourself,* I thought, relieved.

Nimilitzli examined my hand as well. "With some relearning, you should still be able to wield your knife with just those three fingers." She shook her head, frowning. "I owe you an apology, Quetzalpetlatl, for not trusting your claims before. You had every right to be angry with me."

"I shouldn't have been. I expected you to believe me without any real proof beyond an omen and my word."

"I'll never again doubt what you say concerning the god."

"You really should get some sleep, Mother," Little Reed said. "We have much to do if we're going to carry you and Ahexotl out of here tomorrow."

We left Nimilitzli to rest and Malinalli brought me a couple of hot tlaxcallis. I ate while Little Reed and I walked to the water yard to see Ahexotl.

"We've left him there for now, for he's in too much pain to move," Little Reed said. "Would you take a look at him, to make sure there aren't any immediate concerns? I need to get directions to the nearest city and he's the only one of us who knows anything about this area."

"I suppose we need him for something then," I muttered, disgusted. *But maybe the god spared him because he saw something good in him.* I couldn't imagine what that might be, but I had to respect Quetzalcoatl's decision. When Little Reed gave me a shocked frown, I decided it was time to tell him the truth.

And I left nothing out, from what Red Flint and I witnessed in the laundry room to the attack in the water yard last night. When I finished, Little Reed's face was flushed with rage, and he wouldn't look at me anymore, bringing me to anguished tears. "You think I brought this on myself, don't you?"

"No one brings such things on themselves," Little Reed said. "The man's an abomination and he'll pay for darkening the god's good name." Taking his sword in hand, he walked faster towards the water yard.

I cut him off though. "I share your outrage, Little Reed, but the god spared him."

"Only so I could reap justice myself." He stepped around me.

But I intercepted him again. "The god stopped short of killing him for some reason. We'd do best to respect his decision."

"Quetzalcoatl spared him because he didn't realize the magnitude of the man's crimes."

"Of course he knows; he knows everything, and I won't let you anger him on account of my honor, which is hardly clean to begin with."

Little Reed sighed. "Don't dwell on your mistakes, Papalotl. We all make them." He kissed my forehead and smiled. "I will spare Ahexotl because I cannot bear the thought of disappointing you."

Mazatzin limped out of the entryway of the water yard, looking worn but blessedly alive. I laughed as I wrapped my arms around his neck. "I'm so glad you're all right!"

He hugged me back. "Not that the Chichimecs didn't try to sacrifice me. I killed two before they were able to drag me out of your brother's tent."

Little Reed set a hand on Mazatzin's shoulder. "While I lay passed out, he stood in my defense. The Chichimecs would've cut my heart out to their demon Smoking Mirror if not for him."

Mazatzin blushed and murmured something about how it was his honor to defend him, then he led us to the tent set up where I'd left Ahexotl after I'd cut his heel.

Lord Talking Serpent—who was completely unscathed—knelt praying over Ahexotl in a shaky voice. Ahexotl was undressed but covered from the chest down with a blanket. He groaned when he saw me.

"Has he had any tochtetepon yet?" I asked.

"A little while ago," Lord Talking Serpent answered.

I pulled the blanket back, making sure it didn't stick. The scorched flesh started just above his navel and went all the way down to his feet, with everything in between a mess of blackened skin and colorful oozing.

I sent Talking Serpent and Mazatzin to fetch some water from the creek outside town and I gave Ahexotl some more tochtetepon in octli, to prepare him for his bath. "You'd better question him now, before they get back," I told Little Reed. "He won't be coherent once I start working on him."

I feared Little Reed might take the opportunity to confront Ahexotl with what I'd told him, but he kept his temper and asked only about the nearby cities and how to get to them. He finished by the time the others returned with the water, but he remained in the tent with me while I worked, as if not trusting Ahexotl to be alone with me even in his terrible condition.

I cleaned Ahexotl's blisters and smeared ointment over them while he howled in agony. His tepolli was mangled beyond recognition, but it still gave me the shakes having to touch it. *The god made sure he'll never abuse his priestesses again,* I thought, my pity surprising me. I should have relished his pain, but instead I felt sick and wondered if death would have been more been merciful than this. Once the tochtetepon took hold, he lay drooling and only half aware of what was going on as I wrapped him in bandages. We then moved him to the main camp on a makeshift litter.

Little Reed then called everyone to a meeting around the fire. "Having discussed matters with Ahexotl and Nimilitzli, I've decided that it's not safe to remain here. Our leaders need more medical attention than any of us are fit to provide, and though the fire serpent wiped out the Chichimec raiding party, Ihuitimal will send more to finish what the others failed to. We must leave and find help. Ahexotl recommended we head for Acolman, which is half a day journey from here."

"But who's going to carry Ahexotl and Nimilitzli?" Turquoise Bells asked. "Neither of them can walk."

"We'll have to carry them," I said.

"Impossible!"

"Leaving anyone behind while Topiltzin and Mazatzin go to Acolman is impossible. None of us are prepared to defend ourselves if more Chichimecs come."

"You can protect us—"

"The safest option is for everyone to go together," I insisted, annoyed that she would talk about my ability to call on the god as if it were as easy as ordering food from the royal kitchens. "And all of us will help carry the litters."

Malinalli nodded. "The four of us can easily carry Nimilitzli. Quetzalpetlatl and I carried her up the temple steps last night by ourselves, and this time we'll have a litter for her to sit in."

"This isn't impossible," I said. "If we all work together, we can do anything."

Iczoxochitl nodded, but Turquoise Bells frowned.

"And two men can carry Ahexotl," Little Reed continued. "But we'll need to make a new litter so he can lay flat. I need volunteers to gather wood outside the city."

"I can help with that," Malinalli said. "I've felled trees before."

"Go with Mazatzin. Talking Serpent, take a bow and keep sentry on the southernmost wall. Alert me immediately if you see anyone approaching.

148

And you two—" He gestured to Turquoise Bells and Iczoxochitl. "—I need you to cook tlaxcallis for the trip. Quetzalpetlatl and I will go find weapons for everyone. No one is to go wandering alone." As everyone stood to go to their duties, he called for their attention one last time. "And while we all know we're only alive because Quetzalpetlatl performed a miracle, when we get to Acolman, it is sufficient to say we fought off our Chichimec attackers ourselves. If she wishes to tell others what she did, that's her choice, but I won't have strangers cornering her into answering questions she doesn't want to answer. Whatever you saw here is between yourself and the god." He turned a pointed stare at Turquoise Bells and Iczoxochitl. "Understood?"

Everyone nodded but Turquoise Bells cast me a scornful frown as I followed Little Reed out of the yard.

¤

Little Reed and I scavenged weapons from the dead soldiers then returned to camp to help finish packing. At sunset we made prayers to the god for a safe journey, then we left Teotihuacan and struck out west down the road, back towards Lake Meztliapan. While the rest of us carried the litters, Little Reed walked ahead, sword in hand, making sure the road was clear. The moon rose behind us, lighting our way with soft white light.

Soon my shoulder ached under the litter's weight, and no matter where I held my hand, it was uncomfortable. It throbbed if I dangled it at my side but turned numb if I propped it up on the carrying pole, hurting even worse when I lowered it again. With nothing to keep my mind off the pain, we seemed to creep through the night. I felt lightheaded from the constant pain, and the litter's jerking motion frayed my nerves. None of us women knew anything about carrying a litter and so did a poor job of matching strides.

"Are you feeling all right?" Mazatzin whispered as he walked next to me. He carried the front of Ahexotl's litter with both hands at his sides, the better to keep Ahexotl from rolling off in his delirium.

"Why is everyone always asking me that?" I snapped, annoyed.

"You don't look well, and Turquoise Bells said you lost a lot of blood."

My face heated up. "Please excuse my short temper. You're right; I'm not feeling very well. My hand hurts like nothing else, and now my shoulders are numb." I tried to laugh but it came out pathetic. "This hasn't been a good pilgrimage for me."

"Or for any of us," he said with a smile. "I can't wait to get back home and sleep on my own mat in the dormitories again." He called ahead and Little Reed dropped back to walk between us. "Quetzalpetlatl needs a rest, and I'm sure the other women could use one as well."

Little Reed slipped his shoulder under the pole, freeing me of the weight. "We'll be to the forest soon and we'll stop once we're in the trees. I'll carry this the rest of the way."

I offered to carry his pack, but he refused, so I drew my sword and walked ahead to keep lookout. It felt strange and unwieldy in my left hand, so hopefully I wouldn't have to use it.

When we reached the forest, we followed the narrow trail for a while before venturing off into the trees, slowly maneuvering the litters among the trunks. Once we were far enough off the trail to not be seen, we made hasty camp, forgoing any fire to stay as undetectable as possible.

"We're running out of yauhtli for their pain," I told Little Reed after giving Ahexotl a dose when he started moaning and whimpering on his litter. "If I give some to Nimilitzli, we won't have enough for Ahexotl in the morning and our trying to stay quiet will matter for nothing."

Little Reed looked over at Nimilitzli. "You know she'll refuse more if she knows we're running out, but I'd rather she refuse it than us deny her."

When we told Nimilitzli the situation, she told me not to worry about her. "The pain isn't so bad," she told me. "How's your hand?"

"It's fine. I know you're worried for me, but your hip is far worse than my hand."

"As your mother, it's my prerogative to worry about you," she said. "So stop trying to shield me from that honor."

I laughed and tucked her under the blanket. She'd never called herself my mother before; she'd always been Little Reed's mother, for she was the only one he'd ever known, and no doubt she'd refrained from calling herself mine out of respect for my real mother. But it warmed me to finally hear her acknowledge how I'd always thought of her. "Good night to you too, Mother," I whispered, and kissed her forehead.

CHAPTER SIXTEEN

I slept fitfully but after a while I gave up on it. I thought about taking some of the yauhtli, to dull the throbbing in my hand, but both Ahexotl and Nimilitzli needed it more. I sat up and looked around for Little Reed.

"You should be sleeping," he said from behind me, where he sat against a large tree, his obsidian-edged sword balanced on his knees. He turned his head sharply when a jaguar called in the distance, adding its coughing sound to the cacophony of insects and night birds.

I went and sat next to him. "I did sleep."

"Is your hand bothering you?"

"A little."

"I'm sorry."

I laughed. "You have nothing to be sorry about. It saved everyone and that's worth the pain."

He set his hand over mine, giving the good side a gentle squeeze, making my heart soar. "Maybe you should sleep and I can keep watch," I suggested, heat traveling up my body from my belly. Now wasn't the time for such foolishness.

"I can't sleep either. Too much thinking."

"About what?"

"Remember all those reports about Chichimec raiders ambushing the roads along the west side of the lake in the week before we left, when I was supposed to leave for the army? The Chichimecs who came to Teotihuacan were wearing Culhuacan's colors."

"You think there's a spy in Xochicalco?"

He nodded. "Either in Cuitlapanton's court, or in the priesthood. Our uncle had no luck trying to assassinate me inside the city, so it's logical he'd wait until I was setting out on campaign, so he could attack me with actual troops. And he's planted spies once, so who's to say he didn't do it again, to monitor what I'm doing."

"We should alert the king, so he can launch an investigation."

Rustling sounds along the trail brought us both to silence, and Little Reed grabbed his sword. I couldn't see anything in the dark, but the noise grew louder. Soon I heard voices.

"Go wake the men and send them over," Little Reed whispered, then crept to another tree, closer to the trail.

I woke Mazatzin and Talking Serpent and they joined Little Reed at the edge of camp. I also woke the women, in case we needed to leave in a hurry. We huddled around Nimilitzli.

As the voices grew closer, I could distinguish two different ones, but judging from the footfalls there were more people. Mazatzin crept off to the left and Talking Serpent to the right.

"I hope they're friendly," Iczoxochitl whispered next to me. I hoped so too; we deserved a good run of luck.

But my wrist already itched like the previous night. I started to signal Little Reed, but then I heard a bowstring pull tight behind me.

Three men stood over us, all armed with ready arrows. Iczoxochitl squeaked in terror.

Roused by the noise, Little Reed came to his feet and one of the men shot him in the shoulder, flinging him back. I started getting to my feet, but Little Reed held his hand up as more men rushed the camp, swords drawn. Both Mazatzin and Talking Serpent scrambled to stand between them and Little Reed, but the soldiers knocked them aside easily, bloodying Lord Talking Serpent's nose. Mazatzin tried to raise his sword but one of the archers laid an arrow between his shoulder blades.

I reached for my knife, prepared to cut the rest of my fingers off to save us, but the archer nearest me jabbed an arrow at my throat. "Don't," he said.

Still more soldiers gathered around our men. The leader paced in front of them, looking each over by torchlight. None of the soldiers wore Culhuacan's colors, but I trusted my itching wrist.

The leader stopped in front of Little Reed and leaned closer. He then bent over Mazatzin. "Which of you is Topiltzin?"

"I am." Mazatzin ground out the words. Turquoise Bells gasped and he shot her a warning glare but then sat taller, beads of sweat betraying his pain. "I'm Lord Topiltzin, son of Culhuacan's rightful king, Mixcoatl." Beside him, Little Reed watched, shocked.

"Are you now?" The leader knelt in front of Mazatzin. "Are you sure?"

"I know who I am," he panted.

The man grabbed and twisted the arrow, making Mazatzin writhe. I moved my hand towards my knife again, but the soldier poked me again with his arrow.

"Are you still sure?"

Mazatzin nodded, tears flowing down his cheeks.

"Let's just send all their heads back," the torchbearer replied. "Let Ihuitimal sort it out."

An arrow hissed through the air and struck the leader between the shoulders. He whirled, roaring in both pain and astonishment, and was met by two more arrows, one to the shoulder, the other in his eye. He fell atop Little Reed as the torchbearer took an arrow to the neck, and he too collapsed, trapping Little Reed under a pile of death. Still more arrows flew, from both directions.

Shouts and screams filled the night, mostly provided by Turquoise Bells and Iczoxochitl as they clung to each other. I laid low a moment then crawled to help Little Reed claw his way out from under the dead soldiers. Most of the men had gathered at the back of our camp, where the first set of archers had sneaked up on us, and they'd dragged Mazatzin with them.

I grabbed the torchbearer's sparse clothes and pulled him off the pile so Little Reed could finally worm his way out from under the other body. He shoved me behind him and wielded his sword one-handed as a soldier came at us. While he parried the soldier's blows, I snatched up the leader's sword and swung it too, making the man raise his arms and expose his belly. Little Reed swiped him, spilling his guts on the ground. He went down, and Little Reed finished him off with a quick slash to the throat.

Malinalli had found a sword as well and stood guard over Nimilitzli, but the soldiers were too busy dodging arrows or dying to pay her any mind. Soon only two remained, crouched behind a log to shelter from the arrows. She tossed her sword to Mazatzin who crept up behind and felled them one after the other.

More soldiers flooded from the trees and gathered around us, weapons drawn. Mazatzin backed towards Little Reed and me, sword still ready. I refused to drop my sword too when I saw they wore the same green and white as the soldiers who'd beset us.

A man wearing a wooden helmet shaped like an eagle's head and a xicolli covered in brown and white feathers cut through the crowd. "Put your swords down. We're not here to hurt you." Mazatzin refused, so he turned to his men and ordered them to lower their weapons. "We have no disputes with the priesthood of Quetzalcoatl."

"And I protect the god's own flesh," Mazatzin replied.

Little Reed struggled to his feet, gripping onto Mazatzin's arm for support. "Put it away, my friend. Your loyalty is inspiring, and I thank you for it."

Mazatzin lowered his sword but kept his gaze fixed on the man.

The man bowed. "I'm Lord Citlallotoc, son of the rightful king of Acolman. My men and I mutinied when Ihuitimal's spies infiltrated the king's council and assassinated him. One of Ihuitimal's men now sits on my throne, but those loyal to me have joined Xochicalco's allied forces."

"We were on pilgrimage in Teotihuacan when we were beset by Chichimecs bearing Culhuacan's colors," Little Reed replied. "We were on our way to Acolman, seeking aid, but now I must thank you for saving us from my uncle once again."

Citlallotoc squinted at him. "You're Lord Topiltzin?"

Little Reed nodded. "And this is my good friend Lord Mazatzin, son of King Cuitlapanton of Xochicalco, and this is my sister, Lady Quetzalpetlatl."

Citlallotoc nodded to each of us in turn. His gaze lingered on me a moment before he told Little Reed, "It's very good fortune we found you then. We'll take you across the lake to the allied military camp so our surgeons can tend to your wounded. How bad are they?"

"Our high priestess suffered a broken hip and our high priest was severely burned," I said. "And now both my brother and Lord Mazatzin have fresh battle injuries."

Mazatzin looked down at the arrowhead sticking from his chest, then collapsed. Little Reed and Citlallotoc caught and eased him to the ground. "We should tend to both of you before we leave," Citlallotoc suggested. "It'll take until morning to reach our boats at the lake's edge."

"Will you see to Mazatzin?" Little Reed asked me.

"You need your arrow extracted too," I reminded him.

"It barely hurts—"

"For once stop trying to be the big tough warrior and let me help you."

Citlallotoc grinned. "You do need to be tended to. Leave the rest to me."

Little Reed avoided my gaze as Citlallotoc walked away. "We could have discussed this privately, once we were alone," he muttered.

I sighed. "I'm sorry I humiliated you, but a good leader knows when he should see to his own health for the benefit of those he leads, Little Reed."

◘

Only three canoes awaited us at the lake's edge, so half of Citlallotoc's men had to stay behind to make room for us. Little Reed offered to stay behind with them, in case more troops came from Acolman, but Citlallotoc insisted he come along. "I won't leave any wounded man behind. It could mean the difference between your arm healing or having to burn your body for the funeral."

I rode with the women during the crossing and it gladdened me to see Little Reed and Citlallotoc deep in conversation the whole time. "And he thought it would be difficult to gain the other men's loyalty," I told Nimilitzli.

"But he also needs friends," Nimilitzli said. "Someone he can talk to about more than just politics and religion." She set her hand on mine and added, "You need someone too, Quetzalpetlatl." She looked over at Malinalli who sat apart from the other two women. "You two seem to get along best of any of the girls at the calmecac."

Nimilitzli was right. If not for Little Reed, I wouldn't have had any friends at all growing up. Being the high priestess's foster daughter meant most girls didn't trust me not to tell their secrets to Nimilitzli. I hadn't minded it much, but Little Reed wouldn't be around much longer, and without someone to call a friend, I'd grow miserable. *And Malinalli stood up for you to Turquoise Bells that day by the lake....*

Noticing my gaze, Malinalli edged closer to me. "How's the hand?"

"Hardly noticeable anymore." Though now that she'd mentioned it, it started throbbing again. I hoped we'd reach the camp soon so I could get some medicine.

We landed ashore at midmorning and Ahexotl awoke from his drugged sleep shortly after. By the time we reached camp, his wails brought a handful of guards to investigate. They took us to the medical tents and the surgeons immediately divided up among us, most of them hovering around Ahexotl and shaking their heads.

"Did someone torture you?" my surgeon asked when he examined my hand.

"I lost them in the heat of battle." Easier than telling him the truth.

"These seams look pretty ragged, definitely not made by a macuahuitl...." He gave me another questioning gaze but then said, "It should heal well, and once the swelling goes down, you should have normal mobility in the remaining fingers. The tissue looks healthy, but only time will tell whether or not you'll continue having pain. Keep the chapolxiuitl herb on it until it completely heals, and if the pain keeps you awake, take the yauhtli." He put the medicines in a leather pouch and draped it around my neck by a string.

I checked on the others, starting with Nimilitzli. By the time I spoke with Mazatzin and peered over the shoulders of those tending to Ahexotl, the exhaustion struck hard.

Little Reed walked me out of the tent into the day's heat. "You should go and sleep. I don't think you've rested well in days."

"I haven't," I admitted.

He called Talking Serpent over from the nearby cooking fire and asked him to escort me to our tents across camp. "Sleep well," he said, giving my good hand a gentle squeeze.

"Make sure you get some rest too," I said. He smiled and told me he would.

Talking Serpent took me through the heart of camp, into a row of canvas tents painted yellow and white. Turquoise Bells, Iczoxochitl, and Malinalli stood at the communal cooking fire, getting bowls of wonderful-smelling stew from the tattooed woman tending the fire. She gave me a gap-toothed smile when she handed me my bowl.

As we left the fire, Malinalli said, "They gave us tents to share, but if you'd rather share with someone else—"

"I prefer your company, thank you," I said.

Our tent was so small that our bed rolls touched and we had to hunch over to not bump our heads against the slanted canvas ceiling, but the beans were wonderful. We passed the time talking about Nimilitzli's injuries and what they might mean for taking the trials. "Do you think Mothotli will oversee them instead?" Malinalli asked.

"I suspect she will, though I'd rather she didn't."

"She intimidates you too?"

"She's never liked me, but I think she's especially annoyed I wasn't thrown out of calmecac for...well, my poor judgment with the Prince. I'm sure she'll do her best to make my trials too difficult to pass."

"She has seemed unusually hard on you," Malinalli noted. "We could study together, work hard to prepare for whatever silly questions she throws at us."

I smiled. "I'd like that very much."

After we finished eating, we crept under our blankets. I'd hoped to be able to sleep without the yauhtli, but it was impossible to not think about the dull throb in my hand, so I took some from my leather pouch and drank it down with a cup of water.

"I'm glad you're going through with it," Malinalli said, once I lay down again.

"With what?"

"The trials, and becoming a priestess. You have a gift like no other, one the gods don't just give to anybody, and I think you'd regret abandoning that."

"I could never abandon the god, even if I didn't become a priestess."

"Surely the Feathered Serpent has something great in mind for you."

Her words brought my heart to an excited dash. "Maybe," I whispered.

CHAPTER SEVENTEEN

When I awoke the next afternoon, Malinalli had folded up her bed like we did every morning at calmecac and left me alone to sleep. I lay in bed, trying to gather the strength to get up and find something to eat, but a familiar voice in the next tent soon drew my attention.

"What's this I hear about you taking an arrow for that no-good Topiltzin, Brother?" Red Flint said. I sighed, annoyed. I'd enjoyed not listening to his prattle the last couple of weeks. "My poor brother, always so misled. And that's quite a wound! Maybe you'll die and the gods will grant you paradise for giving your life for that whelp."

"Enough," Mazatzin said. "I don't tell you where to put your heart, so don't lecture me. Just because you doubt he's the god's son doesn't mean I must follow you."

"I thought you the smartest of my brothers, Mazatzin, but instead you've turned into a fool."

"Then leave me to my foolishness and I'll leave you to yours."

"I must admit, as your future king, I worry where your loyalties lie."

I raised an astonished eyebrow.

Mazatzin laughed. "My loyalties are to Father, but when I become a priest, my devotion to the god will supersede everything else."

"You'd listen to some *god* over your king?" Red Flint asked.

"So long as Xochicalco's king—no matter who he is—remains faithful to the god, then the king shall have my loyalty."

That brought a smile to my face.

"Someday you'll take an oath to your people, Red Flint, to be their king and protect them from harm, and I won't feel slighted when you put their needs over mine. Quetzalcoatl is Xochicalco's patron god, not your competition, and a wise king consults his god in all decisions. When you're older and Father has taught you about the duties of the king, then you'll appreciate how pointless your concern is."

Red Flint raised his voice. "Then you think I'm not fit to be king?"

"I'm only saying you still have much to learn, hardly unexpected when you haven't yet gone into your first battle."

"Oh, but you—who won't do his military duty until next year—you know more than me about being king?"

"He knows more about everything than you do," I whispered with a chuckle.

"You know nothing!" Red Flint went on. "Spent your whole life locked up in the calmecac, with the cold baths scrambling your brain and priests whispering lies in your ears. Maybe you desire my throne for yourself, is that it?"

"Don't even jest with such talk, Red Flint," Mazatzin warned. "If you think I'm conniving for your throne, then make the accusation in front of everyone and challenge me to a fight. But don't expect me to put up a defense to your stupidity. I'll let you explain to Father why you felt it necessary to strike me down without a struggle."

Just then someone jingled the bells on my tent. I hurried over to find Little Reed standing outside. "I came by to see how you're doing—"

But I shushed him and pulled him inside the tent. "Red Flint's talking about you," I whispered. We both sat on my bed mat and listened at the tent wall.

"Of course I don't think you want my throne, Mazatzin," Red Flint went on. "But sometimes I fear you favor Topiltzin over me, Brother."

Exasperated, Mazatzin said, "I wish you'd abandon this jealousy of him."

"I'm not jealous!"

I started to mutter, "Yes you are," but Mazatzin said it first. "Your jealousy is readily apparent, and someday it'll be your undoing, so I implore you to forget about him and focus on your own path. He'll be an important ally that you may need to call on for help. Put aside your personal sentiments and do what's right for your people."

Red Flint laughed. "I won't need his help. I'm heir to the valley's most powerful throne and he's an exiled prince who will need my help to regain his own small, pathetic one. And I wouldn't doubt it at all if he preferred a man to a woman in his bed."

I gasped, appalled that he'd stoop to such slander, but when I looked over at Little Reed, he merely rolled his eyes, as if he expected no better.

"There you go not checking your tongue again," Mazatzin warned.

"Why? Because you fear what it might say about you, here sharing his tent and defending him with your very life? I at least had the good sense to fawn over the female of the pair, whore though she may be. You weren't at the palace to hear what wondrous things I got her to perform on me—"

My cheeks flared. A breath later, I heard the tent flap swish and I turned to see the tail of Little Reed's robe just as he disappeared outside. *Oh no!* I scrambled after him.

"Get out here, you louse-ridden dog!" Little Reed shouted at the tent next to mine, his fists balled tight.

After a tense moment in which I heard Mazatzin telling Red Flint to leave, Red Flint finally came outside, seemingly surprised to see Little Reed standing in front of him. He darted his gaze to me, then back to Little Reed. "What do you want?"

"Say what you want about me, Red Flint, but you go too far when you speak dishonorably of those dearest to me!"

All around us the soldiers looked up, some standing for a better view. Red Flint flashed his gaze around, ending with me again; but when he turned back to Little Reed, he gave him a sneer. "I'm sorry your sister promised to make a man out of you then backed out on it. The little

159

whore did the same to me."

Little Reed leaped at him and they went down in a heap, taking down half of Mazatzin's tent with them. Mazatzin fought his way out of the back end and nearly fell over into the tent behind it as he tried to get to his feet.

Somewhere in the brawl, Red Flint pulled a knife and swiped Little Reed with it. Little Reed scrambled away, bleeding from a shallow cut on his cheek. "Drop the blade and fight me like a man, Red Flint," Little Reed panted as Red Flint rose to his feet. "Or are you afraid you can't best me without an advantage?"

Red Flint looked around at the others, but after a tense moment, he handed his weapon to Mazatzin. "I'm not afraid of you, you little pile of jaguar shit." He advanced on Little Reed, body crouched.

Little Reed matched his stance and they circled a few times before Red Flint came at him, both hands out for the grapple. Little Reed stepped aside and grabbed him by the arm and jammed it behind Red Flint's back. Red Flint swung at him with his other fist, first one direction then the other, but Little Reed dodged his flailing blows, swinging him around as he did. A wave of quiet laughter swam through the crowd as they continued spinning in circles.

But when they came to the fire pit, Red Flint scooped up a smoldering log and swung it at Little Reed's head. Little Reed let him go, barely avoiding the blow. Red Flint lunged at him, spilling them both to the ground like squabbling dogs. The soldiers whistled and hooted.

I didn't share their enthusiasm. In the blur of fists, kicks, and tumbles, I couldn't make out who was winning, though neither seemed to have the advantage. Soon the fighting became hair-pulling and wrestling. They locked arms around each others' necks, but eventually they both let go and rolled away, panting. I started to rush to Little Reed's side but stopped. He'd never forgive me for mothering him in front of the soldiers.

Mazatzin glared down at Red Flint. "That was all rather pointless. Neither of you proved anything; you just acted like boys rather than men, and that's hardly becoming of a soldier, or a priest."

Little Reed glared at Red Flint but said nothing as he wiped blood from his nose. Red Flint batted away Mazatzin's hand when he offered to help him up. "There you go lecturing me again." He gritted his teeth as he stood and snatched his obsidian knife back from his brother. He then limped away, clutching his scraped thigh.

But Little Reed accepted Mazatzin's help up. "You're right as usual. I'm sorry about the tent. I'll get it standing up again."

"No, Red Flint started this, so he'll help me. You should go and clean up. Hopefully you didn't tear open your shoulder again."

Little Reed and I went down to the lake's edge and he sat on a rock while I washed the blood off him. "If you ask me, it's unfortunate that Mazatzin's mother isn't Cuitlapanton's legitimate wife," he said between gritted teeth as I wiped the dirt off his scraped knee. "Mazatzin would be a far better king than Red Flint."

"Why are you rising to Red Flint's insults? He was trying to make you look like a fool, and he just might have succeeded."

"I don't know what came over me," he admitted, embarrassed. "When he said those things about you...I just snapped."

"You asked me not to mother you in front of the men, but I ask you not to leap to defend my honor either. It only lends weight to Red Flint's claims. It's my shame to deal with; it'll only go away by my own actions."

Little Reed started to argue but then sighed and hung his head. "Then we don't need each other anymore?"

I raised his chin for him. "I'll always need your love, Little Reed."

He smiled back. "And I'll always need yours, Papalotl."

His steady gaze made me hot and uncomfortable, so I wiped the blood from his nose and declared him finished. "How long until we can leave for Xochicalco?" I asked, averting my eyes in hopes I could stop the blush rising up my neck.

"Nimilitzli won't be ready to travel for several weeks and Ahexotl even longer than that, but she already told me we shouldn't wait on her account. She thinks we're safer behind the city walls."

"Then you haven't told her our suspicions about spies?"

"I don't want to worry her."

I unwound the bandage from my hand and put salve on it. I only felt pain now if I raised my hand above my head.

"Now you must give even more next time," Little Reed said, looking frustrated.

"Then let us hope I never have need of it again."

He shook his head. "I fear far greater dangers lie ahead. Our uncle keeps very dark and powerful company."

"I'll make the necessary sacrifice when the time comes, and I shall do it with a smile on my face."

"I pray that Omeyocan doesn't ask so much of you."

His frown left me disconcerted. "Let's not talk about that anymore. We should be making our preparations for returning home."

"We should, but first let me help you re-wrap that."

I handed him my fresh linen and watched him wind it around my hand, my heart racing. For the first time, I saw in him the man he so desperately wanted me and Nimilitzli to believe he was, and it thrilled me more than any of those shameful moments I'd spent in the laundry room with Red Flint. *He looks so much like Father, but also like Nochuatl—like everyone who's ever meant anything at all to me*, I thought, tears blurring my eyes.

Little Reed paused mid-wrap when he noticed me crying. "Am I hurting you?"

I shook my head. "Not at all."

He finished wrapping my hand then asked again, "Are you sure you're all right?"

"I'm wonderful, really."

He started to say more but stopped, an expression of consternation on his face. We walked back to camp in silence.

Back in my tent, Malinalli was preparing to go down to the lake to bathe but I declined her invitation to join her and the others. I lay staring at the tent wall, thinking about Little Reed and the things I wished I had to courage to tell him.

But once I fell into a fitful sleep, I dreamt I was a tree that towered over the lake, its branches heavy with white flowers whose intoxicating fragrance freed the knots not just in people's tongues, but in their hearts as well.

¤

We stayed an extra day to give Mazatzin's wounds more time to heal and I spent the last day sitting at Nimilitzli's side, writing down her instructions for Mothotli. I could write with both hands, though I mostly used my right; and having to hold the quill in the left felt awkward for a while and my writing was less steady at the start. Little Reed came by a few times to check on her but spent most of his time coordinating our military escort.

"He's really taken to his leadership role well," Nimilitzli noted. "Though I heard he and Red Flint got into a scuffle a couple of days ago."

"They did, and neither came out ahead," I said. "I'm sure Red Flint took a thorough ribbing from the other soldiers for being unable to best an injured man." I chuckled.

"Your brother will outgrow that rashness in times. He has the intelligence and the favor of the gods, neither of which Red Flint has nor can ever hope for. Someday he'll make a very fine king. And you will make a very fine priestess; maybe even a high priestess."

"I wish you were administering the trials instead of Mothotli," I admitted with a sigh.

"You'll do just fine. I have faith in you, and so does the god. After what you did in Teotihuacan, I can't imagine you not doing well. And believe it or not, Mothotli really wants you to succeed."

I smiled wanly. "I'll try to remember that."

Nimilitzli gripped my hand. "Trust yourself. You're much stronger than you think."

◻

The march back proved thankfully uneventful, and seeing the city's great white walls again filled me with elation. When I was younger, I'd longed to get outside the walls and run the fields and forest trails like the boys did, but somewhere along the years I'd grown used to staying inside. Now I wouldn't have minded if I never left the wall's sanctuary ever again.

We went immediately to the palace to discuss what happened with Cuitlapanton. I left the telling to Little Reed though, for as soon as I entered the Great Hall, my wrist flared up again. I concentrated on each member of the war council, trying to work out who the spy might be. Was it Lord Necalli, who always looked and sounded angry when he spoke, or maybe Lord Tototl, who always opened his mouth to speak but stopped when someone else started speaking first? I couldn't imagine it could be Lord Spear Fish—who had led me and Mother to safety here in Xochicalco so long ago—but it could very well be Lord Xipil, who kept sniffing and looking bored throughout Little Reed's story. But with everyone crowded around so close, it was impossible to tell.

"The spy is on the war council," I told Little Reed as we left the palace, headed for the bathhouse to clean up after the journey.

"You're positive?" But when he saw me scratching my wrist, he said, "Whom do you suspect?"

I shook my head. "I'm not sure yet. I didn't see anyone who seemed surprised or disappointed to see us alive."

"I did bring up the idea of there being a spy, so they'd be extra careful now. We should have met with Cuitlapanton in private."

"We weren't expecting the viper to be among his trusted advisors. If the spy thinks you're onto him, he might take matters into his own hands, so be extra careful."

"Or now that he knows the god's on our side, maybe he'll thank Omeyocan that the Feathered Serpent didn't come after him."

I looked down at my wounded hand still wrapped in bandages. "And if he doesn't, we do have that option again."

He took my hand in his and gave me a grave look. "We have other options too, so let's not be hasty. We'll find out who it is and we'll deal with him—just you, me, and Mazatzin."

"Of course." I watched him disappear behind the gate into the men's bathhouse. *If only my tongue wouldn't stick to the roof of my mouth every time I think about telling you how I feel about you, Little Reed.* I sighed then headed for the calmecac to deliver Nimilitzli's letter to Mothotli.

¤

I found Mothotli in her meditation room, kneeling in front of an incense burner and rubbing at a strange lump on her hand. She promptly tucked it into her robe sleeve when I announced myself. "Back so soon?" she asked, avoiding my gaze. "I thought you weren't going to be back for a couple more days."

I told her the story of our troubles while she glanced over the letter. I left out the part about me summoning the god though; she was in a calm mood and I didn't want to stir her up with what she'd surely think was lies.

She furrowed her brow as I finished. "Sounds as if we have a spy." She finally looked up at me, but when she saw my bandaged hand, she grabbed it. "Great Feathered Serpent! What happened here?"

Her concern took me by surprise. "One of the Chichimec warriors cut them off when I tried to get away."

She let me go. "At least you made it out alive. More than we can say for most of the men." She looked down at the letter again. "Do you wish for a personal guard?"

"I think Topiltzin is the true target. I'm nobody, just his sister."

That soured her mood. "Go and clean up and get back here by sunset. Nimilitzli wants me to start training you in the fire priestess duties, so be on time. No excuses."

I stood a little straighter. "Of course."

"Now let me be. I have things to do." Mothotli reached into her sleeve to rub at her hand again.

I watched her a moment, wondering if I should ask if she was all right, but then she barked at me to get going, so I scuttled out of the door. *Why must she always be so nasty?* I wondered, disgusted, as I left for the bathhouse.

CHAPTER EIGHTEEN

Mothotli wasn't in better spirits when I met her in front of the calmecac an hour before sunset. She pushed a lit torch at me, which I fumbled with my wounded hand, and I glared at her back as I followed her to the main temple.

"The fire priest's primary duty is to go around the city before dusk and light all the temples' fires," she said when I joined her at the urn outside the Feathered Serpent's temple. "There are thirty-three to light every night, including the ones outside at the rural temples. Each order has its own fire priests and priestesses, and we rotate days. Normally the fire priest would accompany us, but Eztetl has other things to do tonight, so it's just you and me." I didn't relish the idea of an evening stuck with Mothotli, but the frown hit my face before I could stop it. She snapped, "Don't look so disappointed, girl, and get the kettle lit." She shook her head, impatient as I poked the torch into the pile of copal wood in the drum. "Quickly, so we're back before nightfall. Don't dally."

Once I got it lit, Mothotli set off down the stairs, barking at me to keep up. In the lower precinct, we visited each temple and lit the fire kettles outside, Mothotli lecturing me about needing to be quick. "We don't want to be outside the city walls after nightfall. Even two armed priestesses aren't enough to deter some bandits and murderers."

By the time we left the city gates, heading for the first of the three rural temples where the farmers gave their daily offerings, I'd lost patience with her constant snipping. My hand ached and the short nap I'd taken after my bath hadn't lasted me long. I lagged behind, both out of exhaustion and to avoid having to listen to her complaining. But just as we finished up at the first rural temple, I lost my footing on the short set of stairs and dropped the torch into the nearby canal.

"Of all the incompetence!" Mothotli shouted as she stormed back. She grabbed a new torch from the basket inside the door and lit it in the kettle brazier, before thrusting it into my hands, muttering, "Nimilitzli must have gone daft, thinking you're at all worthy of pursuing such important office."

That was enough. I stayed where I was as she started lumbering off towards the east road. "Why do you dislike me so? You've been nothing but mean and spiteful to me since the day we met, but what could I possibly have done to deserve that?"

Mothotli glared at me over her shoulder. "Move it along, girl. Twilight is not that far off now."

I folded my arms. "I demand you answer me."

She looked towards the road again, her temper cooling; but then it suddenly erupted. "Because you're a lazy, self-absorbed wretch who wastes all the potential the gods gave her."

My jaw dropped open. "I've never misquoted a prayer or a sacred story—"

"Oh, you're very good at memorization and repetition, but anybody could do that. Given your royal blood, perhaps it was too much to expect more of you than just another half-witted noble girl."

My cheeks flushed hot. "How dare...who do you...you don't know me at all!"

She strode back, her fists clenched. "I know you haven't the guts to embrace the challenge of living a life of sacrifice for someone whose name will last long after the bones of princes have gone to dust. Instead you'd rather hand your future over to some pretty noble boy who's not even half the man his father is."

I stared at her, too stunned to say anything.

"I see girls like you all the time, doing what they must to please their fathers, just biding their time until they're told to marry, never making the hard decisions for themselves, never grabbing opportunity because they don't dare upset the men. Nimilitzli hoped you would be different, that the god had given you to her for a reason, but that proved foolish. At least she still has your brother to make her proud; he at least has a firm sense of his self-worth and potential. If you believe the only thing you have to offer this world is your womb, then that's all you'll ever contribute, and I'm not going to waste my time trying to make you into something you can't be." She headed down the path again.

You're going to let that slight go unchallenged? I thought, fuming. "And you're just a jealous old woman who can't stand that she's being passed over to be the next high priestess!"

She stopped but didn't turn around.

"Nimilitzli said you'll never be high priestess," I continued, emboldened by her reaction. "That must have really burned, getting her letter telling you to start training me while she's recovering? All those years you spent as fire priestess, and for what?"

Mothotli laughed, softly at first then harder, until it sounded like a deep drum beat. But then that laughter turned to weeping. "You're right that I'm jealous; of everyone who's been spared my fate, who won't die alone in the desert as an outcast from everyone and everything they love because the gods have cursed them for some unknown reason. Who wouldn't be jealous of that?"

At first I didn't understand, but then I remembered how she'd been rubbing her hand then hid it when I'd come to her meditation room. *She was hiding a skin lesion,* I realized, everything suddenly making sense. I'd seen a couple of people with similar ones, all eventually looking like something was eating them from inside, their skin bubbled up into angry blisters that turned black. The priests called it the Divine Sickness because they believed it was a punishment from the gods; though having seen at least one child with the affliction, I had to wonder what one so young could possibly do to incense the gods. Nimilitzli had taught me some remedies for the numbness in the skin splotches, but once they turned to pustules, there was little to be done for them. And based on the size of the one I saw on Mothotli's hand, it could be only a matter of months before they started taking over. Eventually the king would ask her to leave the city, out of fear of spreading it to others.

I felt as though I'd smacked a child and then laughed about it. "I'm sorry. I didn't know—" I said, my voice barely above a whisper.

"But that has nothing to do with why you disgust me," Mothotli said, her anger palpable. "You're an intelligent woman, when you decide to behave like one, but unfortunately you choose to ignore your own potential and look to everyone around you for validation of your worth. You're the cleverest girl I've ever had in calmecac, but you're lazy and consider mere learning good enough. Your brother is brilliant too, but unlike you he looks beyond what the priests tell him. He finds ways to use what he learns to inspire and give others hope, while you look at it as a cage meant to trap you. Being one of the order's leaders is a huge responsibility; you must make sound judgments and be willing to look beyond yourself to make tough decisions that will help everyone. I trust Nimilitzli's judgment, but everything I've seen of your attitude tells me you don't have what it takes to be high priestess."

My shoulders rose like a ruffled bird. "If I don't, then why would the god entrust me with his power on earth?" I held up my bandaged hand. "I didn't lose these to a Chichimec; I cut them off with my own knife to summon the god to defend us. And it wasn't the first time I called on him, either."

Her annoyed skepticism slowly shifted. "The commotion in the precinct that night, when you were just a girl—"

"The god dealt with that treacherous servant," I answered. "Quetzalcoatl has faith in me, and so does Nimilitzli. Why can't you?"

Mothotli scowled. "All the faith of others means nothing when you have none in yourself." She drew her cloak tighter and looked around. "Let's not continue this foolishness any longer and hope we can get back to the city by moonrise." Without another word, she took off down the path at a jog.

I didn't say anything for the rest of the evening as we visited the remaining temples then headed back to the city. Mothotli didn't say anything either but constantly scanned the darkness, keeping close to my side. We still said nothing even as we walked back up to the sacred precinct. At the calmecac we went our separate ways.

As I lay in bed, trying to get to sleep while the younger novices snored around me, her last statement kept dancing around my mind. Nimilitzli and little Reed might have faith in my abilities, but a leader needed to have faith in herself.

So, *Quetzalpetlatl,* I wondered, *do you have what it takes to lead people in the god's name?*

¤

Per Nimilitzli's instructions, I went back to the palace in the morning to check on the three women who were with child. At least one of them was close to her delivery date—Lady Atzi—and she'd begged Nimilitzli not to go on the pilgrimage, in case she went into early labor. So naturally she was near-hysterical when I told her that Nimilitzli wouldn't be back in Xochicalco for a few months.

"Who's going to deliver the baby?" she cried. "What if something goes wrong? Nimilitzli said the birth could be very difficult at my age."

"She gave me instructions to attend to the birth with Lady Ixchell's help."

"You? But you're just a girl!"

"Nimilitzli trained me herself for the last five years, and she trusted me to be the lead midwife at two other royal births just this year."

Lady Atzi relaxed. "Well, I suppose that's all right. Nimilitzli is a good judge of such things. I suppose you'll do." She still looked askance at me.

Laughter echoed from the hallway as I packed up the medicine bag, and a moment later Lady Atzi's two sons—Obsidian Eagle and Pochotzin— came in, fighting each other with toy swords. Pochotzin, who was the eldest of Cuitlapanton's sons, held his sword low to keep his nine-year-old brother from clipping his knees. He let Obsidian Eagle whack away furiously a moment before suddenly knocking the sword from his brother's hands. He laughed while Obsidian Eagle rubbed his wrist and glared at him.

My own wrist was itching.

"Don't come into my room with all your clatter, you two," Lady Atzi replied, lying down on her side. "I'm very tired and you're vexing me."

"We'll be quieter, Mother." Pochotzin knelt next to his mother to catch his breath while Obsidian Eagle snatched up his sword. "I just wanted to come by and see how you're doing."

She smiled back, proud and loving. "I'm quite all right. Thank you for coming by."

Obsidian Eagle came over and watched me finish packing. "Who are you?"

"I'm the midwife who's going to deliver your new brother or sister." I tied the bag closed, eager to be on my way.

"But what's your name?" he insisted, impatient.

"She's Topiltzin's sister, Quetzalpetlatl," Pochotzin said with a good-natured laugh. He seemed so genuine; I never would've suspected him of spying for Ihuitimal.

A bright smile crept to Obsidian Eagle's face. "Oh! You're the one Red Flint says lets men put snakes in her hole."

I frowned at the boy, more annoyed than angry, but Lady Atzi gasped. Pochotzin shot to his feet and cuffed Obsidian Eagle's ears and hissed, "You dishonor Father by saying such things."

Obsidian Eagle cried and rubbed his ears. To me, Pochotzin said, "Forgive my brother for repeating such rubbish."

I gathered my bag. "I doubt he meant any harm, unlike the one he heard it from." I bowed, then told Lady Atzi, "Get your rest and call for me if you're at all uncomfortable and can't sleep."

She nodded, her face red. As I left, I felt Pochotzin watching me still.

¤

I waited until I'd left the palace to break into a run. By the time I reached the calmecac my side ached, but I didn't stop until I reached the doorway to the boys' dormitory. I caught myself at the door and gulped down breaths. "I need to speak to Topiltzin," I told the door monitor once I could speak again. "Right away. Very important."

"He and Prince Mazatzin went out to the exercise yard at the House of Warriors."

And so I raced down the winding stairs to the south gate, where the warrior school was set on the edge of the forest. I found Little Reed and Mazatzin practicing their atl-atl throwing at a set of targets painted on maguey fiber glued to one of the trees. Some of the warriors standing around talking started hooting suggestively as I ran by, but they stopped when Little Reed raised a hand to wave me over. "Forgive their rough manners." He glared at them over his shoulder.

I waved it off. "Pochotzin is the spy!"

Mazatzin startled. "My brother?"

"But he's not on the war council," Little Reed said.

"I think he was listening from a doorway when we were talking with them yesterday," I said.

"But the king's own son?" Mazatzin asked, taken aback. "How could that be?"

"He is the only one of the king's sons who's gone off to war before now, and wasn't he captured briefly last year then escaped?" Little Reed asked.

"He was." After a tense pause, Mazatzin asked me, "How can you be sure, though?"

"The god gave me the ability to sense when the enemy is near, and all the signs point to him," I answered.

Little Reed nodded but said, "The king will need more than just your special sense to convince him, especially when accusing his own blood."

"We could test him," I suggested. "Feed him false information then see if he contacts Ihuitimal."

Little Reed nodded. "We tell the war council that I'm planning on marching out with the next contingent. One leaves at the beginning of next week."

"And I'll keep an eye on Pochotzin, see who he talks to and meets with." Mazatzin sighed. "I still hate to think that a brother would be involved in such treachery."

"I'm sure he didn't do this willingly," I said. "Who knows what he had to agree to in order to save his life."

"And I doubt he's acting alone," Little Reed added. "Perhaps we can draw the rest of the conspirators out as well. We should get started immediately."

Mazatzin followed us out of the exercise yard and back up to the sacred precinct. "It's a good thing you didn't go marching with the army, Topiltzin, for surely the military has been infiltrated as well," he said. "Perhaps Quetzalpetlatl didn't want you to leave because she sensed something would go wrong."

If only it were so selfless, I thought, ashamed. I'd held Little Reed back

171

out of simple selfishness, but I wouldn't make that mistake again. "You can't let Ihuitimal scare you into staying here forever, Topiltzin. I was wrong to not listen to you, and both Nimilitzli and I agree that you're ready. You're a priest in your heart, but only a warrior will win back our throne."

"You're more ready than Red Flint is," Mazatzin added. "I would follow you into battle any time."

Little Reed bowed his head. "Thank you for your confidence. It means a great deal. I can only hope to inspire such loyalty among others as well."

"You will," I said. "And it'll be nothing less than you deserve."

He gave me a warm smile. "I'm still intending to take trials first. It can't hurt to have the god on my side."

Once we reached the calmecac, Mazatzin headed to the palace to speak with his father, and Little Reed and I went to Nimilitzli's house, to make sure there weren't any mice in the meal bags. "There's something I want to talk to you about," I told him as I looked through the sacks of masa and whole maize.

"Is something the matter?"

"Not at all. I'm going to take up the extra studies to become the next high priestess."

"You're sure that's what you want to do?"

I nodded. "I've learned a lot about myself these last couple of weeks, particularly why letting you go has been so very hard. I've spent my life taking care of you, and it scared me to think that you didn't need me anymore—"

"I'll always need you, Papalotl," he insisted.

"And I'll always need you, but neither of us are the kind to sit back and let others rule our lives; we need to lead others, guide them through tough times and get them to the other side, hopefully in one piece."

Little Reed nodded.

"You've always known where you were headed, but my destiny wasn't so clear. Helping people makes me happy and the god is very important to me, so it's only natural I should pursue a future in the priesthood."

He hugged me. "The god will be so very happy to have you in his order. I'm glad you didn't let the difficulties with Mothotli drag you down."

His embrace left me flushed and delighted. "Actually, it was Mothotli who made me realize I was wandering through life, expecting everyone else to tell me what to do. Mother always wanted to be more than she was, wanted a better world for you and me, and she'd want us both to do things that make us happy and bring hope to others. I want to be the high priestess she never could be; I want to be the leader I know I can be."

Smiling, he said, "And you'll do wonderfully."

I kissed his cheek, letting myself linger there a breath this time. "Just promise that you'll write to me often, and that you'll come back home safely. You're taking a piece of me with you, and I need you to bring it back to me."

◻

I spent the rest of the week following Mothotli around the calmecac, observing her while she taught her classes. I hadn't taken much notice of what she did from day to day until now, and having seen the full extent of her duties to the priesthood, I admired her strength to continue on despite her illness. She still hid the lump on her hand, but she was a proud woman who despised rumors, so I neither asked nor said anything about it, not even to Little Reed. I left a jar of medicine in her meditation room though, to help with the numbness, and the next day she let me out of midnight temple duty to attend Little Reed's farewell feast at the palace—part of the ploy to get the spies out into the open.

The war council and Cuitlapanton's sons attended, and I was the only woman there. *Thank the gods there are no courtesans,* I thought. I wouldn't have been able to bear watching them fawn over Little Reed in front of me. There was so much food though, hundreds of dishes ranging from tadpole and tomato casserole to turkey tamales to tlaxcallis made of flour so finely ground that the cooked flatbreads were almost transparent. We ate in courses, starting with tlaxcallis dipped in countless sauces, followed by fruit of every known variety, then the fowl and venison dishes, and finally ended with xocolatl service. I hadn't drunk xocolatl for years, and even then I'd only been allowed to add honey to it, so the sheer selection of ingredients Cuitlapanton had on offer to add was intimidating. I decided on vanilla but kept close watch on Pochotzin while he spiked his with powdered heart flower. He laughed and carried on conversations with everyone around him, including Little Reed, who did a very convincing job of not suspecting anything of him.

I ate until I felt ready to burst; then, after all the speeches and well wishes, Little Reed and I headed back to the sacred precinct, walking close together to keep warm against the wind.

"So are you ready for the trials?" he asked.

"I feel confident I'll do well," I said. "How about you?"

Little Reed smiled. "Not to sound boastful, but I've been ready for this my entire life. I'm ready to start making things happen, and to find out what my father has in mind for me."

I laughed. "Being king of Culhuacan isn't enough for you?"

"It's very important, but sons of mortals don't have a god they have to impress."

I squeezed his hand in mine. "I'm sure he's very proud of you, Little Reed."

We paused at the top of the stairs and stood facing each other, with me still holding his hand. He looked like he wanted to say something but was holding back. I couldn't hear anything over my thudding heart.

But then the itching began on my wrist again, subtle at first but growing quickly. I looked down into the royal square below, searching for signs of Pochotzin or anyone else.

"Are you sensing something?" Little Reed asked.

I nodded, still looking around. I saw no one in the moonlight, but my heart now pounded for entirely different reasons. "We should get inside." I pulled him towards the calmecac.

The itching only grew worse though, and I wondered if we should head to Nimilitzli's house instead. Little Reed had turned down the guards the king had offered him—not wanting to scare off Pochotzin—but now I didn't think that was such a good idea.

I brought us to a stop in the courtyard and looked around, my wrist itching fiercely now. I pulled my mother's sacrificial blade from my belt, taking comfort in the feel of the carved horn handle in my hand.

Little Reed drew his blade as well. "Head for the dormitories. He's after me, not you."

"What if he's brought help? I might not be much use in hand-to-hand combat, but I can call on the god if necessary."

"I'd rather you didn't—"

A shadowy figure leaped down the stairs from the storerooms, an obsidian-studded sword raised above his head. Little Reed shoved me away, almost knocking my blade for my hand, and he ducked into a roll, barely getting out of the way before the sword came down where he'd stood. He sprang to his feet and moved aside as his attacker brought the sword around again. They circled each other, both weapons ready.

I pressed against the wall of the calmecac, looking for an opening, and surprisingly, the man gave it to me, showing me his back. I lunged, my mother's sacrificial knife gripped in both hands, and buried the flint between his shoulder blades.

But when I tried to rip it out, the twist snapped the blade off. The man roared and whirled towards me. Now if I wanted to call on the god, I'd have to let him stab me for the blood.

Little Reed tackled him from behind and they went to the ground in a heap. The assailant tried to buck Little Reed off, but he dissolved into howling pain when Little Reed shoved his knee into the flat side of the blade protruding from his back. "I give up! I give up! Please stop!" he wailed, clawing his fingers into the hard ground.

Shouting from the stairs on the precinct drew my attention, and I saw Mazatzin running towards us, his sacrificial blade drawn as well. By the time he reached us, priests, priestesses and novices were gathered in the courtyard, coming from the dormitories and the bathhouse, some even as far away as the Temple of the Feathered Serpent. "What in Mictlan is going on out here?" Fire Priest Eztetl asked as he cut through the crowd.

Still not letting his attacker up, Little Reed told him, "My sister and I were set upon by this assassin, sent by Ihuitimal."

Mazatzin knelt next to Little Reed. "I've already summoned the guards." He knelt down to frown at Pochotzin, who lay panting and cringing under Little Reed's knee. He frowned. "How could you dishonor father by working for Xochicalco's mortal enemy, Pochotzin?"

Pochotzin shook his head, on the verge of tears. "I'm sorry, Brother. I did what I had to. They were going to sacrifice me—"

"An honorable warrior would've gone to his death rather than betray his family."

Pochotzin let out a loud, sad breath, but said no more as the guards came to take him into custody.

CHAPTER NINETEEN

Cuitlapanton paced before his throne, wringing his hands and shaking his head. "I can't believe this, my own blood conspiring under my nose. If I'd only known...please forgive my ignorance on this matter, Lord Topiltzin. I failed to instill honor in Pochotzin and that nearly cost you your life."

"It's not your fault, your Majesty," Little Reed said. "My treacherous uncle is a master at using fear, and your son was nothing more than a pawn. Hopefully we can uncover the full network of people involved in passing information and we can make the city safer for everyone again. Undoubtedly they are spying on you as well, your Majesty."

Cuitlapanton's face darkened. "Then let's not waste time; I'll interrogate Pochotzin immediately."

"He's being looked at by the royal surgeon right now, your Majesty," I said. "He was injured during the attack."

"Traitors to the crown don't deserve the mercy of the surgeon. He will suffer the pain he's brought on himself." To the guards, he said, "Bring Pochotzin to me immediately. Carry him here if necessary." He sat on his throne and wiped his face with his hand. "We will get to the bottom of this, even if I must cut each finger from his hand to make him speak the truth."

But Pochotzin knelt on the floor before the throne, staring at the floor as he laid out his involvement in the plot to kill my brother. His voice quaked as he recounted the few weeks he spent in captivity in Culhuacan: the daily beatings, the constant starvation, and how eventually Ihuitimal convinced him to be a spy in the royal court. He reported back to him every few months on military plans and trade routes, but mostly on Little Reed's activities. He admitted that he hadn't done it on his own; over the years since returning to Xochicalco, he'd recruited spies in practically every corner of the city. He gave out the names of merchants and artisans, even a priest. The royal scribe recorded them all on a piece of fig-bark paper.

Little Reed said nothing during this, letting Cuitlapanton do the questioning. The king ran the proceedings with a stern frown, and when

Pochotzin faltered on details or showed reluctance to answer, Cuitlapanton had one of the guards twist the knife blade in his back, to encourage compliance. By the end of the interrogation, Pochotzin was pale and sweating and could barely stay upon his knees.

I should have hated him, but instead I pitied him. Had I been in the same situation, might I have chosen a similar path? *Never! Death is preferable to betraying my family.*

"I'm disgusted by your betrayal of your king, but I'm most saddened that you should plot against your own people," Cuitlapanton said. "You've not only put your family in jeopardy, you've endangered the very citizens you swore to protect on the day you first marched to war." He stood and glared down at Pochotzin, his bulky form hunched like an angry bear. "It's with this in mind that I pass judgment upon you."

Pochotzin cast a frightened gaze up at his father, but Cuitlapanton remained firm. "I strip you of your noble title; no longer will you be honored when people speak your name. Second, you will pay restitution to Lord Topiltzin for your assault on him; everything you own now belongs to him—your clothes, your jewelry, all your war prizes. And finally, for your crimes against Xochicalco and her people, you will pay with your life. Because you have exposed Ihuitimal's other spies, I'll spare you the days of torture that normally precede this kind of sentence and you'll instead receive a swift public execution. Your blood shall spill in the name of the god, to avenge his priests, for your actions led to the attack at Teotihuacan that sent many of them to the road to Mictlan before their time."

Pochotzin covered his eyes and wept. "Thank you for your mercy, Father. I'm so very sorry I dishonored you, and I hope to earn back some of that lost honor while I stand before the priests to face my fate."

Cuitlapanton stiffened his lower lip, holding back tears, then motioned the guards to take Pochotzin from the room. "Confine him in the prison yard and send the surgeon to finish patching his wounds." Once the guards had taken Pochotzin away, Cuitlapanton set both hands on Little Reed's shoulders. "I'm so sorry to have been a part of all these troubles, even if it is only through my son." He untied the gold and jade necklace from around his neck and put it in Little Reed's hands. "Please accept this as an apology from me for what my son has done against you. As his father, I share his shame."

"I appreciate the gesture, your Majesty," Little Reed said, trying to give him back the necklace. "But your son is his own master, and his mistakes are his alone. You have been like a father to me in many regards and I cannot in good conscience blame the sins of your son upon you."

"At least take the necklace as an offering to Quetzalcoatl's priesthood, in honor of those who lost their lives to this foolishness."

"That I shall do, your Majesty. The god thanks you for your generous gift."

The scribe handed the paper to Cuitlapanton. "Here's the list of co-conspirators Lord Pochotzin named, Your Majesty."

"The guards will bring in every one who's currently in the city and I'll send a runner to my war chief to have him send the accused soldiers back here for trial," Cuitlapanton finished. "This all will take a while to fully deal with, but justice will be meted out swiftly."

¤

The guards brought in ten people overnight and I sat at Little Reed's side as the war council interrogated and passed judgment on each. At daybreak, the conspirators were publicly garroted with the flowery garland in the royal square, and Pochotzin—called only Pochotl now that the king had stripped his title—was beheaded. It was a brutal yet swift death preferred by most warriors, while those dying by the flower garland lived their last minutes in agony and terror.

I felt a distinct discomfort watching the men writhing under the garrote; the brilliantly-colored flowers looked innocent and beautiful at their necks as their lives slipped away. Little Reed held my hand as the executions played out, the grim spectacle turning disturbingly gory when the guards brought out the beheading stone. I knew such things shouldn't bother me; as high priestess, I'd have to perform the yearly sacrifice: slicing the throat of the sacrificial victim and draining his blood into a bowl until he was dead.

But my sensitivity to such gruesomeness had started very early in my life, even before what happened to my father. The few times I'd gone to witness the sacrifices to the Sun, my gut had wriggled at the gasping cries of dying warriors, and my time in the priesthood hadn't helped at all. Piercing tongues and other body parts didn't bother me; it was the taking of lives. Intellectually, I understood the reason for the deaths, but they still hit me like a knife blow. I'd have to overcome this if I was to be the next high priestess of Quetzalcoatl.

It started to rain once all the unpleasant business finished, but I still took my time returning to the sacred precinct. *You don't suppose you'll have to perform a sacrifice at the trials, do you?* I wondered as I headed towards the temple. I'd only ever seen Nimilitzli and Ahexotl performing any actual human sacrifices, and even then only the highest-ranking priests and priestesses did the sacrifices of snakes and butterflies at the daily ceremonies, so it seemed unlikely. *Stop your worrying. You'll have years to come to terms with this.* But I still shuddered.

Hearing commotion over at Nimilitzli's house, I went to investigate. To my surprise, I found Nimilitzli lying in her bed while a small group of soldiers fumbled around the house, two starting the fire while a third moved her weaving supplies next to her bed. She looked up and smiled when I came in. "You look surprised to see me. You haven't been up to mischief, have you?"

I chuckled as I sat on the floor next to her bed. "I thought the surgeons wanted you to stay until your hip healed."

"I couldn't stop thinking about what you told me about spies. I couldn't leave you two to face that on your own, so I got back here as quickly as I could. There hasn't been any trouble, has there?"

"There was plenty," I said, then told Nimilitzli everything. "I was just on my way back from the executions."

"Is that why you're looking so pale?" Nimilitzli asked.

"Things like this bring back memories of what happened to my father. I wonder if I'll ever get over that."

"Some things stay with us all our lives." She patted my hand. "How's Topiltzin dealing with all this nonsense?"

"With kingly poise." I sat down to grind up some flour on the metlatl stone, flicking beetles away from the pile of dried kernels I'd pulled out of the bag. "He's going to join the army after he takes the trials."

"I'm glad. We underestimated his readiness."

"It's the right time for him to go," I admitted. "He leaves with the rest of the contingent two days after the trials."

"It's for the best."

I nodded. "It is." Though I didn't dare tell her why I thought so.

¤

I spent the rest of the week dividing my time between classes, temple duties, studying with Malinalli, and taking care of Nimilitzli, even though she insisted that her priestesses could look after her. "You've taken care of me since I was a little girl, so I can at least do the same for you," I told her when she protested again the night before the trials.

"You need to be rested for tomorrow. I won't have you doing poorly because you stayed up late caring for me, so off to bed with you. Malinalli will come by and check on me tonight anyway," Nimilitzli insisted.

I finally gave in and went to the dormitories at the calmecac, where I usually slept. All the girls slept on mats on the floor of one large room, the youngest at the far end and oldest nearest the door. Already I noticed that several of the beds closest to the door were abandoned; Turquoise Bells had decided not to take the trials and had already gone home to the palace, and Ixzoxochitl had taken her trials a few days before and had gone home to celebrate with her mother and father for a few weeks. When she returned, she'd move into one of the houses along the edge of the precinct, where the priests and priestess lived. I was already planning on asking Nimilitzli if I could move back in with her once I'd finished the trials, so I could watch over her recovery.

Anxiety kept me from sleeping well though, and I rose before dawn, my stomach sour with nervousness. Initiates fasted from dusk the night before to the dawn after the trials, but I was too nervous to eat anyway and so headed for the temple to make prayers.

Little Reed sat on the cistern wall, and his smile sent my stomach into a flutter. "Feeling well this morning?" he asked as I sat next to him.

"A little nervous," I admitted. He'd taken his trials the day before, so I asked him, "Were the tests difficult?"

"Nothing you couldn't pass. You'll do fine. Were you headed for the temple?"

I nodded. "Would you join me, make some prayers on my behalf?"

In the temple, we knelt on the reed prayer mats before Quetzalcoatl's idol, praying silently until the sunrise bell, then Little Reed kissed my cheek. "Good luck," he whispered, and left. I cursed myself for fingering my cheek as if caressing a precious stone. I needed a clear head today, but instead I sat in the Feathered Serpent's holy temple, thinking about Little Reed in very un-priestly fashion. I nicked my inner thigh, both for luck and to beg the god's forgiveness for my weakness. Ordinarily I'd put a thorn through my tongue, but I had too much speaking to do today. I extinguished the copalli burner and left.

Quetzalcoatl's sacred star—the Morning Star—twinkled on the pink horizon, at the beginning of its months-long ascension into the sky. Today was a good day to join his order.

Mothotli and Eztetl awaited me in the courtyard. Eztetl was a very tall, nervous-looking man, and Ahexotl's embroidered robe looked comically short on him. "Today you seek to dedicate yourself to the service of Our Most Precious Twin?" he asked, stumbling slightly over the words as if he hadn't quite memorized them yet. When I answered in the affirmative, he went on, "Do you seek to place your life and destiny in the hands of he who's greater than yourself? Are you prepared to forsake the desires of the flesh for as long as you remain in his service? And are you prepared to devote your life to ensuring that the people know the will of the Feathered Serpent?"

"I am, your grace."

"Then prove your worth to him." Eztetl turned to the gate in the stone wall that ran along the back of the courtyard.

Until now, I'd only ever seen priests and priestesses going in and out of this entrance, and we students often whispered about what might be beyond it. Eztetl opened the creaking gate and held it open for Mothotli and me.

Beyond it, a vast garden stretched onto terraces, all the way down into the valley below Xochicalco. The trees and bushes grew thick and tall, and the flowers bloomed in brilliant color along winding gravel paths. We followed one to a small temple-like building at the heart of the gardens. Inside, the short walkway came to a vestibule that forked into three doorways with curtains decorated with Feathered Serpents, butterflies, and stars. A slab of wood rang hollow on the floor under our feet.

"First, a priestess will examine you, to make sure you're fit to take the trials," Mothotli said, holding the curtain to the right open for me.

Ixchell stood next to a raised slab of stone in the middle of the room. For the longest time, I'd dreaded this part the most, but now that I knew what to expect, my nerves took a rest. When she finished, she handed me a quetzal feather. "Good luck."

The first half of the day, Eztetl and Mothotli tested my knowledge of Quetzalcoatl's stories, the hymns, the dances, the festival dress, calendar calculations, writing symbols, and charting the movements of both the Morning and Evening Star. We then moved to the last room where all the penance instruments were laid out for me; a sacrificial blade, a basket of maguey thorns and grass balls, a prayer mat woven of green lake reeds, and a jar of copalli incense. I explained why we used them in our sacrificial rituals, recounting the story of the Fifth Sun's rise as I demonstrated the proper use of each, piercing my tongue with the thorns and cutting my upper arms with my blade. My still-healing hand made me fumble a bit, but I persevered. I gathered the grass balls and burned incense while reciting prayers. It was surely close to sunset once we gathered in the vestibule.

Eztetl pulled aside the slab of wood on the floor, revealing a dark hole accessible with a ladder. He opened a box of black and brown dried mushrooms and Mothotli took a few and crumbled them up in a cup of octli. He stirred it with a wooden stirring stick then handed it to me with both hands. "Partake of the sacred teonanacatl then descend into the Underworld. There you will enter the Divine Dream and meditate on your future as one of Quetzalcoatl's priestesses."

I drank the concoction down quickly then climbed down into the cave. When I reached bottom, Mothotli lowered down a lamp. "Ixchell will return for you at dawn," she said, and Eztetl slid the wooden plank back over the hole.

Now I'm stuck down here. A wave of fear coursed through me as I showed my lamp around. Ceramic jars of octli sat stacked behind the ladder, stored there for the cool air blowing up the tunnels. The cavern extended for twenty paces before turning into various passageways that I guessed extended under the city and outside somewhere. At least I could find a way out by walking into the wind if I had to.

I sat on the mats next to the octli jars and tried to meditate, but the wind left me shivering. I huddled under the blanket they'd left me, warming up but growing increasingly concerned that I was still lucid. Had I angered Quetzalcoatl with my unholy thoughts in his temple this morning? *Or worse, did you disappoint him with the whole Red Flint ordeal?*

I am not disappointed in you at all, Butterfly, a windy voice whispered in my ear. I turned to see Little Reed sitting behind me, his arms wrapped around me. My blanket had turned into his cloak of quetzal feathers, and more of them grew from his head, mixed in with his long black hair.

I almost asked how he gotten there, but then the pieces snapped together. "My Lord?" I whispered.

He gave me Little Reed's smile, making my insides roll around like a puppy. *You thought I was Topiltzin?*

"You look like him," I pointed out, red-faced.

A son usually has his father's face, does he not? My heart hammered when he leaned closer, his nose nearly touching mine. *You seek guidance about the future, so let me show you the possibilities.* He stood, leaving me cold without his cloak. *Come, I have much to show you.*

I expected us to walk through the caves, but as soon as I lumbered to my feet, we suddenly stood atop the sacred precinct, outside the temple's door. People went about their routines below us, both in the precinct and the city proper. Lord Sun shone bright against a vibrant pink sky, his tongue sticking out of his open mouth like an artist's rendering. A distant walled city hung among the orange clouds, triggering a feeling of familiarity but no memory. Pointing, I asked, "What's that?"

Quetzalcoatl looked up too. *That is Omeyocan, the home of the gods.* On the wind a strange, snow-like substance floated, forming piles where it landed on the stone. It soaked into my skin when it touched me though, and it smelled wonderful, like bone flowers. *And that is the most precious gift in the whole world, next to life itself,* Quetzalcoatl continued, collecting the flakes on his hands. *Pollen from the tree that grew in Tamoachan, the one the goddess Mayahuel and I created when we came together on earth. I assume you know the story.*

"You stole her from her grandmother, so you could bring octli to the people."

Octli! Quetzalcoatl laughed with bitterness rather than boyish charm. *That had little to do with it, but humanity cannot be expected to know the truth of things that happened long before time was kept.*

"Then the stories I learned in calmecac...they're all wrong?" I asked, shocked.

They are not without a grain of truth, but they are also blurred with prejudice. That is why I sired Topiltzin; I am disheartened with what the priesthood has become, and what sacrifice has come to mean. I want him to speak my discontent and reeducate humanity, show them the path back to true sacrifice. But he needs help. You are quick to question such prejudices, and demand explanation for why some must suffer at the hands of others. That is why I granted you the power to call on me; it is why I am glad you have embraced the priesthood, and embraced me by agreeing to be my next high priestess.

The idea of helping Little Reed with a divine mission from the god sent pleasant chills through me. "I shall do my very best to help your son along his path."

Smiling, Quetzalcoatl motioned me to him. I joined him at the back corner of the pyramid. *Look to the north, so you may see what path he's chosen,* he said.

When I looked, my eyesight became good enough to see far over Lake Meztliapan, past the mountainous temples of Teotihuacan, into the deserts of Chichimec territory. On the border between civilized Tolteca lands and the brutal heat of the desert, I saw a city, shining and grand and overflowing with statues of the gods. Giant stone feathered serpents stood atop a high pyramid in the city's heart, their impassive faces gazing over the land where maize of every color grew twice the height of a man. Flowers cascaded on every roof, and the royal gardens spanned half the city itself. It flickered and faded and re-coalesced, like a mirage.

Topiltzin's future is not just to be the king of Culhuacan, but of all the Tolteca. He will be the high priest of all the gods, ushering in a time of great change that will rattle not only the foundations of the priesthood, but of your people's very culture.

Excited, I asked, "What kind of changes?"

An end to human sacrifice, Quetzalcoatl said with a proud smile.

I blinked, startled. This wasn't at all what I'd expected. I didn't even know what to say.

The sacrifices that take place all over the valley are but a mockery of true sacrifice, he went on. *Who dies on the temple tops now? Criminals and slaves, and captured warriors who honor foreign gods, who grant the power of their spilled blood to the dark sorcerers they follow.*

My mood darkened. "Like Smoking Mirror."

Some believe the time is right for humanity to pay higher sacrificial rites, gods who think themselves the next high deities of the Tolteca. Humanity's lapsed devotion to true sacrifice emboldens them, and they compel men to atrocities through fear. He turned his gaze down to the people below us, fervor in his eyes. *I cannot feel so indifferent about human suffering; my blood flows in them, so I feel their pain and fear. Topiltzin has a difficult task ahead of him; the people will fear the wrath of their gods if they change.*

I chose my next words carefully before speaking. "Forgive my asking, My Lord, but without blood, won't the Sun fall from the sky?"

Quetzalcoatl gave me a patient smile. *We all need blood, but a return to true sacrifice means more powerful offerings. Some among us enjoy the taste of hearts, but a little blood given in earnest is enough to fill anyone's spirit for a very long time. The personal bloodletting performed by the priests and the nobility holds enough power for any god, but these upstarts want to become more powerful than the rest of us. They have manipulated themselves into power among the Chichimecs, and now Smoking Mirror's insidious influence is growing within Tolteca lands, oozing out of Culhuacan. His high priest is sacrificing hundreds of war prisoners every month. Now is the time to act, before he establishes a stronghold and changes the priesthood forever, for the worse. Without this challenge, the day will soon come when it is not hundreds but rather a countless number who die to feed the greedy ambitions of gods who care not a whit about humanity. Seeing my creations brutally killed is more than I could stand.*

Quetzalcoatl was the most merciful of the gods, but hearing this from him startled me. I'd always assumed that, like the others, he found human sacrifice necessary. And the fact that he felt just as I did about human sacrifice pulled my heart closer to him than ever before. "Tell me what I can do to help, My Lord, and it'll be done," I promised.

Quetzalcoatl knelt on the ground and motioned me to do the same. *Stand with Topiltzin against the tyranny of selfish gods. Show humanity the path to true sacrifice and have patience with them when they resist. Even I did not receive the honor of their sacrifices until I had proven myself worthy.*

"I'll do my best, My Lord." I looked at the shower of snow-like flakes floating down from the heavens again and marveled at the warmth it brought me inside as it soaked into my skin. The smell of bone flowers set my heart thudding. "You still haven't told me what this wonderful dust is though."

When he smiled at me with Little Reed's face, I felt I might melt. *It is Omeyocan's most precious gift, of course. Love.*

"Love?" I laughed, turning my chin up and letting it dance down upon

185

me, soaking it up with relish. *I'm covered in love!* When I opened my eyes and looked at Quetzalcoatl again, my heart swelled with longing and desire, stirring my body in ways that even Red Flint's most successful attempts hadn't. He looked so much like Little Reed.... *What must it be like to be his lover?* I wondered.

But to my horror, the words rang out loud. My face burned when he raised an eyebrow and I wished I could end the Divine Dream, so I could escape this mortifying embarrassment.

I have not had a lover since Mayahuel, he said, a thoughtful smile on his face. *The priesthood calls my priestesses my wives, but I have never lain with any of them.*

"Please forgive my uncouth thoughts, My Lord," I stammered. But I forgot how to speak when he set his fingers before my mouth, not quite touching.

Please do not apologize. I would be lying if I did not admit to sharing that same desire. But it is not my way to force anyone—

"But I want to," I blurted out, reckless excitement and desire commanding my tongue. *Dear gods! Will I next brazenly reach out and touch him—actually touch the god without his permission?* The words didn't come out as loud as before, but they still whispered on the wind.

He laughed. *Then you have my permission.*

I hesitated a moment before finally touching his cheek with my hand. His skin looked like smooth flesh but felt feathery, as did his lips when he kissed me, first on the mouth then on the neck, just below my jaw. My pulse sounded in my ears, lust swallowing fear as his hands melted away my robe and the dress underneath as if they were crumbling wet paper. His feathery-feeling hands raised tiny bumps in their wake as they moved over my bare breasts, down my body, and between my thighs.

Overwhelmed with desire, I moved my hands over his body too. Unsurprisingly his tepolli was feathery, though the feel of feathers came and went with dreamlike laziness, sometimes leaving him feeling like a man. I pulled him atop me, savoring his weight on me, pinning but not crushing. With the Sun watching us up in the sky, I couldn't see his face, but the clouds soon rolled over, letting me gaze longingly into those eyes that made me think of Little Reed. He stroked himself against me until I couldn't take it anymore. "Now?" I dug my fingernails into the nape of his neck.

Now. His voice was as eager as my own.

I expected pain, as Nimilitzli told me there would be for any woman's first time, but I felt only pleasure as he eased inside me. It made sense though; this wasn't real, and even after this, I'd still be a virgin, at least physically.

Quetzalcoatl rocked me back and forth with each thrust. *Someday we will make love in the real world,* he whispered. *I have things I must do first, but someday....*

"Promise?" I moaned, wrapping my legs around him. For the briefest seconds I wondered if there had been some truth to Ahexotl's claims; and that we would make love in the real world through some intermediary—gods, let it be Little Reed!—but overwhelming pleasure mounted into a wave that crashed down on me with such intensity that I felt my body in the real world reacting.

He collapsed atop me, spent. *I promise, my dearest butterfly,* he whispered. *As soon as the time is right.*

He faded slowly away after that, the cave gradually re-coalescing around me. My sweating body still vibrated like a drum after the strike as I stared at the jagged ceiling, unable to stop smiling. The god had chosen me for his first real wife.

But why would he do that?

CHAPTER TWENTY

Ixchell came for me at dawn, and she brought a tlaxcalli which she handed to me one small piece at a time, to make sure I didn't gobble it down in my desperate hunger. Once I finished, we climbed the ladder and went out into the garden, my stomach still rumbling.

I'd hoped to still see Love floating down from the heavens, but the sky bled orange with the day's first light. My head swam and my body shook, so Ixchell held my arm as we went down a stepped path along the terraces to two walled courtyards surrounded by tall oak trees. Inside the north one were numerous bath pits and adobe steam baths. We walked under a thatch awning erected over the bath pits and Ixchell closed the maguey cloth screen around one then lit a fire in the clay drum at the back. The stone-tiled pit was already filled with freezing cold water and once I finished bathing, I dried with a piece of linen while standing next to the fire, shivering in the cool morning air. She then helped me into my dress and a fresh robe.

"Did everything go well in the Divine Dream?" she asked as she brushed my hair. "It can be a very intense experience the first time."

My cheeks burned at the memories. "It was...illuminating."

"Nimilitzli wants to see you right away. I'm sure she'll want to hear all about it."

She probably would, but some things would remain just between me and Quetzalcoatl.

□

Little Reed sat at the hearth, stirring something savory in a pot over the fire when I arrived at Nimilitzli's house. His face lit with happiness, triggering that intense flame of desire again. I started to smile back but then averted my eyes. *You can't be unfaithful to Quetzalcoatl, even if it's just in your head.*

"I made a dog stew to celebrate finishing the trials," he said. He sniffed his handiwork then added, "I hope it turns out all right. I'm not terribly handy with cooking."

"It smells wonderful," I assured him. "But how did you get a dog for the pot?" Nimilitzli favored an austere, priestly diet of mostly maize, beans and squash, with the occasional treat of venison, so I hadn't had dog since my days as a young girl back in Culhuacan.

Little Reed smiled. "I have my ways." He offered me a spot near the fire. "Did you have a good experience in the Divine Dream?"

My cheeks burned again.

"I'm sure at the very least it answered many of your questions," Nimilitzli ventured from her bed where she was already working at the loom set across her waist.

I told them about seeing the shining city in the north. "Quetzalcoatl wants me and Topiltzin to end human sacrifice, to curb the influence of gods like Smoking Mirror."

"Sounds very much like the vision you had, Topiltzin," Nimilitzli noted. "That's a lot of expectation to carry. Are you sure you're ready for that?"

"It's what I was born to do, Mother," Little Reed said.

Nimilitzli nodded. "Then go to your destiny, and hopefully something I taught you helps you get there."

Little Reed kissed her forehead and stroked her hair. "You taught me so much, and every bit will guide my heart, now and when I'm king."

"Stop being so sentimental." Nimilitzli shooed him away. "Aren't you supposed to go hunting with Cuitlapanton? One doesn't keep the king waiting."

"I didn't want to spend the day wondering what the god said to Quetzalpetlatl," he said. "The king will understand." He gave my hand a squeeze. "I'm happy you've found a future you can embrace."

I pulled my hand from his, feeling dizzy with lust. I'd really hoped my experience with Quetzalcoatl would cool my feelings for Little Reed, but they seemed stronger than ever now. Why could I not control myself? What was this weakness? It felt at times as though something external were possessing me. "You really shouldn't keep the king waiting any longer, Topiltzin."

Nimilitzli watched him go, then muttered, "Probably a good thing he's leaving now anyway." She cleared her throat. "And you seem very happy with your new assignment from the god."

"I am. It's a tremendous honor," I said, ladling out stew for both of us.

"You don't consider yourself too grown up to listen to an old woman anymore, do you?"

I laughed. "You're not old."

"I'm past my childbearing years, which makes me useful only as a priestess or a servant in the palace."

"I'll always listen to your wise words, Nimilitzli."

"Be very careful taking on this task."

I startled. "What do you mean?"

"It's one thing to serve the gods to honor them. Quetzalcoatl has asked you to become involved in the power struggles of the gods themselves."

I struggled with how to respond. "The Feathered Serpent wouldn't...he'd never...this is about ending human sacrifice, Nimilitzli. Quetzalcoatl cares about humanity and he's tired of seeing us die meaningless deaths to feed greedy gods who only want us for our blood—

"

"That's most of the gods, Quetzalpetlatl. You know that."

"Yes, they all need our blood, and we owe it to the old ones, but he's talking about gods like Smoking Mirror, who want us to fear them so we will feed them extra and make them stronger than the other gods. I've seen the work of Smoking Mirror's followers, and I want him driven back into the desert hole he crawled out of."

The anger rolling off my tongue surprised me, until I realized it had always been there, cooking with the years. And now that the words came flooding out, they brought unexpected pain and despair with them, leaving me feeling like a dying fish gasping for water.

Nimilitzli sat up, the pain plain on her face, and she leaned forward to set her hand on mine. "This Smoking Mirror had no reason to hurt you before, but do you really want to give him one?"

I fought to control my voice as I said, "My father's heart fed that monster, so the least I can do is make sure Smoking Mirror is banished from the temples in his memory."

"I don't want to see you suffer any more than you already have—"

"It's the price I'm willing to pay for my father, for my mother, for Topiltzin, for you. For everyone." I wiped hot tears from my face.

Nimilitzli bowed her head. "Then I shall say no more about it."

◻

Her words stuck with me all through my first day as a priestess, casting a gloomy cloud over everything, and when I returned to warm the stew for the evening meal, I tried hard not to feel angry at her questioning my judgment. She noticed my grumpiness, but kept her word and didn't mention it, and I didn't want to start a fight.

Little Reed was nervous but chatty, regaling us with the tale of his day hunting with Cuitlapanton and Mazatzin. He brought home not deer or peccary, but rather a marriage proposal for me, by the king on behalf of Red Flint.

"He really asked you to make me Red Flint's concubine?" I asked, stunned.

Little Reed shook his head. "It was definitely to tie your dress to Red Flint's Cape."

Turquoise Bells already hated me enough without adding that insult.

"I told the king that I'm not your master, and if Red Flint desires a marriage to you, then he'll have to ask you himself when he returns from war," Little Reed said.

"My answer is no."

Little Reed gave me a smile which he dropped as soon as Nimilitzli asked him, "You're all packed to leave tomorrow?"

With the stress of preparing for my trials and my new god-granted task, I'd forgotten that Little Reed was leaving for the army in the morning. I tried not to feel sick about it, but failed.

"I am packed and ready," he confirmed.

"I won't get to see you off in the morning, so let me say goodbye now," Nimilitzli said.

Little Reed knelt to hug her. She whispered in his ear and he laughed and nodded. "I will, Mother, and I love you too." Nimilitzli kissed his cheek, then he tucked her under the blankets. "I will see you again soon."

Seeing Nimilitzli's tears made my anger at her dissolve away as I shared her pain at seeing Little Reed leaving us, for real this time. This was best for him—and for me. I was Quetzalcoatl's wife now, and it was time that I moved on from this childish infatuation. *He has his future, and you have yours, and someday they'll merge back together again,* I reminded myself as I blinked back tears.

"Will you walk with me?" Little Reed asked. I followed him out of the door onto the darkened precinct.

When we reached the side of the temple, he suddenly stopped and grabbed my hand. "Will you come to see me off tomorrow? I leave quite early, so I understand if you can't—"

"Of course I'll be there."

He averted his gaze, then dashed it back to me. He was trembling. "There's something I must tell you, and tomorrow won't be a good time."

Now I shared his nervousness. "What is it?"

He gathered his resolve then pulled me to him so our bodies touched. "I love you, Papalotl," he whispered, then kissed me, like Red Flint had. Like Quetzalcoatl had.

I should have worried that someone might see us, but the whole world seemed to fall away so it was just me and Little Reed, tangled up in passion and heat, memories of lying with Quetzalcoatl—the god who had

191

Little Reed's face—flooding my thoughts and stoking my desire like a wildfire. Had Little Reed asked to have me just then, I would've let him, right against the side of the Feathered Serpent relief. The desire to ask him grew more intense the longer I held my breath.

Luckily he had better sense than I did. "You should go," he whispered. "I don't want you to get into trouble."

I looked around, dazed and panting. I felt as drunk as that night in Teotihuacan. I checked to see if anyone was watching us, but we were well-concealed in the temple's shadow. "You're right." I separated myself from him and shook my head, trying to clear my thoughts. "People are depending on us; the god is depending on us." *Not to mention that what you've done makes you an unfaithful wife.*

"I'll write to you often," Little Reed said. "You'll write back, to let me know how you are?"

"I will, but we mustn't linger or someone will see us."

I kept at a distance from him as we walked to the calmecac. He wished me good night when we reached the cistern and I mumbled good night too, but didn't look back as I hurried around the corner, towards the girls' dormitories, to get my belongings to take back to Nimilitzli's house.

I lay in my bed next to the fire, trying to sleep while Nimilitzli droned softly in her own bed several arm-lengths from me. But my mind was abuzz as I thought about that moment by the temple again and again. All this time I thought Little Reed hadn't felt anything for me, and now I wanted to cry. He did love me, but I'd already given myself to the god.

¤

Hours before dawn, I was up tidying the house and debating whether or not to go and see Little Reed off. I wouldn't get to see him again for a year at least, but I feared a repeat of last night's madness, so I took my time when I went to the priestesses' steam baths, weighing the decision. By the time I swallowed my fear and decided to go, I had to run to catch up with the soldiers before they left the city.

I skipped down the winding stone stairs behind the houses, into the lower precinct, past the temples to the other gods, then made my way down another set of steps into the Merchant Quarters. I held up my dress's hem as I ran, garnering puzzled looks from the women up early preparing tlaxcallis and atole before their men went to work the market.

I skidded to an unsteady stop when I reached the gates. I looked over the sea of soldiers marching out, the torches hardly shedding enough light to see by. *Am I too late? Curse my indecision!* I should have been at the palace to hug Little Reed goodbye.

But then I saw him, at the end of the marching line. His frown made my heart ache. I waved, trying to get his attention, but his gaze remained fixed on the ground. "Topiltzin!" I called, but when he still didn't look up, I shouted, "Little Reed!"

When he finally saw me, a relieved smile broke across his face. I waved after him as he marched out onto the darkened road, heading away from the safety of Xochicalco. "Goodbye, Little Reed! Please come home safely!"

I continued waving until he disappeared into the darkness, then I leaned against the wall and buried my face in my hands. "And I love you too, Little Reed," I whispered between my tears.

PART THREE
THE YEAR FIVE FLINT

CHAPTER TWENTY-ONE

Two summers after Teotihuacan, Nimilitzli fell on the temple steps and broke her hip all over again, but this time, she didn't recover. I'd moved out briefly, to share a house with Malinalli, but for the next five years I lived with Nimilitzli again, helping her with the daily chores and getting her to the temple for her duties, though in the last year, she did the latter less and less. She developed a cough and soon couldn't leave her bed. I often stayed up late getting her comfortable and fed, but after all the years she'd cared for me, it was the only right thing to do.

Still, someone shaking the bells on the door curtain in the middle of the night irritated me. Nimilitzli woke up murmuring about visitors but I told her, "Go back to sleep. I'll take care of it." I shrugged on my robe as the bells rattled again, more urgent now.

"It's me, Quetzalpetlatl," Mazatzin called from outside. When I opened the curtain, he looked haggard. "I didn't know who else to come to."

"What's wrong?"

"My father collapsed. The physicians are with him now, but I don't even know if he's alive." He rubbed his hands over his face, accentuating the worry. "Will you come to the palace with me?"

I made sure Nimilitzli was settled again then headed for the palace with Mazatzin.

"I'm so sorry for waking you so late," he said as we descended the stairs. "I know you have dawn duties—"

"Please don't apologize," I said. "You were a very good friend when my own life was a mess, so this is the least I can do for you."

Guards stood in the palace halls, whispering in hopes of news while Cuitlapanton's war council gathered in the Great Hall, debating. Red Flint's continued absence was often the subject of discussion; why had he stayed away for seven years rather than assuming his duties as heir apparent?

Cuitlapanton's concubines stood in the hallway near his room, many crying and holding their young children. Mazatzin's brother Mocnelitzin stood outside the doorway, talking to a guard. When we approached, they both looked up, and inevitably their eyes roved to me like vultures spotting a kill.

I'd endured such attention for so long now that I wanted to dismiss it as just something every woman learned to deal with in men. Yet the older I became, the more intense it seemed: not a man passed me by without his attention shifting to me as if dragged by an invisible net. Cuitlapanton's gaze lingered longer now that it used to, and all the priests stared, the world around them seemingly forgotten. Only Mazatzin showed no interest of that kind for me.

But perhaps most disturbing was that even some women, like Malinalli, sometimes became ensnared too. I once caught her staring at me across the priestly gardens, her gaze distant and dreamy, but when I waved to her, she hurried away and didn't talk to me for three days after that. I valued her friendship too much to ever bring it up.

While nothing untoward came of this bizarre effect I seemed to have, I still felt naked and vulnerable for it. I never ventured into the poorer quarters alone, and when I had to light the fires around the city, I always took Mazatzin with me.

Mocnelitzin blinked away his dazed expression and embraced Mazatzin. "The doctors fear he may be cursed, Brother."

"He's alive then?" Mazatzin asked.

Mocnelitzin nodded. "I was about to send for Ahexotl, but since the fire priestess is here, perhaps she can take a look at Father?" He avoided looking at me while the guard stared as if undressing me in his head.

"I'll look at him," I agreed, eager to be out of the guard's sight. I followed Mocnelitzin and Mazatzin inside.

I'd seen many of the king's women in their rooms over the course of my midwife duties, but this was my first time in the king's quarters. It resembled my father's room, with murals celebrating battles and death. Cuitlapanton lay on his bed surrounded by physicians and guards, covered with blankets and animal skins. One side of his face sagged like melted wax, but he tried to raise a hand to me when I approached the bed. "What happened?" I asked as I knelt next to him.

"He was with one of his concubines when he collapsed and stopped breathing," one of the guards answered. "We got him breathing again, but now he can't speak. The physicians suspect a curse."

Physicians were good at curing common ailments, like festering sores and rotting teeth, but if they couldn't see the cause, they assumed it was the work of a dark sorcerer. Nimilitzli said that most ailments could be cured with prayer mixed with strong medicines and time in the steam bath, but some rare illnesses refused to bow to medication, and those never turned out well. She'd only once encountered an actual curse, on a man who had defiled a statue of Tlaloc after losing his children in a flood.

I felt the king's forehead, looking for any bumps or bruises, but there were none. He closed his eyes and moaned, the still-working side of his face turning up into a smile. I emptied my divination pouch onto the blanket, spreading dried maize kernels across Cuitlapanton's chest then chanted various incantations and waited for any response to them. The kernels remained in place as his chest rose and fell. "There doesn't appear to be a curse," I told Mocnelitzin and Mazatzin. "But I can ask the god."

Mocnelitzin closed his eyes, relieved. "Thank you, Fire Priestess."

"Who was with him when it happened?"

"Lady Atzi."

"I'll speak with her first." To Mazatzin, I said, "Please make sure that no one disturbs me while I'm in the Divine Dream."

"I'll have Malinalli take your morning duties." He gave my hand a grateful squeeze. "Thank you for your help, Quetzalpetlatl."

As I went down the hall towards the women's quarters, practically every gaze followed me and not all of them were friendly, especially as I passed the women. In some ways I preferred the childish nagging I'd endured at Turquoise Bells's hands to the silent loathing I felt now from some women. At least if an accusation was spoken, I could address it. I was relieved to finally leave the hallway.

I found Lady Atzi in her room wailing on her bed while her

handmaiden tried to calm her with kind words. They looked up when I cleared my throat, but Lady Atzi looked stricken and cried harder.

I dismissed the servant and sat next to Atzi. We'd had a cool relationship ever since Pochotzin's execution for treason, so she surprised me by burying her face in my robe. I put my arm around her shoulder. "It's all right, My Lady. The king's still alive. Things could have been much worse."

"It's my fault," she sobbed. "All my fault!"

"Surely not."

"It is! He told me he was tired and not feeling well...and now look at him."

"What happened?"

"It was our night to make love, but he told me he didn't feel well. And I told him 'You felt well enough to bed Lady Emerald this afternoon, so don't give me your excuses.' We all deserve our due, right? He shouldn't have gone to her because it wasn't her turn, but then he's always favored her." Lady Atzi wiped her nose on my robe, and as I waited for her to continue, I gave silent thanks to the god that he didn't keep a harem of women like mortal kings did.

"I told him 'no excuses', so he gave in, just to make me stop beating my drum, I'm sure.

"Everything was going fine, but then...then he got this horrible look on his face, as though he had no idea where he was or who I was; and when I asked him what was wrong, he spoke as if he was drunk. Then he just collapsed. I thought he was being dramatic, but then I saw he wasn't breathing...and I called the guards...." She fell against me again and cried so hard her tears soaked through my robe. "I killed him!"

"He's still alive."

"But I did it to him. I should have believed him."

I stayed with her a while longer, offering what comforting words I could, but eventually I sent for her servant to sit with her.

Back out in the hallway, Mazatzin waited for me. "How is she?"

"She blames herself for what happened."

Mazatzin sighed. "Nothing good has happen to her since Pochotzin was executed."

Indeed, the woman seemed to have no luck left to her.

◻

My meditation room in the calmecac had once belonged to Mothotli. She'd been gone five years now; she'd left once the lesions started showing up on her face. She'd said little to either Nimilitzli or I before she departed, but she did leave me a note wishing me good luck in my future and that she was glad she'd been wrong about me. Even now, as I walked in the door, I caught a faint whiff of the incense she used to burn, as if a part of her refused to leave this place.

I kept a wooden box of teonanacatl mushrooms on the shelf above my meditation mat, for consulting the god, which happened more frequently with the years, regardless of whether I needed his guidance or not. It hadn't been very long since I'd last gone into the Divine Dream, but already my desire flared again. *You don't have time for such distractions,* I reminded myself as I drank down the mushroom and octli mixture.

But that was hard to stay focused on when Quetzalcoatl greeted me by pulling me down onto a bed of clouds where he kissed my neck as he undressed me. *I had hoped you would come back soon, my love,* he whispered as he kissed my bare breasts. *I missed you already.*

I stifled my growing arousal. "This isn't a good time, My Lord. I'm here on important business."

But this is *important business,* he said with an all-too-human smile. It surprised me how un-godlike he could be at times, and it drove away my doubts about why I was his lover at all. At times he seemed just like Little Reed.

He dropped the smile when I frowned at him. *Has something happened?*

"The king's ill, and I must know if anything can be done for him."

Quetzalcoatl paused to think. *Ill indeed.* He raised a brow.

"Do you know what's making him ill?"

The blood in his head stopped. He is not a young man, nor was he in the best of health.

"Can we do anything for him?"

The damage cannot be undone, and he will not recover.

I shook my head. "Lady Atzi blames herself for this."

He would have suffered it soon anyway, regardless.

"How long does he have to live?"

A few months, at most. The Deformed One will come when he is ready to collect him. Quetzalcoatl laid his head on my shoulder.

"But Red Flint hasn't returned yet."

It is time he did.

I sighed. "Will he be as good a king as his father?"

Foresight is not one of my gifts, but he will serve his purpose. He kissed me again, trying to coax me back to play.

But I pushed him away gently. "I want to—I always look forward to the time we spend together—but I need to give this news to Mazatzin, and Red Flint must be summoned back immediately."

Of course. Your devotion to duty is why I want you for my high priestess. I will send you back immediately, my love.

His words set my desire aflame and I gave him one last kiss; a promise that I'd come back when we had time to enjoy each other. He stroked my hair, frustrated. *Someday, my beautiful Butterfly. Someday.* He closed my eyes with his fingertips and the Divine Dream melted away around me. I awoke in my meditation room, my heart heavy with its own frustration.

How much longer was someday?

◻

Mazatzin ran to meet me halfway down the palace hallway. "What did the god say?"

I shook my head and he looked like I'd just shot him with an arrow. "Red Flint should be sent for immediately. I'm so sorry, Mazatzin."

Mocnelitzin embraced him around the shoulders a moment before clearing his own throat and saying, "We should inform the Council."

"I'll bring Red Flint back," Mazatzin said. "He should hear the news from a brother."

◻

Mazatzin left at dawn, taking one soldier with him. Even though Chichimec activity had declined since the allied army sent soldiers to every corner of the valley to hunt out the roving camps, I wouldn't want to travel with only one guard; I was moderately skilled with a macauhuitl sword, thanks to Little Reed's training, but little good that would do me against a group of bandits. Men weren't free to have such fears though. I saw Mazatzin off at the gate, giving him a letter for Little Reed, should he see him.

I went back to sleep after eating but Malinalli woke me around noon. "Ahexotl wants to see you."

"What for?" Ahexotl never wanted to see me for anything.

"He didn't say. He's at the palace."

The number of guards had doubled overnight and I felt as if I was walking into an army camp rather than a palace. The guards eyed me when I asked where Ahexotl was, but eventually they pointed me towards the Great Hall.

Ahexotl sat on the edge of the king's dais, his scarred legs stretched out before him. His bloated yellow- and red-skinned feet barely fit into his leather sandals. It amazed me that he could walk on them at all. He leaned against his wooden staff, listening to the Council members argue, but he shot me a glance when I came in. "You called for me, Your Grace?" I asked him.

"Normally I'd call Nimilitzli for this, but with her illness, you've become as good as high priestess." He never held my gaze anymore. "The king is dead."

I blinked. "So soon?"

Before Ahexotl could answer, Obsidian Eagle shouted for silence. To add to my surprise, he wasn't wearing his novice priest robe but rather dressed up in royal splendor. He was studying to become a priest of Quetzalcoatl—and usually followed Ahexotl everywhere, carrying the high priest's books or bags like a scribe. So long as one was a student, he or she was to forsake frivolity and wear only the black or white robes of their chosen order. Had he decided to leave early because of his father's demise?

"We cannot stand here arguing about the punishment. He poisoned Father, and would've killed Red Flint when he came back," Obsidian Eagle said. "Mocnelitzin deserves beheading for his ambitions, and if the Council is too weak to order it, I'll do it myself, with my father's sword."

The nobles muttered to each other, but stopped when I approached. "Excuse my intrusion, but what happened?" I asked. They didn't answer, their eyes all muddled. Annoyed, I turned to Obsidian Eagle, who was as distracted as the others but managed to shake it when I repeated the question.

"Mocnelitzin poisoned the king. He's already in custody and he'll pay for this heinous crime this very evening." He turned to the nobles. "Agreed?"

The leader of the nobles—Spear Fish—replied, "The real question is, who will rule in Red Flint's stead now that the man second to the throne cannot do so?"

"Mazatzin is third in line," I said. "And he's faithful and trustworthy."

"But he's not here," Ahexotl pointed out.

"And I fear he won't live long either." Obsidian Eagle paced. "We've learned that Mocnelitzin sent assassins out to intercept him, to ensure Red Flint never received the news."

"Then we must dispatch troops to stop them," I said.

"I suggested as much." Obsidian Eagle glared at Spear Fish again.

The indecision on the nobleman's face frustrated me. Couldn't any of them make a decision, or were they content to let Mazatzin die? "Who's fourth in line for the throne?"

"Pochotzin was." Obsidian Eagle didn't look at me.

"This is ridiculous." Ahexotl maneuvered to his feet and Obsidian Eagle hurried to help him, but Ahexotl pushed him away. "While we all stand here arguing succession, my fire priest is about to be set upon by assassins. Obsidian Eagle is an heir and he's prepared to hold the throne in trust until Red Flint returns."

Spear Fish wrinkled his nose. "The boy? But he hasn't even spent a day in the military, and he's tenth in line—"

"I'm seventh," Obsidian Eagle fired back. "I've lost three brothers to war in the last two years, but what would you care about such—"

"You're a child barely old enough to wear a loincloth let alone the crown of a kingdom!" Spear Fish shouted back.

Obsidian Eagle reached for his sword, but Ahexotl grabbed his hand.

And my own wrist started itching for the first time in seven years. It wasn't unbearable, more like a tickle deep in my flesh of my wrist. I continued watching everyone very carefully.

"No one else is here, Lord Spear Fish," Ahexotl said. "Camaxtli and Oquitzin are still doing their military service, and we all know that thanks to that fall he took as a child, Prince Stargazer isn't mentally fit to assume the throne; he can barely dress himself, let alone make informed decisions about the kingdom. Obsidian Eagle is young and untested, but he's also well-versed in the priestly arts, and with the Council's guidance, he'll do fine until Red Flint comes back. The Council hasn't the power to act on its own, so let's stop the bickering. The people need a king, even if he's only to lead them for a few weeks, otherwise we become vulnerable to our enemies. If Ihuitimal knew there was a power gap in Xochicalco, don't think he wouldn't try to grab that opportunity."

Spear Fish stared down Ahexotl while the rest of the Council whispered. He then shifted his gaze to me. "What do you think, Fire Priestess? What would the god wish us to do?"

Ahexotl stiffened at the slight, but to his credit, he kept his mouth shut.

"I'd have to consult the god to tell you what specifically he'd suggest, but I know he wouldn't want his holy city to fall into Ihuitimal's hands," I answered. "A son of the king must fill the empty throne, or a foreigner will claim it."

"But him?" Spear Fish pointed at Obsidian Eagle. "Another nobleman with more military experience—"

"Like you?" Obsidian Eagle pressed closer to him. "Are you really so bold as to levy a claim on my father's throne?"

Spear Fish's face darkened. "I was suggesting nothing of the sort. Your father was a lifelong friend, and my own son is best friends with Lord Red Flint. I care deeply about his family and kingdom, so please forgive my doubts. You will be the one to hold the throne for the Prince until this crisis passes, and you will have my full support." He kissed his fingers and swept them across the ground at Obsidian Eagle's feet.

Obsidian Eagle smiled stiffly as he clasped Spear Fish's shoulder in thanks. "I'll need your wisdom during this tumultuous time."

He accepted the bows and oaths of support from the rest of the Council. When he went to his father's reed throne, he sat carefully upon it. "He sometimes let me sit here when I was a small boy, and he'd pretend I was the king and he was my loyal jaguar knight. I never thought I'd have to sit on his throne as an interim king to protect it while Red Flint played his games in the north." He stiffened his chin a moment, but the anger soon passed. "Mocnelitzin will die tonight in the palace square, beheaded as a traitor. But first, I must assemble soldiers to intercept this band of assassins bent on killing Mazatzin."

"And I'll go to the temple and pray," Ahexotl said.

Obsidian Eagle started to rise, but Ahexotl waved him off with a pointed glare. Obsidian Eagle bowed his head, as though he'd been caught doing something stupid.

"Quetzalpetlatl, if you could come with me, we have matters to discuss." Ahexotl headed for the entryway at a stilted limp.

I gave Obsidian Eagle a bow then followed Ahexotl out.

Ahexotl huffed and puffed and wheezed as we walked towards the sacred precinct, but he didn't stop until we reached the stairs. He then sat on the lowest step and massaged his knees. "We need to discuss the next step in your future," he mumbled. "With a new king preparing to take the throne, we can't have leadership disorder in the priesthood. Nimilitzli has chosen you to succeed her as high priestess, and it's time you took on the title and duties formally. Given what happened in the last day, it's all the more urgent."

The news should have brought me joy; I'd finally achieved the first step of my ultimate goal, but instead it left me melancholy. The high priestess served for life, so if Nimilitzli thought it was time I took her robe....

Ahexotl frowned. "Don't look so disappointed with your promotion."

"I'm not. It's just unexpected."

He grunted. "That's life. We'll conduct the formal ceremony in three days, so you have time enough to do the appropriate fasting and to give some thought to whom you want to appoint the next fire priestess."

"I think Malinalli would be a good choice."

"That's fine." He struggled to his feet again, and leaned on his walking stick as he limped up the stairs.

Part of me felt a twinge of guilt at seeing him struggle so much. I moved to take his arm, but he jabbed his stick at my right foot, drawing blood. "I can make it just fine on my own, thank you," he growled and continued on his way.

I watched him go, indignant and furious. What right did he have to speak to me like that?

CHAPTER TWENTY-TWO

When I returned to the palace to make sure none of the king's expectant women had gone into early labor, many of the women still huddled in groups in the corridors, crying. Whatever jealousy had existed before was now forgotten in their shared grief.

As for Lady Atzi, she lay in her room, staring into the hearth, muttering to herself. I tried to explain to her what Quetzalcoatl had told me, but she didn't respond at all. "Watch her closely for the next few days," I warned her handmaiden. "If you see any cause for concern—no matter how minor—fetch Lady Emerald immediately."

The girl paled. "You think she'll hurt herself?"

"I don't know, but it's vital she not be allowed to make decisions for herself right now."

The sun sat low on the mountains when I left the palace in search of Ahexotl. Both the high priest and priestess witnessed state executions, to collect the condemned's blood for the sacrifice, but he hadn't summoned me yet. When I arrived at the temple though, Malinalli told me that Ahexotl had attended the execution without me. "I offered to go and find you, but he said he'd rather spare you the discomfort."

I seethed. True, every time I helped sacrifice a man, I thought about why Quetzalcoatl had chosen me to stand with Little Reed as his high priestess. Watching the victim struggle repulsed me, but I always performed my duty without complaint. The time wasn't yet right to poke that ant hill.

But had I somehow betrayed my real feelings to Ahexotl, or was it a show of contempt and bitterness for not having been able to have me as he'd had so many others?

He brought it on himself, I thought as I headed home. Still, his behavior left me unsettled. *He can hardly walk up stairs, so how can he possibly hurt you anymore?*

While I cooked the sauce for our tlaxcallis, Nimilitzli talked about the few fragments of news she'd heard and I filled in the details; but mostly I sat in melancholy silence, distracted.

"What's on your mind?" Nimilitzli asked, as I set the bowl of sauce between us.

I didn't meet her gaze as I handed her a warm tlaxcalli. "Ahexotl told me it's time I replace you as high priestess."

"It is. I'm not going to get well again, and you're ready."

"I don't feel it."

She patted my hand. "Have faith in the god, and yourself. You'll be a high priestess all will talk about long after you've gone on to Mictlan, just as people will always speak of what Topiltzin does."

Mentioning Little Reed made me long to lie in Quetzalcoatl's arms again and see his son's face. I'd expected my heart to grow forgetful with the years, but instead I longed for him even more, particularly when he signed his letters to me with "Love always." Did he still mean it the way he had the night before he left? I thought about it every time I lay with Quetzalcoatl and imagined he was Little Reed. Having only his letters to hold and touch was no better than having Quetzalcoatl only in the Divine Dream. And the god's constant "someday" had started wearing on me.

Some faithful, pious priestess you are, wishing your divine lover was someone else instead, I scolded myself as I lay awake late into the night. Still, as frustrating as my relationship with the god was, it was all I had, and I craved his feathery touch and airy kisses as much as I needed food and water. *He wouldn't mind me calling on him; he never does.*

Nimilitzli would never abuse the sacred power of the teonanacatl for pleasure. But eventually desire won out. I put extra logs in the fire and slipped my robe on, then woke Nimilitzli to let her know I was leaving. "I have something I forgot to do, but I'll be back soon." Not completely untrue; this particular itch was keeping me awake, but guilt followed me out the door. What if she choked and I wasn't there to help her? I almost went back, but it would only invite questions.

Inside the calmecac, I passed Ahexotl's meditation room. Light glowed beyond the closed curtain. I closed my own curtain silently and forewent a lamp. Better if he didn't know I was there. I cursed softly when I stubbed my toe on my copal burner, but I found the mushroom box up on the shelf.

Hearing footfalls pass my room, I went to the curtain and peeked out. Obsidian Eagle stood at Ahexotl's curtain, tugging it as he looked up and down the hallway. Ahexotl told him to enter and he pulled the curtain closed behind him. "I've dispatched the troops to intercept Mazatzin."

"And you made sure they are all loyal to us?"

"Of course. They're bringing back his head as proof."

I gasped but clapped a hand over my mouth.

"And what about Red Flint?" Ahexotl asked.

"They'll continue to the army camp and bring him away."

"And you made it clear they weren't to mention Cuitlapanton's death?"

"Of course," Obsidian Eagle said, indignant. "I didn't make mistakes with the poison, did I?"

Ahexotl chuckled. "That's because you always do as I tell you, and that's why you find yourself in these fortunate circumstances."

I almost dropped the box of mushrooms, but caught it and set it carefully on the floor, hardly believing what I was hearing. *Mocnelitzin was innocent!* My wrist itched badly and it took all my resolve to not scratch it raw.

"This isn't going to come cheap though," Obsidian Eagle said. "Paying off the soldiers and the palace guards—"

"Who cares? You'll be king."

"Until Camaxtli or Oquitzin challenge me."

"Stop sucking your stones up into your body. Once you have the throne, the army will fall in line and you can openly dispose of them. That's a natural part of succession; you think your own father didn't shed some blood solidifying his power? Ihuitimal will want you to sit unopposed, and once we combine the armies, you can find more than a few honorless Chichimecs who'd gladly bring you their heads."

The god's own high priest conspiring with Ihuitimal to overthrow Xochicalco's royal succession and seize control of the army? The idea of soldiers wearing Xochicalco's own colors falling upon Mazatzin made me sick and furious. *You should summon Quetzalcoatl.*

But my stomach cramped. I'd spent the years since Teotihuacan trying not to think about what I'd have to give to summon him again. I wrung my three-fingered hand, the pain springing back as if I'd just cut those fingers off moments ago. *No, I shouldn't call on Quetzalcoatl if I don't need to.*

"You would be a better king than me," Obsidian Eagle went on. "I've only ever wanted to be a priest."

"Maybe you are as dense as Lord Spear Fish says," Ahexotl growled. "I'm not royal blood, and thanks to Topiltzin's bitch of a sister, I'm a repulsive cripple. The people would never accept me as their king."

My mouth went dry at the venom in his voice.

"She did *that* to you?" Obsidian Eagle asked, his voice tentative.

"Don't worry about being king; you provide the face while I provide the experience. Do what you're told and Ihuitimal will reward you handsomely."

"What's he giving you?"

"Enough." The hardness in Ahexotl's voice raised the hairs on my neck.

Obsidian Eagle pulled the door curtain aside. "I'm still not sure about this. Surely Ihuitimal will outlaw Quetzalcoatl's worship here, just as he did in Culhuacan."

"One god is just as good as any other," Ahexotl said, shuffling out into the hallway. "They're just tools for exercising power."

I clenched my fist so hard my fingernails dug into my palms.

"I worry about Topiltzin, though," Obsidian Eagle said.

"Don't believe half of what you hear about him. He's but a man, just as fragile before the sword as any. Ihuitimal will take care of him."

Obsidian Eagle nodded. "My only regret is that I won't get to see him or Red Flint die like the lake slugs they are."

"You'll honor Pochotzin's sacrifice by fulfilling these plans. Now take me home. I'm very tired."

Even after their footfalls faded, I stayed in my room, leaning against the wall, reeling from all I'd heard. *You can't stay here all night. The kingdom is in danger—Little Reed is in danger—and with Obsidian Eagle buying the loyalty of the soldiers, who can you trust to warn Mazatzin?*

I wasn't safe here anymore either; not with Ahexotl stoking a bonfire of revenge to throw me into. With the god's sacred city under attack from his nemesis, who but his chosen high priestess should act for his interests?

I made sure the hallway was still empty then went to the Council Room. The weapons still hung on the walls; Nimilitzli said they were gifts bequeathed to the temple from warriors who exchanged their weapons for the priestly robe.

My sacrificial blade would be little good against armored soldiers, and was meant for close combat, so I needed a better weapon. The spear was too heavy for me, and I knew nothing about using an atl-atl, so I reached for one particular macuahuitl sword. Little Reed had taught me a bit about how to weild the flat, lightweight wooden sword edged with obsidian blades, so it was my best choice.

But I hesitated. I'd often seen Nimilitzli giving this one extra care, as if it meant something special to her. Would it be disrespectful to take it?

But when I looked closer, it had feathered serpents carved into the wood core, in a design similar to the one on the side of the god's temple. *It's a sign!* I took the sword and headed home.

I crossed the precinct at a sprint then hurried inside the house, trying not to disturb the bells.

I turned to find Nimilitzli awake and sitting up, reading a letter while a man crouched near the hearth. I immediately recognized him as Lord Citlallotoc of Acolman, who had rescued us the night we left Teotihuacan. He looked much the same as he had then, except he'd acquired a lime-white scar on his jaw.

"Good, you're back," Nimilitzli said. "We have news from your brother." But when she spotted the sword in my hand, she asked, "Why do you have that, Quetzalpetlatl?"

Taking a deep breath, I said, "Ahexotl and Obsidian Eagle are moving to seize Red Flint's throne. Obsidian Eagle poisoned the king and now he's sent assassins to kill Mazatzin and Red Flint—"

"Cuitlapanton is dead?" Citlallotoc asked, rising to his feet, alarmed.

"Yes, in a plot concocted by the king of Culhuacan to seize control of Xochicalco."

Nimilitzli sat up straighter. "Where did you hear all this?"

"I overheard them talking in Ahexotl's meditation room."

"What's the sword for?"

"Someone must warn Mazatzin."

"And you thought that should be you?" Nimilitzli asked with an uneasy laugh.

Citlallotoc leaned closer and whispered, "You weren't really going to leave the city unescorted, were you?"

"I'm not completely defenseless," I shot back.

Nimilitzli looked into the fire. "Indeed you aren't."

"You should go to the Council with this news," Citlallotoc suggested.

I shook my head. "Lord Spear Fish might listen, but they all took oaths to Obsidian Eagle, and he's bought off the palace guards. And Ihuitimal promised Ahexotl something involving me for his cooperation and I'm not waiting to find out what revenge he has planned for me."

"You're sure?"

"Him saying 'thanks to Topiltzin's bitch of a sister, I'm a repulsive cripple' is evidence enough for me."

Citlallotoc crinkled his brows. "How dare he speak such vile words? Sounds like he needs be taught some manners with my sword blade."

"I appreciate that, Lord Citlallotoc, but that won't save Mazatzin." Citlallotoc arched his eyebrow, no doubt surprised I remembered his name, but I pressed on. "He knows nothing of this treachery and he and his guard will be helpless as newborn pups when the traitors find them."

"Then we must get to your friend first. And if you truly feel yourself in imminent danger, I could never show my face to your brother again if I left you here." He turned to Nimilitzli. "Topiltzin is back at the camp for a few weeks before setting off to the north again, so she'll be in his care, and I'll gladly lay down my own life to protect her on route."

To me, Nimilitzli said, "If you really feel you must go, then may the god go with you."

"Will you be all right by yourself?"

"I'll be fine. Someone will come looking for you when you don't show up for your sunrise duties and I'll arrange for help then. Worry only about yourself, understood?"

I kissed her forehead. "I'll try, but I can't promise not to worry."

I made tlaxcallis while Citlallotoc went to the cistern to fill some skins for us. When I went to pack the sword, I found Nimilitzli holding it, staring at it wistfully. "I'll leave it here if you'd rather I didn't take it."

She blinked up at me. "What?"

"I can see that the sword means a lot to you, so if you'd rather I didn't take it—"

"No, it should do what it was made for, not hang unused in the Council Room." Nimilitzli handed it to me. "It served its previous owner well, and it'll do the same for you."

I thought to ask who it belonged to, but then Citlallotoc came back. "Are we ready?" he asked as he shouldered the food pack too.

I donned my traveling cloak and strapped on my medicine pouch, just in case. "Ready."

¤

Even with dawn still far off, the Merchant Quarter was bustling with activity. At least five caravans were setting out before first light, their slaves loaded down with packs, and Citlallotoc and I walked among them, to blend in with the stream of departing people. While the gate guards probably weren't looking for suspicious people leaving the city, we wanted to avoid unnecessary contact with them.

Once we passed the quarry, we jogged off into the trees. "Your friend likely took the road, as will those following him, but if we cut through the forest, we can get ahead of them and hopefully intercept Red Flint's brother before they do," Citlallotoc said. "It's a good thing I arrived when I did, so I could help you."

"What brought you to Xochicalco anyway?" I asked.

"I had letters for you and the high priestess. Unfortunately, in our rush to leave, I left your letter with Nimilitzli."

"Was it important?"

"I don't know, My Lady, but your brother did personally ask me to deliver them rather than leave them with a runner."

Little Reed had never done that before, so it surely was very important. It was too late to turn back now though.

By dawn my lack of sleep caught up with me. My steps turned to sluggish stumbles and Citlallotoc often got well ahead of me and had to wait for me to catch up. "I haven't slept well in a few days," I admitted, when we stopped to rest and eat.

"I imagine not, with the king's death and now this treachery." He sat on a fallen log opposite me, eating his tlaxcalli. "I must say I'm surprised you remembered me, Lady Quetzalpetlatl. We only met briefly seven years ago."

"I'm blessed with an impeccable memory."

Citlallotoc chuckled. "You're like Topiltzin in that regard. I don't think he ever forgets anything."

The thought of seeing Little Reed again sent a giddy rush through me. I couldn't wait to hug him again and kiss his cheek. *Or his lips.* But I scolded myself for the thought. *It's been seven years, and you pretty much rejected him before he left. For all you know, his heart's moved on to someone new.* Trying to steer my mind away from my growing disappointment, I asked, "Have you served long with my brother?"

"Five years now, though I was looking for an opportunity to serve with

211

him sooner than that. The moment I first met him...I knew I was standing in the presence of a great man. I can't explain why, but I felt as if he had the very ear of the gods themselves. Do you think me crazy?"

I laughed. "Didn't Topiltzin tell you who his father is?"

"Everyone knows he's Mixcoatl's son."

"Actually, he's Quetzalcoatl's."

Citlallotoc blinked at me, startled. "You're serious?"

"My mother was unable to have any more children with Mixcoatl after me, but the god came to her in a dream and told her to swallow a jade stone he'd left for her. A few months later, she gave birth to Topiltzin. That was seventeen years ago."

"Topiltzin is only seventeen? Impossible!"

"When it comes to the god, anything is possible. I've seen the god's work firsthand, so bearing a human son would be the least difficult thing he can do."

Citlallotoc rubbed his chin. "Topiltzin does heal extraordinarily fast. He took a sword slash to the face a few years back and a week later it was gone, without even a scar. Some think he went to a witch for a magic salve." He laughed. "I'm more willing to believe he's the god's son than that he visits witches for potions." He finished his tlaxcalli. "Are you a child of the god as well?"

"I'm afraid I'm not so special."

"I think you're more special then you let yourself believe. Like Topiltzin, you have...an aura about you."

"Yes well, I'd prefer not to have that aura, for it's sure to cause me trouble," I said, and blushed. I'd never mentioned it to anyone before now.

"Sometimes our gifts are difficult to live with." Citlallotoc swallowed some water. "We shouldn't linger if we're to catch up with your friend before the others do."

After we'd gotten back underway, I asked Citlallotoc, "Does my brother ever speak about me?"

"No. If I hadn't already met you once, I never would've suspected he had a sister."

At first I felt crestfallen, but then how often did I talk to Malinalli about Little Reed? Rarely. Not because he wasn't ever on my mind—not a day passed that I didn't think about him at least a few times—but because

I feared betraying my feelings for him to her. As the next high priestess, I was expected to be an example of unwavering piety. I didn't even mention him to Nimilitzli unless she brought him up first. Maybe Little Reed said nothing about me for the same reasons.

"He's very private," Citlallotoc went on. "He stays silent about what goes on in his heart and in his tent, unlike others. Prince Red Flint crows to everyone about how many women he takes to bed."

I couldn't contain the laugh. "Red Flint?"

"There's no dignified way to put it. He shows no signs of caring for them, or they for him, and he soon gives them to other soldiers to buy their favor. I pity his future wife, for she will surely marry a husk of a man who spilled all his honey carelessly, leaving none for her. Your brother is much more respectful."

A spike of jealousy surged through me. "Then he has lovers?"

"I don't really know. If he does, he's extremely secretive about it, which I suppose makes sense since he's a priest, and aren't priests supposed to live chaste lives?"

"We do take vows of celibacy."

"Your brother is very dedicated to the god, and I dare say he's already a better leader than most kings. He's promised to return my stolen throne to me once he's reclaimed his own, and I know his word is worth every feather in the valley. I'd lay my life down for him without hesitation." To my surprise, he followed this with a heavy sigh.

"But what?" I asked.

Citlallotoc hesitated. "I wish he weren't so closed off. He's very open to listening to his officers and following their advice when he finds it prudent, but...." He averted his eyes as he said, "I consider him my friend, yet I fear he doesn't consider me the same."

The hurt in his voice surprised me, but also made my heart glow. He was unquestioningly loyal to my brother, exactly the kind of man Little Reed needed at his side, and that made me like him all the more. "He never had many friends," I said. "When he was growing up, most of the priests treated him with reverence befitting a god, but he also suffered a great deal of ridicule and hostility from those who didn't believe his divine parentage."

"Some people cannot help being fools," Citlallotoc said with a frown. "I always found his cool demeanor strange though. I thought priests were supposed to be personally involved with the community."

"Yes, but Topiltzin hadn't been a priest more than a few days before he left for the army."

"He does perform the daily sacrifice for the troops, and he's quite the sight to watch. Even the men from the other armies come to hear him talk about Quetzalcoatl. It all makes good sense now that I know his true parentage. He says we should all give a little blood to the god of our choice before a battle, and once I started doing this, my sword fell swifter and I've twice escaped being dragged off by Chichimecs. I wouldn't think to go into battle without honoring Quetzalcoatl with a little of my blood."

Little Reed had told me about such things in his letters. He'd been working hard instilling the idea of bloodletting as a noble and worthwhile practice, especially among the soldiers. *If I can get warriors to believe in the superiority of sacrificing their own blood, converting the general populace will be easy later on,* he'd written in one letter. *They'll be the most difficult group to convert, since they've been trained for so long to shed their enemies' blood in honor of the Sun, not their own.* Over the years such philosophical statements became the staple of his letters, making me wonder if he considered me nothing more than a religious peer he was exchanging notes with.

But he never fails to sign his letters with love, I reminded myself.

CHAPTER TWENTY-THREE

By midday, my legs felt like melting wax, and stopping to take breaks only let my exhaustion pounce on me. When I started feeling dizzy, Citlallotoc had us stop again, but this time he opened the deerskin pouch at his side and took out his pipe and a sleeve of tobacco. "This will help you."

When he handed the stuffed pipe to me and took out his strikers, I pushed it back to him, appalled. "Courtesans smoke, not priestesses."

"You won't be able to go on much further without something to keep you going. You wish to save your priest friend?" When I still didn't pull the pipe back, he added, "I promise to tell no one."

"You won't think me unsavory?"

"Never." He showed me how to hold the pipe. "Take quick, shallow breaths. If you breathe too deeply, it'll add to your exhaustion."

The first inhalation brought me to tears and coughs, but after a few more breaths, I felt the change, like someone had poured glorious sunshine straight into my blood. I could walk all day, perhaps even run some of it. Citlallotoc puffed a bit as well then said, "We need to keep moving. We're probably ahead of the dog-traitor's men now, but they'll travel through the night and so must we."

We stopped only to replenish our water supply in a creek and re-stuff the pipe, to keep us going once the exhaustion peeked in again. We ate while we walked.

Just before nightfall, we came to the road. I waited in the trees while Citlallotoc went to investigate. Now I was jittery and anxious, hopefully from the tobacco, not my intuition. He prowled the road, creeping low to the ground at the opposite edge, bow at the ready. He came back soon. "The road behind us is clear, but I smell smoke, probably from a campfire. We should stay to the shadows until we see who it is. Have your sword ready." We started up the road, but then he stopped to ask, "Do you know anything about using a sword?"

"Topiltzin showed me how before he left for the army."

Citlallotoc chuckled. "That's Topiltzin, never afraid to defy social convention. He'll either change the world or anger everyone by trying."

The cacophony of buzzing insects and monkey shrieks made it difficult to hear much, but Citlallotoc remained alert, arrow nocked and ready. Soon I caught sight of fire flickering through the trees, and Citlallotoc motioned me off the road. "Stay here," he said then went ahead. I lost sight of him when he went down the hill. I waited, my heart thudding as I muttered prayers to Quetzalcoatl. I measured the time by my shaking breaths and pulsing blood.

When Citlallotoc returned, he came with Mazatzin. I wanted to cry out in relief, but allowed myself only a deep sigh. I didn't spare Mazatzin a hug though. "Thank the Feathered Serpent you're all right."

"I'm fine. It's my guard who's not. Last night a jaguar attacked us, and it mauled him."

He led us back to the small camp where the guard lay on a blanket, his head and one arm bandaged up with the remains of Mazatzin's xicolli. I felt his forehead then opened my pouch and took out a small bag of yauhtli. I had nothing for his fever or to keep his wounds from festering, but at least I could relieve his pain. He resisted the bitter medicine but calmed once I sat him up to wash it down with water. "The pain will go away and you can go to sleep soon," I assured him, but he just moaned and rolled his head.

"How is he?" Mazatzin asked.

"I'm not sure he'll make it through the night. He's already in a state of delirium and he's lost a lot of blood."

Mazatzin cursed. "I should have heard the beast, but it came out of nowhere, like a spirit. Perhaps it wouldn't have attacked us if we'd had torches." He rubbed the back of his neck. "Not that I'm displeased with seeing you, but what are you doing out here?" He shot a glance at Citlallotoc, as if to add, *with him?*

"You didn't tell him?" I asked Citlallotoc.

"I thought he might handle the bad news better coming from a friend," Citlallotoc said.

"What bad news?" Mazatzin demanded.

I pulled him back towards the hill, until we were far enough away that we wouldn't be overheard. "Your father died a couple of days ago. Obsidian Eagle poisoned him, then had Mocnelitzin executed for the crime. He's taken the throne and sent assassins out to kill you and Red Flint."

Mazatzin's face flushed dark. "He did?"

I nodded. "And Ahexotl is helping him. They're acting on Ihuitimal's behalf, to secure the army against Topiltzin. I had to warn you and stop this treachery."

Mazatzin clenched his fists, blinking back tears. "Thank you for looking out for me, Quetzalpetlatl. You're a true and loyal friend, and I shall never forget it."

Citlallotoc came over. "We should extinguish the fire so it's not easy for the traitor's men to find us. If we hide near the road and ambush them when they come, we can pick most of them off with arrows before they realize where we are."

We stamped out the fire then did a bloodletting to the god, to bless our weapons. I remained with the guard while Mazatzin and Citlallotoc went back to the road, but I wanted to see what was happening and so crawled up the side of the hill with my sword and lay on my belly near the top. I spotted Mazatzin climbing a large tree while Citlallotoc hurried to the other side of the road and disappeared into the dark forest. Then the waiting began.

I tried to stay alert, but my body turned heavy as a stone. *I'll be better after a moment's rest,* I thought, finally giving in to the desire to close my eyes....

I awoke when someone stepped on me.

It knocked the wind from me and I lunged to the side. A man cried out and tumbled down the hill. Shouting came from the distance, but I returned my attention to the man groaning and cursing at the bottom of the hill. I gripped my sword tighter and stayed still, hoping he couldn't see me in the dim moonlight leaking through the trees.

He stood and backed up a few steps, but then tripped over the guard. He stared at the other man, then, to my repulsion, he drew his knife and cut the guard's throat. He looked around again.

When his gaze stopped on me, I couldn't breathe. We stared each other down a moment.

I sprang to all fours, but when I got to my feet, I only made it a couple of steps before he grabbed me from behind. He clamped a hand over my mouth, holding my arms to my sides with the other and rendering my sword useless. His hard grip sent my mind screaming back to the night in the water yard with Ahexotl and I lashed out, bashing him in the face with the back of my head, breaking his nose. He howled and let me go, but instead of running, I swung the sword and it lodged in his exposed neck. He groped at my hands and I dashed off into the woods, unsure where my panic was taking me.

Someone stepped in front of me and I tried to swerve, but he seized me with strong hands. I went to bite him, but he shouted, "It's me, Quetzalpetlatl!" Mazatzin let me go, backing away.

I flung myself into his arms, my whole body shaking. "Someone came into camp and killed the guard, slit his throat while he slept—"

Citlallotoc jogged to us, his expression hard in the moonlight. "I saw one of the men duck into woods over here."

"She says he came into the camp," Mazatzin said.

Citlallotoc took off through the trees, sneaking from shadow to shadow, but he stopped when he reached the edge of the hill. He pointed his bow at someone on the ground. "Is this him?"

The man lay in the dirt and leaves, my sword sticking out of his neck and blood oozing from his mouth. He blinked up at us. Mazatzin pulled the sword out, letting the blood surge, and the man stiffened and choked, his breath coming quick and shallow. His eyes soon glazed over. I felt sick.

"It was a good blow. Your brother taught you well," Citlallotoc said. He jogged down the hill to check on the guard, but was back in a few moments, shaking his head. "We need to clear the bodies off the road and move on, before the jaguars and bears come following their noses."

Obsidian Eagle's men—ten in all—lay strewn about the road, all driven through with at least one arrow. We carried them back to camp and tossed them on the ground next to the fire where we stripped them of weapons and whatever food, water and medicine they carried. Mazatzin and I muttered prayers over the slain guard, imploring Xolotl to show him mercy and guide him through the trials of the underworld so he might finally find peace.

We set off into the night, following the road north. We walked until the sky turned gray with dawn, then Citlallotoc suggested we fall back into the trees and find a place to rest. The ground was hard with only a blanket to sleep on, but I fell into dreamless sleep as soon as I lay down.

¤

My stomach woke me when I smelled roasting meat. Mazatzin sat next to the fire, tending to a skinned peccary on a spit while he smoked his pipe. Early afternoon sunshine leaked through the canopy. My muscles protested and my stomach gurgled when I sat up. "Where did you get the meat?"

"Citlallotoc shot it a while ago. He's scouting the road, making sure we don't have unexpected visitors."

Citlallotoc came back shortly before the peccary was cooked, looking well rested and ready to march. "We'll be able to make it to the army camp before nightfall," he said as he cut the charred meat into tlaxcallis for each of us. We then got underway, eating as we marched.

I was used to living with little sleep, particularly since becoming fire priestess, but fatigue set in quicker than I'd hoped. The meat lifted me for a while, but after a time I thought only of sleep. I didn't ever go more than two days without a good steady sleep, but I also didn't want to be the reason we didn't make the camp by nightfall. I wished I could smoke a little, but I didn't dare do such things in front of Mazatzin.

I cheered when I saw the first signs of campfire smoke in the distance. We picked up the pace and came to the guard post just as dusk crept over the mountains. My anticipation mounted as we walked through Xochicalco's end of camp; I hardly even noticed the distant, longing stares as I walked by. "I'm going to find Red Flint," Mazatzin told me. "I'm sure you're eager to see Topiltzin, so we'll talk tomorrow." He disappeared into the milling crowd, leaving me with Citlallotoc.

Citlallotoc took me to a large tent near the center of camp. The guard held the flap open for us.

The warm tent smelled of copalli and xocolatl, and cotton armor and weapons decorated a grass man in the back corner. Citlallotoc knelt on the ground then called out, "Are you here, My Lord?"

"Citlallotoc?" Little Reed came through a second flap at the back of the tent, revealing another room behind him as he came out, dressed in a simple white xicolli.

I knew Little Reed didn't age like normal men, and I'd expected him to look older, but I was still shocked by the strands of white snaking through his hair. It was as if those seven years had been fifteen for him. But his smile was the same one I remembered and loved, and he'd grown handsomer with the years.

The smile dropped from his face when he saw me though. "What are you doing here?"

I'd expected a joyful embrace only to get an uncomfortable silence as I tried to gather my thoughts. Citlallotoc rescued me though. "I brought her here to remove her from harm's way, My Lord. Treachery is running rampant in Xochicalco."

Little Reed embraced me, but it was a stiff, formal action. My face burned with resentment. He'd changed much. "Are you all right?" he asked, once he'd made enough space between us again. "What's this all about?"

I told him about Cuitlapanton and Obsidian Eagle, but when I talked of Ahexotl's part, an angry shadow crossed his face. *You should have let him kill Ahexotl back then. You were completely misguided about the god sparing him.*

Little Reed gripped Citlallotoc's shoulders. "Thank you for watching out for my sister. She can take care of herself, but I feel better knowing you could help her if the need arose."

"It's an honor to serve your family, My Lord," Citlallotoc said, bowing his head. "I'm sure you two have much to talk about after so many years, so I'll retire to my tent and catch up on my sleep." He bowed to me as well, and left.

"Your friend is a very good man," I told Little Reed.

"Citlallotoc? Oh yes, a most excellent man." He motioned me to sit down next to the copalli burner, and once we were sitting, he tossed some more incense on the plate. "My first order of business once I've retaken the throne is to send troops to Acolman to punish the traitors who drove him out and return his kingdom to him."

"That will be a fine token of appreciation for his service, but I believe you can still do better for him."

"What do you mean?"

"Far be it for me to divulge a man's heart, but men are loath to admit such things to each other."

"Admit what?"

"He wants your friendship."

Little Reed laughed. "He has it already."

"He wants to be friends like we are." Though I reddened when I thought of Little Reed's last night in Xochicalco and hoped he didn't think Citlallotoc wanted *that* kind of friendship. "What I mean is that he wishes you'd confide in him as you do with me."

"I do confide in him, on every military matter—"

"He wants your ear to talk to you on a personal level, and to offer you his in return. There's more to life than war."

Little Reed smiled. "Indeed there is. I shall do better by him, Papalotl, and thank you for pointing this out to me. I should have true friends, not just loyal followers."

The guard came with a steaming bowl of stew, which Little Reed handed to me. "Could you please bring one more bowl? I wasn't expecting company."

Once the guard left, I said, "You seem to be doing really well for yourself."

"Well enough, though I anticipate a setback once Red Flint takes the throne. I'd hoped to start pushing at Culhuacan next year, while Cuitlapanton was still alive, but I suspect Red Flint won't immediately agree to his father's promise to provide troops."

"Are you two still fighting?"

"We haven't fought in years; we have mutual respect for our differences, but I know Red Flint's heart better than he thinks. He fears appearing subordinate to me, so he won't immediately bow to my request. Maybe in a couple of years...."

The guard returned with another bowl of stew and we began eating.

"He also thinks he holds a strategic advantage over me," Little Reed continued.

"What would that be?"

"You, of course."

"Me?"

"Didn't Citlallotoc deliver my letter?"

"In our hurry to leave, I left it at home with Nimilitzli."

"I'll just tell you what I wrote then. Red Flint was planning to return to Xochicalco next month, to ask you to be his wife. He came to me first, of course, to try to get my permission to have you, but when I told him that you make your own decisions, he called me your little dog and said you always tell me where I can lift my leg."

I rolled my eyes. "You didn't get into a fight, did you?"

"Like I said, we haven't fought in years. I told him I wouldn't grant him permission, but he was free to win your heart on his own."

"I'd have rather you told him to stay away from me," I said.

"Perhaps I should have. I suspect he may try to trick you into believing I was ordering you to marry him, so that's why I sent the letter."

"I would've seen it for the scheme it was," I said. "You already told me how you feel about such arrangements."

"But I also feared he might make threats if you don't accept. Whatever he tells you, Papalotl, I'd rather never get our throne back than see you locked away in a marriage you don't want."

I smiled, feeling achingly warm inside. "Thank you, Little Reed."

He gave me a smile back, making the desire uncoil inside me. "How's Mother doing?" he asked.

The question dampened my lust some. "She hasn't gotten any better, and frankly I doubt she'll last the rest of the year. I'm surprised she's made it this long."

Little Reed watched the white smoke curl off the copalli burner, his expression mirroring some inner conflict.

"I really think you should come home, for a few days anyway," I said.

"We're supposed to cut off a contingent of Chichimecs reinforcements headed for Culhuacan—"

"Nimilitzli didn't give birth to you, but if she'd had milk, she would've fed you at her own breast. She's our mother, and she deserves the honor of us treating her as such."

He tossed more copalli on the plate and sighed. "I should see you safely back to Xochicalco, and I do have a stake in who takes the throne in all this mess. This way at least I can ensure that I can get both you and Nimilitzli somewhere safe, should Red Flint's bid go wrong."

"There's nowhere safe if Xochicalco falls to Ihuitimal."

"Which is why we must make sure Red Flint takes the throne," Little Reed replied. "Through whatever means necessary." He took my three-fingered hand and gave it a squeeze.

My stomach clenched. "Maybe it won't come to that."

"Let's hope not."

The sudden weight of my responsibility must have shown on my face, for Little Reed said, "You should lie down, get some rest. You may use my bed." He helped me to my feet.

"I don't want to kick you out of your bed—"

"I'll get an extra mat from the supply tent."

Through the flap at the back of the tent was a small room just big enough for a bed of reed mats, animal skins and blankets, and a single wicker clothing chest. He lit a second incense burner near the bed, filling the room with the calming aroma of copalli. He hung my cloak on a peg on one of the tent poles. "I'll be out here if you need anything." He turned to leave.

But I did need something, and I wouldn't be able to sleep without it. I'd spent the last day wondering how to bring it up, or if I even should, and over dinner I'd become even more unsure about it. Was possibly ruining our friendship worth satisfying my curiosity? Maybe not, but one thing was certain: I couldn't go on not knowing the truth. "L-Little Reed!" I stammered.

He turned to me. "Papalotl?"

"I...what I mean to say...about when you left," I finally choked out. "I must speak with you about that night, by the temple."

He looked as uncomfortable as I felt. "Well, that was a while ago...."

My hopes fell. *He's trying to explain it away.*

"I'm sorry I made you uncomfortable that night," he said.

"Then you don't feel that way anymore?" I felt as if I were grasping at the wind, hoping to snag it. When he hesitated to answer, I added, "We promised to always be truthful with each other, so please, tell me the truth. I promise not to criticize." *Though I can't promise not to cry if I turn out to be the lovesick fool in all this.*

He finally said, "My feelings for you are the same as they were then, Papalotl."

My heart stopped. "Then you do still...?"

"Love you? Absolutely. And I always will."

I laughed and wrapped my arms around his neck. "And I've always loved you too, Little Reed, just had no idea how to tell you."

He embraced me back with a contented sigh. "Foolish indecision, on both our parts. But no more." He caressed the side of my face. "I'm glad you didn't get to read the letter, for a marriage proposal really should be done in person."

"Marriage?" I asked, giddy. "But what about our future as priests?"

"Once I've taken back Culhuacan and I'm high priest of Father's order, I'll change the laws so priests and priestesses can marry. There is no good reason for them not to."

"And every king needs an heir," I added.

He smiled then kissed me, bringing the desire roaring up again. I drew him closer, desperate for his touch. I giggled when we tripped onto the bed, my head swimming. He chuckled too, nuzzling my neck, but his expression turned serious when I started loosening the ties on my robe. "Help me?" I asked with a smile. I never knew I could be so bold.

He hesitated but then finished undoing them for me. While he draped my robe over the wicker chest, I slipped my dress off, so I wore only my undergarment when he finally turned back to me. He stripped his xicolli off and cast it aside to embrace me.

I missed the feathery softness of the god's caresses, but the intensity of real flesh against mine kept that secluded at the back of my mind. *Seven years I've waited for something real, and that's too long to wait for a god and his promises of 'someday'.* Or maybe I was just trying to justify why I didn't care that I was well on my way to breaking my priestly vows.

But all contemplation of moral nuances ceased once Little Reed started moving down my body, kissing my collarbone, kissing my breasts. When he slid his fingers down between my thighs, the longing inside me stretched tight as a bowstring. Now all I needed was an arrow. *And no limp lizards here to disappoint us this time,* I thought as I worked my hand inside his loincloth. Stroking him with increasing urgency, I whispered, pleading, "Now?"

He untied my undergarment, and I'd just relieved him of his when the copper bells on the outer tent flap jangled loudly. "Come out here and pay respects to your new king, Topiltzin!" Red Flint called out.

Chapter Twenty-Four

For an exhilarating moment, I thought Little Reed was going to go forward as if Red Flint wasn't there, but when Red Flint shouted, "Don't make me the come back there and drag you out of bed!" Little Reed cursed under his breath then rolled away from me.

He pulled the blanket over to cover me then whispered, "I'll be back in a moment." He donned his robe then slipped out through the flap, taking extra care to make sure it closed behind him. I desperately wanted to tell Red Flint to go to Mictlan and leave us alone, but I was too breathless to speak. "Just because I have an anteroom doesn't mean you may barge in unannounced," Little Reed snapped.

"As your king, I will barge in wherever I want," Red Flint answered.

"What do you wish of me, Your Majesty?"

"I'm informing you that I'm marching the full army back to Xochicalco in two days, and I require you to return with me."

"I was already planning to go back, but if you require my help, I'm at your disposal."

"I don't require your help, but as your king, I'll demand it if need be."

"I'll of course serve as you see necessary." The patience strained in Little Reed's voice. "And I trust you'll return the favor once I confront my uncle to take back what's mine?"

Red Flint didn't answer immediately. "I'm amicable to it. But have you given further thought to our discussion regarding Quetzalpetlatl?"

"Brother!" Mazatzin muttered, barely audible.

Little Reed's voice now took on a defensive edge. "My sister makes her own decisions. I'm not going to force her, and neither will you."

I smiled, my heart warming all the more.

Red Flint's voice came closer now. "It would be a pity if you lost your chance to reclaim your throne because of a stupid decision concerning a woman."

"Selling her off for a shaky alliance would be far worse. I haven't hundreds of sisters whom I couldn't care less about; I have one who means far too much to me to see her sequestered in a life of misery."

"How dare you say I'd make her miserable—?"

"Then respect her choice, just as I do!"

I imagined them preparing to tear into each other like that time long ago, but thankfully Mazatzin stepped in again. "Brother, there are far more pressing matters we should be concerned about, don't you agree?"

Red Flint huffed, but he sounded calmer now as he moved away. "We'll discuss this once I've taken care of my throne, but in the meantime, you will coordinate the departure. There's much to do and little time to do it, so get dressed and join me outside immediately. Keep me waiting and I'll have you lashed for disobedience." The bells on the tent jangled as he left.

"A thousand apologies for my brother, My Lord," Mazatzin said, then left as well.

Little Reed finally came back, but he didn't look at me. "I'm sorry, but the king needs me tonight."

Draping the blanket over my shoulders, I stood to hug him. "It's all right. Duty before pleasure." I kissed him on the cheek. "We'll have plenty of time for that."

He sighed. "It's best we wait; I'm not in any position to change the rules of the priesthood yet, and if I got you with child...." He sighed. "Someday...."

His choice of words unnerved me. "We do have to think about the future for everyone, not just for us," I said, guilt creeping up.

"I'll do everything I can to make sure we can be together soon. We've waited a long time already."

I handed him his loincloth. "Better get dressed, before Red Flint comes looking for you again."

He kissed me gently for a moment, making the desire geyser up again, clouding my mind, but next thing I knew he was dressed again and on his way out of the flap. "Get some sleep. It's going to be a long trip back to Xochicalco." He smiled, then left.

My heart thudded so hard I felt dizzy and had to sit down. I hadn't felt tired before, but with the desire fading, my exhaustion showed itself. I slipped under the blankets and inhaled the sweet tobacco and copalli scent permeating the fibers; oh, how much I missed Little Reed, and all too soon I'd have to say goodbye all over again.

¤

I slept late, awakening when I heard the bells tinkling on the tent flap outside. I heard Citlallotoc send off the guard; then he said, "If anything good comes of that man finally taking the throne, it's that he'll no longer be strutting around camp like a dog that doesn't know it's going to be dinner. None of the other kings are pleased with his appointment, surely you know?"

"I think they all hoped he'd get himself killed with his recklessness, forcing Mocnelitzin to take his place," Little Reed answered. "Unfortunately, an even less honorable man is sitting on the throne. I never thought Red Flint would ever be the lesser of two evils."

I pulled my dress on over my head and peeked through the tent flap. Little Reed was lighting his copalli burner while Citlallotoc paced the room like an inpatient jaguar.

"If Red Flint fails, Mazatzin could still challenge for the throne," Citlallotoc said. "We should encourage him to remain behind, just in case."

Little Reed nodded. "I shall speak with him about it, but he's not the kind of man to leave Red Flint to do this on his own. His sense of honor is too good for that."

"It just may get him killed." Citlallotoc stared at the tent wall a moment, then said, his voice lowered, "You know, more than half the army would march at your side if you asked—"

"Take care with your words," Little Reed warned. "Now's the time to get behind Red Flint."

"It shall be done, My Lord. Shall I get us some food?"

"I'm eating with Quetzalpetlatl." Little Reed inhaled the white smoke swirling off the copalli burner, and smiled.

Citlallotoc failed to hide his disappointment. "I'll be off then, My Lord."

"When we arrive in Xochicalco, I'd like it if you'd come to eat with my family," Little Reed said. "My mother should know my best friend."

A shadow of a smile crept to Citlallotoc's face. "I'd be honored, My Lord."

Once Citlallotoc left, I pulled aside the flap. "I believe you've made him the happiest he can be without a wife."

Little Reed laughed. "Did we wake you?"

"No, but some food sounds great."

Over fish tamales, Little Reed told me about his day following Red Flint as he spoke with his generals, making plans. They'd also visited the other armies' generals, who all assured Red Flint that he had their kings' full support and that they would march on Xochicalco with him if need be. "Though they all looked relieved when he told them it wasn't necessary," Little Reed said. "He's so sure of himself."

"To a fault," I told him with a laugh.

"At least he's decided Mazatzin should be appointed the new high priest in Ahexotl's place."

I choked. "That's my decision, not his."

"You already told me you wanted Mazatzin to take the position."

"Yes, but the king doesn't have that kind of power over the priesthood. Red Flint is about as versed in the desires of the gods as I am at the art of spitting tobacco."

Little Reed laughed. "Mazatzin will set him straight when the time comes, but for now let it lie."

Little Reed slept the rest of the afternoon, and I passed the time playing patolli by myself. I wished I had some weaving to keep my mind off thoughts of climbing into bed with him, if only to snuggle and see how tired he really was. These were foolish thoughts though; in my heart I was glad that Red Flint had come when he had, before treacherous desire made us do something I would regret later. Yes, I wanted Little Reed badly, but the thought of getting with child terrified me.

I'd thought I was over that fear, but then last month, one of Cuitlapanton's concubines died in the childbed while I was trying to deliver their baby. I still didn't know what had gone wrong; the baby had been safely wrangled from the gods when suddenly the mother started bleeding like a deer at the slaughter. And nothing I did stopped the bleeding. Eventually I had to have Ixchell take over for me as the poor woman slipped away, for the memories of that night with Mother jumped on me like a silent assassin and my own helplessness rendered me dumb and useless. The nightmares I hadn't had since I was girl plagued me for the next couple of weeks, and I couldn't believe I'd once been so foolish as to actually try to get pregnant by Red Flint.

But did I dare tell Little Reed my fears and risk him deciding that he would be a fool for marrying me?

Once Citlallotoc came back at nightfall, I tidied up the tent and packed a change of clothing for Little Reed while he donned his cotton armor and discussed plans with Citlallotoc.

"I can arrange a litter for you," he told me as he tied his sacrificial blade sheath to his belt.

I tied his cape at his shoulder. "I prefer to walk, actually."

"Red Flint wants me to lead the jaguar knights, so I'll have Citlallotoc walk with you. He'll look after you."

I laughed. "Look after me?"

Little Reed blushed, and Citlallotoc said, "Soldiers can be crass, especially when they're more used to the company of courtesans than Ladies. Your brother just doesn't want you to feel threatened among them."

With a smile, I told Little Reed, "If it'll put you at ease, then I welcome Citlallotoc's company."

"It would, thank you." Once Citlallotoc stepped outside, Little Reed pulled me into a passionate kiss, and I wondered if now would be a good time to talk to him about my worries; but as happened so often when the desire took hold, the world and all its concerns seemed to melt away. There was no past, no future, just the moment. Nothing else mattered.

The world had never felt more perfect.

¤

Citlallotoc frowned at the large litter in the middle of the staging area. "Red Flint borrowed it from the king of Tultepec," he answered when Little Reed asked where it came from. "He said he can't strain himself walking back to Xochicalco like a common soldier."

Red Flint had accumulated significant plunder over the years, most of it packed into wicker baskets. Seven Chichimec women stood among the bounty, each dressed in little more than loincloths, shown off like jewels and treated no better than turkeys.

Red Flint strutted out of his tent but stopped like a startled deer when he saw me. Little Reed slid in front of me, breaking his line of sight, then swept his fingers across the ground. "All's ready for your departure, My Lord."

"Good." Red Flint stepped around Little Reed to approach me. He bowed. "It's a pleasure to see you again, Lady Quetzalpetlatl. I dare say the love goddess Xochiquetzal paid you a blessed visit, for your beauty exceeds words."

I wanted to sneer but instead smiled back, remaining cordial. He wasn't just a prince anymore. "It's a pleasure to see you again as well, Lord Red Flint. Or should I say Your Majesty?"

"From your lovely lips, I much prefer Red Flint. Please, allow me to help you into your litter."

"I'm not traveling by litter."

"Nonsense! The daughter of my father's best friend won't walk like a commoner. You must ride in the royal litter."

Little Reed stiffened but said nothing. *Nor would it be wise to humiliate Red Flint in front of his men,* I thought. Red Flint was waiting for my answer, looking intense. "Far be it for me to reject the kind offer of my king."

Red Flint smiled and took my hand to help me up into the royal litter. I stole a glance at Little Reed to find him whispering to Citlallotoc, who was nodding. "Make yourself comfortable and I'll join you once we're ready to leave." Red Flint motioned Little Reed to follow him as he went down the line, inspecting the baskets and his soldiers.

"I doubt Lord Red Flint would be foolish enough to try anything unbecoming where everyone could hear him, but I'll be here should you need anything." Citlallotoc looked over at Red Flint, then added, "Don't hesitate to call on me, My Lady."

I smiled. "I can handle the king."

◻

Once Red Flint climbed inside the litter, he tried to close the curtains, but I grabbed his hand. "It's stuffy in here," I said.

Red Flint grinned as he lounged back on the blankets next to me. "You must be happy to see your brother again after so long," he said after we'd ridden in silence for a while. "And as you can see, he's done very well for himself."

"He has," I agreed.

"He does all this for you, you know?"

"Does all what?"

"All this fighting and recruiting. He wants to be king for your benefit, to make sure you're taken care of. It's all that matters to him."

I wrinkled my brow, wondering what possessed him to speak as if he knew—let along respected—Little Reed.

"He'd do anything for you, even throw away his chances at his throne." Red Flint held a bowl out to me. "Fried grasshopper, My Lady?"

I held up my hand, struggling to keep the look of loathing off my face. *He thinks he can use guilt to persuade me to marry him, does he?* Yet when I thought about Little Reed never regaining Culhuacan's throne because Red Flint refused to help him—

Give yourself over to this man you hate and abandon any hope of ever being with Little Reed? I shook away the creeping guilt. Perhaps I shouldn't have accepted Red Flint's hospitality after all.

He spent the day plaguing me with stories of his many battle victories and near-death escapes. "I was in Chichimec hands twice, and once put upon their sacrificial stone, but both times the Feathered Serpent sent men to rescue me. He is the greatest of all the gods."

But the arrogance on his face told a different story. Who did he think he was fooling with his lip service?

The litter's constant bobbing combined with Red Flint's prattle exhausted me, and it took more energy than I had to keep from nodding off.

"You look very tired," he noted after he'd gone through the list of war booty he'd claimed. "I imagine the journey to camp took much out of you."

"It wasn't so bad. Priestesses are tougher than most people would think."

"I wasn't demeaning your physical prowess, My Lady." Red Flint smiled. "I know better."

"I prefer manual labor to lazing around," I replied. "I'm not made for a life of luxury."

"I wouldn't say that, but yes, it must be tiring to be a noblewoman, as my mother can attest. How is she? She and Father were very close, so I imagine his passing hit her hard."

"I haven't seen her in weeks, but I know she'll be glad you're returning. As will Turquoise Bells."

His smile wavered. "I'm sure many of my sisters will be pleased to see me again. I, however, am more looking forward to seeing you again every day, as the next high priestess of Xochicalco. I'm lucky; my father had only an old woman to look upon all these years."

"Nimilitzli is very beautiful," I said, biting back the urge to snarl the words.

His smile turned catlike. "You should rest, for I'd like you to join me for dinner tonight, and it won't do for you to fall asleep in your food." He jumped from the litter after calling for a halt. "Sleep well, My Lady." He bowed, then closed the curtains.

I situated myself under the blankets, glad to finally be able to rest. *And to think you tried to marry yourself to that braggart.* I felt luckier than ever that fate had saved me from that unfortunate future.

¤

Over dinner in Red Flint's tent, Little Reed suggested that Red Flint should put away his royal regalia and disguise himself as a common soldier and march with his ranks when we reached Xochicalco. "Let Obsidian Eagle believe the assassins killed both you and Mazatzin," Little Reed said. "We'll send a runner ahead to tell Obsidian Eagle that Camaxtli and Oquitzin haven't been heard from in months and that they're presumed dead. I'll say I'm bringing the army back to pledge loyalty to Obsidian Eagle as the new king. Then the four of you can ambush him when he's feeling relaxed."

"I suppose that's as good a plan as any," Red Flint conceded. He'd been furious when Little Reed rejected his idea of marching into the city with full pomp. And even now it was obvious Red Flint didn't like this plan but had no better suggestions. I wanted to tell him to stop pouting and that he'd get his royal reception eventually, but Little Reed had worked too hard to get him this far just for me to ruin it all with a nasty comment.

"I know you think hiding is dishonorable, but we're dealing with a dishonorable man," Little Reed reminded him. "If he knew you were coming he'd send more assassins, or worse yet force you to lay siege to your own city. Let him believe all went according to his plan, and then you can jump out and challenge him in fair hand-to-hand combat, may the best warrior win. There is nothing dishonorable in that."

Red Flint harrumphed but said nothing more about it. When Little Reed and I stood to leave, Red Flint said, "I would like to speak with you before you retire, Lady Quetzalpetlatl."

"What for?" Little Reed asked.

Red Flint glared at him. "It doesn't concern you, unless you've changed your mind about allowing your sister the freedom to make her own choices?"

Little Reed glared back, but I touched his shoulder. "I'll be fine."

When Little Reed finally turned to go, Red Flint added, "And don't listen outside my tent, or I'll have the guards escort you away."

"Of course I wouldn't, Your Majesty," Little Reed replied with a perfunctory bow. "Good night." He shot me another glance then ducked out the tent flap.

"Brothers can be so overbearing," Red Flint said with a smile.

"I appreciate him looking out for me."

"But also not making your decisions for you."

His small talk grated on me. "You said you wished to speak with me about something?"

Red Flint poured two cups of xocolatl from the small steaming pot. "Yes, about something very important." He held one cup out to me but I declined. "I'm sure your brother has told you by now that I'm intending to ask you to be my wife."

"He mentioned it—"

"Before you say any more, allow me to address some concerns I'm sure you have. First, the little matter of my...poor showing, that evening in the laundry room. I admit I had a problem for a long time, but now I chew roots every day to cure that. It takes a man to accept he needs help with such things and seek out assistance, wouldn't you agree?"

"I wouldn't argue otherwise, Your Majesty."

"And I'm sure you're concerned about my father having betrothed me to Lady Turquoise Bells. You may be surprised to know that your father first intended to betroth you to me, to strengthen his ties with Xochicalco, but he ended up marrying you to Lord Black Otter to mend a disagreement with Ihuitimal. Our own fathers had intended us to marry, and to be frank, I prefer you to my sister. I'm sure she's grown into a beauty, but she's self-absorbed and never quite grasped concepts of cordiality and public image. Not good qualities in Xochicalco's future queen, wouldn't you agree?"

I'd been listening so as to not appear rude, yet he startled me when he asked me to denigrate Turquoise Bells like this. He probably knew something about our mutual hostility when we were younger and thought I'd willingly take the bait. Well, to Mictlan with him. "I haven't spoken to Lady Turquoise Bells in many years, so I don't know anything about her fitness to be queen."

"I know you're more than up to the task," Red Flint replied. "Your extensive priestly training will help me lead the kingdom in a direction pleasing to the god. The people deserve a strong queen who cares about their welfare, don't you agree?"

"Of course, but Red Flint, I'm not—"

"I know I've been like an angry hornet in the past, and I was completely dishonorable to you before I left. I particularly regret the harsh names I called you for showing common sense in the situation. I beg your forgiveness for that."

"Red Flint—"

"I'm a different man now; battle-hardened, but also appreciative of how the company of a good woman can make me a better man. And you're that woman—no, don't shake your head. You're a very good woman and I love you, so—"

"I've already promised myself to someone else!" I shouted, practically breathless. I immediately snapped my mouth shut, my heart pounding. *You shouldn't have told him that.*

Red Flint stared at me, taken aback. "You lie!" When I didn't answer, he roared, "To whom? Topiltzin said you were free of obligation!"

Without waiting for his dismissal, I ran from the tent. *Fool! Now Red Flint will never help Little Reed reclaim Culhuacan's throne.*

¤

I was almost in tears when I reached my tent to find Little Reed waiting for me. He opened his arms to me, the concern plain on his face, but I couldn't accept his comfort. What if Red Flint had followed me? I couldn't risk him finding out Little Reed was my intended.

Little Reed dropped his arms awkwardly. "Are you all right? Did he do something to you?"

I looked over my shoulder before shaking my head. "I'm sorry, Little Reed. I didn't mean to tell him anything...." The tears finally came.

Little Reed looked around as well, then led me into the trees across from my tent. We zigzagged among the shadows until we reached a clearing next to the lake, where the moonlight shone bright as morning on the water's smooth surface. This time when he pulled me into a hug I didn't resist, welcoming the strength of his arms around me, the smell of sweat and tobacco, his breath warm on the top of my head. "What happened?"

I shook my head, keeping my forehead buried in his chest as I cried, "He kept pushing the issue, no matter what I said, and before I knew it, I just blurted it out, to make him stop."

He stroked my hair patiently. "What exactly did you tell him?"

"I said I was already promised to someone else."

I felt the tension in his body as he kept his voice even, unconcerned. "What did he say?"

I rested my cheek against his chest. "He said you promised I was free of commitment, then he demanded to know to whom I'd promised myself. But I ran from his tent before I could say anything more stupid than I already had."

Little Reed chuckled. "You're not stupid, Papalotl."

"If he finds out it's you—"

"He'll find out eventually anyway," he said. "I don't intend to marry you in secret, as if I'm ashamed of it."

Seeing only laughter in his eyes brought a relieved smile to my face. "Then you're not angry with me?"

"If anything, I'm glad that's out of the way. He should worry about his throne, not who he'll marry when he gets it back. Though maybe I haven't the right to talk, since I'm doing the exact same thing."

"I would still marry you even if you never became king of Culhuacan," I said.

He kissed me gently, his grip on my hand light and undemanding, but still the desire welled up like a jaguar preparing to pounce. I imagined pushing him to the ground and making love to him under Lord Metzli's pale light. I pressed up against him, knotting his cape in my fingers, demanding; and when he parted his mouth from mine, I felt as drunk as I had that night in Teotihuacan so long ago…and strangely hungry despite having just eaten. Often when I fasted for more than a meal or two, intimacy with the god helped take my mind off the hunger, at least for a while, so had the years trained my body to inextricably mesh the two desires together? Still, it troubled me how easily I could forget everything and become so focused on ignoring good sense, all for the possibility of pleasure. *Pleasure that could lead to your death,* I reminded myself.

Little Reed's smile melted away, replaced again with concern. "What's wrong?"

I found it too difficult to look him in eye as I said, "Perhaps I'm not a good choice for a wife, Little Reed."

"Why not?"

"A king needs heirs, and I...." My voice broke.

He set his hands on my shoulders. "You're shaking."

"You need someone who wants children, Little Reed."

After a pause, Little Reed said, "You're afraid that what happened to Mother will happen to you?"

"It's foolish, I know—"

"Not at all. I always thought you'd make a wonderful mother, but I understand."

"You should marry someone who isn't afraid to give you a future."

He shook his head. "Children or no children, I want you, Papalotl. I've loved you so long…forever, it seems, and at the risk of sounding more selfish than the god's chosen high Priest should, you're all that matters to me. I've hated only being able to talk to you in letters these last seven years. I can't count how many times I wanted to just up and go home to you. I'm more powerful with a quill in my hand than a sword anyway, and the turmoil of the battlefield...it's insane, Papalotl, and I don't understand why we do these things to each other. I long for the rational discussions with Nimilitzli, where we solve problems with logic and diplomacy rather than brute strength." He laughed dejectedly then added, "She was right that real war is nothing like what they teach you in the House of Warriors. I wasn't created for such pointless violence."

The raw, exposed emotions on his face broke my heart and I pulled him into a hug of my own. He rested his head on my shoulder with a sigh. "If you find it so difficult...then why not come home?" I whispered.

"Because it's gone too far," he said. "I played by our uncle's rules instead of staying in the priesthood and using faith to turn people against him. I've pushed him into going after you, to get at me, and it has cost so many people their lives. I'm sorry, Papalotl."

I looked up at him. "You can't blame yourself for everything, Little Reed. You did what anyone would have done."

"Yes, but I'm not just *anyone*, am I?"

"No, but you're human, like the rest of us, and we all make missteps. Quetzalcoatl didn't make us perfect."

Little Reed chuckled and looked out over the moonlit lake as he muttered, "No, I don't suppose humanity can be any more perfect than he whose blood gave them life."

The slight against Quetzalcoatl unnerved me, but what did I know about their relationship? Years later I still felt ambivalent about my own father, whom I knew to be anything but perfect.

He sighed. "I will get this done soon, Papalotl. I promise. Then we'll have the peace we all need to move forward. No more waiting." He took my face in both hands and for a moment I thought he was going to kiss me again, but he merely set his warm lips against my forehead and whispered, "We should get back. Morning comes all too soon." A heated flush still traveled lazily up my neck at his touch.

It was on the tip of my tongue to ask him to share my tent tonight, so I could keep him close, but when we reached my tent, Citlallotoc called out to him from further down the row. Little Reed squeezed my hand, and just before he turned away a mask seemed to go up over his face: the vulnerability he'd shown me earlier vanished, hidden behind a facade of absolute confidence and staunchness. How had I not noticed it before? I suspected that tonight had been the first time in many years he'd let it slip away, if only for a little while.

CHAPTER TWENTY-FIVE

The next day I walked among the slaves, afraid to go anywhere near Little Reed, fearing Red Flint might realize that he was my intended and perhaps confront him. I also stayed away from both Mazatzin and Citlallotoc, to spare them from being dragged into this stupid mess. Thankfully, Red Flint didn't come looking for me.

It rained the morning we arrived at Xochicalco and Little Reed and I huddled inside the litter, passing the time in nervous silence. The weather broke around midday as we approached the plain outside the walls. Conch shells sounded from the city, and our frontline soldiers answered with a similar tune. The farmers gathered at the edge of their fields, watching us pass.

"Let's hope Red Flint doesn't rush out too soon," Little Reed said as we came into the city. "When we get there, please remain in the litter. You'll be safer in there once the battle begins."

I swallowed hard. I hadn't thought about there being actual fighting.

The caravan wound through town, towards the palace square. People gathered outside their houses, and the many mothers calling out to their sons and crying reminded me of the joy of seeing Little Reed again after so long.

The soldiers filed into the palace square, spreading out to the edges to make room for all. Those carrying the litter marched to the base of the palace stairs, and once there, Little Reed stepped down and ascended to where both Obsidian Eagle and Ahexotl waited at the top. I sat concealed behind the curtains, peering around from the side, my stomach knotted.

Ahexotl looked ill-tempered as usual but Obsidian Eagle smiled, looking regal in his father's quetzal and turkey-feather headdress, gold-woven sandals, and hummingbird-feathered xicolli. Around his neck he wore the heavy gold necklace Cuitlapanton had worn to that fateful council with Ihuitimal. It forever reminded me of what happened to

Nochuatl, and seeing Obsidian Eagle wearing it now was a taunting reminder of whom he'd betray us to.

Reaching the third from the top step, Little Reed swept his fingers across the step before him. Obsidian Eagle inclined his head. "Thank you for bringing my army back to me, Lord Topiltzin. Your loyalty to Xochicalco is not only noted, but admired."

"You're most gracious, My Lord," Little Reed said. "Culhuacan was my parents' city, but Xochicalco was and always will be my home." Little Reed turned to the crowd behind him, and when he raised his hands all the soldiers went to their knees. "Xochicalco once again has her king!" He bent to one knee too.

But then the four soldiers standing in front of the litter jumped up, swords drawn, and charged the stairs. They wore concealing wooden helmets—a jaguar, an eagle, and two coyotes—but I instantly recognized Mazatzin's bulky build under the eagle head. Red Flint—who wore the jaguar head—leaped over Little Reed's bent body, sword swinging.

Obsidian Eagle had been taking in the scene beyond the litter and only at the last moment saw Red Flint and his brothers coming at him. By the time he shouted for his guards, Red Flint was almost upon him. Ahexotl stumbled out of his bow and took a slash across his chest from Little Reed, turning the cloth crimson along the cut.

The guards rushed forward, wedging themselves between Obsidian Eagle and Ahexotl and their attackers. Obsidian Eagle retreated into the palace, but the guards had to carry Ahexotl.

"I'm not done with you, you abomination to the Feathered Serpent's good name!" Little Reed shouted after him, but when more guards pushed towards him, spears ready, soldiers flooded up the steps to defend him. The guards retreated back to the palace.

Red Flint paced the top step. "Come out and claim Father's throne like a man! Or are you still that bawling little boy Mocnelitzin and I tied naked to the sacrificial stone on the ball court? Come out and fight me, you cowering woman!"

"I told you to wait until the signal," Little Reed snapped. "And you were supposed to come out and challenge him, not drive him into hiding."

"I don't need your lectures! He's a dishonorable dog who would never agree to a faithful duel. I saw my opportunity and I took it."

Obsidian Eagle strode out of the palace, flanked by guards. Ahexotl hobbled behind him, clutching his chest. "I'm not your little dog to whip, Red Flint," Obsidian Eagle snarled.

"Then step away from your nursemaids, draw your sword, and claim Father's throne honorably, you puddle of dog piss."

Obsidian Eagle laughed. "You're a brute of a man who can't even coax a turkey in from the rain. A king should have more skills at his belt than just his arm muscles."

I chuckled to myself. "You should listen to him on that one, Red Flint."

"You'll see all my skills in action right before I lop your head off," Red Flint said.

"Is that what you'll do when Ihuitimal threatens you? Your problem, Red Flint, is that you only know how to stomp on those smaller than you, but Culhuacan's army outnumbers our own now. That makes you a fool."

Red Flint hunched his shoulders like a bear. "Of course you'd speak that butcher's name since it's him you honor, not our family. You and your treacherous priest chose the wrong place to discuss your sedition; you were overheard by someone loyal to Father. Do your guards know that you—not Mocnelitzin—poisoned Father? Do they know you plan to hand our great city over to Ihuitimal?" To Ahexotl, he added, "And do they know that you—old man who defiles his priestesses for his own gratification—do they know that you betrayed our city's god with plans to hand his temple to the Smoking Mirror?"

Ahexotl grinned. "I at least didn't have troubles rising to my plans, Lord Red Flint."

Red Flint made to spring at him, but Mazatzin held him back.

Ahexotl was enjoying this far too much, so I jumped out of the litter and ran up the steps. "After the god showed you mercy by leaving you only a cripple, I'd think you'd have better respect for his power." I stopped next to Little Reed, who in turn went up a step to stand between me and Ahexotl.

Ahexotl sneered. "You speak about the god as if you're his chosen one, but it was you who set fire to the courtyard that night. You burned down half the sacred city trying to murder me, you bitch."

Little Reed pressed forward again but the guards closed around Ahexotl. "You know not whom you meddle with, priest," Little Reed growled. "Quetzalcoatl won't extend mercy to you a second time."

"Then call on your god to punish me, and he can also settle this sticky matter of royal succession. Red Flint and Obsidian Eagle should meet on the Tlachtli court and battle this out like kings of the past. The man with the god on his side will prevail."

"Excellent idea," I agreed. The gods had passed the ritual ball game down to us precisely to settle disputes of honor, particularly among kings, and with Quetzalcoatl on our side, there was no way we could lose. "Your man against ours; one backed by the Feathered Serpent, the other backed only by your bragging, and we'll see who comes out victorious."

Red Flint flinched, but I ignored him.

"Then it's settled," Ahexotl snapped. "Lord Red Flint and Lord Obsidian Eagle shall match wits and skill on the battlefield of the ball court tomorrow afternoon, and the winner claims Xochicalco's throne. The loser says goodbye to his head, and his brothers swear on their honor and the risk of committing treason to abide by the results."

Obsidian Eagle's grin stretched from ear to ear. "I'm glad we're dealing with this like honorable men, Brother. Aren't you?" Red Flint looked sick, and he laughed. "Feel free to set up camp for yourself and your men in the palace square. I'd invite you to stay inside, but I don't trust you to be as honorable a man as myself." He turned and disappeared back inside.

A din of conversation rose and Red Flint turned to the crowd. He feigned a smile when they started chanting, "Hail the rightful king!" He glared at me before following Mazatzin down the stairs into the throng.

"It's about time Ahexotl understood the power he spits in the face of," Little Reed said, still glaring back at the palace.

"He's had it coming a long time," I agreed.

"It should never have come to this."

I cringed. "I'm sorry I stayed your hand back then, Little Reed—"

He shook his head. "I admire your desire to believe the best in people. We just must be mindful not to show so much mercy that it costs us our own lives." He took my right hand and looked down at it. "You're very brave, sacrificing so much for all of us."

I hadn't thought about that part yet, or that I had to think it through by tomorrow afternoon. My stomach churned.

¤

After camp was set, Little Reed accompanied me up to the sacred precinct. My mood lightened at the sight of the temple turning yellow in the day's aging sun, the colorful Feathered Serpent slithering along its side.

Malinalli was sweeping out the hearth when we arrived home. She squealed in delight as she embraced me. "I was sure something terrible had happened when Ahexotl kicked you out of the order and named me your replacement. Where were you?" When she saw Little Reed standing behind me, her cheeks flushed and she bowed her head. "Welcome home, Lord Topiltzin."

"It's good to see you again too," he told her with a smile that sent a spike of jealousy through me. My envy immediately shamed me though, and I could barely meet Malinalli's eyes when I asked her about Nimilitzli, who was sleeping.

"Her cough hasn't gotten any better, but it hasn't worsened," Malinalli answered. "I've been coming by four times daily."

"I'm sorry to have dropped this responsibility on you like this, but I had to leave quickly."

She gave me an understanding smile then turned to Little Reed, who was kneeling next to Nimilitzli. "You can wake her. It's time for her medicine."

I joined Little Reed at Nimilitzli's side as he gave her shoulder a gentle nudge. "Mother, it's time to wake up," he said.

Nimilitzli stirred and coughed. I eased her up to rub her back and when she saw Little Reed, she broke into tears. He smiled and kissed her cheek, letting her cry on his chest a while before she smiled up at him. "My little boy, all grown up and handsome, and home again!" She fingered a long white strand of his hair, then sighed. "Your aging hasn't slowed much, has it?"

"Don't fret, Mother," Little Reed assured her. "I look older than I feel. I have many good years left in me."

Nimilitzli turned to me. "I'm very glad to see you made your journey safely."

"Citlallotoc was an excellent guide, and your sword served me well." I set the weapon on her lap.

She ran her fingers over the carvings, her mind suddenly distant, then smiled and said, "I'm glad it saw proper service again."

"It's a very fine sword." Little Reed picked it up and slapped the flat side against his palm. "Light but sturdy. Whose is it?"

"It belongs to the order. Do you like it?"

"The carvings are exquisite, and it's a good weight. The one Cuitlapanton gave me is heavier and doesn't fit my hand so well."

"Then it's yours."

"Oh no, I couldn't steal from the order—"

"It's hardly stealing, Topiltzin. As the high priestess, it's mine to give to whomever I wish, and I know the sword's previous owner would want you to have it. It just gathers webs hanging in the Council Room, so better it should be carried at your side, helping you bring Quetzalcoatl's worship back to Culhuacan."

"Then I shall carry it with honor and dignity, Mother."

While Malinalli and I cooked dinner, I told Nimilitzli about what had happened outside the palace that afternoon.

"And Red Flint agreed to it?" Malinalli asked. "Obsidian Eagle is the city's leading Tlachtli player. He's on the royal team and practices every day after his priestly duties."

"I don't keep up with the sport," I admitted.

"That's why Red Flint looked like he'd swallowed a leech," Little Reed said with a grin as he smoked his pipe. "When the men would go to the ball court in Tultepec to practice, Red Flint was always busy making rounds of the camp, "overseeing" his army or indulging in the courtesans; you know, 'princely matters'. I'm sure he's regretting that now."

"It won't matter how good he is," I replied. "The god will see him to victory."

"You're going to summon Quetzalcoatl again?" Malinalli's gaze wandered to my hand.

"I'll do what I have to." I didn't want to ruin the evening with anxious thoughts about that, though.

After Malinalli left for her temple duties, Citlallotoc arrived. Little Reed greeted him with an embrace, and after the meal they stayed late into the evening, sharing stories of their military exploits while Nimilitzli regaled Citlallotoc with stories of Little Reed's childhood rivalry with Red Flint. It felt wonderful to laugh and remember times past.

"We haven't heard much from you tonight, My Lady," Citlallotoc said once he'd finished his last story. "Tell me what happened to your fingers?"

"That's nothing, really. It happened the day before we met you and your men over by Acolman."

"Your group was set upon by Chichimecs, right? Did you lose them in the skirmish?"

"Sort of. They'd killed most of the men and had the women cornered atop the Pyramid of the Moon, so I cut off my fingers as a sacrifice to Quetzalcoatl, to ask for his help."

"And he came as a giant fire serpent," Little Reed continued. "Burned down half the city and killed every Chichimec warrior."

Citlallotoc looked from me to Little Reed then back again. "You can summon the god?" Reverence—or perhaps it was fear—shone in his eyes.

"I haven't in years. It costs a great deal to use the power," I said.

"Will you use it tomorrow, to help Lord Red Flint win the game?"

"It's in the god's best interest that Red Flint take the throne."

"Then you'll cut off some more fingers?"

"I haven't decided yet what I'll do." Seeing the worry on Little Reed's face, I added, "But I'll know by morning."

The guards outside jingled the bells then told Little Reed that Red Flint had sent for him. "My king calls me," he said; he kissed Nimilitzli on the cheek, and once Citlallotoc disappeared through the curtain, he kissed my cheek too, though he lingered at mine. "Sleep well, my love," he whispered, and left. I watched the curtain swing a moment before turning back to the room, hoping my face had cooled down.

But Nimilitzli was gazing into her cup of medicine, so I set up my weaving next to her bed, so she could watch me work. "Your brother seems to be getting along just fine out there with the other men," she noted as she sipped. "I'm glad he's made a trustworthy friend like Citlallotoc. That can be a difficult task for the heir of any throne."

"Citlallotoc is a good man," I agreed. She had the distant look in her eyes again, and now that we were alone, I said, "Who did the sword belong to?" When she shot me a sharp look, I added, "You needn't answer if you'd rather not."

She sighed. "No, I've kept this to myself long enough, and honestly, I know I haven't much time left."

My chest constricted. "You have longer than you think—"

"I've always embraced the reality of any situation and I'm not afraid of death, Quetzalpetlatl. I spent my time here well, as attested to by both yourself and your brother, but I haven't walked in two years; and honestly, I'm looking forward to facing Death's road, swimming the Black River, navigating the storm of arrowheads, and scaling the mountain of obsidian blades. In death, even women can be warriors, and I've only lingered here to know that you and Topiltzin will be all right. But it's time for me seek council with the Eater of Filth, so I can ready myself for the next leg of my journey."

I was numb. "Perhaps you're ready, but I'm not."

"You are. I taught you everything I know, and the rest you have to learn for yourself. But there is one last thing I want to tell you."

"I'm always ready to learn from your wisdom, Mother." I tried to be the strong woman she thought me to be, but the tears won out.

Nimilitzli closed her eyes. "I've spent most my life preaching the values of the chaste life to all the young priestesses passing through my tutelage—yourself included—but the truth is I'm not going to Mictlan unbroken."

I blinked, caught off guard. She was the woman who never made a false step, who was completely infallible. I should have felt indignant about all those lectures she'd given me about staying true to our priestly vows, but instead all I could think about was Ahexotl cornering her in some remote part of the priestly gardens— "Who?" I sputtered.

My face must have betrayed my thoughts. "Don't worry; it happened before Ahexotl was the high priest. In fact, it was the former high priest who…well, he was my first love, and my only. I've had my share of fluttery hearts and sweaty palms, but what I felt for Xochimecatl…it was unlike anything I'd felt before, or since." A smile slid onto her lips. "He had one blue eye, 'the color of the ocean', he always told me. My heart still skips to think of him."

I smiled. "He must've been very handsome."

"I found his fierce devotion to the god the most endearing; he too had been committed to serving the god since an early age and we both saw it as our greatest duty. We spent hours in deep discussions of the god and devotion, and ironically, that's what brought us together. We resisted taking the physical path for years, but it became torturous to continue denying our love for each other. It was utter weakness, but truthfully I felt closest to the god in those moments I spent in Xochimecatl's arms."

I thought of all the times I'd spent in the god's arms, wishing he were Little Reed. "The god wouldn't consider you weak," I said.

"Priestesses are supposed to make sacrifices for the god, but as high priestess, we make the hardest sacrifice of all. We should be able to devote ourselves to the god alone in spite of what our hearts feel, and in that regard, I was weak and unworthy."

I disliked the change in her tone. "I've always admired your piety and strength, Nimilitzli, but I admire you even more for knowing this. It gives me hope for myself."

Nimilitzli laughed. "You have the ear of the god himself and are his chosen high priestess, but you doubt your worthiness?"

"This whole chosen future...it's a robe that doesn't fit me as well as I'd hoped. I don't think I can devote myself completely to the god alone." Nor did I want to.

Nimilitzli nodded but then pulled a letter from the basket next to her bed. The copal wax seal on it was broken, but she didn't open it, just held it out to me. "If it gives you any comfort, your brother—son of the god though he may be—feels the same way. He has big plans for the priesthood once he becomes king of Culhuacan."

I nodded, avoiding her gaze. "He told me."

"Then you know what's in the letter?"

"He wants us to rule together as both king and queen, and high priest and priestess of his father's order."

"Have you given him an answer yet?"

I ventured my gaze up at her, fearing disappointment on her face, but there was none. "I've loved him all my life, just as I've loved the god." I sighed, frustrated. "It's not right I should have to make a choice between the two. My loving Topiltzin doesn't diminish my love for the god; it makes it stronger. My mother wished she hadn't had to make that choice either, and it wouldn't have made her any less of a priestess or mother for having been both."

Nimilitzli nodded. "I could never imagine leaving the priesthood, but I also couldn't imagine living without Xochimecatl. That's why we conducted our affair in secrecy." Tears formed in her eyes. "But then a fever took him three winters before you and your brother came to live with me."

My gut twisted. "Oh no!"

Nimilitzli shook her head, lips pursed tight. "For years, I thought it was the god's punishment for having broken our vows, but then he'd never have entrusted me with his only son and his chosen high priestess if he truly thought me an oath-breaker."

"I know for a fact that he thinks very highly of you."

She dried her tears on the sleeve of her night robe. "The god put Topiltzin in this world for a reason, so I trust him not to lead us astray. He's going to change the world for the better, for all of us; both of you will. And it's only appropriate that it should be through love and devotion, strengthening each other. My only regret is that I won't live to see the two of you take the steps that neither I nor your mother thought we could."

Tears swelled my throat closed, so I held her hand tight.

She looked very tired but insisted I go to fetch the high priest of Tlazotlteotl. "I'm in a confessing mood, so I should unburden myself now. I doubt I have enough time left to sin too severely against the gods."

ȹ

I wept all the way down the stairs to the smaller temples, but I dried my eyes before entering the Temple of Tlazotlteotl. I might not wear the robe of the high priestess of Quetzalcoatl yet, but I wanted to appear a wall of great strength. The high priest was meditating, but when I told him the reason for my visit, he agreed to go and see Nimilitzli immediately.

One's final confession was a private time, for what was spoken was for Tlazotlteotl's nourishment only, so I walked through the lower precinct, the guards Little Reed had assigned to me following at a respectful distance. My mind wandered to the sacrifice I had to make by tomorrow afternoon. The conversation with Nimilitzli had given me a clue of what that might be, but how could I abandon my love for Little Reed to make sure that a man who spoke the god's name with a faulty tongue won the throne?

I descended another set of stairs and came upon a ritual ball court. The one where tomorrow's match would take place was next to the palace, while this smaller secondary one was where the peasant teams and young noble boys practiced. It was the very same one where Red Flint and his friends had attacked Little Reed when they were just boys. Paintings of feathered serpents ran the length of both walls in white, red, and green, crushing skulls under their meandering coils. Two stone rings stuck out into the court from the top of both walls. I stood up next to one of them, peering down at the men practicing below.

Red Flint wore his royal Tlachtli gear: a woven yoke to protect his gut and groin; leather elbow and knee pads with a polished curved stone glued to each; and a wooden helmet decorated with white heron feathers. Mazatzin stood next to him, clutching the maroon ball at his side while his brother and Little Reed argued strategy.

"This is stupid," Red Flint snarled as he grabbed the ball from Mazatzin. "You can talk all night about techniques, but I haven't played Tlachtli in seven years. Obsidian Eagle plays every day; that's all he's ever done."

"Had you not tied him naked to the ball court's sacrificial stone when he was just a boy, perhaps he wouldn't have taken such an intense interest in the game," Mazatzin said.

"That was a long time ago!" Red Flint snapped. "We were all just children."

"The deepest wounds never heal, just fester and grow," Little Reed said. "Now continue practicing."

Red Flint grumbled but readied himself. Other men dressed in Tlachtli gear took turns hitting the ball at him, but he only returned one volley before hitting the ground and scraping his chin. He tore his elbow pads off and threw them at the wall, breaking one in half. "I might as well walk to the palace right now and offer my neck to Obsidian Eagle!" When he saw me, he yelled, "You set me up to die so you wouldn't have to marry me!"

"My Lord, rest assured, you're not going to lose," I said, suppressing the urge to laugh at him.

"I had him cornered into accepting my challenge, under my terms, but then you had to go spouting off about the god to Ahexotl."

"Then why didn't you turn down the challenge?"

"And look like a coward? Honorable men don't follow cowards. You gave me no choice and now you've handed my father's throne to his murderer."

How could this pathetic man be worthy of being the next king of Xochicalco? He spewed false faith, always moaning, "Oh Merciful Quetzalcoatl this" and "Thank be the Feathered Serpent that", to look pious, but he had no true belief. He would win tomorrow's match and he would owe it all to Quetzalcoatl, and to me, but he would never acknowledge that. This ungrateful wretch was what I was supposed to sacrifice my future with Little Reed for? It was ridiculous.

But with all his men around, looking uncomfortable, and him looking like a cornered jaguar, this wasn't the time to speak my mind. "Have faith, My Lord," I said, taking great care to moderate my voice. "I was just on my way to the temple to speak with the god, and he will see to the proper victory. I promise you that." I whirled around and left, desperate to be away before my temper got the better of me.

But Little Reed caught up with me. "I don't think you should make any sacrifices right now, Papalotl. You're angry and you might do something you'll regret later."

"I'm fine, Little Reed," I snapped, the rage rising in me. Seeing him flinch, I took a deep breath, ashamed for having let my anger at Red Flint slip out. "I'm not about to do anything stupid on his account." I touched his cheek and whispered, "I'll see you tomorrow, my love." I sealed that promise with a kiss. I expected the usual desire to well up, but instead my insides were boiling with anger.

"Papalotl, please, know what you're doing—"

"I know what I'm doing."

My anger and indignation carried me all the way to the temple and I cleared the two priests out so I could be alone. I cut my palm and bled it into the wooden bowl at my knees, then bowed my head, my anger still bubbling. *Red Flint doesn't deserve to be king, but I said I'd do this. I'll let the god decide what's best, for who should know that better than he?*

"Oh Great Quetzalcoatl,
I need your guidance again.
If Red Flint is truly meant to be king,
Then make him worthy of it.
Protect him tomorrow as he goes into battle for his throne.
Whatever sacrifice you deem necessary,
I will accept.
I trust in you always, My Lord,
And ask you to give me strength."

The anger and tension drained out of me with the words, as if a great weight had been lifted off my chest. I opened my eyes to see the blood gone. *Then he's agreed,* I decided. *But what did I agree to?* For a panicked moment I wondered if he'd frozen my heart, but when I thought of Little Reed, the familiar pleasure raced through my veins. I sighed, relieved. *So long as I still have that, everything will be all right.*

CHAPTER TWENTY-SIX

*W*here is he? I watched the door curtain while I boiled the opossum tail for Nimilitzli's medicine, hoping Little Reed had just slept late. *You should have listened to him last night, and gone to the temple this morning instead of letting your temper do your praying.*

I poured the medicine in a cup and held it out to Nimilitzli, but she shook her head. "I'm going to pass on it today."

"But your cough—"

"It's not bothering me." When I started arguing, she said, "Please humor an old woman. Leave it next to my bed and if I feel the need for it, I'll drink it."

I finally agreed, and promised to come back after the match.

"There's no need to hurry back," she said. "I'm sure you'll have much to celebrate after the game."

My stomach still churned as I headed for the stairs down into the city, but I breathed a sigh of relief when I saw Little Reed sitting on the edge of the cistern. I went over and sat next to him. "You didn't come to eat."

"I had things to do this morning." He didn't look at me.

I didn't know what to make of that, so I said, "We should hurry, so we don't miss the opening of the match."

"I'm not going. Red Flint asked me to make sure Ahexotl doesn't get away." He took my hand and clasped it between his. "Whatever happens, just remember that I love you, and I always have."

"I know you do." Though how he said it disturbed me. I watched him leave, headed for the house, and I was on the edge of going after him, but Mazatzin came over from the calmecac.

"Are you all right?" he asked. "You look upset."

"I'm fine," I replied, forcing on a smile. It seemed to help.

"Then everything is ready? You've spoken to the god?"

"I have."

"Good. I made my own sacrifice as well. You saw Red Flint play last night. He needs all the help he can get."

¤

The palace square bustled with soldiers, citizens, and merchants. People meandered into the sacred ball court with its yellow and white feathered banners fluttering in the wind while a band played drums and flutes for the waiting crowd. Mazatzin took us in through the royal entrance and out to the stone-paved court. "Red Flint asked me to extend his apologies about last night, and to say that he'd like you to sit on the sidelines to cheer for him and tend to his wounds."

"He couldn't apologize himself?" I asked.

"I was concerned that I wouldn't get the chance to before the game," Red Flint said, coming out of the hallway dressed in his Tlachtli gear. He looked like a man who knew the point of backing out of the battle had passed and now he must do whatever he could to escape capture. That alone softened my anger and I accepted his muttered apology. "It means a great deal to me that you think I can do this," he admitted. "I should have as much confidence in myself."

Now wasn't the time to tell him that I had no confidence in him, but instead was betting on the god saving all of us. I just smiled and bowed, wishing him good luck.

The court was three times larger than the other, with gently-sloping walls decorated with reliefs of feathered serpents, which would make for interesting bounces. The polished stone rings near the top of the walls glimmered in the sunshine.

Mazatzin and I sat on the stone bench where the extra players usually sat. "Where's Topiltzin?" he asked.

"Making sure Ahexotl doesn't run for it when Red Flint wins."

Mazatzin cracked a smile. "As if Ahexotl could run."

I laughed, then searched for Ahexotl in the crowd gathered in the seating overlooking the court, but he wasn't there.

Uproarious cheering came when Obsidian Eagle strode out of the hallway opposite us, wearing his father's yellow and white feathered robe and the enormous quetzal-feathered headdress. Red Flint—who'd been pacing by himself—clenched his fists. Slaves hurried the robe off Obsidian Eagle's shoulders, revealing his elegant, jewel-encrusted Tlachtli gear. They also replaced the headdress with an eagle-head wooden helmet with feather-covered flaps over his cheeks.

Lord Spear Fish came out of the same hallway, carrying a maroon rubber ball under his arm. He called both Red Flint and Obsidian Eagle to center court.

Red Flint flashed me a weak smile then ran out to Lord Spear Fish. Obsidian Eagle strolled out, waving to the cheering crowd.

Lord Spear Fish raised his hand, and when he spoke, the crowd fell silent. "The first player to win five points, or to knock the ball through one of the rings, will be the winner."

"I've put balls through them three times myself," Obsidian Eagle announced, smiling up the crowd. "And I intend to make my fourth today." The audience cheered.

"Today will be my first one," Red Flint said. "Though it shall be done with your head." Some whistles and shouts for Red Flint broke out among the laughter from the crowd.

I'd never attended a ritual ball game before, but I'd picked up some of the basic concepts listening to Little Reed talk about it growing up. From what I gathered, different cities played by different rules, depending on their idea of skill and stamina, but certain rules were universal: you couldn't touch a ball in play with hands or feet, and points were scored when the opponent allowed the heavy solid rubber ball to hit the ground. It could bounce as much as it wished on the walls themselves, but not roll, and one couldn't climb the wall to fetch it either. Bouncing a ball through one of the two rings way up on the wall automatically won the game, though it was a rare occurrence. The fact that Obsidian Eagle had done it three times gave credence to him being the best player in all of Xochicalco.

But this is the favorite game of the gods, so once Quetzalcoatl shows up, all of Obsidian Eagle's skills will mean nothing, I thought with a smile.

Lord Spear Fish implored both men to play fair, then he bounced the ball hard into the ground and dashed out of the way.

Red Flint sprang at it, but Obsidian Eagle knocked him backwards. On the ball's downward fall, Obsidian Eagle slammed it with his glittering elbow pad and Red Flint moved his knee to intercept it. The ball hit the ground next to his foot. The crowd broke into frenzied cheers as Lord Spear Fish called the point for Obsidian Eagle.

Red Flint bounced the ball off his knee pad, sending it high. Obsidian Eagle backed up, repositioning himself, then he struck it with his right knee pad, sending it catapulting at Red Flint. Red Flint dove to return it, scraping his shin, but Obsidian Eagle whipped around and sent it flying back at his head. Red Flint scrambled to block it with his yoke, but the ball clipped his shoulder as he came up. It spun off behind him as he crumpled to his knees, holding his arm and gritting his teeth.

Obsidian Eagle leaned over and said something inaudible over the crowd noise, and Red Flint shoved him away and limped to fetch the ball. When he neared the bench, he gave me another angry look.

Trust in the god, you idiot, I thought.

Red Flint put the ball into play as he ran back towards center court. He and Obsidian Eagle exchanged a couple of volleys before Obsidian Eagle kneed the ball into his chest, sending Red Flint to the ground, writhing. Obsidian Eagle leaned over him. "I think he wants to forfeit," Obsidian Eagle crowed, but Red Flint struggled to his feet. Blood poured from a gouge under his kneecap. He picked up the ball and took a deep, pained breath before sending it back into play.

The high, arching serve brought a triumphant smile to Obsidian Eagle's face. He watched the ball as he took three quick steps then threw his left knee into it, sending it flying towards the ring on the right side of the court. The crowd fell silent as the ball sailed, many rising to their feet. My own heart stopped as I followed the ball's progress.

The ball hit the ring's inner rim and ricocheted into the wall. Obsidian Eagle leapt to put it back into play before it bounced off the wall but it hit the ground at his feet. The crowd exploded with hoots and hisses.

"I gave him that point!" Obsidian Eagle shouted, a sneer on his face. "I didn't want him looking so pathetic that he couldn't score at all!"

The crowd laughed.

"That was too close," Mazatzin said, letting out an anxious breath.

I shared his worry. Where was Quetzalcoatl? *Perhaps he didn't accept your stupid not-a-sacrifice after all.*

Obsidian Eagle set the ball into play off his elbow, and Red Flint took one step to intercept it, but then he collapsed, his whole body shaking.

The crowd fell into stunned silence.

Mazatzin sprinted to his brother. I hesitated a moment then followed. Red Flint thrashed on the ground, his mouth foaming and his eyes rolled up inside his head. Mazatzin held him down. "He's having some kind of fit!"

"He's trying to gain pity for himself," Obsidian Eagle accused, keeping his distance. "The point still counts!"

Lord Spear Fish knelt over Red Flint as well. "He's in no condition to play. We'll have to call the game off."

"Then he forfeits, and by the rules, I win."

Lord Spear Fish looked to Mazatzin, but just then Red Flint fell still. He blinked a few times, bewilderment in his watery eyes, but when he saw me, a shadow of a smile crossed his lips. "I'm here, Papalotl," he whispered.

I let out a held breath and bowed my head. "My Lord."

"Are you all right, Lord Red Flint?" Spear Fish asked.

Red Flint blinked a couple of times then sat up. "I just need a moment to gather myself." Mazatzin helped him up; but when they locked gazes, Mazatzin gasped and bowed his head.

Red Flint turned to Obsidian Eagle. "Did you say something about forfeiting?"

Sneering, Obsidian Eagle threw the ball at him, but Red Flint caught it and smiled back. "Whenever you're ready," Obsidian Eagle said.

"You're ready then?"

"More than you'll ever be."

"You're sure?"

"Let's get this over with," Obsidian Eagle insisted.

Red Flint shrugged then played the ball off his knee, right into Obsidian Eagle's face.

The crowd gasped as Obsidian Eagle lay on the ground, holding his bloodied face and moaning.

"You said you were ready," Red Flint pointed out, a whisper of amusement on his face.

Obsidian Eagle rolled to his knees and spat out a couple of teeth with his bloody phlegm. "That's how you want to play?" he snarled, getting to his feet. "Then let's play."

Red Flint backed up and motioned for me and Mazatzin to get out of the way. We both ran back to our bench.

Obsidian Eagle served the ball hard off his knee pad, aiming for Red Flint's crotch, but Red Flint returned it with little effort, sending it sailing high. Obsidian Eagle backpedaled then dove in front of the ball, bouncing it with his knee as he slid sideways. Red Flint jogged backwards a few steps then hit it off his yoke, delivering a light return. Obsidian Eagle scrambled for it, diving belly first to the ground, but it hit the stone in front of his face and bounced off behind him. He lay on the ground, panting as the crowd broke out into ear-piercing cheers of "All hail Lord Red Flint!" starting from the soldiers sitting on the wall behind me.

"I've never seen Red Flint move so fast," Mazatzin said with an excited smile. "I doubt he knew his body could do that."

Obsidian Eagle struggled to his feet, his chest and left leg scraped raw and bleeding. "You need a break to cover your wounds?" Red Flint asked, his voice sincere, but Obsidian Eagle spat at him and snatched up the ball again. He limped halfway to the back of the court then turned and served the ball off his knee. It arched high, towards the right side of the court.

Red Flint moved in the opposite direction, watching it fall towards the wall. It hit and bounced high, and when it came back down, he returned it with his own knee.

Obsidian Eagle stumbled backwards and returned it with his yoke, but when Red Flint headed towards center court for it, Obsidian Eagle ran into him with his shoulder, knocking them both down. The crowd broke out into boos and hisses.

Red Flint never took his eyes off the falling ball though. When it came within reach, he kicked his leg up, striking the ball with his shin. It streaked towards the south wall, towards the ring, bringing the crowd to its feet in a collective gasp. Even Mazatzin leaped off the bench.

The ball hit inside the ring and spun like a leaf in a whirlpool. It eventually fell out the other side, still spinning as it bounced down the wall towards the court. The crowd burst into riotous cheers.

Obsidian Eagle stared at the ball then scrambled to his feet and ran for the exit hallway. But the guards closed ranks across it.

I followed Mazatzin back out to Red Flint, who was lying on the ground, groaning and looking around as if he had no idea where he was. "My Lord, are you all right?" I asked, but when he looked up to me, I saw Quetzalcoatl was gone.

Mazatzin helped Red Flint sit up. "It was the most frightening thing, Brother," Red Flint gasped. "I could see everything, but I couldn't do anything. My very insides burned."

"You'll be fine soon," I said. "The god has left your body."

"The god?" For a moment I thought he was going to vomit, but then shouting distracted him.

Obsidian Eagle was climbing the wall, trying to escape into the crowd, but the people sitting in the front row shoved him back. He struggled against them, but he slipped and fell, rolling and thumping down the wall back to the feet of the waiting guards.

"Seize him immediately!" Red Flint stood up with Mazatzin's help. When Mazatzin handed him his sword, he took off for the guards at a limping run. "Strip him down!" As he came upon the ball, he scooped it up with his free hand.

Obsidian Eagle squirmed as the soldiers tore his equipment off, not even leaving him the dignity of his loincloth. Red Flint broke into a full run the last few lengths, then threw the ball as hard as he could into Obsidian Eagle's chest. Obsidian Eagle gasped and would have crumpled to his knees, but the soldiers held him up, even when Red Flint finished by ramming his stone-padded knee into his crotch. Obsidian Eagle gagged, his mouth hanging open in a silent scream, his eyes bulging and face straining.

I stopped short, keeping a distance from the murmuring crowd around Red Flint. *This is only going to get uglier,* I thought, nausea growing in my stomach. I tried to step backwards but the crowd of soldiers pressed in behind me.

Red Flint shoved Obsidian Eagle to the ground. "Did you really think you'd get away with stealing my throne? Or with killing Father and inviting his greatest enemy to share in the spoils? And did your precious high priest think I'd let him get away with insulting my manhood in front of the entire army?" He whipped around. "Come down here and face your destiny like a real man, Ahexotl! Or did the fire burn that away too?"

"Ahexotl isn't here, Brother," Mazatzin said.

"Coward! Send guards to find that vile excuse for a man immediately!"

"You already sent Topiltzin to do that before the match," Mazatzin reminded him, though Red Flint looked at him as if he spoke a foreign language.

"It's no matter anyway. The true traitor is caught and he shall pay for his crimes now." Red Flint punched Obsidian Eagle across the face then spat on him. "Bring me the sacrificial stone! And some rope," he added with a coyote-like smile.

Two soldiers lugged out a rectangular slab of stone decorated with carvings of ballplayers playing Tlachti with skulls, and when Obsidian Eagle saw it, he broke out into a keening cry that raised the hairs on my neck. It rose louder as the soldiers dragged him to the stone and tied him down, his neck stretched across its concave middle. "Have mercy, Brother! Ahexotl tricked me! I trusted him as a friend but I see now that he wanted the throne for himself! He's the true traitor, Brother! Have mercy, I beg you!"

Red Flint stepped up to him. "I am having mercy on you. I could have my soldiers molest you like a war prize in front of the entire city, but I'll spare you that humiliation." He poised the sword blade over Obsidian Eagle's neck. "And you're no brother of mine, you little maggot." And he brought the blade down.

I flinched, suddenly drowning in that same feeling I had whenever I dreamed of my father's murder, or when I saw the sacrifices dying for the god—sacrifices the god didn't want.

It took two swings to behead Obsidian Eagle—one with each side of the sword, for half the obsidian blades shattered after the first hit—but once it finally fell, Red Flint picked up the head and threw it at the north courtside ring. It hit the wall, splattering gore before rolling back down to the ground.

Everyone fell to their knees around Red Flint, but then Mazatzin rose again and shouted, "Bring forth King Cuitlapanton's royal robe and headdress!" He beckoned me to join him next to Red Flint.

My sense of duty made me obey, but every hair on my neck stood up when Red Flint draped his arm over my shoulder as if we were friends.

Two slaves hurried through the crowd with the pieces of the royal garb. Mazatzin helped Red Flint into the yellow and white robe and I placed the quetzal feather headdress on his brow. The men rose and shouted his name, raising their swords and fists in the air. He smiled and raised his hands too, glorying in their chant, looking every bit the king.

¤

"Why wasn't Topiltzin at the match?" Red Flint asked as he lounged on his reed throne, a dozen serving women washing his wounds and combing his hair. Mazatzin sat on the high priest's mat next to him, smoking his pipe as he scribbled on a piece of parchment. I could have taken the high priestess's mat on Red Flint's other side, but he was still on edge and stared at me as though he thought I'd set the god upon him rather than helped him win the match. "Stop pulling my hair!" he snapped at one of the serving girls, looking ready to hit her.

"He was out finding Ahexotl, just as you'd ordered, your Majesty," I reminded him.

Red Flint thought a moment then said, "Oh yes, I did. Didn't I?" He looked at Mazatzin, who nodded in confirmation. "Well, maybe I did or maybe I didn't. My head is out of sorts right now."

"There's been far too much excitement for all of us," Mazatzin said.

"I'm thinking of putting him on my war council, you know?" Red Flint rambled on. "So I can consult him on important matters. He'll be honored by the offer."

An administrative role would put an indefinite hold on Little Reed's plans to reclaim Culhuacan; surely Red Flint's way of keeping control of when he could march on Ihuitimal. That was the last honor Little Reed needed.

"And of course, my dearest brother will be the next high priest, now that Ahexotl has forfeited his life," Red Flint went on.

I couldn't remain silent about that though. "Traditionally the high priestess chooses the next high priest, Your Grace."

Red Flint ignored me. "You should bring Nimilitzli to pledge loyalty to me and counsel me about these rituals I must perform prior to my coronation."

"I will do that for you, your Majesty—"

"I'd rather the high priestess do it," he interrupted. "Let's maintain tradition."

I bit back the barb on my tongue. *Fine, fetch Nimilitzli and she'll set him straight. He's always been afraid of her.* "I'll go tell her of your wishes, Your Majesty." I bowed, then left the Great Hall.

Mazatzin jogged out after me and called for me to stop. "Please excuse Red Flint," he whispered. "He's impetuous—we both know that—but I'll speak with him about proper protocol and authority. He'll listen to me; he always has."

"Tell him he'd do well to remember who put him on his throne. He must keep his hands out of the order's concerns, like choosing the next high priest."

"I'll remind him." I turned to leave, but he set a hand on my shoulder. "If you don't believe me to be the right candidate, I'll gladly step aside—"

"You're absolutely the right choice," I assured him. "You were born for the position and I'm glad to see you finally receive what you deserve."

Mazatzin bowed his head. "Thank you for your confidence in me."

"You're the best and most loyal friend, and I'm honored to have you at my side."

"The honor is all mine."

I sighed, exasperated. "Will you let me praise you for once and just accept it?"

"Well, if you insist," he said with a smile.

I headed up to the sacred precinct, to share the good news with Nimilitzli, and hopefully get some even better news from Little Reed. Finally Ahexotl would pay as he should have long ago.

Strange how things just go on as normal, I thought when I reached the summit to find the novices gathered around the cistern, talking over their afternoon break. *That's because priests are strong and they persevere regardless of the circumstances,* I told myself with pride.

"What do you want to eat, Nimilitzli?" I asked as I elbowed aside the curtain. "I'm thinking something celebratory, something with meat...."

But my words trailed off when I saw the blood splashed across the far wall like a red sunset. My stunned gaze immediately fell to Nimilitzli, lying face down on the floor next to her mat. Slashes and deep rents left her looking more like a butchered animal than a human being.

My stomach heaved and I vomited, bringing myself to my knees. I looked up at her again, bewildered, my mouth raw. "Mother?" I whispered.

She didn't answer.

Hearing shuffling behind me, I turned, only to receive a heavy blow to the head that knocked me into darkness.

Chapter Twenty-Seven

Pain dragged me awake and I had no idea where I was; my back was hot, but when I tried to move away, intense pain shot up my right leg. I grabbed my thigh and my hand came back covered in blood. I tried again to stand, but my foot dangled lifeless at my heel.

"Difficult to move, isn't it?" Ahexotl asked. Seeing him sitting in the corner behind the doorway, the nightmare rushed back at me: the blood on the walls, Nimilitzli's cloven remains, the reek of death in the air.

My eyes watered. "Topiltzin will kill you for this."

"He's going to kill me anyway, so what does it matter? I've waited seven years for justice, and I'll die with a smile on my face." He hobbled over to me, relish in his eyes.

I tried again to get up but he grabbed my hair and shoved me back down. "Help me!" I screamed, but he clamped his sweaty hand over my mouth.

"Save it for when the flames are eating you," he panted, then shoved me.

I grabbed the hearth's outer lip with both hands and pushed back hard. He punched my stomach, knocking the wind out of me, and I finally fell in, but I caught his robe and dragged him in with me.

"Ayya!" he cried, flailing to catch hold of the hearth's opening. I groped around to pull myself back, but when I finally found solid purchase, he yanked us both out, shrieking, "Get off me, you bitch! Get off me!" I finally let go and he slumped to his knees, holding his groin. "You filthy whore!" He grabbed a flaming log and flung it at me.

It hit the side of my face, but the pain was only a distant cry in my head as I crawled behind Nimilitzli's body. He threw another and it missed me, but the bright tinder set the sleeping mat smoldering. I slapped at it, but tiny flames began jumping up with alarming speed.

Ahexotl lumbered towards me and tripped over Nimilitzli, crushing me under him. I tried to claw my way out but he closed his fists around my neck. I raked him across both cheeks, leaving trails of oozing blood. "I'll see you on the path to Mictlan and I'll bend you over Lord Death's sacrificial stone and have my way with you while he eats your heart!" He started squeezing, euphoria spreading over his face.

Blood pulsed in my head. I went for his eyes, but couldn't reach them, so I beat on his sides. He only seemed to enjoy my struggling. Panic swooped in and I groped around for any part of him I could claw or twist to make him loosen his grip.

By the god's grace, my fingertips found the smooth handle of the sacrificial blade hanging at Ahexotl's belt. I pulled at it until it dislodged from the sheath, then I gripped it tight and plunged it into his ribs.

His eyes bulged in surprise but he didn't loosen his grip, even when I twisted the blade. I took another jab at him, this time going for his neck.

I missed my mark but buried the blade in the fleshy jowls hanging over his jaw. This time he let go to grab the knife, looking half-dazed. Able to breathe finally, I found a second burst of energy and stabbed him again, this time squarely hitting his neck. The next time I impaled his hand as he tried to shield himself from me. With my last strike I opened his jugular, and the shooting blood splattered wide across the wall behind me.

Ahexotl clutched the blade, blood streaming over his hands. He got it halfway out before his fingers slipped off the handle and he stared down at me with astonishment. His gaze wandered up and he flinched.

I turned my head to see the Black Dog standing in the corner, watching us.

"How was one to know?" Ahexotl gasped, and fell over sideways.

The Black Dog peered down at me. *This is what you get for not being strong enough to make the necessary sacrifice,* I thought, closing my eyes and waiting to feel his tongue on my cheek. *It probably feels like a blade of ice, cutting through flesh and severing all mortal bonds. I pray Little Reed isn't the one to find my body.*

¤

When I came to again, I recognized the weapons hanging on the wall of the Council Room in the calmecac. Malinalli leaned over me, her harried expression changing to ecstatic relief. "Quetzalpetlatl? Can you hear me?" She leaned closer.

"Little Reed," I whispered, my mouth tasting like ash. The strong smell of burning flesh stuck in my nose. "Where's Little Reed?"

"Who's Little Reed?" Malinalli asked.

"He's Lord Topiltzin," Ixchell answered. She was tending to my injured foot. "We'll try to find him for you, High Priestess, but for now, rest."

I shook my head and tried to sit up. "We must save Nimilitzli. The house is on fire—"

Malinalli pushed me back down. "It's too late, Quetzalpetlatl," she whispered, tears in her voice. "She was already gone by the time we found you."

I overflowed with tears. "I must see Little Reed. He must know what's happened." And why didn't he get to Ahexotl before that monster could butcher Nimilitzli?

"I'll find him." Malinalli had me choke down some tochtetepon and octli. "Ixchell's going to try to fix your heel. Everything's going to be all right."

"Tell him I must see him immediately," I pleaded, holding onto her hand as she stood to leave.

She gently removed my fingers from her wrist. "I promise I will."

I didn't remember falling back asleep, but Malinalli wasn't at my side again when I awoke much later, and my throbbing heel made the knife wound in my leg seem like an annoying insect bite. Ixchell soon gave me another dose of tochtetepon and I fell back into dreamless sleep.

◻

I stayed asleep most of the next couple of days, hardly aware that time passed. Coming down off high doses of yauhtli took a while, and though Ixchell stopped pouring it down my throat by the second morning, I still slept as if I hadn't rested in days. Dreams slowly returned, fuzzy at first, but then taking on terrible coherence; I came home to find Little Reed as mutilated and dead as Nimilitzli. I awoke with a start, shaking and sweating.

"You're all right," Malinalli whispered, gently stroking my back. "It's just a dream."

I looked around, my heart slowing again. I sat in her bed in her house, and she'd laid out an extra mat next to the hearth where she usually kept her weaving. I clutched my stomach as it battled back and forth between nausea and hunger, and she brought me a warm tlaxcalli. "Eat slowly.

You've had nothing but yauhtli and water for almost two days."

I gritted my teeth at the stiff pain as I sat up. "I feel like I'll never walk again," I panted, out of breath already.

"Ixchell thinks you'll get most of your foot's mobility back again, but you'll probably have a limp, and some difficulty running. You should move it as much as you can, so the muscles don't freeze."

I did so, despite the extreme pain in my tendon. I felt faint. "Has Topiltzin been by to see me yet today?"

Malinalli's gaze dropped. "About Topiltzin, Quetzalpetlatl...."

I tightened my grip on the tlaxcalli until it was crumbling between my fingers. "Is he all right?"

She hesitated then said, "Mazatzin wanted to talk to you as soon as you were awake, so I'll go and get him." She cast a worried glance back at me before hurrying out the curtain.

I sat in stunned silence the whole time she was gone, thinking about the nightmare. "That's all it is," I assured myself, but already I felt myself dying inside.

When Mazatzin arrived, the pained smile on his face told me everything I needed to know. He kept his hands behind his back as he said, "Feeling better? Make sure you're doing your ankle exercises, even if it hurts."

"What are you hiding?" My own voice sounded distant.

He hesitated. "I hate being the bearer of such news, but...you risked your life to tell me of my father, so it's only right I return the favor." He finally brought his hands around and held a sword out to me.

I immediately recognized it as the sword Nimilitzli had given to Little Reed. It was covered in dried blood. I felt like someone was throttling me all over again as I took it with trembling hands. "What happened?"

"He didn't report to the palace after the match, and no one knew where he was, so Red Flint sent troops out to find him." He struggled to speak before finally continuing. "They found his remains out in the limestone quarry, burned. We caught those who did it—and Red Flint executed all of them, but...I know that's little comfort. If we'd only known earlier...."

Or I could have made the hard decision and none of this would've happened. Now I wished I'd let Ahexotl choke the life from me. *This time it's all my fault.* I doubled over, unable to hold back the tears any longer.

Mazatzin put his arms around me and whispered comforting words, but I didn't deserve any of them.

◻

Malinalli cared for me while I recovered from my physical injuries, but the others—the ones I buried deep and showed no one—for now there was no helping them. Losing Mother and Father had taught me that though such wounds healed with time, there would always be the ghost pains, like the ones I sometimes felt in my hand.

For now I focused on putting it out of my thoughts with work. I officiated over Nimilitzli's funeral, using the strength she'd taught me to encourage my priests and priestesses to trust in the god to lead us through this dark time. Mazatzin and I buried Nimilitzli's ashes under the stone floor of the temple.

He offered to let me officiate over Little Reed's funeral, but everything I wanted to say was private. I suggested that Citlallotoc give the speech, but no one had seen him since the day of the match. I wondered if he even knew.

Red Flint rambled at length to the crowd gathered in the rain about Little Reed's valor and intelligence, but he stared at me when he started talking about my brother's dedication to family. "Everything he did was for the benefit of his poor, orphaned sister, she who meant everything to him, she whom he leaves behind alone. May she find his tremendous strength in herself to take up the mission he leaves unfinished."

I'd been so busy transitioning to being the official high priestess and preparing for the funerals that I hadn't given any thought to what would become of Quetzalcoatl's plans now that his son was dead. Who would overthrow Ihuitimal and bring the Feathered Serpent's worship back to the people?

Long ago war queens did rule the Tolteca, but those times were dead and I was already at the top of what women could achieve. The people demanded a king, but in my carelessness I'd cost them the future they deserved. Would Quetzalcoatl expel me from his priesthood for this? That was all I had left anymore, and the thought that he might take that away from me.... *I can never face him again. My service is the only thing getting me through this now.*

"The king wants to see you," Mazatzin said, interrupting my thoughts. The Great Hall was mostly empty after the mourning feast, with only a handful of nobles sitting near the hearth, smoking pipes. Red Flint wasn't there though.

I handed my bowl of cold food to one of the servants. "What does he want?"

Mazatzin looked away, grumbling under his breath. "I told him the whole marriage issue is pointless since you're the high priestess now, but he insists on talking to you about it."

"But he's marrying Turquoise Bells at the end of the week."

"Mother said if he could gain your consent, she wouldn't object."

Mazatzin said little as he led me out into the torch-lit garden, down a stone path to a circle of carved wood benches. Red Flint paced between them, muttering, but he stopped when we approached. Mazatzin cast him a hard glare then left.

"Thank you for seeing me, My Lady," Red Flint said. "If I might be so bold, you're looking better these days. You seem to be walking well on that foot now."

"It's getting better," I acknowledged.

"Wonderful, wonderful." He gazed around nervously before saying, "I never did extend my condolences on your loss. Truly tragic, My Lady."

He could ramble all day about my injured leg or the weather, but I wouldn't talk about either Nimilitzli or Little Reed. "Forgive my bluntness, My Lord, but I have temple duties before dawn."

"Of course. I'll get directly to the matter. I know you meant a great deal to your brother and he'd want someone to step up and look after you now that he's gone on to Mictlan—someone who would also look after his affairs here on Earth. I can be that man, Quetzalpetlatl."

His words felt like knives stabbing my throat.

"It makes perfect sense. Ihuitimal wouldn't stand a chance against my army if I ordered a full assault on Culhuacan. Marry me and I'll go to war to reclaim your father's stolen throne; it's my wedding present to you, and when our eldest son comes of age, he can rule Culhuacan until I pass on, then another of our sons will take his place there. I'll finish what Topiltzin started; I will be his replacement."

For all his sincerity, those last words snapped the fragile string holding my mask of politeness in place. "Have you any idea why Topiltzin was here to begin with? Why Quetzalcoatl put him in my mother's belly and gave him life?" Red Flint tried to say something but I cut him off.

"Getting Culhuacan's throne back...that's merely a small mark on the battle plan Quetzalcoatl laid out. Topiltzin was going to be the king of all Tolteca and end human sacrifice in the valley, bringing everyone together in peace and prosperity and leading us all into a great new age. And you—who scoff at the god's power as if it's nothing—you believe yourself worthy of being both the people's high king and the god's high priest?"

Red Flint went livid. "Who do you think you are, daring to defy the request of your king?" he snarled.

"I am the high priestess of the god, chosen by the lips of the god himself; the god who put you on your throne. And if you're not careful, he will withdraw support for your reign."

"How dare you threaten me?" He lumbered at me.

I backed a few steps and drew my knife, holding it poised over my palm. "All I have to do is cut, Red Flint, and you can discuss this with Quetzalcoatl himself." My voice quaked.

Anxiety danced in Red Flint's eyes and for a moment I thought he was going to call my bluff, but he stepped back, his face pale as he realized what had almost happened. "Get out of my sight." The rage had drained from his voice, leaving him raw and vulnerable.

I sheathed my sacrificial blade then hobbled off, not looking back.

◻

I prayed in front of the Feathered Serpent's idol a long time, waiting for the shakes to wear off. When they finally did, I felt exalted by what I'd told Red Flint. Perhaps Little Reed had left me a bit of his strength after all.

I finally looked up at the shimmering gold idol. I'd given serious consideration to going into the Divine Dream and saying what needed to be said to the god, but dread held me back; not of facing him, for I'd finally found the truth in my heart: no matter how much I might have erred, Quetzalcoatl would always care about me, and he would forgive my faults. But I couldn't handle seeing Little Reed's face in his and feeling the pain and guilt.

But I could stare all day at the serpent idol and think only of Quetzalcoatl. Had the god come to me that first time in the Divine Dream as a feathered serpent, would our relationship have turned in the same the direction it had? *I'd have seen him for the god he is, not as a human being; especially not one I yearned for. It was wrong to treat him as if he were merely one of us.*

I touched the statue's smooth nose. "I've made a complete mess of your battle scheme, My Lord, but rest assured I'm more dedicated than ever to seeing your reforms to victory." I pierced my tongue with a string of maguey thorns and threaded it through, the familiar, comforting pain of sacrifice calming me. "Please forgive my mistakes and trust me to do what's necessary to see human sacrifice ended. Guide me through these dark days, help me grow stronger for them, and give me the faith necessary to help my people find their way to brighter days."

I extinguished the copalli incense in the burner. In the morning, I'd tell Mazatzin and Malinalli everything Quetzalcoatl had told me about his plans, and together we'd see it through.

Part Four
The Year Seven Rabbit

CHAPTER TWENTY-EIGHT

I wanted to start making progress on Quetzalcoatl's plans, but not long after the tragedy on the sacred precinct, everything started falling apart. A mudslide wiped out half the city's crops and later that summer, just before harvest, swarms of grasshoppers devastated the remaining half. Higher numbers of Chichimec traveled the roads with their families, and the royal nursery remained empty. "The god has cursed us all," the peasants whispered. "He's outraged at his high priest having slain the high priestess a hundred paces from his temple."

But the only real curse on Xochicalco was her king. A few months into his reign, Red Flint publicly executed all his concubines, accusing them of sneaking chipahuacxihuitl to keep from begetting his children. The incident outraged several of his allies—all his concubines were royal daughters from cities like Tepenec and Xochimilco and Cholula—and they rumbled about withdrawing their military support, but he threatened to march on their cities if they did.

He also implicated Turquoise Bells, but Mazatzin talked him out of executing her. "They're all trying to sabotage the royal bloodline," Red Flint insisted. "If she doesn't beget a child in the next two months, then I'll use her head for a ball at the next Tlachtli match!" He beat her, usually to shouts of "inadequate whore!" that could be heard even in the royal gardens. How did she manage to live in such an environment?

Soon his strange behavior crept into his political dealings too. He sent his war council north to demand tribute from the Chichimecs and only Spear Fish returned, carrying the others' heads in a bag. He executed Camaxtli and Oquitzin for sedition when he saw them practicing on the ball court, but when he mentioned Mazatzin conspiring with them, I warned him, "Keep your hands off the high priest, or the god will pay you a visit, Your Majesty." He sneered, but said nothing more about it.

But when he set the royal turkeys loose in the market because they'd been "lecturing him", I had no doubt that he'd become deranged.

"He's always been rash," Mazatzin protested as we sat whispering about it in my meditation room. "That's just Red Flint."

"You would be a much better king than him," I said.

"Don't say such things." He looked over his shoulder. "If we're overheard by the wrong people.... I was Red Flint's most loyal supporter, and for me to turn on him—"

"Who's more important? Him, or your city and your people?"

"I can't talk about this anymore." But the look in his eyes said he knew I was right.

Not that I was above Red Flint's scrutiny. He'd abandoned any notion of marrying me, but instead focused on haranguing me into his bed. Sometimes he spoke sweetly, trying to appeal to my "womanly gentleness", but mostly he screamed and raved, calling me a difficult bitch. "You're a rebellious city in need of conquering," he told me with a chilling grin that seemed to reach to his ears. I'd never seen him look crazier.

But then the new morning dawned.

¤

I sat in my meditation room when a young priest tore aside my door curtain, panting. "High Priestess! You must come quickly! The king—!"

Oh, what's he done now? Yesterday he'd ordered the guards to shoot down any birds over the city, because they were spies for Ihuitimal, and their constant singing was keeping him awake.

"He's at the temple and he...he ordered me to fetch you immediately." The priest looked frightened, so I followed him out to the precinct.

Priests and novices were gathered at the foot of the Feathered Serpent's pyramid, a storm of conversation going. I made my way through, aggravating my ankle when I tried to jog up the stairs, so that I had to hobble the last few steps.

Red Flint stood in front of the idol, flanked by guards. He looked around like a harried, nervous deer, so I knew if I lectured him about bringing weapons of war into the god's house, he would set off into a tirade, and might even damage the temple.

His face lit with joy when he saw me. "I'm so glad you hurried! I have such good news!"

"What is it, Your Majesty?" I tried to sound patient but wanted him out of my god's temple now.

"I know why all my women have failed to give me children!"

Not at all what I'd expected. "That's...wonderful, Your Majesty."

"Not so wonderful, since I had all them garroted when it wasn't their fault. But it's not my fault either. The Feathered Serpent cursed my reign; he hates me—"

"Quetzalcoatl doesn't hate you—"

"Of course he does! He's a fertility god, yet no children run the halls of my palace, knocking over my statues, or tromping in my flowerbeds or stealing my armor for play. He blessed my father with countless children but turns his nose up at me. Well, to Mictlan with him!"

The guards gasped. One even muttered, "The king cursed the god in his own temple!"

"Shut up or I'll stuff you inside this foul idol!" Red Flint screamed, pointing at the gilded Feathered Serpent behind him. He then stood very still. "Do you hear that?" He jumped atop the altar and cupped his ear.

The crowd murmured outside, but surely that wasn't what he was talking about. "What do you hear?" Hopefully he'd admit, in front of his own guards, to hearing nonexistent voices, so they could see him for the madman he was.

He smiled that same crazy smile again. "I cursed the name of the supposedly mighty Quetzalcoatl in his temple and he does nothing. Some all-powerful god!"

"You've held the god's power in your body, so you know he's not weak," I snapped.

Red Flint sneered. "All gods have power, but who put that into me? Mazatzin told me how you summoned the god before, as a fire serpent to ravage attacking Chichimecs, and a stone serpent that peeled off the walls

270

of this very temple. You, My Lady, are the one with the real power."

The calculating look in his eyes startled me. "Not at all true, My Lord—"

He leaped off the altar and landed in front of me like a pouncing jaguar. "We've been worshiping the wrong god the whole time. Or should I say, the wrong goddess...."

"This is crazy, My Lord—"

He slashed his hand at me for silence. "I'm outlawing the worship of that weak Feathered Serpent and instead every citizen shall offer sacrifice to you alone! You'll bring prosperity back to Xochicalco!"

I looked imploringly at the guards, but they whispered to each other, watching me warily. Surely they didn't believe this craziness?

"I'm taking this temple for you," Red Flint continued, advancing on me. "I've already commissioned a new idol fashioned after your enormous beauty—" He reached out to me but I moved away. "Once everything is consecrated, I'll make love to you on this altar, and your divine powers will cure my curse and you'll bear me a son rich with the blood of the gods. The whole city will gather to witness the miracle rebirth of Xochicalco's royal line!"

"I won't have sex with you, Red Flint." Why did it always come down that?

He smacked me hard and I fell backwards onto the stairs, sending a shock of pain up my spine. "Or perhaps I should consecrate the temple's altar with the goddess's virgin blood, shed during the forceful planting of the seed."

I looked to the guards for help, but their fervent expressions chilled me. If I ran, would they catch me and hold me down while Red Flint made good on his threat? Did they really think this would help the city?

Screams rose outside.

Red Flint flashed me a smug smile, so I scrambled outside.

Smoke billowed to the east, and down in the lower precincts, soldiers ran from temple to temple, setting them afire while the priests stood outside, shouting and crying. The high priest of Tlaloc tried to stop two soldiers mounting the stairs of his god's temple, but they threw him down and he lay motionless at the bottom of the pyramid, crowded by his priests.

"So beautiful, don't you think?" Red Flint asked beside me. "The glow will light the entire city when night falls."

"We haven't had rain in over a month! A single wind gust could spread it to the rest of the city!"

"Consider this my last effort to persuade you to do what's best for your people," he said, unmoved.

Malinalli rushed up the steps. "They're setting fire to the calmecac, My Lady!"

"Where's Mazatzin?" Only he could talk sense into him.

"Tucked away." Red Flint sighed. "He was unenthusiastic about my idea too; he even dared challenge my fitness for the throne, so I put him away."

My guts twisted. "You killed him?" When he grinned catlike at me, I pulled my blade.

But Red Flint batted the knife away and seized my hair. "Always so stubborn, you stupid woman." He turned to the guards gathered at the doorway, dragging me with him. "Our uncooperative goddess requires a sacrifice. Take torches down to the Merchant Quarters, lock every man, woman and child inside their homes, then burn them down." To me, he hissed, "I will sacrifice five more people every day you resist taking my royal seed."

A rumble of outrage finally passed among the guards. "Surely you don't mean for us to kill our own citizens—" someone ventured.

"Go or I'll sacrifice the whole lot of you instead!" Red Flint screamed, so they scrambled down the stairs. "Not you!" he shouted at one young man who looked barely old enough to have served a day in the army. The man cringed but stopped.

Red Flint yanked me back to the temple. "I need a witness to the capture and claiming of the goddess."

The guard paled but followed us inside.

I tried to scramble away when Red Flint flung me onto the altar, but he shoved me back, laughing as he started cutting my robe off with his knife. Jerking the blade through the ties at my neck, he nicked my chin, then he grabbed my head and latched onto the wound like a sucking leech. I beat my fists against his head but cut my arm on his blade. "Can't waste any of that divine blood," he panted, then moved his lips to mine, his sweaty, groping hands crushing my breasts. I wiggled like a trapped dog, trying to find some angle that would allow me to slip away, but he knotted his fingers in my hair so tightly I couldn't move my head anymore. He held his blade to my throat. "You don't want me to hurt you, do you?"

Tears finally broke free—not from the searing pain in my scalp but because I realized I could do nothing to stop him. And the intoxicating desire rose up like a hungry cat, growling, *Go ahead, and see what happens to you, fool!* But I bit back the challenge and squeezed my eyes shut, horrified. What was wrong with me?

"I knew you'd see reason." Red Flint smiled at me with a caring expression. "I'm going to make you so happy, Quetzalpetlatl; I'll make you far happier than Topiltzin ever could have."

That broke through the haze building in my head. "What?"

He grinned like a caiman. "Oh, don't think I didn't know. I'm not stupid." He looked up and laughed, as if recalling a fond memory. "He paid for his treason; I won't tolerate anyone trying to steal from me."

My anger raged past my desire like stampeding deer and I spat in his face. He stared at me, astonished. "You really are nothing but an impotent lizard, you murderer," I snarled.

He sat up and wiped the spittle from his eyes with his fist. "You insolent bitch!" he growled and raised the knife to stab me.

Someone shattered a clay censer across the side of his head, and he fell sideways, crying out in surprise. But when he cracked his head on the sharp edge of the altar, he went down the rest of the way in silence.

Malinalli stood with the handle of the broken censer clutched in both hands, her breath hissing between her clenched teeth. Red Flint sprawled on the floor, blood bubbling out of the deep gouge in his forehead.

The guard stared at him, stunned, but once he looked at Malinalli and me, he ran out screaming, "Please don't curse me! Quetzalcoatl is great! Have mercy on me!"

Malinalli dropped the censer handle and gave me a hug. "Thank the god you're all right," she whispered, tears in her voice.

I couldn't hold back my own tears. "Thank you, Malinalli. I owe you my life."

We looked down at Red Flint. "Dear gods, what have I...is he dead?" Malinalli asked, half crying, half laughing.

I felt a faint, erratic pulse at his neck. He gurgled but didn't move. "No, but he hasn't much longer."

Malinalli clutched her sides, breathing rapidly. "Dear gods, I've killed the king!"

I took her shoulders with my hands. "You did what you had to." Still seeing uncertainty on her face, I picked up Red Flint's blade and slid it into his jugular.

"Show mercy on this lost soul,
My beloved Lord,
Hold not the Black Dog from him.
Let him suffer in this world no more."

A few breaths after I pulled the blade out, Red Flint's gurgling fell silent. "You didn't kill him, Malinalli; I did. And it was the merciful thing to do."

We carried Red Flint's body outside and tossed it down the temple stairs, bringing gasps from the crowd. "The god has laid judgment on King Red Flint's reign," I announced. "We're without a mortal king but we still have the gods, and we must do all we can to save their temples. I need our fastest priestesses to spread word of the king's death to the soldiers, so they know they need not follow mad orders anymore. The rest of you, grab anything you can find that'll hold water. We must get this under control." To Malinalli, I said, "Stay here and oversee. I must go and see the war council."

¤

The war council was gathered among a crowd of guards and servants in the Great Hall, and to my disbelief—and utter joy—Mazatzin sat in the middle of them, nursing a cut head. I smothered him with a hug. "Dear gods, he said he killed you!"

"He would have, if not for Lord Spear Fish," Mazatzin said, his face flushed. "He left ranting that he was going to bring the wrath of the gods down on me." He shook his head. "I should have dealt with him a long time ago."

"We must seize the king and strip him of his headdress, for the people's safety," Spear Fish said.

"The god has already done so," I said. "Lord Red Flint has been struck down by the god's wrath."

"You called on him again?" Mazatzin asked. I'd told him that I'd never again use my powers; it came at too high a price.

"He made his will known through the hands of his servants," I assured him.

"Then matters are settled." Spear Fish went to his knees and the rest of the room followed. "We honor you, Lord Mazatzin, king of Xochicalco." I knelt too.

Mazatzin frowned, uncomfortable. Even as high priest he'd never grown used to the attention his status afforded him.

"But there's more, My Lord," I said. "Red Flint ordered all the temples burned and he sent men to torch the Merchant Quarters. I've already sent people to stop the soldiers, but hearing the news from other soldiers might help this end quicker."

To Spear Fish, he said, "Dispatch messengers immediately. I'm going to the sacred precinct—"

"With all due respect, Your Majesty, I'd rather you didn't," Spear Fish said. "You should evacuate from the city, in case the fires spread."

"We should evacuate the whole city," I added. "Our soldiers don't need to be worrying about rescuing women and children while they're also battling the fires."

Flustered, Mazatzin said, "I can't run out while the gods' temples are threatened."

"You're the king now," I reminded him. "You're no good to anyone if you're dead."

Mazatzin frowned but relented. "I'll take my father's women and children and get a camp established out by the quarry. Lord Spear Fish, will you stay to oversee the evacuation and fire operations?"

"I'd be honored, Your Majesty," Spear Fish said with a bow.

I was about to head back to the sacred precinct when Mazatzin grabbed my hand. "I did as you asked, so please do me the same honor. I want you to come with me."

"I should be with my priests—"

"They'll evacuate along with the rest of the city. Xochicalco needs her spiritual leader just as much as she needs her king, so please, you must come with me to ensure the order's leadership." He lowered his voice before adding, "I promised Topiltzin long ago that I'd do my best to look after you in his absence. Please don't make me break that promise."

I wanted to argue, but the plea in his eyes stilled my objections. "Very well."

¤

By noon, Malinalli arrived at the quarry leading a group of soot-covered priestesses and novices, including the youngest male students. The priests and older male novices had remained behind to help fight the fires.

Mazatzin's tent was set up in the middle of a makeshift camp east of the limestone quarry with the rest of the citizenry's tents pitched around it, the classes clustering together like petals of a sunflower. Farmers gathered in their fields to watch the fires rage.

News trickled in slowly; the fires had spread to the Artisan Quarters, and the Merchant Quarters had burned down completely. Roofs were now smoldering in the Noble Quarters.

"There's just not enough water in the cisterns," one soldier reported at dusk. "And it takes so long to get it from the canals."

"I have Tlaloc's priestesses praying and making sacrifices," Mazatzin said. "Let's hope he hears our prayers and responds."

"We haven't had rain in months," I pointed out.

"We have to hope the gods will show us mercy."

Mazatzin spoke little over the evening meal, then we sat outside, watching our city burn down in a glowing inferno. Even when shifting winds brought the smoke into camp, making it difficult to breathe, I sat with him until dawn, not saying anything but staying in case he needed to talk.

In the morning, gray smoke blanketed the land like fog and it was impossible to see whether or not the city was still ablaze; but a steady stream of soot-covered soldiers wandered into camp, all looking shocked and distraught. There was no laughter, only wailing and prayers as the news spread.

Xochicalco was no more.

¤

We waited two days before going back into the city to inspect the damage. While Mazatzin checked on the palace, I went to the sacred precinct, praying Quetzalcoatl had protected his temple from the flames.

The temple's basic structure had survived, but the wooden roof supports had collapsed. The fire spared nothing; not the reed mats, the baskets of grass balls and maguey thorns; even the idol had melted into a grotesque parody of the god. I knelt next to the altar, shocked by how warm it still felt. I rested my cheek against it and closed my eyes against the stinging tears.

"Horrifying, isn't it?" Mazatzin stood outside the rubble, looking around like a lost child.

"It's like losing my mother—both of them—all over again."

Mazatzin sat on the altar. "I feel so much worse than when I found out that Obsidian Eagle murdered Father; I stood by and did nothing, and now my family's city is destroyed."

"You weren't a coward for leaving. You had to."

He shook his head. "How many times did you tell me we have to do something about Red Flint? If I'd been stronger and did what I should have, this wouldn't have happened. I was too cowardly to stand up to him, because I loved him." He covered his face. "I wouldn't make the difficult choice and now we're all paying for it. I'm king of a pile of burnt rubble."

His words tore open my old wounds. I knew exactly what he was feeling right now. I joined him on the altar and put my arm around him. "Sometimes things are out of our hands. The god has reasons for everything that happens."

Mazatzin chuckled dejectedly. "Should I be angry that he wanted Xochicalco destroyed? He put Red Flint on the throne after all."

It made sense that Quetzalcoatl would have wanted a power void for his son to fill, if he were still alive, but that struck me as too calculating for the god I loved. *My faith in the god is all I have left,* I thought, shaking off the unsettling thoughts. "Good things can come from tragedy. I lost my mother and father, but it brought me here, to Nimilitzli, to Malinalli, to you, and the god. You're like a brother to me, Mazatzin, as dear as Topiltzin, and I wouldn't trade that for anything."

He nodded. "Neither would I. Still, seeing everything my father and his father built turned to ash...I must trust the god to show me the way forward from here."

"We all must," I said with a smile.

A conch shell alarm sounded in the distance and we looked towards the camp barely visible in the haze. More blew, one after another, the sound travelling toward the city.

Mazatzin's guards emerged from the smoky haze at the temple stairs. "We should return to camp, My Lord." They both held their swords.

But we only made it to the palace square before a runner found us. "Your Majesty," he panted, looking ready to fall over. "Our scouts just came in from the outpost along the north road. Culhuacan's army is marching this way!"

CHAPTER TWENTY-NINE

"There must be several thousand men, My Lord," the scout gasped between gulps of water. We gathered around him in Mazatzin's tent, anxiety hanging in the air. "They shot the other scout. I barely made it out of there myself."

"What kinds of soldiers?" Spear Fish asked.

"Spearmen and archers mostly. And Lord Black Otter is among them."

Spear Fish stood straighter. "You're sure?"

"The other scout said as much, but I didn't see the man myself."

A tense silence followed. "Is that bad?" I asked.

"Black Otter commands Culhuacan's general army, which is four thousand strong," Spear Fish answered. "Our own is five thousand strong, but it'll take them a week to get here. Red Flint kept only seven hundred and fifty soldiers in Xochicalco, thinking our reputation alone would defend us. Reinforcements are coming in from the outposts, but we only get a couple of hundred men every other day, so we might have fifteen hundred by the time Culhuacan's army arrives."

"But surely we have several thousand able-bodied men just in our peasantry."

Spear Fish nodded. "We'll arm them, but they'll be fighting mostly with gardening tools since we managed to only save half the armory's spears. We stand a good chance against the infantry, but a third of Culhuacan's army is archers, and they will wipe us out fast."

"How long until they get here?" Mazatzin asked.

"The first wave will reach us by nightfall, My Lord," the scout said.

"Could the walls withstand a siege until the army gets here?" Mazatzin asked Spear Fish.

"The walls aren't the worry. All the gates suffered massive fire damage. They wouldn't even need scaling ladders to get inside. Our best hope is to leave."

Mazatzin let out an exasperated breath and thought a moment. "We could head for Xochimilco. We've already sent them messengers, letting them know what's happened."

"If the runners had arrived, we would've heard back from King Growling Monkey by now. I think it very likely Ihuitimal's men intercepted our messengers. We've lost countless runners along that road in the last year and a half."

"The north road is already blocked," the runner confirmed.

"Then we must try to go around and meet up with the army on the west side of the lake," Mazatzin replied. "Let's start preparations to move out. Send soldiers through camp and the fields to give the evacuation alert."

As Spear Fish and the other Council members bowed out of the tent, I told Mazatzin, "I'll get the priests and priestesses ready to move out."

"Make sure everyone wears civilian clothing, in case they're captured," Mazatzin said. "Ihuitimal gave standing orders to execute all priests of Quetzalcoatl on sight."

"I'll make sure."

He pulled me into a fierce hug. "Be careful, and good luck."

"I'll do my best, Your Majesty, and you do the same. You're the strong king the people need now; you're the king I need." I kissed his cheek and headed out.

¤

Rumors of the approaching army spread even before the soldiers gave the evacuation order, and as I went through camp men everywhere were arming themselves with whatever weapons they could find or fashion in short order, while the women made tlaxcallis on every cooking stone.

By mid afternoon, the first caravan set off into the northwestern forest, the same direction Citlallotoc and I had taken to intercept Obsidian Eagle's assassins. It buffered the royal caravan, which set off to the west, and my entourage of priests and priestesses followed behind while the longer columns of peasants took up the flank. A member of the war council led each group, to provide military guidance.

"I feel naked without my robe," Malinalli told me as we marched.

I nodded. "And it's cold now that it's getting dark." I wore a dress that Lady Turquoise Bells had given me and it barely covered me compared to my priestly robes.

"I still can't believe any of this happened." Malinalli shook her head. After a pause, she added, "I had the worst dream last night, that we were back at the temple and Red Flint was...well, you know. Except I did nothing; I just stood there with the censer in my hand, watching." Shame filled her eyes. "But that wasn't the worst of it. The drought ended, Lady Turquoise Bells had a whole bundle of children, mostly boys, and the entire city prospered like never before."

I understood her distress. I'd dreamt of that moment myself; except that, in my dream, when Red Flint made good on his threats, my body drank the life completely out of him as if it were sweet, nourishing octli. He'd then fallen onto the temple floor dead, a dried-up husk of a man with an eerie smile on his face, and I'd awoken, flushed with vengeful pleasure. But even thinking of admitting any of this to Malinalli—especially that unsettling desire that had come on during the attack—left me feeling horribly ashamed.

"How could anyone think that what he was going to do would fix anything?" She shook her head. "It could have been any of us, year after year, feeding his delusion. I'm glad he's dead. He would've locked every one of us in the city to die."

I nodded. "You saved us all, not just me."

Ahead of us, our war council member held up a hand. In the distance came shouting followed by conch shells blaring. "Move the women over that way and take cover," he told me, then ordered the priests to arm themselves.

I dragged two of the younger priestesses into the forest and Malinalli followed with several more. We huddled behind trees, waiting in the dark. I couldn't see much, but as the sounds of fighting grew closer, I gripped my sacrificial blade tighter.

Silence fell over the forest, but then a soft *swoosh!* filled the air, followed by *thunk! thunk! thunk!* into the tree I hid behind. *Arrows!* We squeezed closer together as still more arrows came, so fast that the sounds of their strikes blended together into a continuous drone punctuated with cries of agony. "Keep those shields up!" Lord Spear Fish shouted. "And keep moving, no matter what!" I prayed he was getting Mazatzin to safety.

But now we're on our own, I thought. As the cries of battle rushed towards us, I took the two priestesses by the hands and pulled them up with me. I shot a glance over at Malinalli and motioned them to follow, hoping they could see me in the shadows. I struck off into the trees, not looking back to see if they were following.

The others ran while I did my best to keep up at a swift limp despite the growing pain in my bad foot. My lungs burned, but I pressed on until I couldn't hear fighting anymore. I dropped behind some bushes, glad to be off my feet. A breath later Malinalli and her group came as well. "Where's Tayanna and Paper Flower?" I whispered.

Malinalli looked around. "They must've gotten lost."

Soon I heard footfalls crunching leaves. I rubbed my wrist against my side, trying to relieve the vague itch. Dark shapes moved in the trees and one of them stepped into a strand of moonlight falling through the canopy, revealing his muscled, tattooed body. He looked right at me. In the distance Tayanna cried and my stomach clenched.

"Run!" I whispered to the others.

The other women sprinted from the bushes and I tried to follow, but my tender heel hobbled me. I got no more than ten steps before a soldier sent me sprawling to the ground with the handle of his spear. I crawled away but he pounced, pinning me down. I scrambled for my dropped blade but he kicked it away.

Whooping and shouting filled the night as Chichimecs swarmed through the trees. Women screamed. I strained to see what was happening but my captor held my head down with his knee as he bound my hands behind my back. He dragged me to a clearing where the other men had gathered the rest of my priestesses, all bound.

A tall Tolteca nobleman looked us over. His gaze lingered on me, but when he noticed the other men doing the same, he barked, "Don't stand there gawking! Get them ready to take back to camp." He resumed leering while the Chichimecs bound us together with a length of rope.

His expression reminded me all too well of how Red Flint used to stare at me. I prayed to the god that it wouldn't end like that very nearly did.

¤

By the time we reached the camp north of Xochicalco—at the crossroads where Ihuitimal's troops were also intercepting the trade caravans—we were all stumbling from exhaustion. The soldiers prodded us along to the center of camp, to two cordoned off areas; stacks of caged prisoners filled the first, while women and children roamed like turkeys in the second. Guards watched the perimeter.

The Tolteca Captain shoved us one after the other into the holding pen after the Chichimecs released our bindings, but when my turn came, he gave my left breast a hard squeeze.

I instantly flashed back to the temple: Red Flint pinning me down to the altar, his crushing grip making my breast feel ready to rupture. And just like then, a strange mixture of overwhelming helplessness and vengeful desire struck me—

Malinalli punched him, knocking him over with a startled cry and breaking my unsettling trance. He stared up at her in disbelief. Even the guards gaped at her with open mouths.

"Don't just stand there, you idiots!" he shouted. As they took hold of her, he lumbered to his feet and wiped blood from his mouth. He slapped her so hard she lost her footing then he hit her again, this time with his fist. "She wants to fight like a man? She can die like one. Throw her in with the sacrifices."

"You shouldn't have done that!" I cried to her as they dragged her away.

"You shouldn't have to put up with such dishonorable behavior, even as a prisoner of war," Malinalli called back.

I wiped tears away. "Keep your spirits high and say your prayers. The gods may yet show us mercy!" Seeing the Captain scrutinizing me anew, I hurried my priestesses away, wanting as much distance from him as possible.

A strange mix of emotions pervaded the crowd; some women wailed while others tended to their children as if nothing had happened. Most sat in shocked silence, looking around like rabbits expecting coyotes to descend. We found Tayanna and Paper Flower, and they both wept to see us. "But where's Lady Malinalli?" Tayanna asked, looking worried.

"She punched a man for disrespecting the high priestess, so they took her to the other pen," one of the young priestesses said.

"Do not speak any of our religious titles," I warned, looking around. "We are among enemies of the god here."

"What will happen to her?" Tayanna asked me.

"She'll be sacrificed, as will the rest of us if we're found out." *Though it should have been me. I should have been strong enough to defend myself against that dog, not stand there like a frightened young girl.*

We sat around, some sleeping while soldiers brought in more prisoners. I could have nodded off at any time, but I made myself stay awake, listening for news about Mazatzin. Once night fell, the guards gave us each half a tlaxcalli—less than even a peasant child would live off per day—and it was gone all too soon. I gave mine to the younger priestesses who were less used to fasting than me, and I did my best to ignore the bouts of desire and hunger that kept swooping in and out on me. Focusing on conversation seemed to help.

"What do you suppose they're going to do with us?" Paper Flower asked as she ate. "Will we become slaves?"

"Some of us will," I said. "But a good number of us will be taken as concubines by the noblemen."

Tayanna shivered. "Mother told me I'd regret joining the priesthood and rejecting Night Snake's proposal."

"I heard that the road into Culhuacan is lined with the corpses of the Feathered Serpent's followers, on display as a warning," one of the younger priestesses whispered.

Paper Flower glared at Tayanna. "Hopefully no one reveals us."

My wrist had itched constantly since we arrived, but it flared now. I looked around to see the Tolteca Captain snapping at everyone to get out of his way as he came towards us. "That's her, right over there," he told the guards behind him.

My priestesses froze, but I whispered, "Keep to yourselves and say nothing."

The guards hauled me to my feet and took me out of the pen, the Tolteca Captain following behind.

"So who are you? One of Red Flint's sisters? One of his concubines? Maybe even his wife Turquoise Bells?" he asked as we approached the large tents circling the center of camp.

"I'm just a servant," I said. Not exactly a lie, since I served Quetzalcoatl.

"Servants don't wear such nice clothing. Not even a top-ranking noblewoman could wear a dress that nice, so either you stole it, which makes you a thief, or you're being dishonest about who you are, which makes you a liar."

"Turquoise Bells gave it to me."

"You're one of Red Flint's sisters then?"

"I'm not related to the royal family, nor have I ever been a guest in any of the princes' beds, or the king's."

"Lord Black Otter will sort out who you really are and whether you're of any use; even if you aren't, I'm sure he can find *some* use for you." He showed me a toothy smile.

My heart crawled up in my throat as the guards pushed me through the flap of the largest tent.

A fire burned in a clay brazier in the center where three men gathered around a wood slab, examining an open roll of paper. "He'll go north, towards Chapultepec," one man said. "We can send soldiers to intercept them, but we should ask your father for reinforcements to cross the lake."

The man who responded could have been my uncle Nochuatl, had I not known he was dead. The resemblance made my heart ache. "We can also pull off part of the contingent fighting near Tultepec and surround them. With Xochicalco's army bogged down in the north, King Mazatzin should be easily captured before reinforcements can rescue him."

At least something was going right today. Mazatzin was still alive, thank the gods.

"I'll send the messengers immediately," the third man said, getting up. He cast me an interested glance as he left.

The Tolteca Captain stepped forward and bowed. "My Lord, here's the woman I told you about earlier." He yanked me forward with his stony grip.

I glared at him before sliding my gaze over to Black Otter again. I didn't see recognition in his eyes; he looked me over with mild interest, perhaps assessing my beauty rather than actually trying to see beyond it. But then his gaze lingered at my eyes.

In his, I saw his mother. Despite my efforts to ignore this, my heart warmed and a tingle built up deep inside me—that same giggling feeling

I'd often felt for him when we were children, but more intense. A flush crept up my cheeks and I swallowed hard, unnerved.

Black Otter wagged his finger at me, a smile coming to his face. "I've seen you before," he said, still unsure, but then he clapped his hands. "Quetzalpetlatl!"

CHAPTER THIRTY

The Captain's eyes bulged. "You mean Mixcoatl's daughter?"

Black Otter laughed lightly. "Why didn't you tell me immediately that she'd been captured?"

"I didn't know she was your wife, My Lord. If I had—"

"You wouldn't have treated me like a camp courtesan?" I snapped.

Black Otter sat straighter, dismayed. "You did what?"

"She wouldn't tell anyone who she was, My Lord, not even when asked. I'd never intentionally behave so reprehensibly to your wife, My Lord!" The words came out in a rush.

Black Otter narrowed his eyes. "Return to your post. We'll speak later." To the other remaining man, he added, "Leave us, please."

Alone now, Black Otter came to me with an amused smile. "You really wouldn't tell him who you are?"

"Would you be forthcoming with your identity in an enemy camp?" My pulse jumped as he neared me.

"My enemies would have no trouble identifying me. I make it a habit of looking them in the face before I send them to Mictlan. Though why would you consider me an enemy? I haven't done anything to you."

"We both know why I'd wish to keep my identity secret."

He set a gentle hand on my shoulder. "You'd really risk becoming some stranger's concubine rather than embrace your birthright? Our parents married us. You're the future queen of Culhuacan."

"My father dissolved our marriage," I snarled. The conversation didn't upset me so much as the fact that I'd said little more than a few words and already I was as flush-faced as a young girl. This growling, hungry lust was far more intense than I'd ever experienced before and it scared me;

especially since the god wasn't here to soothe it for me. *Someone else is though,* I thought, heat creeping between my legs and my breasts tingling. I felt as lightheaded as after a night of octli and meditation.

Hardness seeped into his eyes, finally showing me a flash of the man who'd raised him. "Mixcoatl doesn't rule Culhuacan anymore and my father calls our marriage binding. But you still haven't answered my question: is the thought of being my wife so horrible that you'd rather end up someone's whore?"

"Of course not," I muttered, tearing my gaze away from him. "I've hardly eaten anything in days and I've slept even less, and with being chased by your soldiers, bound and groped, and seeing my best friend dragged off for defending me against that dog of a Captain of yours...I'm feeling half out of my mind." Which wasn't far from the truth.

Black Otter's expression softened. "Forgive me. You've surely been through a great deal and I shouldn't have pushed the matter. I'll get you something to eat." At the open tent flap, he told someone to bring a fresh plate of food. "And tell Captain Storm House that I want to see him right away too." He then led me to the wood slab. "Make yourself comfortable. My tent is now yours as well."

I sat and focused on the grain of the wood, for that seemed to calm the desire. A servant boy soon came with a plate of food and a pot of xocolatl, and he filled cups while Black Otter stoked his pipe opposite me. I dove into the food as quick as I could while still retaining some dignity, and didn't hear anything Black Otter said until he tapped the wood in front of me, breaking my concentration. "What?" I reddened when half a mouthful of tamale tumbled out of my mouth, and finished chewing more delicately.

Black Otter smirked. "Do you need more to eat?"

My face burned, but at least now the desire didn't resurface. "No, thank you," I murmured.

He chuckled. "I was saying I know another reason you wouldn't want anyone knowing who you are. The high priestess of Quetzalcoatl would make a powerful sacrifice to the Smoking Mirror."

I almost asked him how he knew that, but caught myself. How many times had Ihuitimal's spies infiltrated Xochicalco over the years? *He probably knows how many times you bathe per week. This food you're eating is probably your last meal.* I grimaced.

"You needn't worry though," Black Otter said. "If you forsake your vows to Quetzalcoatl and embrace your duties to me, he'll let you live."

I choked on my food and had to wash it down with a swig of xocolatl. "With all due respect, my devotion to the god goes back to before we were married, and only my faith saw me through the disaster Ihuitimal made of my life. Do you know he put my father's heart in my hands? Told me it was a gift, like it was nothing more than a pretty little bracelet?"

Black Otter pursed his lips. "No, he never told me that."

"He also threatened to kill me, told Nochuatl he was going to pluck off my wings. I had nightmares for years, and only prayer brought me comfort. If you make me choose between Quetzalcoatl and my life...there *is* no choice." *And I'll use my death to call the god down on Culhuacan to put an end to your father's reign,* I thought. *Maybe that's the true path Quetzalcoatl has set out for me.* Unsurprisingly, the notion didn't bother me.

Black Otter stared at me, startled at first, but then amused. "Let's not talk about my father anymore. I understand why you feel as you do, but he's my father and I ask that you respect that."

"And I remember you as a kindhearted boy who once promised he'd never make me forsake the god I love. What happened to him?"

"And I wonder what became of the girl who promised on the god's name that she would keep my secrets," Black Otter fired back.

I felt pierced with an arrow, until I considered what kind of beating he must've gotten for my betrayal; severe enough that almost twenty years later, he still held a grudge?

A guard announced Lord Storm House, and a moment later the Captain knelt, trembling, in the tent. "You wish to see me, My Lord?"

"You took one of my wife's friends to the slave cages," Black Otter said. "Bring her to me immediately." My stomach dropped as he cast his hard gaze back at me. What trouble had I got Malinalli in now?

"Anything else, My Lord?" Storm House asked.

"Just go and fetch the woman." Once Storm House left, Black Otter puffed his pipe and answered my gaze. "You'll need a handmaiden, and just to show you what a bad man I am, I'll spare your friend's life. I presume she's also a priestess? Call it a wedding present that she's not standing first in line at tonight's sacrifice."

Storm House returned with Malinalli, bruises shining on her swollen face and a wooden slave collar around her neck. I gave her the remainder of my food, and she too ate as if she hadn't had anything in days—which was true.

Once Black Otter finished his pipe, he donned a jaguar cape. "While I'm making my rounds, clean my wife up for bed," he told Malinalli. "Get a basin and soap from the supply tent on the other side of the bonfire, and don't do anything stupid like trying to escape. The guards will kill you on sight if you do." He gave me a pointed glare then stepped outside.

Malinalli gave me a puzzled look. "His wife?"

My cheeks burned. "My father married us when we were very young, before he found out my uncle was plotting against him. Seems Black Otter still considers that binding." I shot a hesitant glance at the tent flap. *Does he intend to exercise his rights as my husband tonight?* The thought made my stomach clench and I felt I might vomit up everything I'd just eaten. I almost wished for the desire to return, if only to feel stronger—it never made me feel weak or afraid.

Malinalli fetched the supplies and we sat down to work. I admired her adaptability, so strong compared to me as I sat shivering next to the fire while she washed my hair and body. "Are you cold, My Lady?" she asked as she combed my hair.

"It's disturbing, suddenly having as much control over myself as a dog being fattened for the king's table," I admitted.

She nodded. "You're scared about tonight."

"I'll do what I must." Fear broke my voice, and I had to clear my throat and sniffle to keep from losing some of the tears I was holding back.

"I'm sure the god won't see it as a violation of your vows. He'd rather you survive."

I nodded, trying to convince myself.

Like Little Reed's army tent, Black Otter's was divided into two rooms, with the sleeping quarters in the back behind another tent flap, but it was four times larger than Little Reed's. Wicker clothes chests cluttered the open areas around the bed of mats and animal skins that could easily accommodate four people. A room befitting a Prince.

We went through the baskets looking for something for me to wear for the night, and settled on a long white xicolli that hung past my knees. "Your dress should be dry by morning," Malinalli said as she turned to leave. "Do you need anything else before I go?"

I stared down at the bed. "Maybe a little of your strength?" She smiled back and I added, "Be careful out there."

"You too."

Alone, I knelt and offered murmured prayers to the god.

See me through this difficult night, My Lord,
Show me how best to serve you in these circumstances.
My heart is forever devoted to you and your mercy.

Not wanting Black Otter to catch me at it, I hurried into the bed and stared up at the shadowed ceiling, trying to ignore my irritated wrist. *Do what he wants and he'll have no reason to hurt you.* I fidgeted, listening for Black Otter's return, but I heard only distant laughing and singing, as if the soldiers were celebrating their victory. *I wish I was waiting for Little Reed instead.*

Sadness washed over me and I covered my face with the blanket. *Dear gods I miss you so much, my love.* The pain hit like a lightning strike, leaving me freshly wounded.

¤

I awoke with a start when something tickled my face. I looked around groggily, not recalling where I was until I saw Black Otter peering down at me with a kind smile. "I didn't mean to wake you," he said with a chuckle. He glided fingers over my chin, studying me. "Have you any idea how beautiful you are?"

"My mother was beautiful." I rolled over, eager to get back to sleep.

"You look just like her."

"And you look just like your father." The memory of Nochuatl's head lying at Cuitlapanton's feet made me frown. "I miss him."

"You miss my father?"

With my brain addled with sleep, it took me a moment to realize my mistake. Of course he wouldn't know who I was really talking about—I doubted Ihuitimal would admit to anyone that he'd been cuckolded, least of all by his own brother. Rubbing the sleep from my eyes, I said, "I'm sorry, I'm half-asleep. I meant our uncle Nochuatl."

Black Otter lay next to me, resting his chin on my shoulder. "A lot of people tell me I look like him." He smelled of the same tobacco Little Reed used to smoke, awakening the wanton desire I'd thought I'd finally banished. The dread I'd felt before bed was thankfully absent, replaced by a pleasant fog, like the beginnings of a divine vision descending upon me. His closeness felt so wonderful, so right....

You need more. The voice in my head commanded obedience, so I moved closer, turning to face him when I felt his breath on my ear. He brushed his lips against my cheek, sending tingles racing through me. He continued the tease for a moment before smiling and whispering, "Will you punch and curse me again if I kiss you?"

I stared at him, confused—and vaguely annoyed—but then I remembered: that's what I'd done the first time he'd kissed me. I laughed. "I was just a girl back then, but I'm not anymore, am I?" The suggestion alone should have made me blush, but then I topped it by pressing firmly against his groin. "And I see you're no mere boy anymore," I added, responding to the hardness I felt there.

He kissed me with an earnest, eager passion. He rolled on top of me, his weight stoking my want, so I tore at his loincloth, desperate to have him inside me. He separated his lips from mine long enough to yank my xicolli off and toss it aside, but he had less luck with my undergarment, fumbling with the knots before tugging with bruising ferocity. I finally untied them for him, my patience wearing thin. "Now." An order rather than request.

He coupled with me fast—painful, but not as much as I'd expected— and didn't slow down after. Unlike those long, drawn-out sessions with Quetzalcoatl where I reached climax after a slow, delicious buildup, this time the pleasure rose fast and crashed over me so hard that a surprised moan slipped past my lips. Black Otter jolting inside me brought the wave cresting again and I felt energized, the tips of my toes and fingers tingling. I felt so alive, as if I'd just done what the gods had created me do!

Black Otter collapsed next to me, panting and trembling. "Dear gods! I've never felt so good."

I almost said, *I know what you mean,* but all those thoughts evaporated as I stared at the ceiling. Surely I was imagining this....

The tent cloth looked no thicker than a thin veil, and outside white flakes of Love fell from the sky like snow. And the night sky had that peculiar hue of purple indicative of a vision. *I'm seeing into the Divine Dream!* I realized, amazed.

My awe soon gave way to concern. *What if Quetzalcoatl finds me here like this, naked and flushed with pleasure?* I reached over Black Otter—who was already asleep—to grab up the xicolli.

But when I looked up again, the tent's transparency was fading away, and within a moment, I lost my connection to the Divine Dream completely. With nary a whisper from Quetzalcoatl. I should have been happy, but instead tears welled in my eyes. Two years I'd stayed away, and until now I hadn't realized just how much I'd missed the Divine Dream, and the god.

CHAPTER THIRTY-ONE

It was still dark when I left Black Otter sleeping as still as a dead man and went out into the anteroom to reheat the pot of xocolatl. I kept quiet so as not to wake Malinalli, but the smell of the boiling xocolatl soon roused her. We huddled around the brazier, sipping our drinks.

"You're positively glowing, Quetzalpetlatl," Malinalli said after we'd sat in silence for a while. "I don't think I've ever seen you look so...I don't know if 'happy' is the right word, but maybe contented?"

"I am feeling better than yesterday," I admitted.

"So it wasn't as terrible as you feared?"

I averted my eyes. "It was...nothing like I was expecting. I'm glad it's over though."

Malinalli chuckled. "It certainly sounded like you were enjoying yourself."

I gasped. "You heard us?"

"It woke me up, though if it makes you feel better, he was much louder. I bet half the camp heard him."

Dear gods, how horrifying! I thought, my ears burning. After a moment of awkward silence between us, I asked, "What if I just failed a test of my faith and loyalty, Malinalli? Isn't it a slap in the god's face to enjoy losing my maidenhood to the son of the high priest of his arch enemy?"

She shook her head. "We trust the god to show us the right path, so maybe tonight he showed you yours."

Maybe she was right. After so thoroughly messing everything up, it was my responsibility to see Quetzalcoatl's plans fulfilled through whatever means necessary, so maybe embracing a fruitful marriage to Black Otter could help bring the god back into the temples in Culhuacan and ensure the future of the order. And maybe, with time, I could learn to love Black Otter; not as much as I'd loved Little Reed, but enough to be happy.

¤

Black Otter said little when he came out of his room at daybreak, but once Malinalli left to see about my dress, he asked, "Feeling all right this morning?"

"Fine," I said, not meeting his gaze as we sat eating our morning atole at the wooden table. "And you?"

A smile quirked at his mouth. "I can't remember the last time I slept so soundly. I trust the bed was comfortable?"

"Sufficiently." I tried to hold back the blush but failed. I focused on spooning up my atole to keep from looking at him.

"What happened to your fingers?" he asked after taking a few more bites of his own.

I couldn't possibly tell him the truth—if he knew I had the ability to call on Quetzalcoatl, he might kill me immediately. Better to lie and get a better assessment of his intentions first. "I smashed them between some stones and had to have them removed."

He cringed but thankfully didn't press the matter.

Once he'd finished eating, he said, "We're heading home today. A boat from Xico will meet us north of here and we'll be back in Culhuacan before nightfall."

"So soon?" I'd hoped for a few more days to prepare myself for seeing Ihuitimal again.

"The army camp is no place for the future queen," Black Otter said. "And don't worry. The women of my household will make you quite welcome."

I hadn't given any thought to there being others, nor did I want to think about it. I'd seen enough jealous bickering among my father's concubines to know I wanted nothing to do with such drama. *I suppose it can't be much different from running matters in the priesthood,* I thought, but then my priestesses were there because they wanted to be, not because their fathers made an alliance with the god. It was also accepted that some priests and priestesses had a closer relationship with the god than others, and as high priestess I didn't need to make sure the god divided his time equally among all of us, or that my priestesses were caring for themselves while carrying his children.

You could be with child yourself now. And in nine months you could be dead, just like your mother. My stomach twisted.

Black Otter's expression turned to concern. "Are you all right?"

I shook my head, panic cresting. "This is…overnight I've become a Prince's wife, and guardian of a group of women I've never met, and I could be with child." I couldn't catch my breath. "My mother died giving birth!"

"That doesn't mean you will. Women give birth all the time and live to have still more children."

"I know they do!" I snapped.

"I understand this is all very sudden, but the others will help you transition; and as for the other thing…it's too soon to worry about that, don't you think? It was just one night—"

"It takes only once!"

He set his jaw. "You're overreacting."

"Overreacting? When I refuse to forsake Quetzalcoatl, your father's going to torture and kill me, and put my body on display with the rest of the corpses decorating the road into Culhuacan. Don't tell me I'm overreacting!"

"You're too valuable to do that—" he said, but then regret crossed his face. "I didn't mean that the way it sounded—"

"Of course you did. I'm well aware of my worth to both you and your father. I sat in Xochicalco's court, not as a meek wife but as a powerful high priestess who commanded respect the same as any nobleman, and I know love and fondness have nothing to do with marriages like ours, so stop trying to sweeten the truth. I prefer knowing exactly where I stand."

Black Otter set his bowl down with a clank that surely left a crack in the pottery. "You want the grim truth, My Lady? Here it is: you're only of use to me so long as you give me an heir of Mixcoatl's blood. And though you were a high priestess in Xochicalco, in Culhuacan no woman sits in on court. You're not your mother, and I'm not a fool like your father was.

That doesn't mean I can't make life good for you, but if you'd rather I be the cruel and vile man you believe I am, I can oblige you." He stood, shaking. "Once we reach Culhuacan, you can tell me which you prefer." He slashed aside the tent flap as he left.

"What a fine mess you've gotten yourself into now," I muttered, then kicked aside his bowl.

◻

I spent the morning praying and meditating, hoping Quetzalcoatl would show me the way from here, but without teonanacatl, or even a blade to cut myself, the gulf was too large. *You could always seduce the man again,* that other voice suggested with a lurid laugh. *That will get you back into the Divine Dream.* I shoved the notion aside immediately. That other voice was starting to irritate me.

Black Otter returned before noon to take me to the boat, still stone-faced and short with his words. But we went no more than a step outside the tent before he suddenly stuck his arm out in front of me. I looked down to see a black and white banded snake sliding across the path.

When the guards pointed their spears at it, Black Otter snapped, "Leave it be. It's not hurting anyone." The snake disappeared around the corner of the tent.

I gave Black Otter a sideways glance he didn't return. Perhaps I'd misjudged him and the god wanted me to trust him?

The boat was moored against the bank among the reeds, and several polers stood aboard. It wasn't a very large boat, but it had an enclosed area in the middle made of hide-covered reed walls, to provide protection from enemy arrows. I followed Black Otter inside the enclosure, welcoming the shade of the canopy in the already hot afternoon. Malinalli sat outside, at the bow of the boat. We sat on mats on the floor, neither saying anything as the polers pushed us away from shore and out into the lake. Guards stood stolidly at the doorway, no doubt to make sure I didn't attempt to jump overboard to escape.

I stared at the carving marks in the floor, contemplating the snake again. If it was an omen from the god, it would be foolish not to listen; I'd messed up Quetzalcoatl's plans enough already. Perhaps I could turn this situation around to the god's benefit again. *If you embrace being Black*

294

Otter's wife and earn his affection, maybe you can convince him to allow Quetzalcoatl's worship back into Culhuacan.

I glanced up at Black Otter, assessing exactly what kind of man he was. He carried none of his father's hardness; if anything, sadness hung over him like an invisible cloud as he stared out of the doorway. And thinking back on how he'd smiled at me last night in bed....

I'd hoped the memory might spark some affection for this man who'd once been my best friend, but it only brought forth memories of Little Reed. More than once over the last two years I'd wished Red Flint hadn't interrupted us, and that Little Reed had left me with something more than just memories and pain. Though if he'd left me with a child, I'd have more than myself to worry about now, for any son or daughter would have been as much a target as he had been. Feeling both relieved and regretful at the same time left me befuddled.

Despite my fanciful regrets about the past, the truth of here-and-now pressed heavy on me. Accepting my role as Black Otter's wife meant accepting the risk of childbirth. But if this was the path the god wanted me to take.... *I must believe he will protect me so I can accomplish his goals,* I thought. *He's giving me a second chance, and I can't disappoint him.*

I looked up at Black Otter again, then took a deep breath before speaking. "I'm sorry about this morning. I was cruel, and disparaged your good name for no reason, and I let fear take over the conversation. I don't really think you're vile; in fact, you've been kind and shown care for my well-being, and I thank you for that."

His shoulders rose a bit and a shadow of a smile came to his lips. "Can you forgive me for my sharp tongue as well?" he asked. "I realize this is a lot for you to cope with—probably even frightening, now that I'm taking you back home to Culhuacan, but rest assured I only want you to be safe and happy."

"What about your father?"

"I will protect you." His vehemence surprised me, and for the briefest of breaths, he got that strange, intense look in his eyes I'd seen too often in other men. But it disappeared as quickly as it came. "But you needn't worry, Quetzalpetlatl. You're my wife and the legitimate heiress to Culhuacan's throne. He will want you to stay, if only to quiet critics who still think he's an interloper."

He is an interloper, I almost said, but I caught my tongue in time.

He tentatively reached his hand out to me, smiling when I finally accepted it. His grip was gentle yet possessive. "Everything will be all right, I promise."

◻

Ihuitimal had made Culhuacan's gray basalt walls higher and thicker, filling me with foreboding as we slipped into the docks. Tolteca archers watched the lake front from on high while Chichimec spearmen guarded the street level. The city didn't look bigger than I remembered; in fact, it seemed overcrowded. The Chichimec men were grubby and barely dressed, and the women wore their hair matted, and most had thin, naked children clinging to their hips.

They all vanished once our porters took us through a stepped archway into the Noble Quarters. There hadn't been any walls around it when my father was king, but here the streets were clean-swept and children played behind courtyard walls, the sounds of their laughter giving the only evidence they were even there. Everyone was Tolteca—even the servants—and dressed in fine clothing, looking proud. We even passed a dedicated Tolteca market—another new addition. The stark class division shocked me. Xochicalco's peasants had lived in their own quarters of the city, but no walls warned them to keep out, nor did the nobles have their own market so they didn't have to mingle with the farmers.

At the palace's front steps, three Tolteca women and a number of children and servants awaited us. Black Otter helped me down from the litter and escorted me to the stairs where he kissed each woman. All but one were younger than me, and the latter had a boy of no more than a year old on her hip while a little girl—probably three or four years old—crouched behind her, squashing ants on the stone with her fingers. The woman smiled with veiled hostility. I couldn't shake the sense of familiarity I felt when I looked at her, and after some thought I finally figured it out: she was my sister, Jade Flower.

The next woman in line was heavy with child and looked the youngest, while the last woman held another little girl's hand—this one about five. Next to her stood a girl of twelve or thirteen, but Black Otter addressed her as "My Lady" and kissed her hand. She wasn't too old to be his daughter, but given the flush on her face when he spoke to her, I doubted she was. *A token of some alliance, the poor girl.* But judging from how quickly he let her hand drop, I knew he must not be sleeping with her yet. Moral tradition dictated that consummation of such arrangements be left until the girl had been through a year of monthly cycles, and I respected him for taking that obligation seriously.

Black Otter brought me forward. "Allow me to present Mixcoatl's daughter, Princess Quetzalpetlatl."

A long pause ensued while the younger women exchanged puzzled looks. Jade Flower's expression remained unchanged though; she already knew who I was, which made her hostility all the more alarming. The pregnant woman asked, "Do you mean the same one your father married you to when you were a boy?"

Black Otter nodded. "She's finally returned home."

Jade Flower took my hand with a practiced smile. "Allow me to be the first to welcome you home, Quetzalpetlatl. I don't imagine you'd remember me, not after so many years."

"I do remember you, Jade Flower. Our mothers used to sit together and weave in the Women's Hall every day, and we spent many pleasant afternoons playing in the gardens." I answered her calculating expression with a careful smile. "You're looking radiant."

Jade Flower replied, "My heart bursts with joy for seeing you again, especially since I was sure I never would." She then introduced me to the others. Lady Corn Flower had the eldest child while Lady Papantzin was swollen with her first, and the girl not yet of age—confirmed by Jade Flower—was Lady Anacoana. While the others' greetings felt perfunctory—and I was sure there would be much whispering between them after I left—Anacoana was the only one who remembered to bow as was proper.

"I must meet with Father, so Jade Flower will help you settle in," Black Otter said. "I'll come for you later." He gave me a gentle kiss then bade us all goodbye before ascending the stairs into the palace.

When I turned to Jade Flower, she was watching him go too, looking melancholy and ready to cry. She put on a brave face when she turned back to me, but I knew that resentful look in her eyes that she couldn't quite cover up. It looked as if I'd just landed in the middle of a domestic quagmire.

◻

"I will have the servants bring all your things out of storage," Jade Flower said as we walked down the hall towards the living quarters. Malinalli followed us, looking around with keen interest.

"I don't think my old clothes will fit me anymore," I said with a laugh.

Jade Flower laughed too. "I meant your wedding presents, though I'm sure a good many of them won't fit either. You were supposed to trade them once you were older anyway. The royal seamstress will put something together for you tonight. You can't appear before the king in an ill-fitting dress."

When we reached the living quarters and Jade Flower started down the left-hand hallway, where Father's concubines once lived, I stopped. "Aren't the royal quarters this way?" I asked, pointing to the other curtain decorated with Culhuacan's royal crest.

Jade Flower shook her head. "Only the king and Princes live down there. We're not allowed beyond that curtain." She turned into the first doorway on the right side of the left hallway.

Rugs, screens, and wood carvings of animals and various goddesses decorated the room, and a small gold-plated idol of Cihuacoatl—goddess of the childbed—sat next to the bed of mats and blankets.

Malinalli started a fire while Jade Flower took me out on the patio. The garden wasn't as big as the one off the room where Black Otter and I spent those four days after our wedding, and it looked as if it hadn't been properly cared for in months. The pond was small and overgrown with broad-leafed bushes, and gangly flowers overflowed the beds. A copal tree's spiny branches fanned across the yard to all three vine-covered walls. At the back wall, I pulled aside the vines to find the opening into the passage beyond sealed up.

"Isn't it wonderful to be back?" Jade Flower asked.

"It's strange," I said. "Some things haven't changed, yet when you pull aside the curtain, the things that matter most have." I sighed, saddened by the thought.

"I'll leave you to bathe and get some sleep before the feast tonight. I imagine it will be a late night for you and Lord Black Otter," Jade Flower said. "I'll see you tomorrow morning, in the Women's Hall."

I nodded. "I look forward to it."

Once Jade Flower was gone, the servants arrived carrying basket after wicker basket loaded with clothing and jewelry. I helped Malinalli go through them, sorting out what needed trading and what was worth keeping. Each piece of clothing brought a memory of who'd given it to me and soon I was regaling Malinalli with stories about the people who gave me specific gifts.

"The old woman who gave me this necklace just about boxed my ears when I acted bored at her ritual chastisement before the wedding. My mother promised I'd make her a blanket. And my father's feather-worker gave me this one, though it looks like the feathers could use replacing."

"Your memory astounds me, Quetzalpetlatl," Malinalli said. "I can hardly remember what I ate for dinner last night but you recall things you told me on some lazy afternoon when we were both seventeen. You never forget anything, do you?"

"It's good for some things," I conceded. Like the way I could remember Little Reed with absolute clarity, from the smell of his skin to the tenor of his voice. I hated it for the very same reason.

The dress I found at the top of the last basket brought a smile to my face. "My aunt Eloxochitl made this for me. She and Mother each worked on a piece of it months before I'd heard anything about marrying Black Otter. They used to smile and laugh together all the time, and she'd doted on me even more than my own mother had, for she had no daughters." If anything pleased me now, it was that I'd soon get to see her again. I'd surprise her by finally wearing the dress she'd helped make to dinner tonight.

¤

Everyone who'd ever known my mother always said I looked like her, but I rarely saw it. She'd been far more beautiful than I could ever dream of being.

But after Malinalli braided my freshly-washed hair with feathers and flowers, I finally saw in the obsidian mirror what everyone else had seen, and it overwhelmed me.

"You look very queenly," Malinalli said, awed.

"My mother always did," I whispered through the knot in my throat.

The bells on my door curtain jingled and a moment later Black Otter stood in the bathhouse doorway, wearing a jaguar-pelt loincloth, a handsome cape of turquoise fabric, arm and calf bracelets of black feathers, and a small feathered headdress with two quetzal feathers tucked between brown eagle feathers. He stared as if he were seeing me now for the very first time. "You're ready?" he asked, finding his tongue again.

"As ready as I can be." Noticing he was holding a necklace, I asked, "What have you there?" It was made of feathers and turquoise, a stone reserved for royalty.

"Oh! I forgot," he admitted, blushing. "My father says it was your mother's, and I thought you would want it. Here, let me help you put it on." Black Otter moved behind me and drew it around my neck, smiling in the mirror. "Now you truly look like the future queen."

It was the necklace Mother had let me wear on my wedding day long ago; my favorite of her jewelry. I'd lost my mother's sacrificial blade—the only thing I'd had left of her—so it brought tears to my eyes to have this now. I smiled back at him in the reflection. "Thank you, My Lord."

He squeezed my shoulders and kissed my cheek as if we were old lovers.

◻

A sea of noblemen knelt as Black Otter walked me to the head of the Great Hall, his arm hooked in mine as if it were perfectly natural there. There was only one royal banner now, directly above the dais, but large polished obsidian mirrors hung on the side walls, casting shadowy reflections of ourselves as we went by. Did I only look so frightened and pallid in the mirror or had Culhuacan truly grown so dark in character that the mirrors showed reality?

Ihuitimal rose from my father's reed throne. His skeletal smile made the scar on his cheek turn into a crevice, lending him a sinister, sunken appearance. His sparse silver hair showed off his thinning skin, and he wore a flowing red and black feathered robe, with an obsidian mirror dangling from a cord around his neck. A diamond-shaped jade shard hung from his pierced septum. The sight of him raised the hairs on my neck, and I felt defiled when he embraced me. "My dearest Quetzalpetlatl, the last of my brother's bloodline," he said, his voice like sand between stones. "Welcome home at last." My wrist felt afire. I wished I still had my sacrificial blade so I could have plunged it into his eye, to make the itching finally stop for good.

To my disappointment, the woman next to him, sitting in my mother's throne, wasn't Eloxochitl, but rather someone at least a couple of years younger than myself—and though she smiled, it lacked any true interest. Where was my aunt? And why was my mother's throne devoid of flowers? It looked so naked and small without the stalks of bone flowers crowning it.

"A pity what happened to Xochicalco," Ihuitimal said. "But every great city sees its sunset eventually. We're grateful you're back at your husband's side, to see the rise of the next great city here in Culhuacan."

I knew I would blast him with spiteful words if I said anything, so I merely bent my head.

"Let's conduct the ceremony, so we may celebrate your return." Ihuitimal motioned me and Black Otter to kneel, but I only did so when Black Otter tugged my sleeve. Ihuitimal placed his hands on our heads and pushed me down so my nose touched my knees. I could hardly breathe.

"Oh Mighty Smoking Mirror,
Who knows everything,
Who sees everything!
Bless this union,
Grant us your favor,
Make our children know your greatness
And tremble before it.
I bless this marriage with the blood of your enemies!
Most Powerful,
Most Terrible Tezcatlipoca!"

Cold liquid dribbled into my hair and turned the white fabric of my dress red where it dripped. *He's pouring the blood of Quetzalcoatl's priests on me!* I thought, struggling to stand up. But he held my head down with his claw-like hand. *Protect my heart from fear and tyranny, My Lord,* I prayed. *Give me the strength to remain true to your teachings in the den of your nemesis!* When he finally let me go, I nearly launched over backwards. Blood wormed down the side of my face and the back of my dress, leaving my flesh crawling. It ran out of Black Otter's hair too, but he remained calm.

Ihuitimal tied the edge of my dress to Black Otter's cape, giving it a sharp tug. "Let us feast for the restoration of my children's wedding vows!" he announced, then cleaned his hands with a cloth while a black-robed priest took away the empty blood bowl.

Like before, Black Otter and I shared the traditional tamales, though we stayed for the remainder of the feast this time. All night Ihuitimal watched me, his gaze sometimes lingering like a man watching his lover, and at other times as if he were plotting revenge. I avoided his gaze, chilled at the thought of his eyes groping me the way most men's did. He didn't speak to me beyond that opening greeting—thank the gods, for I knew I'd say something that would land me in the prison yard for the night. *Though denigrating him in front of all his allies and noblemen might be worth the flogging,* I thought, but this wasn't the time to be careless with my life. Quetzalcoatl still had better plans for me.

I breathed a sigh of relief when Ihuitimal finally dismissed us for the night. I couldn't wait to wash all the dried blood out of my hair, and get to know Black Otter better; and to see how difficult it would be to implement my goal to get Quetzalcoatl back into Culhuacan.

But a whole new trepidation cropped up when Black Otter followed me into my own bath house and stood stock-still with his arms out at his sides while his two body servants undressed him one bit of clothing at a time. I fussed with my teeth in front of the obsidian mirror, so as not to look at his nakedness. Malinalli waited with her back turned as well, the uneasiness plain on her face.

Once he dismissed his servants, he asked, "Don't you think you've picked your teeth enough yet, my precious flower?"

I risked a glance over my shoulder to find him sitting submerged to his chest in a large tub of hot water next to the steam bath. A hungry smile stretched across his face. "Surely you haven't forgotten how to stand so your handmaiden can undress you?" he teased.

I looked away again, flushed. It was one thing for Malinalli to help me dress when it was just the two of us, but the thought of having her undress me in front of him.... "That will be all for tonight, thank you," I murmured to Malinalli, not meeting her gaze.

"Thank you, My Lady." She quickly disappeared back into the room like a mouse chased by a dog.

I undid the ties at the neck of my dress, but when I noticed Black Otter watching me, I squeezed my eyes shut. "Must you do that?"

"Do what?"

"Look at me like that."

"Like what?"

"Like...like...I don't know what, but I don't like it," I sputtered, glaring at him.

He laughed. "Why so embarrassed? It's not as if we haven't enjoyed each other before now."

The flush burrowed deeper as I recalled last night's frantic lovemaking, and I half-expected the desire to well up again, but instead I felt humiliated, reduced, and trapped. Like that night in the water yard when Ahexotl had stared at me lying half-naked on the ground. "I was raised to be very modest, as priestesses should be," I choked.

Perhaps the stress in my voice bore through the lust, for he muttered, "Sorry I made you uncomfortable. I promise not to look." And to show his seriousness, he moved to the other side of the tub, with his back to me, then proceeded to wash his hair.

I undressed quickly—and clumsily—then scrambled into the tub too, and by the time he finished rinsing his long hair, I'd submerged myself up to my shoulders. The water's heat was dizzying; for years I'd taken mostly cold water baths, and even the few that were hot had been lukewarm compared to this. Already sweat beaded on my forehead.

Black Otter wiped the water from his face then grinned at me boyishly. "How can you wash your hair with all that in it?"

In my hurry to gain the cover of the water, I'd forgotten to take my hair down. I started picking the bits of flowers and feathers out, but he sidled over next to me and insisted, "Please, let me help you with that."

I wanted to elbow him away—what would he know about untangling a woman's intricate hairstyle anyway?—but he worked with surprising gentleness and deliberate slowness, so as not to tug my hair as he removed the gold pins holding it up. He unwound the two braids one at a time, letting my wavy brown hair fall around my shoulders with a rousing sensuality. He then poured water over my hair from a clay jar, carefully tilting my head back so it didn't leak into my eyes.

But when he started washing my hair with the soap, the first hints of haziness settled over my mind. I tried to shake it away, but the caress of fingers on my scalp only made it worse. Desperate to not lose control like last night, I blurted, "Can I ask you something?" My heart throbbed painfully in my chest.

He smiled. "Of course you may."

"How dedicated are you to your father's chosen god?"

Black Otter blinked at me just before an invisible shield went up behind his eyes. "Why?"

"You know where my heart lies, My Lord, but I know little about yours."

He didn't say anything as he continued massaging my head with his soapy fingers. Eventually he said, "My father wants me to take his place as Smoking Mirror's high priest once he's dead, though I don't know why. I have no priestly training, and while he has shown me some things...I'm a soldier, not a priest. He wants me to go north and live in the desert for a year like he did, so I can have a vision and know what the Smoking Mirror expects of me when I'm king."

The haze still clung to my brain, so I focused on his face above me, taking note of the consternation, the indecision, the unhappiness as he rinsed my hair out with a small water jar. "You don't want to do any of that?"

"I oversee the sacrifices on campaign, and I say my prayers before battle, but...shouldn't serving the gods be a life's calling, not something forced on one?"

"True devotion can't be forced, not the kind you'd need to be a high priest. Faith comes with time and experience, not at spear point."

"Must we talk about such things now?" he asked, setting aside the jar then wrapping his arms around me.

As soon as he kissed me, I tried to fight off the intense desire swelling up inside me, but something sprang up and blocked all control of my body. I felt just like that time when I was a girl, when the god had spoken to Ihuitimal with my tongue.

Though when I settled onto Black Otter's lap, I knew this couldn't be Quetzalcoatl controlling me. So then whose magic was this? Panic rose inside me, but then that voice I disliked whispered, *Watch and learn, little girl.*

This time, when Black Otter's gaze fell down to my exposed breasts, a peculiar confidence cut through the anxiety and I felt lulled and content.

"Do you plan to continue your father's policies once you're king?" It was the exact question I'd wanted to ask him all day, but I hadn't willed my tongue to form the words now; they just spilled out, unbidden and exerting a strange authority. It was the voice I used with students, but more calculating. The tone demanded truthfulness, and anything less wouldn't be tolerated. I felt awed that I could sound this way.

Black Otter stuttered a moment, distracted by my naked breasts, but then he said, "I don't...I promised my father...."

I leaned closer, our noses almost touching. He reached up to pull me into his arms, but I pushed them away with gentle but firm hands. "You promised you would never make me give up Quetzalcoatl."

"I did," he conceded, breathless. He trembled under me when I moved in to kiss him.

But again I held back at the last moment. "Wasn't last night good for you?" I asked.

"Incredible," he whispered, his voice pained. "I've never felt so good.... Was it not so for you too?"

I smiled but said nothing. This other me didn't care about such things. "It can be even better, My Lord, if I knew I could trust you to keep your promise."

"I will," Black Otter insisted.

"Then you will let Quetzalcoatl back into the temples?"

"I will!" He said it so fast I wondered if he even understood the question.

A smile tugged at my cheeks then I finally kissed him. He hugged me so tight I thought he would crush my ribs, but I did nothing to stop him. Instead I laughed and whispered, "Now get to the bed, so I may satisfy your hunger."

Next thing I knew, I sat atop him in my bed as he writhed in ecstasy under me, knotting his fists into the blankets as I squeezed him between my thighs. I didn't care about the quenching pleasure coursing through me as the octli-like haze dissipated. I just wanted to see into the Divine Dream again; see the flakes of Love floating down from Heaven and glimpse the tall stone walls of Omeyocan high among the night clouds.

But most surprising, I longed to see Quetzalcoatl swirling down from his heavenly abode, not even caring that he'd find me still coupled with Black Otter. *What I wouldn't give to see Little Reed's face one last time, even if only in the face of his father!* I searched the sky, trying to will the Divine Dream to last longer, trying to call out to him with my mind, but it faded without any sight of the face I loved.

Hot tears wound down my cheeks. *Your heart will never mend if you keep doing this, Quetzalpetlatl. You must accept that he's dead, and focus on making a new life for yourself.*

Fearing Black Otter might see my tears, I wiped them away quickly, but it didn't matter. He was already asleep.

CHAPTER THIRTY-TWO

Black Otter slept through breakfast, so I left him in my bed, not wanting to wake him from his very sound sleep. I'd hardly slept at all last night, feeling too awake after we'd finished; strange, since I'd always thought such exertions would be exhausting.

I joined the others in the Women's Hall and we passed the morning weaving while Black Otter's daughters spun our thread for us. Not much had changed in here: the walls were painted with the same floral patterns and there were a lot of women of varying ages at their weaving, all chattering away as they worked. I'd half expected some veiled hostility when I entered the room, like my mother often had to endure, but to my relief most of them just smiled then returned to their work. Even Black Otter's other women gave me pleasant greetings and made room for me at the circle of mats where they gathered.

Jade Flower was the same mediocre weaver she'd been as a girl, but she made up for that lack with her strong leadership of Black Otter's women. They sought her opinion on a multitude of issues, like dealing with a cruel servant calling Lady Corn Flower's daughter "Little Lizard" because the girl's toes splayed too wide, or distinguishing between real and fake labor pains. She even recommended I send Malinalli to the market for a special skin cream for my inflamed wrist, which had been constantly irritated since I'd arrived in Culhuacan.

Only Anacoana seemed out of place in the group. She rarely said anything, but the others didn't pay her much attention either. While they spent more time talking than working, she wove some of the most intricate patterns I'd ever seen, and with incredible speed.

"I think it's the only thing her mother ever taught her," Jade Flower confided to me as we headed to the kitchen to get something to eat that afternoon. "I shudder to think that she might know nothing about sex and I'll have to teach her all too soon. Though I suppose that will be your duty now, as the Prince's wife. But then you're probably just starting to learn about such things yourself."

"The woman who raised me taught me everything I needed to know about that," I said. "She was always forthcoming with answers, regardless of subject matter."

"You were raised by one of Cuitlapanton's wives then?"

"No, the high priestess of Quetzalcoatl. Topiltzin and I were very lucky to have her once Mother was gone." Uncomfortable with the stiffening in my chest, I changed the subject. "Speaking of mothers, I didn't see Eloxochitl at the wedding feast last night."

Jade Flower shook her head. "She died a few months after your mother, in childbirth too, if you can believe it. The baby survived though; Amoxtli is his name, and he and Black Otter are very close."

"Black Otter has a brother?"

She nodded. "The last few months have been especially difficult though, since Amoxtli was taken prisoner. We do know he's still alive and we're hopeful we'll get him back. I pray to the Smoking Mirror every day for it."

You're praying to the wrong god, Jade Flower, I thought, suppressing an ironic smile. *The Smoking Mirror thrives on your pain and fear, so why would he do anything to lessen it?*

I saw the woman who'd been sitting on my mother's throne last night talking with some of the old matrons by the kitchen doorway. "The king's wife looks younger than us."

"She's not his wife, just his latest favorite concubine. He never remarried after Eloxochitl died."

We took our tamales out into the yard where the children ran yelling and laughing. There were far fewer than I remembered when I was a girl, and hardly any boys at all. "Is this all the royal children?"

"Not all of them are royalty. The boys over there are sons of the nobles who live in the palace, but those three girls over in the corner—the older ones—those are the king's daughters."

"The king has only two sons?"

Jade Flower nodded. "Having lots of daughters can buy favor with his allies, and he sends them off to new households as soon as they come of age."

I watched Jade Flower's daughter sitting with Lady Corn Flower's daughter, braiding the maguey fiber hair of their dolls. "Do you worry Black Otter will do the same to your daughter?"

"Why would I worry?" she asked, puzzled. "That's what girls are for."

Her attitude shouldn't have surprised me, but I couldn't suppress the spike of anger. "That's a sad thing to think, Sister."

"Why? Men cannot make more men without us, so that makes us very important and valuable."

"True, but why should we be so narrowly defined? Men can be a multitude of things."

"What men do is insignificant."

I laughed, incredulous. "A city future or its spiritual well-being is hardly insignificant."

Jade Flower stared at me, taken aback. "You don't think being a mother is important?"

"Of course it's important, but what's wrong with wanting everything, for both our daughters and our sons? Wouldn't you rather your daughter marry someone who loves and respects her, and whom she loves too? Do you really want her to end up like you, second best in this farce nobles call marriage?"

Jade Flower's eyes bulged. She stood, face flushed. "How dare you.... Not all women are as fortunate as us, Quetzalpetlatl! Just remember that." She hurried back inside.

¤

Jade Flower didn't return to the Women's Hall after the meal break. Lady Corn Flower and Papantzin talked in hushed whispers while Anacoana focused feverishly on her weaving. My own mind was distracted by what Jade Flower had said, and the fact that I'd left behind my priestesses to be given out as war prizes. *And what could you have done about it? There's no point dwelling on things you have no control over.* Still, I felt I *should* have done something.

Determined to focus on other things, I edged over next to Anacoana where she was working on a tapestry. "That's wonderful work," I whispered.

She gave me a shy smile. "Thank you."

"Your mother taught you?"

She shook her head. "My servant girl, when I was growing up. Mother said I needed to excel in at least one skill if I ever hoped to find a place in someone's house, since I'd inherited my father's rough looks."

I nearly laughed, though such cruelty from a parent was hardly funny. "One doesn't find one's true beauty until one's grown, but I'd wager that you won't be disappointed."

Her smile relaxed into something more natural. "Thank you, My Lady."

"You're certainly the best weaver I've ever seen. Would you mind showing me how you do that exquisite pattern?"

We passed the rest the afternoon talking about weaving and palace life. Anacoana was exceedingly sharp, picking up easily on the tone of conversations around her, but as soon as a man—be it a nobleman or a servant—came into the room, she spoke no further words until they'd left again. Another thing her mother taught her? And when Black Otter came to fetch me for dinner, she hurried to cast aside her weaving, getting herself tangled in her thread, so I helped her up.

"I see you're settling in nicely," he said. "I trust the others have given you a warm welcome?"

Lady Corn Flower and Papantzin fidgeted but I said, "Everyone has been exceedingly kind, My Lord."

Black Otter took my arm. "Please excuse us," he told the others. "We have preparations to make before dinner tonight." I felt Lady Corn Flower and Papantzin's piercing gazes on my back as we left.

"I didn't see Jade flower in there with you," he noted.

I sighed. "I upset her this afternoon at lunch."

Black Otter laughed. "So you girls are right back where you left off twenty years ago?"

I cast him a scathing glare. "What's that supposed to mean?"

Still smiling, he said, "Nothing. I just noticed that your friendship was always...contentious? What did you say to her?"

I shook my head. "Nothing important. Just foolishness. I'm used to speaking my mind, but that isn't going so well anymore. Maybe you can talk to her, let her know that I didn't mean to upset her. I'm not looking to cause grief in your household."

"It's your household now too." He patted my hand. "The others just need to understand it will take time for you to settle into your new position and responsibilities. And speaking of responsibilities, the prisoner caravan has arrived and I must hand out war prizes at the feast tonight. Father also wants us at temple services, for sacrifices to honor our marriage."

"No doubt to sacrifice all the priests of Quetzalcoatl that you captured," I muttered.

"If we had any, I'm sure he would."

So the civilian disguises worked, I thought. *Perhaps you can turn this in your favor.* I thought about how that other me might deal with this opportunity, but the thought of using seduction to get what I wanted felt unbecoming of Quetzalcoatl's high priestess. Besides, if this marriage was to work, sexual blackmail was ill-advised.

But if I could harness that confidence and authority....

"May I request a gift from you, My Lord?" I asked, gripping his hand tighter in mine.

He smiled down at me. "What kind of gift?"

"A wedding gift."

"I thought I already gave you one."

"Am I really only worth one handmaiden to you?"

He fixed his gaze on me again, a grin quirking at the corner of his mouth. "Of course not."

I granted him a smooth smile, pleased at the influence of my mere words. "A woman of my social status should have at least five handmaidens, to help me dress and bathe. And there must be no royal gardeners, for my garden is a shambles. Let me pick some from the prisoners." I thought to add "please", but that other voice never asked, and that worked quite well.

Black Otter contemplated a moment before asking, "These men and women you're planning to pick...they wouldn't be priests and priestesses of Quetzalcoatl, would they?"

I fought back the spike of panic. If they died because I exposed them, I could never forgive myself. "What does it matter if they are or aren't?"

"Of course it matters. My father—"

"And what about the promise you made me last night?" I demanded, the fear nearly taking over, but I gulped a lungful of air. Words alone weren't going to save my priests and priestesses. I put on a sultry smile that made my stomach crawl, then I played the tips of my three fingernails over his chin, gently tracing his lower lip. His whole demeanor changed, like a predator spotting movement in the bushes. "You do this for me, and I return the favor, My Lord," I whispered, and kissed him.

He embraced me hard, pulling me off my feet. I expected the desire to flare up, but my whole body remained steady, in control of itself. When he backed me up against the wall and reached for the hem of my dress, I stopped him. "Not yet. First, my servants; then I promise I'll make it very worth your while."

Black Otter looked me up and down with longing and frustration. "If my father found out about this, he'd hold my face against the cooking stones." I read the rest on his face: *But I don't care at all.*

I felt disgusted with myself.

Don't denigrate the gifts Heaven gave you, the voice suddenly snarled in my head. *It's his fault for being weak.*

¤

Black Otter took me to the palace prison in the north courtyard. I'd never been there before, but Black Otter had told me numerous stories about it when we were children. I'd been too enthralled by the descriptions of the cages and punishment tools to give any thought to why he and his father must have been going there at all. Stacks of cages lined the yard, but the male war prisoners sat in the middle, tied to each other by a rope looped around their necks. They all looked ragged and scared.

"Get some wooden collars ready with my name carved in them. I need workers for my wife's garden," Black Otter told the guard. He took my hand and led me over to the prisoners. "Pick the ones you want, my precious flower."

Now that I stood in front of all these condemned men, I felt horrible. Why were my priests more important than that farmer or that merchant, or that twelve-year-old boy crying for his mother? How could I choose to save some people while leaving the rest behind? I waited for that stronger voice to speak up, but it remained maddeningly silent.

Black Otter gripped my hand tighter then pointed to a man sitting in front of us, dressed in a dirty xicolli. "How about this one?"

He was a merchant who sold beautiful painted pottery I'd bought for the temple once or twice. The plea in his eyes almost had me nodding. *But if you say yes to every desperate look, you might end up saving none of your priests.* It wasn't the voice I'd hoped for, and my own, familiar one was far from certain, but as high priestess, my loyalty above all else was to the god and his servants, even before king and family. I finally shook my head, my eyes stinging at the grave disappointment on the merchant's face. Not even the relieved expressions from my priests could keep the haunted feeling away once I'd finished. Black Otter had the five low-ranking priests fitted with slave collars.

"I want all my wife's flower beds weeded and thinned before nightfall," he told them, as the guard led them out of the courtyard. He then took me back inside. "Are you all right?" he asked.

"I don't think I'll ever be all right again," I whispered. I'd just left two hundred men to die for no good reason. *It's all a needless waste, and some day I'm going to have the power to stop this nonsense.* It was still my familiar voice but this time loaded with confidence, and anger. *No human should have to die for a god who doesn't give a damn about them.*

The women were in one of the small banquet halls off the kitchen. I picked out my priestesses quickly and tried, unsuccessfully, to not dwell on it; by the time we arrived in the Great Hall for the victory feast, I thought I might throw up if I ate anything. I ventured a glare at Ihuitimal when I caught him watching me. *Someday you'll pay,* I thought. *For what you did to me, my father, to the followers of my beloved god, to those prisoners in the yard, to men and women alike.* He grinned at me as if amused.

And it's going to be sooner rather than later.

CHAPTER THIRTY-THREE

I decided that night that I needed to speed Ihuitimal on his way to Mictlan. I watched him very closely after that, observing his habits. He came to the occasional feast, but I never saw him in the hallways, nor did he ever touch a bite of food or drink without it first passing a taster's testing. Guards formed a shield around him, and manned the curtain separating the royal living quarters; and still more came and went from within, no doubt guarding the king's quarters from possible treachery by his own sons. If only Father had been so cautious...

"Why's he never around?" I asked Black Otter as we lay in bed.

Black Otter shrugged. "I'm usually with the army, so I don't spend much time with him. This is the longest I've been home in years." He kissed my bare shoulder.

"The others must miss you if you're never home."

"I imagine they do." He glided calloused hands over me.

And of course his being here with me right now didn't help matters. By the end of my first two weeks in Culhuacan, I'd become a pariah among the others, except for Anacoana. Jade Flower kept a cool distance, speaking to me only when I spoke first, but she kept conversation short and rarely smiled except in a simpering, forced fashion. Initially her rude behavior angered me, but eventually I decided it wasn't unwarranted. Black Otter had spent every single night since I'd arrived with me, and I'd stupidly assumed that he was seeing to his other obligations during the day. I'd failed in my duties to the others and I feared my own sister might start plotting against me soon if I didn't fix things.

I pulled away from Black Otter, annoyed by his touch. "When's the last time you actually spent the night with Jade Flower? Or even Lady Corn Flower, or Lady Papantzin?"

He stared at me, incredulous. "What does it matter?"

"You have duties, My Lord, and you've been neglecting them."

"Says who?"

"No one dares speak a word about it, but they know exactly how much time we spend together, and they compare it with how little you spend with them."

He shook his head, irritated.

"A good man doesn't keep more women than he has time for."

His face darkened. "Now I'm a bad man?"

"Sometimes even good men need reminding that they're making a wrong step. Do something about it before it's too late."

He sighed. "Very well." He tried to move in again, but I stopped him with fingers against his lips.

"Now."

He looked irritated but said, "Fine. I'll go and see Jade Flower."

"And stay the night with her." When he started protesting, I said, "She loves you, you know."

He looked as though I were speaking a foreign language, but then he blinked and nodded, that distant look vanishing from his eyes. "Of course she does." He donned his cape and left.

Finally! I knew men had big appetites when it came to sex, but he hadn't gone a night without bedding me since I'd come here. Not even the arrival of my monthly cycle deterred him—though its arrival right on time both surprised and relieved me; I would be spared pregnancy at least another month. I supposed one had to be insatiable when one kept multiple women, as all kings do. My own father had had over thirty women in his household, most of them keeping track of who he was with on any given night and whispering their disapproval about it in the morning.

But something was odd about Black Otter; in particular, he'd started looking gaunt, even weak at times, as if he couldn't replenish his strength with food, even though he ate like a ravenous wolf. And he slept like a dead man. Was he sick? If illness took him, what would happen to me? If his oldest son died, might my horrid uncle marry me off to this other son of his whom I'd never seen before? Or if he lost that son as well, might he replace that favored concubine of his with me? The thought sent chills racing up my spine like a giant centipede.

When Malinalli answered my summons, she brought a pot of xocolatl and we took it out into the garden. Servants weren't allowed to partake of xocolatl, but whenever we were alone I made sure she got a cup.

"At least he's leaving at the end of the week," I said, as I poured us each a cup.

"Is it really so bad?" she asked.

I chuckled. "Life could be worse. Still, I've been reduced to little more than a toy. I shudder to think that this is how most women must spend their lives. I had it very good."

"And you will again. The king won't live forever."

But I couldn't wait around years for the Black Dog to finally visit Ihuitimal's bed. Growing up, I'd assumed Little Reed would make my uncle pay for his crimes, and so I'd only fantasized about ways of killing him—most of them involving him holding his own heart in his hand—but now that responsibility was mine alone. I couldn't stab him to death with all the guards around, so my attack required stealth, and hopefully would make the death look natural. In his declining health, it shouldn't take much.

"I'm going to need some poison. Like the kind we used in the laundry room to keep the mice from nesting in the clean robes," I said.

Startled, Malinalli looked around a moment before lowering her voice. "What for?"

"Rodents are eating my bone flowers."

Malinalli nodded, understanding. "How much do you need?"

"Just a spoonful or two," I said lightly.

"I can have it for you by morning."

I shook my head. "I need to observe them more. They come and go like phantoms, and I want to make sure it's mice, not insects, otherwise all this is useless."

"And if the poison works too quickly, you might scare off the others," Malinalli said with a pointed look. "It would be better to poison them slowly, so it builds up and they can't smell it on any of the bodies."

Yes, that definitely was a consideration. I needed to spend more time planning this out in better detail.

I heard the bells on my door curtain jingle and I hurried to my feet, my stomach sinking. *We were overheard!* But it was only Black Otter, fresh-faced and excited. I calmed my racing heart. "What are you doing here?"

"I did as you asked, so now I'm back." He tried to take me into his arms.

But I slipped out of his reach. "You're supposed to stay the night with her."

"She's asleep, so what does it matter? And I still must do my duty to you." He tried again to embrace me.

"I don't need that tonight," I said, avoiding him again.

"But I do." He backed me up against the tree so I couldn't escape, and kissed my neck, making my head cloud.

"But you were just with Jade Flower," I murmured, trying to fight back the desire but failing. "How could you possibly need more?"

"Because I saved it all for you." He pushed up against me, sliding his hands all over me.

My resistance began melting faster. I'd completely forgotten Malinalli was still there—watching us with a blank look on her face—and I imagined her bare breasts pressed up against me, Black Otter caressing us both, her delicate fingers raising my flesh as they glided down my hips, over my abdomen, down between my legs....

The voice crawled forward in my mind, ready to ask my best friend to join Black Otter and myself for the rest of the evening, as if it were the most natural thing to do. I often blushed at remembering the things Black Otter convinced me to do while in the throes of passion, but I couldn't take the chance of wrecking my friendship with Malinalli. It was the only relationship I had left that meant anything to me. "You should be off to bed now," I told her, panting and bewildered. "Thank you for the xocolatl."

Malinalli blinked as if waking from a trance and muttered about talking to me in the morning, her cheeks flushed. Black Otter watched her leave, but I grabbed his chin and pulled him back to kiss me.

Afterwards I was sore from scrapes on my back—he took me against the copal tree—but those were just a minor inconvenience. Among the pants and trembles, he'd murmured, "I think I'd die without you, Quetzalpetlatl," in my ear, then collapsed into the grass, too weak to move. I struggled to drag him to my bed on my own—surely the guards would think I'd done something horrible to him if I asked for their help—and eventually I got him there. He groaned and fell immediately into a deep sleep.

But I stood there a long time, staring down at him, my mouth dry and my whole body trembling. I couldn't stop thinking about that dream of Red Flint, dead on the temple floor with an eerily contented smile on his face, as if having me even once was worth dying for.

◻

The week dragged by, and I tensed every time Black Otter came to see me, especially in the Women's Hall. He'd stare at me as if the rest of the world didn't exist at all, and Jade Flower's attitude had grown worse. She completely ignored me, walking away if I spoke, and I tried every day to get him to spend more time with her—or even one of the others—but he'd disappear for a little while then return to my quarters, eager to indulge himself.

Black Otter even made his farewell ceremony miserable for me by kissing the cheeks of the others while saving his most passionate embrace for me. Only after Ihuitimal cleared his throat did he finally let me go, leaving me half-drunk with lust in front of the disdainful glares of the others.

Ihuitimal whispered something to Black Otter but his son shrugged and snapped back at him, leaving Ihuitimal fuming. "I should have news in the next couple of days, so look for my runner," Black Otter told him, then ventured a smiling gaze back at me. I kept my eyes downcast until he was gone from the courtyard.

"I'm not going to the Women's Hall," I told Malinalli once we arrived back at my quarters. Everyone else had left ahead of us; Jade Flower had run from the courtyard, sobbing. I couldn't face her after all that.

"You want me to bring your weaving to you?" Malinalli asked as she gathered my laundry.

I shook my head. "It's been far too long since I've had time to meditate and pray."

"I know what you mean. Ihuitimal requires all servants to give prayers to the Smoking Mirror once a day, so I've taken to whispering prayers to the god in the steam bath in the middle of the night so as not to be overheard."

Anger flushed my face. "How are the others handling it?"

"Tayanna nearly lost her life by babbling about refusing to worship her beloved god's mortal enemy. Luckily the head servant chose to have her whipped rather than turning her in to the king for the sacrifice." She finished packing my laundry in a wicker basket then asked, "Do you think the prayers still count, even if I don't mean them?"

"Real prayers are always stronger than fake ones." As Malinalli turned to leave, I said, "Meet me by the pond in the main garden this afternoon and

I can hear all the news you've gathered this week."

Malinalli nodded knowingly and left.

I knelt in the morning sunshine in my garden. My priests were doing a wonderful job, and under their care the bone flowers were starting to bloom. The sharp, sweet smell brought memories of childhood; of Mother, of my wedding day, and of Little Reed bringing me bundles of flowers back from palace visits. I plucked one of the waxy white flowers and crushed it between my fingers, releasing a concentrated burst of sweet vanilla aroma. If love had a smell, this would be it.

Someone clearing their throat broke my reverie. Two guards stood behind me, making my heart stop before it took off at a frantic sprint. "Yes?"

"The king requests your presence," said one, motioning me to stand.

I wasn't about to show fear and condemn myself, so I rose and followed them back inside. But when they turned down the men's hallway, I hesitated; not even female servants were allowed in the men's quarters. The guard gave me a gentle push to get me moving again.

There were only four doors beyond the curtain; there'd been at least ten doorways here before, so the missing six had been sealed up and plastered over and decorated with murals of birds and jaguars. As we passed the first doorway, I recognized my old nursery, still painted with birds and butterflies. Black Otter's son sat on the floor, babbling as he pushed a toy jaguar around on its little wooden wheels. An old man smoked a pipe in the corner, watching over him. Two of the remaining three doorways presumably belonged to Black Otter and his lost brother, but both curtains were closed off.

The lead guard held the last door curtain open. Memories of my father's mutilated corpse and death's foul stench made me freeze until he prodded me forward.

The room smelled very different now—sweet with tobacco, incense and xocolatl. Where Father's bed once sat, a servant crouched, tending a bubbling kettle in the middle of a sitting area. New murals of blood sacrifice stretched across every wall, but the weathered wood hearth mantel looked the same. The wall between Mother and Father's rooms was gone and Mother's quarters were now a sanctuary or sorts, devoted to a painting of a giant, strutting god, human-looking save for the small mirrors in his eyes and the large obsidian mirror in place of his left foot.

His skin was so black it seemed to suck the light from the room, as if the picture were a constantly shifting cloud of smoke. Hearts poured into his open mouth from the hands of priests, the color of the blood so dark I doubted it was paint.

Ihuitimal knelt in front of the large mirror; but even when he struggled to his feet, he didn't look at me, just wheezed lightly as he walked by. He drank his xocolatl then waved the servant and his guards from the room.

I hadn't expected that. What was he playing at?

"I trust you've settled into palace life again?" he asked, still not looking at me.

I hesitated to answer at first, but when I finally spoke, I kept my tone cool. "It was a little difficult at first."

"And seeing family again is always good. I'm sure you've missed that a great deal since losing both Topiltzin and that woman who raised you."

A storm of emotions stirred inside me: anger that he'd even dare speak about Little Reed and not even take the time to find out Nimilitzli's name; devastation over being reminded yet again that they were gone; and resentment that this demon-worshipping filth even presumed to say anything about the joys of family. I took a deep, calming breath before speaking though. "I'm glad to see Jade Flower again. And Black Otter."

Ihuitimal chuckled. "If only Jade Flower were as happy to see you. She thinks your being here is a very bad thing for Black Otter. And I'm starting to agree with her."

I couldn't help scowling at him. "Black Otter is his own master, and I cannot make him spend any more time with her than he's willing to—"

"She thinks you're poisoning him," Ihuitimal cut in, his gaze like a dagger. "And given how terrible he's looked recently, I have to wonder as well."

I tried to laugh, but part of me wondered if someone was indeed poisoning him. *Maybe you're doing it without even knowing it.* But I pushed that outrageous thought aside. "I'm trying to make a life for us here."

"By tearing down everything I built to bring that weak Feathered Serpent back into the temples?" Ihuitimal grinned at me. "Let's not play games, Quetzalpetlatl. I'm not afraid of losing face to you; I'd have to believe that you're someone of importance for that to happen. And I know you've waited a very long time to have this chance to confront me, so go ahead, speak your mind. Let us deal honestly with each other."

I wavered only a moment before the anger surged enough to loosen my tongue. "You sneer at Quetzalcoatl, but the truth is that the Feathered Serpent loves everyone, even you; yet you chose to reject him for that demon that hates us all. Don't think you're some exception to that; when you fail your dark master, does he pat your head and say 'try again', or does he make you pay a high price? What did he do when you let my mother escape? Or how about all those failed assassination attempts? At first I found it odd that you have so many daughters, but now I think the reason is clear: you failed the Smoking Mirror so he punished you by denying you any blood sons of your own, and you must rely on your brother's illegitimate son to carry on your legacy. This other son is probably no more yours than Black Otter is, is he?" When Ihuitimal stared at me, surprised, I added, "I was in the room when you confronted Nochuatl. Your murderous rage must have been too thick for you to remember."

A smile crept over his scarred face. "I remember telling Nochuatl I was going to pluck your wings off." He chuckled but soon turned serious again. "He was no better than your father; scoundrels, the whole lot of them. They both got the destiny they wrote for themselves."

"My father deserved nothing you handed him that night," I said, my voice shaking. "You have a nerve calling my father a scoundrel. You earned your exile. You broke the law—"

Ihuitimal turned away to contemplate the hearth with his hard gaze. "Your illusions about Mixcoatl are pathetic. Your father did more damage to me than any other man. He was a filthy, lying dog who sneaked his way onto Culhuacan's throne—the throne I was promised by your grandfather. Never knew that, did you?"

His words shocked me into silence.

He smiled coolly at me. "Everyone always talked about how honorable and noble your father was; even as a child, Father gave him just a little more tlaxcallis than he gave the rest of us." He went back to the kettle to pour himself a new cup of xocolatl. "We were on campaign in the north when we were beset by Chichimecs and I was captured. Mixcoatl vowed to return and free me, even if it took the rest of his years. I spent three years in captivity, forced to fight with one ankle bound to my opponent for the amusement of the chief and his allies, half starving and constantly defending my life, and dreaming of the day when Mixcoatl would keep his promise and raze their miserable village to the ground. I dreamed nightly of finally taking my throne and seeing Chimalma's smile again; that kept me from succumbing to the misery of my waking hours," he added, with a surprisingly nostalgic expression.

I blinked, stunned. "My mother?" The thought of him pining for her made my skin crawl.

Ihuitimal frowned as if I'd interrupted a pleasant dream. "Of course your mother. Your grandfather promised her along with the kingdom, and we were to marry when I returned from my last campaign." He gulped down the xocolatl as if it had angered him. "But Mixcoatl never came. Instead the Chichimecs granted me freedom, won with scars uncountable." He pointed to the one on his face. "So I walked home, eager to see my brothers again after so long." He paused as he stared down at the kettle. "Imagine my surprise when I found that Mixcoatl had told our father that I'd died, and claimed Chimalma for his own. And when her father died, he inherited the throne. He'd already reigned for two years, and he never sent anyone to find me; claimed he thought me already sacrificed. But he couldn't hide the shameful truth from me: he'd left me to die so he could claim my throne."

I knew my father was flawed—he'd made me cry too many times for me to not know—but I never would've suspected him capable of such backhanded deception. *You can't believe Ihuitimal's spiteful lies,* I thought, but I'd heard enough from my own father and others to give the claims credence. Nochuatl had told me that Ihuitimal had a right to be angry. "You should have challenged him for the throne back then," I said, my resentment leaking through.

"I should have," Ihuitimal admitted. "But I clung foolishly to Mixcoatl's promises to make things right. He gave me Chimalma's younger sister, but then Nochuatl wanted to fight me for her." He chuckled. "Mixcoatl wouldn't let him. Eloxochitl wasn't half the beauty your mother was, but she had her own charms, and your father promised to betroth the first compatible set of children we each had."

He extinguished the burner, then sighed. "But even then, I couldn't find a shred of happiness for myself, so I left for the north again. I was determined to find that Chichimec village again and burn it to the ground, for all those years they'd made me suffer and kept me from my rightful future. They cost me everything that mattered."

How often had I felt that same, blinding feeling since I'd returned to Culhuacan? The notion unnerved me.

He stood up, his eyebrows raised in surprise. "But to my amazement, the chief remembered me. He welcomed me into his home and called me a son. He gave me a house and all the women I could want for, saying I'd earned them with my bravery and tenacity. I hadn't received anything like such a kind welcome when I returned home from my captivity, and in my confusion, I fell into a dark despair."

He hobbled over to the mural of the black-painted god. "The village shaman told me to seek guidance from the Smoking Mirror, so I lived out in the desert for two months. I was starving and near death before the god finally came to me as an obsidian jaguar. He set his giant paw upon me and said 'You are my high priest, destined to bring my worship out of the desert. Be my voice and I'll reward you with everything your heart has ever desired.' And for the first time in years, I felt I had purpose again; I'd finally found my life's calling." He stared up at the mural with reverence.

Chills rose up my spine. *That sounds like what Quetzalcoatl told me....*

"After a year in the north, I returned to Culhuacan to find my wife pregnant and Nochuatl unable to look me in the eye," Ihuitimal said, amused. "I considered killing the baby and his mother, but the kindness the Chichimecs had shown me stayed my hand. I prayed to the god to decide their fate for me; if the child lived to learn his true name, it was because the god had use for him." He turned away from the mural finally and came back, not meeting my gaze. "So when Black Otter survived, I accepted him as my son, the same way my Chichimec father accepted me. Since he'd come from Eloxochitl, everyone would accept him as my son, so I raised him, molded him as if he were my own blood. And Chimalma had finally carried a daughter to birth after years of failure and the ordeal left her barren. Everything was falling into place finally."

"But then you had to go and ruin it all by worshiping your beloved god in my father's city," I pointed out.

"My only mistake was telling Black Otter anything about Smoking Mirror before he'd earned the right to know," Ihuitimal corrected me. "The final arrow in my heart came when Mixcoatl once again broke his promise, betraying my son. As soon as he discovered Chimalma was carrying the Feathered Serpent's bastard, he pushed Black Otter aside, proving his word was worthless. What I did was the only right thing to do."

I laughed. "To make sure Black Otter got the throne?" When he nodded, I asked, "Then why isn't he king yet? You were the throne's custodian until he was old enough, but yet he's still not king."

"Do not doubt my love for my son," Ihuitimal snarled. "I will see him on the throne I was wrongly denied and I won't let a conniving woman stand in his way."

"How am I standing in his way? You're the one who's still holding onto it like some pet monkey clinging to its master. It would be best for everybody if you just stepped aside for him now."

Ihuitimal flicked his gaze back to the mural again. "He can only take the throne when the god says he's ready, and as long as you're poisoning his mind with whispers of bringing Quetzalcoatl back, that will never happen. He will only take his rightful throne when he's willing to take up my mantle as the next high priest of the Smoking Mirror."

"You and your god do him a disservice by forcing him to be something he doesn't want."

"Kings sometimes have to do things they don't like. If he hasn't the stomach for it, then he won't take the throne, but I trust my son to do what needs doing when his master demands it."

A smirk crept onto my lips. "You give yourself far too much credit when you claim you've molded Black Otter in your image. I see far more of his true father in him—a failure for you, but a victory for the goodness of mankind."

Ihuitimal flashed his sharpened teeth in a grisly smile. "Then why don't you just do it for him then?" He tossed an obsidian knife to me. "I'm sure it's crossed your mind more than once; I see it in your eyes. How many years have you dreamed of this, Quetzalpetlatl? Since the night you stumbled in here to find I'd slain your father? Does it still haunt your dreams, little girl? Do you wake in the middle of the night in a cold sweat, crying for your Tatli?" He laughed, showing off pointy teeth.

I tightened my grip on the knife's wooden handle, my anger surging and my wrist feeling afire. I'd gotten used to the constant itching so I hardly noticed it anymore, until now. *Plunge the blade into his throat, just like you did to Ahexotl; watch his blood splash across the face of his demon god,* I thought, sweating with anticipation. *Oh who will be the one laughing then?*

"The hatred feels good, doesn't it? As comfortable as a worn pair of sandals." Ihuitimal took my hand and put the blade to his throat, the expression in his eyes intense. "You know you want to do it, so do it!" he growled.

But why was he goading me?

Who cares? Slice him from ear to ear and he'll bleed to death in no time. You know how to do it; you learned it for the spring sacrifices. He deserves the same fate as murderers and thieves.

I started pressing the blade.

But he's my uncle, my blood, my family, what little I have left of it, I suddenly thought.

He's nobody! He deserves to feel the pain you've felt all these years!

Ihuitimal stepped closer still, pushing so hard that the blade cut into his neck's flabby, wrinkled skin. "Do it, Quetzalpetlatl! Resolution will only come from killing me; trust me, I know all about it."

And become just like him, and his demon god? My grip on the knife loosened. I let it slip from my fingers and it clattered on the stone floor between us. *That's not what Quetzalcoatl would want; that's not the person I am.*

Ihuitimal sneered. "And that, dear, is why women have no business in politics; they haven't the loins to do what must be done for the good of their people. That's why Culhuacan has no queen, nor will she ever again. Your usefulness is just about finished, and thankfully I'll soon be rid of you, and Black Otter can regain the good sense you've stolen from him. Jade Flower at least knows her place, something Black Otter's own mother never quite understood either. Don't make me deal with you like I did with her." He turned away and leaned against the hearth, as if the whole discussion had tired him out. "Now get back in your place and don't darken my doorway again."

CHAPTER THIRTY-FOUR

I met Malinalli by the pond and we went to where my father used to keep his exotic birds. Most of the cages were falling apart with disuse, their doors hanging open. We sat under the large oak tree sheltering the remains of the macaw cage and ate our lunch.

"You're upset," Malinalli noted.

I shook my head. "I had the chance to do it, actually had a blade to his throat with no one around...but I just couldn't do it." I sighed.

Malinalli gripped my hand and gave it a gentle, reassuring squeeze. "What did he say?"

"He spent most of the time justifying what he did to my father, but he thinks me meddlesome. And Jade Flower thinks I'm poisoning Black Otter."

"She's just a fool."

"Maybe she's not." I looked up at her after a hesitation. "I'm...I think there's something wrong with me, Malinalli."

Frowning, she asked, "Why would you think that?"

"You've seen how Black Otter has been behaving. He won't stay out of my bed, and I can't get him to spend any time with the others. And the other night, he told me he couldn't live without me. He's becoming obsessive."

"What does that have to do with you though?" Malinalli asked puzzled.

"What if I'm making him like that? What if I drove Red Flint crazy?"

Malinalli shook her head. "Red Flint was a terrible man. You can't blame yourself for the things he chose to do. Nor can you blame yourself for the kind of man Black Otter is."

I bowed my head. "No, I can't. It's just...when we make love...." My face burned to even speak of such embarrassing, private things, but I needed to talk to someone about it, and who could I trust not to judge me if not my best friend? "I'm not myself; I turn into someone else, and this other woman I become...she scares me. I completely lose my head, and I'm afraid of what I might do."

Furrowing her brows, Malinalli asked, "What do you mean what you might do?"

I thought of the dream again, about drinking the very life out of Red Flint in the throes of ecstasy, but I couldn't bring myself to speak of it. How could I possibly talk about the fear that I was slowly killing Black Otter without sounding completely ridiculous, and crazy? *Because it is ridiculous,* I told myself, and shook my head. "I don't know. I feel like I have absolutely no control of the situation."

Malinalli gave my hand another squeeze. "Granted, I don't know much about sex—not from experience anyway—but maybe all this is completely normal."

"I don't think so." I almost blurted out *because it's nothing like it is with the god,* but I bit my tongue in time. It was difficult enough talking about all this without bringing the true nature of my relationship with Quetzalcoatl into it. "My own experience is limited too, but…I just know that this isn't normal, and I'm afraid something bad is going to happen."

She gave me a sympathetic smile. "I know you, Quetzalpetlatl, and whatever it is that's worrying you…maybe it's in fact a good thing? Maybe it's why the god chose you for his high priestess? He gave you that most important task of ending human sacrifice, after all."

"He gave that task to Topiltzin," I corrected her. "It's only fallen to me because I erred and he's dead." Thinking about Little Reed made the ache in my chest intensify, and I couldn't hold back the tears. "So what if I mess this up too? What if Black Otter ends up like Red Flint?" *Or worse yet like Little Reed?*

Malinalli's face turned serious—and a bit scared. "Has he threatened you, the way Red Flint always did?"

"Oh no, Black Otter is nothing like that," I insisted, embarrassed for even insinuating it unintentionally. "He's a good man, but Ihuitimal…he's already warned me about remembering my place or he'll kill me, like he did my aunt." I wiped my tears away with a fierce swipe of my fist. "Eloxochitl was a wonderful woman, so kind and generous…." *And an adulteress,* I imagined Ihuitimal hissing. *Don't forget that!*

"Do you think it's dangerous to stay here now?"

"I don't know. He did say that my usefulness was almost over, so maybe he is planning to kill me after all." Though why hadn't he yet, especially now that Black Otter wasn't here to protect me? *Something else is going on, something that requires him to keep me alive. I'm too valuable for him to kill, at least just yet.* The thought gave me a shiver.

Malinalli glanced around, then whispered, "Then I'll make sure he's dead before morning."

I shook my head, adamant. "I can't ask you to do something I couldn't do myself."

"You shouldn't have to live like this, constantly subjected to terror and dishonor. It's an insult to the god's honor; I should do it to defend that."

"The god wouldn't want you to do it either. He despises gaining power by murder, and it was my mistake to forget that. We can't let fear drive us from our convictions."

Malinalli bowed her head. "Of course, My Lady. Forgive my angry outburst."

I shook my head. "I'm grateful for your loyalty, to both myself and the god. We'll find a way out of this without compromising our principles. I trust the Feathered Serpent to show us the way."

"And so do I," Malinalli replied. "I have faith in the god, and in you."

¤

For the next week I made daily appearances in the Women's Hall if only to avoid looking like a guilty woman hiding away in her quarters. I wouldn't let Ihuitimal's threats deter me.

While I saw little of him after that day, his guards followed me everywhere, even keeping watch outside my quarters. But the most troubling development came when a serving woman I'd never seen before came to bathe and dress me the day after my meeting with Ihuitimal. I asked where Malinalli was, but she refused to answer, and just brushed my hair with a ferocity that made my eyes water. Once a few days passed and Malinalli still didn't return, I began to really worry. *She's been arrested or maybe even sacrificed,* I thought as I lay on my bed crying. *And once again it's your fault. You put those silly schemes into her head.*

"She's been reassigned to one of the noblemen's wives," Paper Flower told me when she brought me my afternoon atole. I cried still more, relieved Malinalli was alive, but shaken that someone had thought she ought to be taken away from me.

Something else was going on, though. Guards were everywhere, and Paper Flower informed me that the city was crawling with soldiers now. "Three times as many archers are on the defensive wall, and packs of

Chichimec warriors are patrolling the Noble Quarters." Everyone—particularly the women—whispered about armies coming around the lake. It appeared that war was on its way to Culhuacan's gates.

But why hadn't Black Otter returned yet? He'd promised to return within a few nights, but a week had passed and I'd heard nothing from him. I started fearing that he'd been taken prisoner, or worse yet killed. I dreaded to think what might become of me if that were the case.

Or maybe his father sent him away, to get him away from you, before he does something stupid, I thought as I climbed into bed. *Whatever has been affecting you, Black Otter, please don't bring it back with you.* For the first time since he'd left, the bed felt so empty without him there with me.

◻

A noise woke me in the deep of night and I sat up, alert: I'd been sleeping more and more lightly as the days went on and my anxiety grew. And my cheek felt wet and tingly; but I'd been dreaming about that day in Teotihuacan when I first saw the Black Dog, so maybe it was all in my mind. I shivered as I looked around. "Who's there?"

"Shhhh!" Black Otter stepped out from behind the screen that shielded my bed from the doorway at night, and an overwhelming desire to hug him fell over me. The worry on his face stopped me though. "Get dressed. We have to go," he whispered.

"Go where?"

"No time to explain." He glanced over his shoulder. "Just get dressed."

I put on a dress and sandals while he glanced repeatedly at the door, as if expecting unwelcome company. He draped a black cloak over my shoulders then led me out into the garden, his sweaty grip painfully tight. My heart started racing. He climbed the copal tree then surveyed the walkway behind the wall. He beckoned me to climb up after him.

I froze. I hadn't climbed a tree since I was a girl and I wasn't even sure my bad heel would allow me to. But when he beckoned again, impatient, I hiked up my hem and made my way up unsteadily. I used to run up trees like a monkey, but now I was clumsy and slow as I shimmied up to the branch where Black Otter crouched. Sweat dripped off my brow and I could barely catch my breath before he wanted me to follow him up to the next large branch, which reached out over the garden's back wall. "Where are we going?" I finally choked out, once we reached the top. To my surprise there were no guards behind my wall.

"I'm getting you out of here," Black Otter whispered, then jumped down to the ground. He held his arms out, so I jumped down too, letting him cushion my fall. He looked both ways down the walled passageway then took my hand and pulled me to the left. "It's not safe for you here anymore," he continued as we walked.

"What do you mean?"

He held up a hand for silence. At the bend in the passageway, he pushed me gently against the stone wall and held a finger to his lips. He stepped around the corner. "What are you two still doing back here? We have an invading army on the way and all able-bodied men are to report to the main gate for orders."

A man answered, "The king told us to guard the corridor, My Lord—"

"My father sent me out to make sure everyone was reporting as ordered." When silence followed, Black Otter asked, "Are you deaf and dumb? Your war chief just gave you an order!"

"We'll go immediately, My Lord," another man squeaked. Once the slapping of their sandals on the ground faded away, Black Otter came back, grabbed my wrist and pulled me along after him.

"There's an army coming?" I panted, jogging to keep up.

"It'll be here by sunrise," Black Otter replied. "I was worried I wouldn't make it back in time to get you."

"Which army?"

"Xochicalco and its allies, of course."

Joy quickened my heartbeat. "King Mazatzin is coming?"

He hesitated before saying, "Mazatzin abdicated his throne."

"To whom?"

He didn't answer, so I repeated the question, refusing to go further. Why didn't he want me to know?

We'd reached the mouth of the cave leading out into the lake. Black Otter peered into the dark before finally saying, "To Topiltzin, all right?"

"Topiltzin's dead," I replied; but when he wouldn't meet my gaze, my throat felt tied in a knot. "What are you getting at?"

He tried to pull me along again but I stood firm. He sighed. "Topiltzin's alive."

"You're lying!" I snarled through tears. "Red Flint had him murdered.

Mazatzin brought me his sword."

"He escaped."

"If he was alive he would've let me know...he would've written me letters," I insisted, bordering on hysterical.

"He did, but my father intercepted them."

His face was a watery blur behind my tears. I wanted to punch him for telling me such a cruel lie. "I don't believe you!"

After an uncomfortable silence, Black Otter said, "He calls you Papalotl, like I used to, and he signs his letters as Little Reed."

Little Reed! My eyes widened, a smile tugging at my lips. Though my mind was in turmoil, my heart knew it was true. "He's really alive?" *My Little Reed—my love!—he's not dead! He found out Ihuitimal was holding me prisoner and he's come to rescue me!* The pain that had squeezed my heart for so long loosened, letting joy pulse inside me and a relieved laugh escape my lips. "He's really alive!"

Black Otter took my arm. "You must keep your voice down or someone's going to hear you." We advanced into the darkness, taking no torch with us.

Soon I couldn't see my own hand touching my nose. "How do you know where you're going?"

"Just keep hold of me. I've gone through here many times."

My whole body was abuzz. *This is why I'd never convinced my heart to move on, because it always knew Little Reed wasn't dead. Of course he'd outwit Red Flint, and that dog wanted you to believe he was dead, so you'd fall into his arms in despair and look to him for comfort.*

But Black Otter too had known all this time that Little Reed was alive and said nothing, not even when I mentioned him. *So he could impregnate you and solidify his claim to the throne, making Little Reed the interloper.* Anger and betrayal roiled in my chest, and I couldn't stand his sweaty hand shackling my wrist. I tore it away from him.

He stumbled and I moved away as he floundered around in the dark, calling out my name. With at least ten steps between us, I finally spoke. "Where are you taking me?"

"Why didn't you answer when I called for you?" His irritation couldn't conceal the panic underlying his voice.

"Where are you taking me?" I repeated.

I imagined Black Otter muttering to himself, trying to decide what, if anything, to tell me, but finally he said, "Topiltzin captured my brother Amoxtli in battle three months ago and offered to trade him in exchange for our surrendering Culhuacan's throne. And my father—if you can believe it—was on verge of accepting the compromise, to save Amoxtli, but then Xochicalco burned down and I captured you. We'd been intercepting Topiltzin's letters to you for several years already, so I knew he'd be willing to trade my brother and the throne for you."

"Then why lie about Topiltzin being dead if you were just going to trade me away?" I demanded. "Why go through all that trouble of making me your wife and convincing me we were going to build a life together?" When he didn't answer, I thought my insides would collapse under the weight of my fury. "Because you knew he wants to marry me, and you couldn't resist claiming me for yourself just to spite him, right?" I didn't want to cry but tears muddled my voice anyway. "Or maybe you just wanted revenge against me, for that broken promise when we were children?"

"Absolutely not!" Black Otter insisted. "I do love you, Quetzalpetlatl, more than anything. Maybe it started out as a callous deception, but now...I feel horrible and wonder how I could have ever justified it to myself. You're everything to me. You must forgive me—"

"You convinced me to break my vows to the god, you dog! I could be with your child right now!"

"I know, and that's why I can't let my father trade you back to Topiltzin."

I hadn't heard him moving during our conversation, but suddenly his hand closed around my wrist and when I tried to wrench away from him, he held firm. "Let me go! I'm not going anywhere with you!" He dragged me by the wrist but when I kicked him, he pinned my arms behind my back. "You're hurting me!" I snarled as he pushed me onward.

"It's for your own good," he said, his voice regretful. "I can't let Topiltzin hurt you."

"My brother would never hurt me, Black Otter," I insisted as I stumbled in the dark, tripping, but he caught me before I fell.

"You say that now, but I know what men do to secure their own power. My father killed all your brothers, to make sure none of them would avenge your father, and if Topiltzin found you pregnant, he would kill our child."

"Topiltzin is nothing like your father."

"He can't be trusted, and neither can my father, so we must leave Culhuacan. It's the only way I can guarantee your safety."

Usually it was easy to argue against Black Otter—especially given how prone to irrationality he'd become with the passing days—but he sounded downright coherent now. Not that I believed for a moment that Little Reed would kill any child of mine, regardless of who the father was, but I couldn't call Black Otter crazy for fearing it. *And funny how after a week away from you, he seems almost normal again, as if being around you affects his reason.* The thought sent a chill through me.

A glimmer of light eventually appeared ahead, but it still took a long time to reach it. The glow came from a torch held by a guard standing at the bow of a canoe; an eerily reminiscent scene. We climbed into the boat and sat facing each other as the soldier pushed off from the shore, turning the bow towards the mouth of the cave.

"Where are you taking me?" I asked, glowering at him in the moonlight as we moved out onto the open lake.

"I don't know yet," Black Otter admitted. "There won't be any safe haven for us anywhere in the valley, so we'll have to travel past the mountains, to the south. We'll find somewhere where no one knows us."

"Topiltzin won't stop looking for me, Black Otter. We won't be able to hide from him forever."

He stared at me with eerie dispassion. "I'll die before I let him have you."

My heart quickened. So much for the rationality. "But what about Jade Flower and the others? Surely you wouldn't run out on them?"

His expression didn't change. "You said a good man doesn't keep more women than he has time for, and you're right. I have but one wife to devote my heart and soul to, someone I love and am willing to lay my life down for—"

"But what about your children? Why would the son you already have be any safer than one I may or may not be carrying?"

"They don't matter."

His indifference sickened me. "You can't mean that—"

"They aren't your children, so they are meaningless." He frowned, perplexed. "This is what you want too, isn't it? Isn't this how marriage *should* be? Don't you love me?"

I felt so numb with disbelief. "How could you say such things?"

But he shook his head like an obstinate child. "The gods gave you to me for a reason, and who are you to argue with them? Say you love me, Quetzalpetlatl!"

"Enough!" I cried. *It's like Red Flint all over again,* I thought, tears stinging my eyes. *But worse. You actually care for Black Otter.*

A shadow of anger crossed his face, but a soft whistling distracted him. The guard suddenly gagged and tried to stand up, grasping at an arrow piercing his throat, but he tipped over sideways, almost dumping the boat over with him.

"Get down!" Black Otter pushed me to the floor of the canoe and crouched next to me, sword drawn as he scanned the lake over the boat's edge. Eventually he stood up and waved his arms, shouting, "Hold your fire, you fools! You're attacking your war chief's boat!"

But another arrow whizzed by and Black Otter dropped down again. "I don't think those are your men," I whispered.

"That dog Topiltzin has disguised his men to fool me," he growled.

"Topiltzin isn't an unreasonable man. We should surrender."

"And be taken as a sacrifice?"

Such foolishness. "The god doesn't want the lives of war prisoners; he doesn't want lives at all. The guard dropped the paddles, and they're going to get us anyway, so surrender is the only reasonable option. Don't throw away your life."

Black Otter peered around wild-eyed. "You promise to negotiate with your brother on my behalf?"

"I promise."

He kissed me hurriedly but the excitement of seeing Little Reed again kept any desire gagged. We remained crouched until the approaching canoe neared, then I told Black Otter, "Call out for our surrender."

He sighed, disgruntled, but did so.

Someone called back, "Stand and toss all weapons overboard." We did so, struggling to not capsize the canoe as Black Otter located three blades and dropped them into the dark water.

In the growing dawn, I saw three men in the other canoe, each dressed like Culhuacan's soldiers. One held a drawn bow pointed at Black Otter while the other two paddled. I started crying, trying to keep it quiet. My captivity was nearly over and I could finally be rid of this constant itching that had me clawing ruthlessly at my own wrist....

As the canoe slipped up next to ours, Black Otter dropped his hands. "What is this outrage?" he demanded, the wildness returning. "These are my father's personal guard. How dare you fire on your future king?"

In answer, the man shot Black Otter in the chest, catapulting him backwards into the water. I nearly fell overboard too, but someone grabbed and dragged me into the other canoe. "Let me go!" I searched around in vain for signs of Black Otter, but I saw only waves where he'd fallen in. The man tightened his grip so I sank my teeth into his arm, tasting blood. The metallic tang brought a strange spike of hunger.

The man ripped free of me, but I claimed a chunk of his flesh. Roaring, he shoved my head into the water.

I thrashed, kicking and clawing, holding against the urgent need to inhale. When the man finally hauled me back up after what felt like days, I sucked in deep, panting breaths, my wet hair plastered across my face.

"You almost tipped us over!" another man shouted.

"Look what she did to my arm!"

"I ought to toss you to the caimans. Can't even handle an unarmed woman! Let Tenoch deal with her."

He let me go but I lay on my stomach on the bottom of the canoe, giving no fight while someone bound my hands. I had none left.

As the men paddled back towards Culhuacan, a strange, strangled cry rang out across the lake, making them pause to look back the way they'd come. "Lake monster," the one called Tenoch said, and the leader told the others to pick up the pace. He shook his head and murmured, "Oh, such a bad omen. I fear none of us will live to see the Lord Sun set on Meztliapan ever again."

Chapter Thirty-Five

The assassins returned me to the palace and took me to the prison yard, leaving me bound in one of the cages. My muddy, wet dress chilled me but I still fell asleep for a while, plagued by dreams of strange, giant lake otters dragging Black Otter to the bottom of Meztliapan. He broke free of them, but when he reached the surface, he'd turned into one of them, shouting in a high, crying voice, "Mine! Mine!"

I awoke when someone kicked the side of my cage, and I squinted up to see Ihuitimal glaring down at me. His face was painted black with gold stripes across his eyes and mouth, and he gripped an obsidian-tipped spear so tight in his right hand that the veins stood out on his surprisingly thick upper arm. I'd taken him for a frail old man under his bulky royal robes, but now—in just a loincloth and feathered arm and calf bands— it was clear he wasn't nearly so weak. He didn't smile; there was no smug gloating; he was livid, and if not for the cage he probably would've throttled me awake.

But with the dreams of Black Otter's murder still fresh in my head, I refused to melt under his fury. "How could you kill your own son? Does no one matter to you?"

"Kings must make difficult decisions, for the good of their people and god...." Anguish choked the anger in his voice. "I should have kept you locked up in the prison yard instead of showing you compassion you don't deserve. Whatever you did to him—" He shuddered, then looked down at his palms. Blood dripped between his fingers where he'd balled his fists too tight. He stared at it a moment before barking at the guards, "Get her ready to take out." The loathing in his glare intensified as he told me, "Someday you will pay for this. What I did to your father will look like a mercy compared to what Amoxtli will do to you when he hears you forced me to kill his brother." He stormed away as the guards dragged me wet and shivering from the cage.

¤

Troops spread out over Culhuacan's eastern plain like swarming ants, blackening the ground as far as I could see. Ihuitimal's infantry stood between them and the walls, all armed with spears or slings. Archers crowded the walkways atop the walls, their bows pulled tight and ready as Ihuitimal and I set out from the gates.

We walked through the ranks down a gap. A pack of well-armored soldiers formed a circle around us, and the lead guard held up a long wooden pole with a feathered banner attached, displaying the city's royal crest.

A group of soldiers split off from the front of the opposing line, the lead man carrying a standard as well; a white feathered serpent with slender green feathers trailing around its neck. The serpentine flag flapped in the cool breeze from the lake behind us.

As we continued out onto the field to meet them, my anxiety soared, but so did my hope. Any moment now, the nightmare of these last two years would finally end and I could hold Little Reed again.

Both groups stopped about a hundred paces apart, but I saw familiar faces now. Mazatzin stood next to Citlallotoc at the front, both of their faces painted white with vertical green stripes running from their hairlines, over their eyes and down to their jawbones. Everyone wore cotton armor under their feathered xicolli shirts. But still no sign of Little Reed in the serried ranks.

Ihuitimal grabbed my arm with his stony grip and pulled me forward. Our group opened up to let us by, and two soldiers broke off to follow us. We stopped a few paces away when the other group parted as well.

Little Reed stepped out, wearing no face paint but a tall crown of white heron feathers and a matching cloak. The shirt over his cotton armor bore the feathered serpent emblem, done in shimmering jewels. Hardness resided in his eyes. His hair had gone still whiter, so the dark strands were mere accents now.

A young man wearing only a loincloth walked next to him, and I was struck by how much he looked like Ihuitimal; Amoxtli obviously was the king's natural son. They stopped a few paces beyond their group as well.

"I've come here on your terms," Little Reed called across the gap between us. "I'm returning your son and disavowing any claim to Culhuacan's throne, so now return my sister to me, as unharmed as your son is."

Ihuitimal still frowned, but he said nothing, just shoved me in the back to get me moving. I glared back at him before heading off alone towards Little Reed.

Little Reed nodded and Amoxtli started walking as well, towards me. Little Reed kept his gaze focused on me though. I picked up the pace, eventually passing Amoxtli without a word, then I broke into a limping run for the remaining distance, tears blurring everything.

By the time I flung myself into Little Reed's outspread arms, the reality finally hit with painful force: he truly was alive. I sobbed as I crushed him in my arms. He whispered to me, but in my incoherent joy, I didn't understand any of it. It was enough to have his arms around me and feel his pulse thudding against my nose as I buried my face in his neck. *I will never let you go again,* I thought, squeezing him tighter. "I'm sorry, Little Reed," I wept. "You were so close to getting the throne back if not for me—"

"You mean more to me than any throne, Papalotl," he whispered. "So long as I have you, everything will be just fine." I smiled at him through tears when he took my face between his hands and leaned in to kiss me.

But shouting from the other side of the field broke the moment. I turned to see Amoxtli running back to us. Ihuitimal still stood where I'd left him, a panicked, bewildered expression on his face.

Amoxtli fell to his knees before Little Reed. "My Lord, I beg you, accept me into your ranks!" he panted. "I have seen the goodness of Quetzalcoatl and I cannot risk going back into the cradle of his enemy. Please do not turn me over to the mercies of such a dark god!" He groped at Little Reed's legs with pleading hands. "You are the rightful king of Culhuacan!"

Little Reed opened his mouth to answer, but Ihuitimal screamed, "You son of a dog! You poisoned my son! You turned him against me! Just like that whore of a sister of yours turned Black Otter against me!" He ran towards us like a charging bear, but his guards cut him off, trying to hold him back. He tussled with them, cursing, and clawing at the atl-atl baton hanging at one of the soldier's belts.

Little Reed's men started yelling too, and everything turned into chaos. "Close in around your king! Now!" Citlallotoc shouted. "Ready your weapons!"

A burning sting hit my chest as the soldiers shuffled me backwards, as if I'd taken an elbow to the sternum, but the pain grew hotter and sharper, radiating deep through my chest as I breathed. I tried to reach for it, but everyone pushed and shouted. Then I couldn't breathe at all. I gasped for air, but it was like inhaling water. My heart pounded, a strange numbness replacing the pain. Dizziness swooped in on me, and I fell backwards against Little Reed. My hand finally reached my chest; a stiff shaft of wood stuck out. I stared dumbly at the red and blue feather fletching for a breath before recognizing it.

An arrow.

In my growing numbness and confusion, I wrapped my hand around it and pulled. I doubted my muscles had the strength left, but it finally came free, and blood gushed out of the open wound, pulsing in time to my frantic heartbeat. The world fell silent even as the men shouted and the jostling continued. All I heard was my own heart, slowing and faltering with each beat until it stopped altogether.

A startling calm spread over me. The sky turned pink and the clouds melted into orange, like in the Divine Dream. I felt no pain, no cold, no heat, just lightness. I watched the clouds laze by. I'd never felt so peaceful. Why had I fought so hard to remain in that terrible world of pain and misery?

But then I saw Little Reed looking down at me, and his anguished expression shattered my contentment. *Go back and comfort him, tell him he needn't worry about you.* I tried to move my lips, but they refused.

Suddenly I stood at a distance, watching him weep over my body while Citlallotoc and Mazatzin crouched over him, shields raised to protect him from the storm of arrows raining from the city walls. His troops surged forward and the enemy readied their weapons. Ihuitimal's men did the same, those closest holding their shields up to protect their king from enemy arrows and spears. I saw the atl-atl baton lying on the ground, the arrow missing from the slot. Ihuitimal had made good on his promise of vengeance.

I looked down to see the Black Dog sat next to me. *Xolotl?* My voice came disembodied, as if it whispered on the wind.

I am the guide for the dead, he confirmed. While I flinched at soldiers rushing past, he remained steady. *I help them earn their eternal rest on the road to Mictlan.*

I touched my cheek, remembering the strange tingling when I'd woken. It was no dream after all. *You marked me, like you did those atop the temple that day in Teotihuacan?*

I came while you slept. Xolotl reached out and licked a passing man's ankle. A few steps later, the man took a spear to his leg and two men pulled him off behind Culhuacan's line. *War is hard work, requiring many nahuals. Most times I enjoy my job, until days like today. Depending on the outcome, I may be marking people well into the night.*

You don't know who will win?

The future is rarely so clear.

But you chose me for death. How can't you know?

He tilted his head quizzically. *I do not choose; Heaven chooses, based on sacrifices, and I obey. Nothing more, nothing less.*

So then you decide how people will die? A strange, disembodied hostility rose around me like a foul mist. *You're the one who decided that Nimilitzli would be hacked up by an evil, god-hated man wanting revenge on me?*

Xolotl laughed like a coyote. *You assign me importance I do not have. You gave the blood and called on Heaven's mercy when you knew not what to do, and Omeyocan showed you compassion. It found someone willing to pay the tax for you, but now you begrudge it?*

Willing? No one would choose to die like she did.

You would not give your life for someone you love? Xolotl asked, startled. *She saw you struggling with your fear, so when Destiny came to her she embraced it, for you and the Feathered Serpent. Whatever another marked man did to her shell afterwards shouldn't overshadow the sacrifice she made for you.*

She was already dead when Ahexotl...?

She is in the Heaven of the Feathered Serpent, who takes excellent care of his sacrifices.

I felt as if he'd rolled a giant rock off my shoulders. What I wouldn't give to see Nimilitzli one last time, to hug and thank her for all she'd given for me. I stared back at my own dead body barely visible behind the line of shields around Little Reed. *What's to become of me?*

You'll walk the road the same as last time, but since you have no heart to pay to Lord Death for your rest, you must sit and wait, until the day when Smoking Mirror finally earns his own heaven.

What do you mean I don't have a heart to pay with? And what does Smoking Mirror have to do with anything?

Your heart fed the Smoking Mirror in sacrifice, Xolotl answered matter-of-factly.

Suddenly, a deep rumbling shattered the preternatural silence and I took a step back. If I could hear it in death, it must not be good. *What is that?*

As if in answer, thunder crashed even louder and Xolotl looked up, ears perked. He sniffed the wind then turned to me, his black eyes gleaming. *Smoking Mirror always underestimates his opponents' strengths. He doesn't understand the true power of sacrifice.*

What's going on?

See for yourself. He tilted his head towards Little Reed.

I looked to see Little Reed clutching me in his arms while my body jolted like I'd just been pulled from the lake after almost drowning.

Xolotl set his front paws on my shoulders. *I haven't much time, and I'm again bound by deals I helped craft, but listen closely and remember: you are the fire in women who won't bow to the whims of men or gods. Quetzalcoatl gave humanity life, but you give them reason to want that gift.*

What do you mean? I asked, but immediately had to cover my ears against the painful roar of battle. The sky flashed, blinding me.

Feeling fingers stroking my hair, I opened my eyes to see Little Reed gazing down at me. My heart beat hard and fast in my chest, and to my amazement, when I gasped, air not blood filled my lungs. "Omeyocan help me, I thought you were gone for good," he wept, resting his head against mine.

My tongue was heavy as stone and my muscles felt as if they were finally getting blood again after being deprived, but I fought past the painful stinging to give him a one-armed hug. "How am I...what happened?" I finally said, my words slurred.

A piercing roar broke over the battlefield and the group of soldiers that had been sheltering Ihuitimal suddenly flew apart, bodies tossed aside as if they were little more than dead leaves in the wind. Smoke roiled up from the ground, followed by the form of a monstrous jaguar, blackness curling off it like vapor on the lake on a cold morning. Hot coals burned for its eyes. When it spotted Little Reed and me, it bared long obsidian-bladed fangs and screamed, spitting soot and singeing-hot air.

"Great Feathered Serpent!" Citlallotoc grabbed Little Reed under the arms, hauling him to his feet while Mazatzin scooped me into his arms. As he got Little Reed's arm around his shoulder, he yelled, "Behind you,

Mazatzin!"

The giant smoke jaguar tore into the nearby crowd, scattering men in a pummeling fan of bodies, knocking Mazatzin off his feet. I hit the ground, lighting up my already painful muscles even more, but I only managed an extended gasp. "Get the king back behind the lines!" Mazatzin shouted.

I rolled onto my stomach and searched desperately for Little Reed. He lay dazed while Citlallotoc stood between him and the jaguar, sword drawn. And to my horror, Xolotl was dragging his tongue up the side of his cheek. Little Reed saw him but showed no surprise, only resignation.

"No!" I cried, but the terrible din of battle swallowed it. The jaguar raked up Citlallotoc and Little Reed, as well as ten other men and threw them through the air. The front ranks closed in around Little Reed, sheltering him as the beast came again, clawing through the scrum and scattering the soldiers like sparrows. They launched spears and arrows but everything passed through the smoke as if the beast didn't exist.

Only Quetzalcoatl can save Little Reed. And this time I wouldn't hesitate to do what I must.

I pulled a dagger off one of the dead men near me and cut my hand. I clasped the knife with both hands, pointing it at my heaving chest.

"Lord Quetzalcoatl,
I call on you now!
Save your son,
And I give you my life,
Taken in your name,
By my own hand!"

But Xolotl snapped the blade from my hands and tossed it aside. "What in Mictlan are you doing?" I demanded. "I'm trying to call on Quetzalcoatl to save Topiltzin."

A noble thought, but Heaven has already accepted your life on behalf of another god, so that sacrifice won't bring forth the Feathered Serpent.

"What could possibly be more powerful than giving one's own life?"

Take counsel with your own heart to find your answer. Xolotl trotted off into the melee, marking soldiers as he went.

My heart, I thought. *I can't literally give it anymore, but emotionally....* I

341

raised my hands again.

"Lord Quetzalcoatl,
I promise to love none but you.
Turn my heart to stone for all others—"

But Xolotl still shook his head. Still not good enough? But why?
Because the high priestess makes the hardest sacrifice of all, Nimilitzli's
voice spoke to me for memory. *We devote ourselves to the god alone in spite
of what our hearts feel.*

Of course! It wasn't a true sacrifice if I didn't feel the loss, didn't suffer
on the god's behalf, and didn't keep the path in spite of it.

I raised my hands and closed my eyes, this time confident.

"Lord Quetzalcoatl,
I will follow your path,
I will see your good works to fruition,
And I will give my body and soul to none but you,
For the remainder of my mortal days.
Give me the strength to save your son,
Oh Great Lord!"

Tingles filled my flesh and I opened my eyes to see glowing white
feathers sprouting from my skin. My body elongated and coiled like a
snake until the agony melted away and I stood taller than the city walls.

Papalotl, my love! the god's familiar voice whispered, making me ruffle
my new feathers with a shiver of joy.

Everyone stopped to stare in awe up at me. The jaguar bared his fangs,
bringing a deep rumble. Behind him lay Little Reed, unconscious and
bleeding from a deep gash across his chest. *He's not breathing,* I thought,
panic welling up. *Was I too late?*

He still lives, Quetzalcoatl whispered. *Hope is not lost.*

So you've finally come to face me, have you, Brother! the jaguar said. *And
you've brought your most powerful follower. Let's see how strong she really is.*
He sprang, obsidian claws outspread, smoke streaming off his body.

I expected Quetzalcoatl to take control but the jaguar crashed into me,
snapping at my exposed throat. I thrashed aside, feathers and flesh

singeing as I escaped. *You asked for the power to save Topiltzin,* Quetzalcoatl whispered. *I cannot give more than what was asked for.*

Solidifying my resolve, I struck back at the jaguar with my fangs.

But he leaped away and laughed. *Faith proves itself slow and dumb when pitted against fear. I look forward to eating both of your hearts!*

Trust yourself, Papalotl, Quetzalcoatl continued. *He underestimates you. Smoking Mirror's pride would have him abandon his host rather than risk fair defeat.*

I ducked and slithered away as Smoking Mirror sprang again. He crashed into the city wall, leaving a gaping hole, and as he struggled to free himself of the rubble, I sank my fangs into his shoulder and threw him over my head. His enormous body dug a crater where it hit the ground, knocking people off their feet.

He scrambled to his feet again, lips curled back, and this time I met him halfway, slamming into him with all my strength. He ripped into me as I wrapped my coils around him, each swipe opening a gush of gold dust and pain. I squeezed tighter, panicked when he grabbed my throat, but he had neither breath nor bones for me to crush. *Surely this isn't how it ends!*

Keep faith, Papalotl, Quetzalcoatl whispered. *You have more power than you can imagine.*

I suddenly felt re-energized, as if untapped magic now opened to me. *Puff your neck feathers,* the authoritative voice told me, so I did.

Smoking Mirror howled and wrenched free of my coils, turning up a flurry of white feathers in his wake. I slunk away, feeling gutted, but my wounds healed fast, feathers re-growing. He pawed at the long emerald feathers sticking out of his jowls and neck like daggers. Maguey thorns formed the tips of the quills. When Smoking Mirror lunged again, the voice told me to push magic into the ground beneath me, and this time thousands of lime-white roots shot from the dirt and lashed around Smoking Mirror's body, binding him.

Smoking Mirror howled and slashed the ground with his claws as the roots dragged him under the dirt, hind legs first. *My priest's faith can withhold whatever you can hurl at him! When he gives me his heart, you will pay for your trickery, little girl!*

"What would you know about faith, Smoking Mirror?" I panted. "You'll send your most faithful follower to sit on the banks of the Black Lake in Mictlan, never knowing rest nor peace, spending eternity wishing he'd known that before devoting his last breath to you."

Smoking Mirror shuddered, his smoke wavering. *Give it to me now, priest!* he shrieked. *Don't be a fool!*

Behind the smoldering coals, Ihuitimal's own eyes—afraid and unsure—showed, awakening unexpected pity in me. "Resist him, Uncle! It's not too late. Let go of everything that's bound you as his prisoner all these years!"

The smoke jaguar howled then slowly dissipated, leaving my uncle screaming as the roots pulled him further under. *Stop!* I thought, and they obeyed. As I knelt next to him, my human body returned, but magic still pulsed inside me. "Let me help you, Uncle."

Ihuitimal stared at me with wide, frightened eyes. "Why is it only now, with Death's dank breath on my neck, that I finally see the truth?" He shook his head. "My son had no chance against you; no man does."

His words shook me. "What do you mean?"

But he just stared at me, his breath completely gone.

CHAPTER THIRTY-SIX

Citlallotoc had Ihuitimal's body dug up, to show at the gate as proof that the king had fallen. He wanted to leave him for the buzzards to eat, but I refused. "He was family, so he'll get proper burial rites and we'll make sacrifices to honor his passing," I told him as we watched the surgeons gathered around Little Reed's sickbed in the Great Hall. "We will honor Lord Black Otter too." When Citlallotoc cast me a puzzled look, I said, "He is in the Land of the Drowned."

Hearing a strangled cry, I turned to see Jade Flower standing paralyzed in the doorway beyond the sea of soldiers. When our gazes locked, she fled from sight.

"Who's that?" Citlallotoc asked.

"My sister, Jade Flower." I sighed, feeling horrible. "I must go and talk to her, but let me know immediately when Topiltzin wakes up."

Women poked their heads out of their doorways, whispering as I went down the hall to Jade Flower's quarters. Over the quieter sobbing came my sister's wails, like a dying heron, and when Lady Corn Flower saw me, she ventured out of her room like a frightened mouse. "What's going on?"

"I need you to gather Anacoana and Papantzin and take them to the Women's Hall," I said. "We must have a meeting."

"What about Jade Flower?"

"She probably won't come, so I'm going to go and talk to her."

I continued past the few doorways, down to my sister's quarters, stopping in front of the curtain. *She's going to blame you, but you owe the truth to her.* I took a steadying breath, then tugged the curtain, jingling the bells.

"Go away!"

"Please, I need to talk to you," I said.

"I don't want to talk to you!"

"Please, Jade Flower." She said nothing this time, so I went inside.

She lay crumpled on her bed, sobbing. The sight made me cringe; that was me two years ago. Blinking back tears, I said, "I'm sorry you found out like that, Jade Flower. I wanted to tell you myself."

She turned to me, her face lit with anger. "So you could rub it in my face?"

The accusation stung but I kept my composure. "Of course not. The king betrayed him, Jade Flower. He sent assassins to kill him."

"That makes no sense. Ihuitimal loved Black Otter; he'd never do that!" Jade Flower sobbed harder into her hands.

Seeing her pain made the old wounds reopen. Sniffing back tears, I sat and hugged her. "I'm truly sorry, Sister."

But she shoved me away and stumbled to her feet. "You ruined everything! We were happy before you came back! He even used to love me!"

"He still loved you, Jade Flower. I understand how you feel right now—"

"You know nothing! You haven't shed a single tear for Black Otter, so how dare you tell me you understand?" She made to leave but then whipped back and cried, "Ihuitimal should have killed you the moment you arrived!"

I flew to my feet, shaking with fury. "I cared about Black Otter too, and don't tell me that I don't understand how it feels to lose someone so dear, how it hurts so deep you can't breathe, how you struggle to drag yourself out of bed every day to face a future that doesn't include them anymore." Hot tears wound down my face.

Jade Flower stared at me, stunned, then ran into her garden. I rushed from the room too, back to the Great Hall, desperately needing to see Little Reed again with my own eyes, to verify that this day wasn't a dream.

The surgeons still gathered around his bed when I clutched his hand in mine. *I need to tell you how much I missed you and still love you,* I thought, but he was asleep, drugged with tochletepon for his stitches.

"Quetzalpetlatl!" Mazatzin hugged me, holding on tight and laughing. "Isn't today a miracle? Topiltzin has risen from the ashes and we're all alive to see the dawning of the new era."

I gave him a fierce hug. "I'm so glad to see you again too, Mazatzin. I was really worried for you."

"I'm fine." He glanced at Little Reed as he said, "The surgeons think he'll be fine too. He just needs to rest and heal." His expression then turned anguished. "I'm sorry, Quetzalpetlatl. If I'd known Red Flint lied about Topiltzin—"

"There's nothing to forgive."

He nodded, looking relieved. He cleared his throat. "We should start making plans for cleaning up the road outside Culhuacan. You wouldn't believe all the bodies out there; some must have been lying out there for years."

I nodded. "The god will want them honored for giving their lives to remain faithful to him. We'll need priests and priestesses to help out with that, so if you go to the servant quarters, you'll find some of them there, including Malinalli."

"You hid them right in the belly of the demon?"

"Right in plain sight. Go and see about freeing them. I'm sure they're anxious to be rid of their slave collars."

Mazatzin hurried to find the others, and though I wanted to stay at Little Reed's side, I had to keep my appointment with Lady Corn Flower, Papantzin and Anacoana.

¤

The meeting remained thankfully civil. Lady Corn Flower and Lady Papantzin wept while Anacoana sat in stunned silence for a while before asking, "Will your brother take us as concubines now?"

"And what about our children?" Papantzin asked.

"Topiltzin's reign is a bright new beginning for everyone, men and women alike, so you needn't worry. Tell me where you wish to be, and I'll see it done."

Lady Corn Flower and Papantzin both looked skeptical, but Anacoana piped up, "Can I go home to Xico, to live with my sisters again?"

I smiled. "Absolutely. What about the rest of you?"

"I want to take my daughter back to Chimalhuacan," Lady Corn Flower said, trying for hopeful. "My mother misses her grandchild."

"And I'd like to go home too," Papantzin added. Her smile soon faded, though. "What about Jade Flower? She has no family to go home to...and she has a son."

"Topiltzin isn't going kill all the male children, like Ihuitimal did when he took Culhuacan from my father. And as for Jade Flower having no family, that's not true. She's my sister and Culhuacan is her home, and she and her children are welcome to stay. Topiltzin and I are her family."

"You really mean that?" Jade Flower suddenly asked behind me. When I nodded, she rushed to hug me. "I'm so sorry for all those awful things I said, Sister," she whispered. "Can you ever forgive me?"

My tears came again. "Can you ever forgive *me*, for causing you such grief and heartache?"

She hugged me tighter.

¤

Jade Flower didn't stay any longer than the others, though. When Papantzin's father came to bring her home, Jade Flower went with them. "Too many ghosts here. I can hardly sleep, and Papantzin will need help with her new bundle when it arrives."

I understood. I too felt the old conflicts haunting the hallways, and I hated visiting the royal quarters but did so to care for Little Reed. Workers had whitewashed the mural of the Smoking Mirror with five layers of paint, but still the god's shadow showed through, persistently lingering.

The surgeons had said Little Reed would be fine that first day, but the next day his wounds started festering and medicine did nothing—

unsurprising, given they'd been inflicted by a god. But whispers of residual magic still tingled inside me days after the battle, and when I set my hands on his forehead or shoulders, it eased his discomfort and began, slowly, to heal him.

But he wasn't the only one healing. The scars on both my hands and my ankle were gone. I could run again for the first time in two years, and the puckered skin where I'd cut my fingers off had become smooth, as though I'd been born without them. But most notable of all, the itching was gone. Maybe that meant I'd never again need its warning?

I'd expected Amoxtli—having once been a contender for the throne—to follow Jade Flower's example but he insisted on staying. I wanted nothing to do with him though, not even when he visited the temple, asking how one became a priest and offering to help clean up twenty years' worth of blasphemous mess his father had left in Quetzalcoatl's old temple. I let Jade Flower give him the unfortunate news about Black Otter since I knew nothing about Amoxtli and I didn't trust him to not share more than his father's looks.

Little Reed didn't mind his presence though, and even allowed him into his quarters while he was recovering. I had no idea what they talked about, for I couldn't bear being around someone who reminded me of Ihuitimal.

I needed something to help heal that hole in my heart that felt as if it had been raw all my life, so with the bone flowers in my garden now in splendid bloom, I cut off a dozen stalks and inserted them into the hollow reed slots along the back of my mother's old throne, just as the servants used to do when I was a little girl. I could almost see my mother sitting there, regal and proud, but it wasn't Father who sat next to her; it was Little Reed, wearing a crown of emerald quetzal feathers and the robes of the high priest of Quetzalcoatl. And I realized it wasn't really my mother sitting in the bone flower throne next him; it was me.

¤

Little Reed spent most of his first week as king sleeping while Citlallotoc and I oversaw pressing city matters, but by the second week he finally left his bed for short stints, with the help of a wooden staff. As his strength grew, I took him on walks through the palace, showing him where everything was; and once the weather turned nice, I took him out into the gardens and the menagerie.

"Can I ask you something?" I asked as we walked by the tapir cage.

"You may ask me anything you wish, Papalotl," he said with a smile.

"What happened the day of the ballgame? Red Flint said he had you murdered."

"You didn't get any of my letters?"

"Ihuitimal intercepted them."

The look on his face puzzled me—simultaneously frustrated and relieved, but he went on before I could say anything. "Well, I went to find Ahexotl to arrest him, but some of Red Flint's men jumped me and beat me unconscious. I came to in the limestone quarry when they started stabbing me."

I cringed. The thought of what that must have been like...he had no physical scars, but I wondered how often he woke in the night, panicked and thinking he was dying. "I'm so sorry, Little Reed. I never should have said anything to Red Flint," I whispered, my voice cracking with guilt and shame.

He patted my hand. "It's all right. I made it through alive, thanks to Citlallotoc. He dispatched two handfuls of men. I owe him everything."

"How did he find you?"

"He left the match to use the public bathhouse and saw Red Flint's men dragging someone through the city, so he followed them. He not only killed my attackers, but he took me half-dead upon his shoulders and ran from the place, tending to my wounds when we were far enough away to stop. After that he carried me all night to Xochimilco to get me to a surgeon. Red Flint's men continued pursuing us, so we fled again, to Tultepec. The king took me in and offered protection."

"Xochicalco's army could have easily crushed his city trying to get to you," I noted.

Little Reed nodded. "Luckily Ihuitimal started ramping up his attacks in the north, keeping the army distracted and giving me time to heal. And from what I heard, Red Flint was falling apart, so confidence in his leadership was diminishing. That allowed me to come out and negotiate with his generals. I still had a good many allies in the army, so when word of Xochicalco's destruction reached us and Mazatzin abdicated his throne, the army didn't hesitate to declare loyalty to me."

"I suppose it shouldn't surprise me that Mazatzin abdicated his throne.

He didn't seem very comfortable in the role the last time I saw him in Xochicalco."

"I didn't ask him to; I didn't want it, but everyone agreed that if we were to move on Culhuacan, the army needed a leader with more military experience. This is probably all for the best, really." Little Reed sat on a bench to catch his breath. "With the drought south of the valley, Xochicalco would have been abandoned eventually anyway."

I sat too. "So we truly never can go home again?"

"You don't like it here?"

I hesitated before answering. "We've been through so much to get Culhuacan back, but...it doesn't feel like home, and I doubt it ever will."

Little Reed nodded. "Father wants us to build that new city and I plan to get started before too long. Amoxtli tells me that he knows where his father buried Mixcoatl's bones, so once he shows us, we can get started building our new city. I just have a few things that need working out first...." He gazed around a moment then took my hand between his. "Some things I've been putting off far too long." His voice shook and he laughed. "I'm nervous as a boy facing his first battle!"

I gave him an encouraging smile.

He sobered, then continued, "I love you deeply, Papalotl; you're the tiny butterflies tickling my heart and you would make me the happiest being in all the Heavens if you would be my wife, the queen at my side, my best friend and partner, the one whose smile makes every day of my life worth living, forever and always. Please marry me."

Leftover magic danced joyfully inside me. Ten years I'd waited for this, and I desperately wanted to tell him, absolutely, without a doubt, *yes*.

I was unprepared for the crushing feeling as I realized, *But you can't*. He looked so eager with that smile I dearly loved, but if not for that sacrifice my heart now cursed, I wouldn't have gotten to ever see it again. *It's only a true sacrifice if you suffer for it*, I thought, close to tears.

But I didn't want him feeling like I did right now. I couldn't even hold his gaze, afraid he'd see the answer in my eyes, so I looked away, scrambling for the kindest way to disappoint him.

My gaze found the pair of lake otters frolicking in the pen behind him. It brought back the dream about Black Otter, of the creatures dragging him under the dark water until he became one of them, screeching, "Mine! Mine! Mine!" *The end I brought him to, just as I pushed Red Flint over the edge. And eventually Little Reed will end up just like them,* I thought, and before I knew it, tears streamed down my cheeks. Why would I even think that?

Little Reed looked over his shoulder too, and the smile fell from his face. His shoulders sagged as he turned back to me. "Please forgive my thoughtlessness. He's only been gone a few weeks, surely not enough time to properly mourn the loss of a loved one."

I blinked, startled. "Oh, Little Reed—"

"No, it's all right." He cleared his throat then said, "You thought I was dead, so of course your heart moved on. I understand completely. If I'd truly been dead, I wouldn't want you holding onto my memory forever and never finding happiness. I love you too much to wish that upon you. I just...I didn't think, and I'm sorry. Please forgive me."

It's you I cry for, Little Reed, I wanted to say, but stopped myself again. Perhaps it was better if he thought this, so I didn't have to reject him. Maybe then he could move on sooner. "I'm not angry, Little Reed," I said.

"Thank you." He tried to smile.

I hugged him. "No, thank *you.*"

"Can I beg you for one thing though?" he asked when I let him go. "Will you still co-rule with me? The god never intended me to do this on my own, and I need your help building the best possible future for our people."

I gave him a smile, and it felt like my first genuine one in years. "I can definitely do that."

¤   ¤   ¤

AUTHOR'S NOTE

Ce Acatl Topiltzin Quetzalcoatl is often thought of as the "King Arthur" of Mesoamerica: he was the great uniter, the father of Toltec civilization, and the champion against human sacrifice.

Given the Aztec preoccupation with blood sacrifice, it's easy to see why his story was so compelling to them. The importance of the Topiltzin myth in Mesoamerican thought and history cannot be overstated: some stories of the Spanish Conquest point to Emperor Moctezuma the Younger becoming frozen with fear and indecision because he thought Hernan Cortes was the fulfillment of Topiltzin's promise to return and reclaim his throne. The Mexica (Aztecs) derived their right to rule through connecting their own royal families with the bloodlines of the legendary Toltec priest-king, and they considered themselves the beneficiaries of the culture he created for the Toltecs. He is so inextricably intertwined with the god from whom he took his name that often the lines between history and mythology become so blurred as to be indistinguishable from each other.

The legends of Topiltzin Quetzalcoatl are many and diverse. Practically every area of central Mexico had its own version. Who his father and mother were varied with the telling, as did the name and number of his uncles, where he was born, and how he spent his formative years; but one element remains firm through all the stories: he outlawed human sacrifice in defiance of the gods, and for that he and his followers were driven from Tollan through cruel—and often magical—trickery. Some versions have him disappearing into the southern jungles to build new cities, while others say he immolated himself upon a raft of serpents, rising into the sky as the planet Venus. Often these tales promised he would return someday in the future to reclaim his throne.

But what do we know of the woman Quetzalpetlatl? Very little. Her name appears in only one rendition of the stories, recorded in the Anales de Cuauhtitlan, a collection of Nahuatl narratives from the basin of Mexico and Puebla. She is called Topiltzin's "sister", though it's unclear whether she's an actual blood relative or merely a priestess under his authority. Regardless, through the dark influence of the sorcerer god

Tezcatlipoca, Topiltzin committed transgressions—religious and/or sexual—with Quetzalpetlatl, and left Tollan in shame. But what became of Quetzalpetlatl, whom the gods used to destroy Topiltzin's reputation and power? She's never mentioned again.

This book—and the ones to follow—sets out to posit answers to these mysteries: who was Quetzalpetlatl, what was her relationship to Topiltzin, what role did she play in his greatest accomplishments, and, eventually, what became of her once the gods finished using her to destroy Mesoamerica's most famous hero?

INDEX OF CHARACTERS

Ahexotl – high priest of Quetzalcoatl

Amoxtli – son of Ihuitimal

Anacoana – concubine of Black Otter

Atzi – concubine of Cuitlapanton, mother of Obsidian Eagle and Pochotzin.

Black Otter – son of Ihuitimal, husband of Quetzalpetlatl, heir of Culhuacan

Blood Wolf – friend of Nochuatl

Camaxtli – brother to Red Flint

Chimalma – wife of Mixcoatl, mother of Quetzalpetlatl and Topiltzin

Cihuacoatl – the Snake Woman – goddess, the mother of mankind

Citlallotoc – Topiltzin's best friend and war chief

Corn Flower – concubine of Black Otter

Cuitlapanton – king of Xochicalco

Eloxochitl – Ihuitimal's wife, Black Otter's mother, sister to Chimalma

Emerald – sister and legitimate wife of Cuitlapanton, mother of Red Flint

Eztetl – a fire priest of Quetzalcoatl

Iczoxochitl – novice priestess

Ihuitimal – brother of Mixcoatl, king of Culhuacan, father of Black Otter and Amoxtli, high priest of the Smoking Mirror

Ixchell – priestess of Quetzalcoatl

Jade Flower – Quetzalpetlatl's half-sister, concubine of Black Otter

Malinalli – priestess of Quetzalcoatl, Quetzalpetlatl's best friend

Mayahuel – goddess of the maguey plant

Mazatzin – priest of Quetzalcoatl, brother of Red Flint

Mictlantecuhtli – Lord Death – god of death and ruler of the underworld, Mictlan

Mixcoatl – king of Culhuacan, brother of Ihuitimal and Nochuatl, father of Quetzalpetlatl and Jade Flower

Mocneltzin – son of Cuitlapanton

Nanahuatzin – Tonatiuh - god of the sun

Necalli – lord on Cuitlapanton's war council

Nimilitzli – foster mother to Quetzalpetlatl and Topiltzin, high priestess of Quetzalcoatl

Nochuatl – brother of Ihuitimal and Mixcoatl

Obsidian Eagle – son of Cuitlapanton

Oquitzin – son of Cuitlapanton

Papantzin – concubine of Black Otter

Paper Flower – priestess of Quetzalcoatl

Pochotzin – son of Cuitlapanton

Quetzalcoatl – the Feathered Serpent – god of civilization, father of mankind. Also known as Ehecatl, god of the wind.

Quetzalpetlatl (Papalotl) – legitimate daughter of Mixcoatl, sister of Topiltzin

Red Flint – Cuitlapanton's legitimate son, heir to Xochicalco

Spear Fish – Cuitlapanton's war chief

Stargazer – son of Cuitlapanton

Storm House – a captain in Culhuacan's army

Talking Serpent – novice priest

Tayanna – priestess of Quetzalcoatl

Tecuciztecatl – god of the moon

Tezcatlipoca – the Smoking Mirror – Chichimec god of war and sorcerers, god of the night

Tlaloc – god of rain

Tlazolteotl – Eater of Filth – goddess of sex and childbirth

Topiltzin (Little Reed) – son of Quetzalcoatl by Chimalma, brother of Quetzalpetlatl, heir of Culhuacan

Tototl – lord on Cuitlapanton's war council

Turquoise Bells – sister and wife of Red Flint

Xipil – lord on Cuitlapanton's war council

Xolotl – the Black Dog – god, guide of the dead

Zeltzin – concubine to Mixcoatl, mother of Jade Flower

FURTHER READING

Richard Blanton, Stephen A. Kowalewski, Gary Feinman, and Jill Appel, *Ancient Mesoamerica: A Comparison of Change in Three Regions*, Cambridge University Press, 1981.

Burr Cartwright Brundage, *The Phoenix of the Western World: Quetzalcoatl and the Sky Religion*, University of Oklahoma Press, 1981.

David Carrasco, *Quetzalcoatl and the Irony of Empire: Myths and Prophecies in the Aztec Tradition*, University Press of Colorado, 2001.

Sophie Coe, *America's First Cuisines*, University of Texas Press, 1994.

Nigel Davies, *The Toltecs Until the Fall of Tula*, University of Oklahoma Press, 1977.

Richard A. Diehl, *Tula: The Toltec Capital of Ancient Mexico*, Thames and Hudson, 1983.

William Gates, *An Aztec Herbal: The Classic Codex of 1552*, Dover Publications, Inc, 2000.

Rich Holmer, *The Aztec Book of Destiny*, BookSurge, LLC, 2005.

Miguel León-Portilla, *Aztec Thought and Culture*, University of Oklahoma Press, 1963.

Roberta H. Markman and Peter T Markman, *The Flayed God: The Mythology of Mesoamerica*, Harper San Francisco, 1992.

Mary Miller and Karl Taube, *An Illustrated Dictionary of the Gods and Symbols of Ancient Mexico and the Maya*, Thames and Hudson, 1993.

H. B. Nicholson, *Topiltzin Quetzalcoatl: The Once and Future Lord of the Toltecs*, University Press of Colorado, 2001.

Guilhem Olivier, *Mockeries and Metamorphoses of an Aztec God: Tezcatlipoca, "Lord of the Smoking Mirror"*, University Press of Colorado, 2003.

John M. D. Pohl, *Aztec, Mixtec and Zapotec Armies*, Osprey Publishing,

1991.

John Pohl, PhD and Adam Hook, *Aztec Warrior, A.D. 1325-1521*, Osprey Military, 2001.

Fray Bernardino de Sahagún, *The Florentine Codex: The General History of the Things of New Spain*, translated by Arthur J. O. Anderson and Charles E. Dibble, The School of American Research and The University of Utah, 1975.

Jacques Soustelle, *Daily Life of the Aztecs*, Dover Publications, Inc., 2002.

ACKNOWLEDGEMENTS

This book slowly came together over a four-year period and many a failed draft, with lots of people's help.

I couldn't have even thought of writing this without the support and encouragement of my husband Jeff. He made sure I was able to go to Clarion West in 2002, and he supported my move to becoming a full-time writer after college. Thank you for giving me the room to pursue my dreams.

Douglas Cohen, former assistant editor at Realms of Fantasy pulled this story's original novelette out of the slush and championed it, and though Realms ultimately passed on it, his continued enthusiasm for the story convinced me that it really belonged at novel-length.

Andrea Somberg, thank you for taking a chance on me and helping me see that I indeed had something really good here. If not for your faith in this book, I might have let it languish in a drawer, forgotten.

I also want to thank Samuel Tecpaocelotl Castillo and all the folks over at the Mexica History Facebook page, who welcomed me into their community so I could listen and learn about the culture and history from those it means the most to. So many of the conversations made me reconsider and reevaluate everything I'd learned about the Mexica in text books and school.

A big chunk of my thanks goes to my writing group *Written in Blood (WiB)*. They endured two completely different drafts of this beast, both of them bordering on 200k in length, but with their help, I whittled it down to what you just read. Juliette Wade and Janice Hardy both brainstormed some pretty significant changes in plot and character with me between drafts, and Genevieve Williams challenged me to explore Mesoamerican spirituality on a deeper level. Doug Sharp and Keyan Bowes provided enthusiasm, and encouragement along the way.

An extra special thanks goes to Aliette de Bodard, fellow WiBby, my friend, my con buddy and kindred spirit who's always available to bounce every crazy idea off of. She always knows exactly what I'm trying to do and knows just how to help me get there.

And finally, to Dario Ciriello, my tireless editor, fellow WiBby, Clarion

West classmate, dream-chaser and all around inspiration. Thank you for taking a chance on my book and making that final push to help me make it the best it can be. I hope it's an investment that makes you proud.

ABOUT THE AUTHOR

T. L. Morganfield lives in Colorado with her husband and children. She's an alumna of the Clarion West Workshop and she graduated from Metropolitan State University with dual degrees in English and History. She reads and writes way too much about Aztec history and mythology, but it keeps her muse happy, which makes for a happy writer, so she has no plans of changing her ways.

You can join her mailing list at www.tlmorganfield.com to receive updates on her latest work.